T0367878

SHAME
THE DEVIL

Praise for Shame the Devil

"Full of twists and turns to find the wrong-doer,
who will elude you to the end"
—Best Chaplit

"Joel Mark Harris does not fail to deliver!
Make sure you have time to spare because
you won't want to put this one down!"
—Allison Cosgrove, author of the *Stan Brookshire novels*

"Joel Mark Harris strikes it rich with Shame the Devil"
—Mike Cantwell, author of A *Beautiful Song*

SHAME THE DEVIL

JOEL MARK HARRIS

iUniverse LLC
Bloomington

SHAME THE DEVIL

Copyright © 2013 by Joel Mark Harris.

All rights reserved. No part of this book may be used or reproduced by any means, graphic, electronic, or mechanical, including photocopying, recording, taping or by any information storage retrieval system without the written permission of the publisher except in the case of brief quotations embodied in critical articles and reviews.

This is a work of fiction. All of the characters, names, incidents, organizations, and dialogue in this novel are either the products of the author's imagination or are used fictitiously.

iUniverse books may be ordered through booksellers or by contacting:

iUniverse LLC
1663 Liberty Drive
Bloomington, IN 47403
www.iuniverse.com
1-800-Authors (1-800-288-4677)

Because of the dynamic nature of the Internet, any web addresses or links contained in this book may have changed since publication and may no longer be valid. The views expressed in this work are solely those of the author and do not necessarily reflect the views of the publisher, and the publisher hereby disclaims any responsibility for them.

Any people depicted in stock imagery provided by Thinkstock are models, and such images are being used for illustrative purposes only.
Certain stock imagery © Thinkstock.

ISBN: 978-1-4917-0457-8 (sc)
ISBN: 978-1-4917-0458-5 (hc)
ISBN: 978-1-4917-0459-2 (ebk)

Library of Congress Control Number: 2013915758

Printed in the United States of America

iUniverse rev. date: 08/27/2013

To Chelsea Manning and whistleblowers around the world.

The Don Juan

THE SOUTH OF FRANCE WAS having a Saint Martin's summer.
The sleek one-hundred-foot yacht, named the Don Juan—so
named by its previous owner, a Kuwaiti prince—had cast itself
from St. Tropez, delving into the expansive, crystal-white water.
The boat, by all accounts, was a magnificent specimen even in
the elegant St. Tropez harbour, where millionaires and billionaires
flexed their fragile egos. Fair to say, the Don Juan stood out among
its rivals. Even the locals, used to such massive phalluses, stopped
to gawk and gape at the brilliant, angular, white hull.

At sea, the fishing boats, rug boats, cruise boats, sail boats and
motor boats all tried to snuggle up alongside the Don Juan, which
had been meticulously imagined by the Kuwaiti prince and brought
into existence in the docks of Hamburg.

The yacht had thirty stunningly furnished rooms, including
a fully stocked wine cellar, a gym complete with swimming pool
and sauna, a fifty-seat concert hall, an entertainment room, a study
room and a plethora of bedrooms and bathrooms. Each room was
a marvel of architecture, both modern and ancient. Gold-trim,
marble counters and ornate carvings inhabited each room as well
as heated floors, platinum-plated appliances, and brass-knobbed
cabinets.

One could invite thirty friends aboard and not see any of them
for the entire voyage.

The Don Juan sailed out of the dozy, jutting gulf. Its large,
powerful engine purred casually along, taking the passengers and
crew further away from the beaches and sandy-coloured buildings

with quaint red rooftops with the low-top mountains like jagged stencil drawings behind them.

The Don Juan sailed past a slender lighthouse and past a dozen or so other yachts that likely carried more captains of industry than true captains of the sea.

The boat travelled lethargically down the white coastline for several nautical miles before hitting open water where there was nothing but the brisk blue horizon, which stretched on and on until the end of the world.

The heat hit a sweltering forty degrees. The sky was clear and windless and the large glaring sun was midway through its daily march.

On the top deck there were four people—three blonde women and one deeply tanned man—lounging in the pool, and a fifth woman was sunning herself in a lawn chair.

The woman in the lawn chair was in her mid-forties but could have been thirty or even twenty-five. She wore a white bikini over her pale skin. She looked like she had been kept in the dark for most of her life, and indeed she probably had.

She had blue eyes, so deep you could swim in them, soft round shoulders and, as a whole, an Eastern European beauty. Her long, unruly, chestnut-coloured hair was tied back in a ponytail.

"What was he in now? *The Last Wind*?" one of the bee-coloured blondes asked the other, slowly shifting her hair around her shoulders.

The three pool girls were all a little inebriated and as a result had discarded their bikini tops long ago and were baring their fake basketball-sized breasts to the Mediterranean sun.

"What is it with the French?" another girl chimed in. She had a bony neck and a plum-coloured complexion.

"I thought I saw him back there—you know the actor, what's-his-name?"

The first blonde rolled her eyes and looked around ruefully. "All I want is a refill on my fucking drink."

"Maybe you should give him fellatio. It's the only thing the French understand."

"What's fellatio? Is it a cocktail?"

There was an unsuccessful suppression of giggles.

"Yes, it's a type of cock . . . tail."

More giggles.

The first blonde squished her face up. "You guys think you're so fucking smart."

"You should ask the waiter. He'll tell you."

"Didn't he play a navy captain in something? I would definitely perform fellatio on him."

"Speaking of the waiter, where is he? I'm thirsty."

One of the blondes suddenly turned to George Hopkins. "What did you say you did again?"

George Hopkins was looking at his blonde companions with a mixture of amusement and bewilderment. He was a slightly pudgy man with thick forest-like chest hair and mahogany-coloured skin.

"I'm an oil and gas prospector."

The blondes frowned synchronously. "What's that?"

"A geologist."

"You look for oil?" one of the girls asked.

George nodded. "That's right."

One of the blondes kicked her feet up, splashing water over the edge. "Is that how you can afford this boat?"

"How do you look for oil?" another blonde asked.

"Well, what I generally do is a seismic survey, which is basically sound waves designed to map out the ocean floor and find oil pockets."

"Do you go to the Middle East much?" the plum-coloured blonde asked. Then without waiting for an answer she said, "I would like to go to the Middle East—all the hot weather and those beaches."

"Don't be silly. There aren't any beaches in the Middle East," one of the girls said.

"It's all fucking desert," George said, definitively. He then smiled wryly at his companions. "No skinny dipping there."

The girls giggled shrilly, causing a ripple of water to splash over the side of the pool.

Andrea Drashkov, who was in the lawn chair, wished George and his harem would just move to the bedroom and get on with the orgy and leave her alone, but when the waiter appeared she knew she was out of luck.

"Fucking finally," one of the blondes whispered under her breath.

The three blondes rudely waved their glasses at the waiter who took them with the reserved look of utter contempt that only the French can pull off with success.

"Five more, please," George smiled apologetically at the waiter.

The waiter nodded and turned, but Andrea stopped him. "Actually, I'll stick to water."

George gave a deep frown. "Why don't you have another drink for once in your life?"

"I've had enough," Andrea replied, turning her head away and closing her eyes. The heat was making her feel dehydrated.

"We're on vacation. We can do what we like," George insisted.

Andrea opened her eyes and sat up on one elbow and stared at George. "Please remind me why I invited you onto my boat?"

One of the blondes turned to George. "I thought it was your boat."

He smiled and his cheeks turned a little flush. "Well . . . technically, I think, it's the company's boat."

Andrea let out a gust of hot air from her lungs. "It's my boat. I bought and paid for it."

The geologist opened his mouth, but hesitated. He turned to the blonde girls as if to ask for help, but they all just frowned at him, their bodies slowly recoiling from him.

Andrea smiled. Perhaps there would be no orgy after all.

"Well, I thought it was company property. How was I to know?"

The waiter appeared from below deck, saving the two from further squabbling. In the waiter's hand was a satellite telephone. He gave it to Andrea. "For you, Madame Drashkov."

Andrea frowned, putting the phone to her ear. Who could be phoning her? Very few people had this number.

"Andrea, it's David."

David Kahn was the chief executive officer of Nerno Energy. He sounded worried.

"Is there a problem?" Andrea asked.

"You could say that," David paused, sounding on the verge of saying something else. It always annoyed Andrea when people were afraid to speak their minds.

"You know I like things blunt," Andrea said. "It's the Russian in me."

She got up from her chair and slipped into her sandals, careful to avoid the scorching deck, and made her way below. She walked along a narrow metallic-walled hallway. It was humid and unpleasant without the sun's warmth.

"You know the Ko Chang Project?"

Andrea stopped. "Of course."

"There seems to have been a mistake."

"For fuck's sake, David. Just tell me."

"There's no oil. At all."

Andrea was suddenly aware that she was holding her breath. She tried to let it out but her body was unable to move, seemingly frozen. "What do you mean?"

"I mean we're totally dry."

"Nothing at all?" Andrea gasped in disbelief. Her mind tried unsuccessfully to grasp the gravity of the situation. "Shit, David," Andrea said, "who fucked this one up? I mean how could we be so wrong?"

"George Hopkins did all the field work."

Instinctively Andrea glanced upwards as if she could pierce him with her gaze. *I am going to kill him*, she decided. She would throw him off the side of the boat.

"What are we going to do? What are we going to tell the investors?"

"We don't tell them anything. We sit tight until we sell and then it becomes somebody else's problem."

"David, that won't work. You know it won't. The Chinese are going to audit the shit out of us."

"Have a little faith."

"People will eventually find out."

"So what? We'll be rich beyond our imaginations."

"I want that prick George gone."

"Soon we can all retire and sit on the beach in the Caribbean."

"This whole thing is a bad idea."

"Andrea, we've been over this," David said, sounding irritated. "It's what everybody wants."

"I guess I'd better come home." Andrea sighed inwardly. Part of her was distraught that her first vacation in about six years was being cut short, but part of her was glad. Being stuck on a boat with George and those girls was too much to bear.

"No, you can stay," David said. "Enjoy your vacation. There will be plenty of time to talk over things when you get back."

"How the fuck am I supposed to enjoy my vacation when I have this hanging over me? And especially with George on board."

"You have George there?" David said, sounding worried.

"Yes, I told you. In fact you were the one who convinced me to let him tag along."

"Of course," David said. "Listen Andrea, don't tell him any of this. Let me do it."

Andrea rubbed her temples with her thumb and forefinger. She felt a headache materializing. Not a good sign. "Okay," she said. "I can go get him."

"No, we should do it when the time is right. When you guys are rested and back from vacation."

Andrea closed her eyes. Something wasn't right. What was David doing? What was he planning? "David, what's going on?"

"Nothing. I just want to make sure everything is done correctly."

"Why won't you tell George?"

"I just don't want him to know right now, that's all. He screwed up. It's going to hit him very hard."

"Okay, fine. I'll see you when I get back."

"That's a good girl."

When David hung up, Andrea could start breathing again. She felt the blood rush to her head. *Don't patronize me, asshole*, she thought. *What was this good girl crap?*

She was furious. She knew that she should have just gone back to her room and let her temper soothe itself. But she couldn't do that. She was never the type to suffer in silence and so she felt her body turn and climb the stairs back up to the sundeck, as if she wasn't really in control of it. She marched over to the pool where the girls were laughing at something and threw the phone at George, narrowly missing his head. The phone hit the deck with a resounding cracking sound of plastic splitting, then skidded for several metres until it fell overboard into the ocean.

"Son of a bitch!" Andrea screamed.

The three girls immediately climbed out of the pool, grabbing their abandoned bikinis and towels, and ran for safety.

George shrank into the corner, looking up at Andrea. "What now?"

"How could you screw up so badly?"

"What are you talking about?"

Andrea paced agitatedly along the edge of the pool like a predator who couldn't quite reach its prey. "There is no fucking oil in Ko Chang. That's what I'm talking about."

George frowned. "Of course there isn't."

Andrea stopped pacing and looked at George, stunned. That wasn't the reaction she had expected. "You knew? You were on all those conference calls, those meetings, and you said nothing?"

George creased his large forehead. "I don't understand . . . are you saying you didn't know?"

"Of course I didn't know! Why would I know? We told the shareholders . . . you realize you could go to jail for this?"

George nodded, crossing his hands across his stomach. "I went to David about a year ago and told him my findings."

Andrea could hardly believe what she was hearing. Was he telling the truth? Why should she believe him? She took a deep breath. "What did he say?"

"He said to keep quiet. He wanted to buy some time before telling the investors. I'm sorry. I thought you knew. I thought he told you."

Andrea shook her head in disbelief. "Time for what?"

"Time to find oil elsewhere? Time to sell the company? I don't fucking know. I really thought we would get lucky with the other sites."

"Okay," Andrea said, sitting back down on the lawn chair. Her anger had subsided somewhat. "Why do you think he's telling me now? While on vacation?"

"I have no idea."

"He didn't want me to talk to you about it. He had forgotten you were here with me, in fact." Andrea picked at the frayed ends of her stringy hair. "I feel like he's plotting something now. Plotting for us to take the fall for this. He didn't want us to conspire together."

Andrea suddenly stood up, knocking the lawn chair over. George cowered in the pool corner again, probably afraid Andrea would throw something else at him.

Without a word, Andrea turned and walked towards the hatch below. She could hear George call out after her, but to her he was barely distinguishable from the soft wind as it fluttered across the deck. "Andrea, wait! Where are you going?"

Andrea once again disappeared below the deck and walked towards her room.

David Kahn was a shrewd, cunning businessman. She wished she knew exactly what he was planning. A press conference? Would he leak the information through somebody? The real question was, was she ready to match his wits?

And what was she going to do when she got home? What should she do? The responsible thing would be to come clean, but that would mean a loss of hundreds of millions of dollars, and she wasn't sure if she was ready to live thrifty again.

Andrea's room was large with oak floors and large Impressionist paintings bunched together unceremoniously and tastelessly on the wall. A king sized bed with neatly folded silk sheets dominated the room.

Andrea quickly stripped out of her swimwear and for a moment she stood naked and paralyzed. She wondered if she should have a shower. Did she have time? Her white skin was sticky from lotion. But it wasn't just her indecision about a shower that had stopped the woman who was somehow always perpetually in motion.

Andrea realized that she was about to make the biggest decision of her life, and she wondered how one moment she was lounging by the pool and the next moment life had thrust upon her such a weighty responsibility.

Andrea opened the walk-in closet and selected a sleek maroon-coloured blouse from about a dozen others. She repeated the process for her skirts and then laid her clothes out on her bed. She then went to her drawers and, with less effort this time, picked a bra and a pair of panties which she slipped on.

Why do I always have to do everything myself? Andrea asked.

Andrea finished getting dressed and had just managed to fix her hair when she heard a knock on her door. Expecting to find the waiter with another phone call, instead she found George with a towel wrapped around his waist, dripping wet.

"What do you want?" Andrea asked. "You're getting water all over the hardwood."

"Are you leaving?"

"I'm going back to Calgary."

"You have to take me with you."

"No, you're staying here. I can't be seen with you."

Andrea walked over to the intercom and buzzed the crew.

"Madame?"

"Yes, can you get the chopper ready?"

"You mean the helicopter?" the man's crackling, French-accented voice floated through the room.

"S'il vous plait."

George stepped uninvited into the room. "Please . . . we need to be together on this." George's eyes were wide and puppyish.

Andrea had never liked the geologist—he had been David's recruit—and nothing George was doing persuaded Andrea to alter her perception.

"Look, George, the bottom line is I can't trust you. You've withheld the truth and whatever happens, in my opinion, you deserve it."

Andrea then placed two palms on his wet chest hair, pushed him out the door and locked it.

George pounded on the door but Andrea ignored him. She finished applying her make-up and gathered her things into a small suitcase. The rest she left.

Before she stepped out into the hallway, she listened for George but he seemed to have retreated, presumably to his own room. Andrea briefly wondered what had happened to the girls who, until recently, had been fawning over George.

Before Andrea left, she turned to look at the room that had briefly been her home. It was clean, unblemished and practically unused. It was too bad she hadn't gotten the chance to invite the waiter or perhaps the captain back. It made Andrea sad she had left such a small imprint.

The helicopter was ready as she had asked. The pilot wordlessly but chivalrously took her suitcase and placed it in the back of the helicopter. Andrea climbed into the passenger's seat and the pilot climbed in after her. He was wearing a grey jumpsuit and smelled of sweat and grease. He handed Andrea a pair of scratched earmuffs, which she donned.

It's going to be a long flight, Andrea decided.

The pilot flicked a couple of switches on his complicated control panel and then pulled slightly on the throttle. There was a surge of sound and power as the helicopter seemed to convulse and then lift off from the boat, upwards and upwards, and Andrea got a strange feeling of vertigo as the boat grew smaller and smaller beneath them.

Andrea tilted her head slightly and looked at the gold-trimmed shoreline and the white frothy surf crashing and sputtering in torment. The famous beaches stretched into the distance, seemingly for miles. As the helicopter skimmed low and fast across the water, Andrea could make out the hundreds of swimmers, surfers and sun tanners. Colourful umbrellas were clumped together like cattle.

About an hour later, the helicopter landed in Nice. Andrea stepped out into the sunshine, the heat visibly rising from the tarmac.

Andrea took out her cell phone and looked at the bars on her screen. She had reception again. She felt a great temptation to call her broker and sell everything. She could already hear the incredulous response. The chief financial officer was in the dark? Really? How was that possible?

She knew David Kahn still had his shares. He wanted her to sell, to make her look guilty so he could point the finger at her. He wanted her to blink first but she wasn't going to.

How much was she worth? Last time she looked she was worth 2.4 billion dollars. How much would she be worth in a month? Two months? A third of that if she was lucky.

She had worked so hard for it all: college, all those internships, thankless jobs for ungrateful bosses, and in a single broad stroke it would be wiped away. It seemed so incredibly unfair.

Andrea looked around at the curving promenade, the puffy palm trees, the Baroque-style architecture and wondered why not just stay here? They couldn't touch her. She could go Roman Polanski on everybody. Take an assumed name. Home seemed so far away, so unimportant.

But could she live with herself, knowing that David Kahn had won?

Andrea walked slowly over to the Lear jet with her suitcase in tow. There a flight attendant greeted her. Andrea barely registered her as she walked up the stairs and into the air conditioned cabin.

As the Lear jet taxied down the runway, Andrea thought of her time with the company. David Kahn had personally head-hunted her from Chevron.

"How far do you think you'll get in a prehistoric leviathan company like Chevron?" David had said. *"Come join Nerno. We look to the future."*

Andrea opened the menu to try and distract herself, but nothing seemed appetizing. Everything seemed so heavy . . . pork chops . . . steak . . . fettuccini Alfredo. In the end she ordered a Caesar salad with a glass of white wine.

The jet engine rumbled to life and Andrea pressed her back against the chair. She watched through the narrow glass window as Nice passed through a layer of smoky, white clouds, and at that moment she knew that she was flying into another life.

The Rollercoaster

JOHN WEBSTER INSTINCTIVELY GRASPED HIS son's hand as they slowly chugged up the colossal tracks, but Byron slipped out of his father's hand.

Of course, John thought. *What am I doing? He's not a kid anymore.*

Byron looked calm, almost half asleep. John glanced sideways at Byron in disbelief. Was it reckless youth that made staying cool so easy?

There was a slow, metallic noise that vibrated through the October afternoon air as they climbed higher and higher. John barely noticed the autumn sun which was midway in the sky and glowed onto the rutty wooden carriage. He held his breath, a tingle of anticipation, adrenaline coursing through his body.

Something about the moment made him think about waiting at the airport, his chartered flight ready to go to unseen places. Places most people only saw on the weekend news or in photographs. It was the same kinetic nervousness all over again.

The cart reached its pinnacle and for a brief moment the fun-seekers were suspended, weightless in the air, free of the brace, free of all restraints. Then, as if they were going in slow-motion, the whole reel at quarter speed, they descended the track, picking up speed. The cement rushed perilously towards them. John couldn't help but close his eyes and grit his teeth as his shoulders pressed up against the back of his seat. He heard a collective scream. Hands were thrown in the air. Wind crushed against his chest and thrashed his face. They dipped and curled. Then in a few moments they reached the end and it was over.

John got out and shakily headed towards the exit. Byron was several paces in front of him and seemed to have suffered no ill effects. John stopped and looked at the rest of the crowd. They were at least twenty years younger than he was.

John had the dark brown restless eyes of somebody who had seen combat. His complexion was whitish offset by his wavy brown hair that curled across his forehead. He was tall, wide-shouldered with a sharp jaw. His youth was lost to him—faded away like an ancient mural and what was left of John was a middle-aged man who walked with slow long strides, knowing things and people would arrive and depart whether he wanted them to or not.

It was John's first rollercoaster ride and it had taken some cajoling from his son for him to even try it. A much younger, less battle-weary John would have hopped onto the rollercoaster without a second thought. But that was before John had been shot twice, before he had seen too many bloody corpses, too many needless deaths, too much of everything the world had to offer.

John and Byron stepped from beneath the rollercoaster's shadow into the thick light and found themselves among a group of teenagers and kids carrying balloons and eating cotton candy and mini-donuts, all shuffling zombie-like towards the petting zoo or the superdogs, or the Hellivator.

It was Byron's thirteenth birthday. John had planned on watching Byron enjoy the rides from a safe distance, but Byron would have none of it, and shamelessly goaded him into joining him, knowing the exact right buttons to push with his dad.

They braved the crowd, walking aimlessly and savouring the moment, letting people wash over them like they were floating down a stream. Kids running everywhere. Strollers used as battering rams. Elbows used as weapons. Several years ago, John wouldn't have been able to handle the large crowds, the childish laughter, the constant jostling without feeling like somebody was squeezing his chest, a feeling that untold dread was about to occur.

John turned to his son. Byron already had the distinctive awkward teenage incongruous facial features and the same lankiness and body thickness John had had at his age. A lady-killer he was not. Byron wore baggy pants and a Grateful Dead T-shirt with holes in it and a red Yankees baseball cap slightly off centre.

Was this really the style? John wondered. He doubted Byron even knew who the Grateful Dead were, but he knew that the best way to further alienate his already alienated son was to question his questionable taste in clothes.

John looked around at the other kids who were roughly Byron's age. They also wore questionable clothes and so John decided he wasn't one to judge.

Byron said something to John but John wasn't paying attention. "Pardon?"

"I said let's go again," Byron said.

"Can't, my leg is stiffening up. I need to walk around some," John said, instinctively touching the cavity in his leg where a chunk of flesh had once been. John thought it was funny that the older gunshot wound from Afghanistan was the one which ached more than the one from the gangster.

"Just once more," Byron said. "You don't want me to tell Mom you were chicken, do you?"

John smiled. "She'd never believe you."

Byron stopped walking and looked up at John. "Come on Dad, don't be an old fart."

"Okay, once more."

They got back in line. John peered up at the rollercoaster, not believing they had just gone on the rickety thing and were planning on going back.

"You scared?" Byron asked.

"Why would I be scared?"

Byron shrugged his shoulders. "Don't know. Because you're chicken."

John laughed good-naturedly and patted Byron on the back of the head—a gesture Byron tried unsuccessfully to dodge.

What was it about experience that makes me so cautious? John wondered. A kid has so much more to lose but thinks so little about chance and mortality.

"I used to be brave once," John said, looking back up at the looming wooden structure. John used to ride into battle with Marines and barely flinch. Even the stoic Marines, known for their bravery and their prowess, had praised John for his coolness.

Where had that man gone?

"So you keep telling me," Byron said, incredulously.

The lineup went slowly, stretching out the dread, but eventually they made it to the front. After they finished the rollercoaster for a second time, John exhaled in relief. He was glad that was over with.

They next wandered over to a stand and bought two hotdogs. They found a bench to sit on and watched as the crowd went by.

"Dad . . . you ever think you'll go back?"

"We've talked about this before," John said, between mouthfuls of hotdog.

"No, I mean to Afghanistan. I mean, it's a lot safer now."

John felt stupid. He had thought that Byron was talking about his ex-wife. "Oh, I don't know. Probably not. That period of my life is over. Why do you ask?"

"Well, I just thought it would make you happy, that's all." Byron studied his food overly carefully.

"No, that wouldn't make me happier. It makes me most happy when I spend time with you. Don't ever think otherwise, okay?"

Byron looked up and smiled weakly. "Sure thing, Dad."

John put an awkward arm around his son and for a brief moment Byron let it rest there before he shrugged it off.

Was it really such a ridiculous suggestion? John wondered.

Was Byron picking up on some undercurrent that was always there? Sure, perhaps he had once longed to be back in a place where he felt he could make a difference, but the hues and colours had all but faded and he was content to be far away from the messes of the world and be with his son and watch the crowd with nothing more than narcissism on its mind.

John and Byron finished their hotdogs and joined the crowd. They took in the salty air, the smell of grease, the white lights, golden tents, the shoot 'em up games, the roulette tables and the loudspeakers announcing the monster trucks.

Byron lumbered around with the disinterested swagger native to early teenagers around the world. John always thought parenthood was a sort of curse, a cosmic joke—the way your kid always turned out a better, youthful, more helpful version of yourself.

"What are you doing tonight?" John asked.

Byron shrugged. "Probably just watch a movie or something with a couple of friends."

"What movie?"

"Something PG—don't worry."

"That wasn't why I was asking."

"I don't know. I'm not really sure what's out. You want to get some cotton candy?" Byron asked as he stopped and surveyed the park ground.

They shuffled over to the vendor, a thin man with ruddy skin and a big smile. John brought out his wallet and paid eight dollars and fifty cents.

"You remember the last time you bought me cotton candy?"

John shook his head. "I haven't a clue."

"We were on a vacation—in New York at the Yankees game. You had some sort of meeting there or something."

John nodded. He had gone to New York to meet with his editors about a possible book deal that eventually became *Putting Hell Together*. "The Yankees came back to tie it up in the bottom of the ninth."

"I heard they built a new Yankee Stadium."

"It's not the same."

"You've been?"

John shook his head. "No, and I'm not going to. It just wouldn't be the same."

"Apparently it cost like a billion dollars to build."

"Yes, but Ruth didn't build it. That's the difference."

Byron frowned. "Who's Ruth?"

John shook his head and sighed nostalgically. "Never mind."

They walked past a promotional booth advertising a cable company, or perhaps a new flat-screen television, where two boisterous, long-legged women were smiling their best smiles, practically draping themselves over the screen, proving that minimum wage could at least buy sex appeal.

"How's school?" John asked his son.

A month or so ago, Byron's teacher had emailed Hayden to say she was concerned a bunch of older boys were picking on Byron. Hayden had phoned John in tears, asking what she should do about it. Byron had refused to say anything or tell anybody.

John, so adept at crisis management, drove over to calm Hayden down and talk to Byron. Byron admitted to his idolized father that there was one boy named Ben who would kick him in the back on the way to class.

John had told him to stand up for himself, while Hayden had told Byron to tell his teacher. It was yet again one of their many different parenting styles.

"Not really," Byron said, staring at the television screens.

"What does 'not really' mean?"

"Forget it, Dad."

On the three televisions in the booth there were different stations—one sports station, one nature channel and a news station. John, forever the news junkie, instinctively stopped to see what was making the broadcast.

On screen was a handsome reporter talking about a banker who had defrauded his client out of millions of dollars. The reporter called it one of the largest Ponzi schemes in history.

"Come on, Dad."

"Just a moment."

"Questions are being asked about why the authorities didn't suspect anything for such a long period of time," the reporter said. "In fact, the police failed to act even after they received several tips."

John watched until the report ended and the newscast cut to commercials.

"What do you want to do now?" John asked Byron.

"Let's go to the arcade."

They walked over to the arcade tent and John watched as Byron played several video games.

"Do you want to play?" Byron asked. He was playing a game where he had to shoot various types of aliens.

John tried to conceal his disgust at the computer-animated gore and guts. "No, I don't think so."

Just then John's phone rang. Byron let out a soft groan. John looked at his phone. He didn't recognize the caller; it wasn't a local area code but John decided to answer anyway.

"Is this John Webster?" It was a soft, hesitant female voice.

"Speaking."

"You write for the *Daily Globe*?"

"Yes, the same. Who is this?"

"I . . . may be in some trouble."

"What sort of trouble?" John asked, his interest piqued.

There was a long period of silence, but then the woman spoke so fast that her words got garbled together. "I think I've done something really terrible. I thought I could trust him, but I'm not sure."

"Trust who?" John asked. "I'm sorry but you're not making any sense."

"Have you heard of the Ko Chang Project?"

John glanced at Byron, who had gone back to his video game and wasn't listening to the conversation.

"No," John replied. "Should I have?"

"Nerno Energy has the rights to a field in the Gulf of Thailand, several hundred miles off of the island of Ko Chang. Only the project has been delayed several times."

"So what are you saying?"

"They say the delay was caused by environmentalists but I have my doubts."

"Why do you doubt it?"

The woman hesitated. "I've heard rumours that there is no oil there at all. Possibly even intentionally faked to drive up stock prices."

"Where did you hear this rumour?" John hoped she had something more than just rumour.

"I can't tell you that."

"Well, I'm sure there are many legitimate reasons as to why the project was delayed."

The woman hesitated again. John held his breath. He knew it would come down to what the woman said next, whether she was legit or just somebody with an axe to grind.

"I have proof," she finally said.

"What kind of proof?"

There was another long period of silence which was beginning to frustrate John. "Look," John said. "I'm not going to help you unless you offer me proof."

John waited but the woman hung up. John sighed. He was disappointed because it sounded like it had potential. John redialled the number but the phone just rang and rang. John decided that just in case there was some credibility to the story he would phone his boss, managing editor of the *Daily Globe*, Charles Dana.

John knew that Charles Dana would be working on a Saturday because he always worked six days a week. Charles answered on the first ring.

"Hey boss, do you know anything about Nerno Energy? You have somebody covering it?"

"Not much and not to my knowledge. Why?"

"I just had an interesting conversation." John then relayed the conversation he had just finished having with the unknown woman.

"You don't know who she is?"

"You haven't heard anything?"

"You should try asking Michael Chu. He would know better than I," Charles Dana said. "But what's your gut on this?"

"I don't know. From what the woman said I think it's just somebody trying to get Nerno some bad coverage, but I want to make sure."

"Okay, keep me posted."

Next John phoned Michael Chu. John didn't know Michael well but he knew he was from Toronto originally, and had worked as an investment banker before moving to Vancouver to work for the *Daily Globe*.

"John Webster, what can I do for you?"

"You following Nerno?"

"Somewhat. Why?"

"Do you know anything about the Ko Chang Project?"

"I've heard of it, but I don't really know much about it."

"You think it could be fake?"

"What do you mean fake?

"I'm talking cover up."

"What makes you think that?"

"I have a source but I'm not sure of the credibility of the info."

"Well, not knowing anything about your source I would have to say it's extremely unlikely. There are many hoops a company has to go through in order to secure those drilling rights and it wouldn't make much sense unless they were certain oil was there."

"Okay, thanks," John said and hung up.

John found Byron, who was over in the corner playing a racing game. John stood watching Byron as he navigated virtual corners, passing virtual cars. Soon Byron would be old enough to drive real cars and demand his own wheels. The thought made John sad. Time passed so quickly, especially when you weren't paying attention.

"Byron, I'm sorry . . . I've got to go."

"What? But we haven't even been on the Zoom Accelerator yet," Byron said.

"You can stay here if you want. I can come pick you up in a couple of hours."

Byron got up from the racing game. "Just forget it, Dad."

"I'm sorry."

"I know, it's work."

"It could be something. I'm not sure yet."

Byorn crossed his arms, looking very childish and slightly comical, yet again reminding John of his childhood self. "It can't wait a couple of hours?"

"You know how it is . . . old news is no news."

The ride home was a silent one. Byron curled up with his feet on the seat and stared out the window. John understood his disappointment.

John thought back to his conversation with the mystery woman. He was skeptical about her, but the more he thought about it, the more curious he became.

John scanned the radio stations for any mention of Nerno but there was nothing. John couldn't decide if that was a good sign or not. It could mean the woman was a fraud, or it could mean something really big that nobody had gotten yet.

In the back of his mind, John kept wondering why the woman had phoned him of all people. Why hadn't she picked somebody who reported on business, somebody like Michael Chu?

John pulled up to his old house. His ex-wife had decided to keep it in the divorce. John wasn't sure if it was malicious intent or she just didn't want to move. Every time John saw the house, it filled him with remorse of how he let things get so bad.

John debated whether to just drop Byron off, but he felt he should at least say hello to his ex-wife. He didn't relish facing her, especially since she would likely be angry at their early appearance.

John turned to Byron but he had already jumped out of the car and was walking up the stone steps. John got out of the car, locked the door and followed Byron who, at the top of the stairs, dug deep into his pocket and pulled out a set of keys, which he then inserted into the lock. The door clicked open, and Byron stepped in, and not waiting for his father, shut the door behind him.

John stood looking up at the door, slightly aghast. Had his son just shut the door on him? *I knew it was his birthday but he had better grow up,* John thought.

At the top of the steps John could hear Hayden through the wood siding, her soft voice sort of floating through the air.

"Byron? Is that you? What are you doing home so early?"

John turned the door knob but it was locked and so he knocked. John stood looking around at his old neighbourhood in the moments before Hayden opened the door. She stood with her arms crossed and one hip slightly higher than the other in a defiant attitude. She wore a grey turtleneck sweater with jean capris. Her thick black hair fell over her shoulders.

"John?" She looked surprised. "What are you guys doing home so early?"

John was grateful she didn't seem mad. At least not yet.

"I got a call to go in to work."

Hayden nodded distractedly. "Big story?"

John nodded. "Yeah, could be big."

"all right then," Hayden said, looking back up the stairs.

"Everything okay?" John asked. He was relieved he wasn't going to receive the usual lecture, but at the same time worried. Something was going on.

"Yeah, sure."

John stared at his ex-wife. He knew if he kept pestering her she would just clamp up tighter. "Okay. I'd better go then."

Hayden looked down at her fingernails. "John, can you give me a call some time . . . you know, when you're not so busy."

"Of course. What's this about?"

Hayden frowned. "Not now. You have to go."

"Give me the brief version. Just so I don't worry."

Hayden's nut-brown eyes were large, almost pleading. John couldn't remember the last time he had seen her look so . . . vulnerable. He instinctively took a step forward but then stopped himself, remembering he couldn't take her in his arms anymore. The thought physically pained him.

"It's better if we sit down," Hayden said, crossing her arms tighter. "And have a stiff drink."

John frowned. Hayden had never been a big drinker and if she needed alcohol to tell him then he knew it was bad.

"Is it something to do with Byron?" John asked.

Hayden smiled, almost laughed, and it made John feel better.

"No, nothing to do with Byron."

John waited. The silence was uncomfortable, but John was determined not to be the one to break it. Eventually Byron ended the stalemate by barrelling down the stairs, stopping just short of Hayden. He looked at his parents.

"You guys okay?"

"Yeah, everything is fine," Hayden said, putting a hand on Byron's shoulder. Unlike with his dad, Byron let it rest there. A female's touch, John supposed. What men would do for a female's touch.

The Office

THE DIM AUTUMN SUNLIGHT FLOODED the porch, illuminating Hayden and Byron who were standing, watching John, who sat in his Honda Civic, his curiosity unsatisfied. John smiled and waved at them before turning the key in the ignition.

John remembered when he would go on some dangerous war assignment and his family would watch from the same porch and wave him goodbye. Hayden, younger would hold Byron in one arm while waving with the other as John climbed into the taxi, airport bound.

As John turned onto 10th Avenue, this snapshot of the past faded. Was it some ill omen? John thought about Nerno Energy and Ko Chang and his unknown caller. The woman caller bothered him for some reason. Was it the stress in her voice? Call it a journalistic sixth sense.

John drove across the Burrard Street bridge, looking across to downtown, the stately buildings in profile against the blue mountains.

John stopped at a traffic light. He felt an unsettling feeling in his stomach, but he didn't know if that was from Hayden's reluctance to tell him whatever was bothering her, or from Nerno Energy. Perhaps it was from both.

The traffic light changed and John slowly pressed down on the gas pedal, laying his two forefingers on the steering wheel. The engine groaned under strain. The unsettling feeling increased, as if he was in some kind of danger, always in his periphery.

Could Nerno Energy really be dangerous? Generally John knew who his enemies were, but if he went to Calgary his enemies would be unseen, unspoken, undefined. Was he ready for such a battle?

John arrived at the *Daily Globe* building, parking in the underground lot. Usually John just walked to work since he lived only about twenty minutes away, so he didn't have any specific spot and he found he had to go down to the second level before he found any empty spaces.

The *Daily Globe* building had once been the most impressive building in the city, but decades of neglect and weathering had left it a shattered version of its truer, nobler self. The building was an apt metaphor for the newspaper itself. The *Daily Globe* used to be dropped off at every doorstep, every business. You wanted to know something, you went to the *Daily Globe*. But those days had long gone, along with vinyl records and bell-bottom jeans.

John took the elevator up to the fourth floor. The news room was the hub, the hive, the nucleus, the epicentre. John nodded to the secretary, a temp he didn't recognize. The editors had just finished their afternoon pow-wow to check on stories and any updates. Computers were buzzing, phones were ringing. A couple of the younger Saturday interns were herding at the coffee machine like fretful caribou, talking about their most recent sexcapades.

John walked past them on his way to his desk, greeting them with a tight-lipped smile. He was mostly wary of them, as they all wanted his job and would stab him in the back to get it.

John booted up his computer. He searched online for Ko Chang and found several offers for hotels and flights. Judging by the pictures of the sprawling beaches, it was a popular tourist destination. He searched further and found it was the third largest island in Thailand on the eastern seaboard.

Next John typed "Nerno Energy" into Google. The first thing that popped up was their website. He scanned over it and clicked on the most recent annual report. They seemed to have had record profits; their stocks had skyrocketed, said a post from the CEO, a man named David Kahn.

On page fifteen of the annual report was the first mention of the Ko Chang platform. Once it was up and running, it would produce 200,000 barrels of oil a day, the report said, and had an estimated life span of twenty years. John sat back in his chair, digesting what he had just read. He didn't know anything about the oil business, but that seemed like a staggering amount of oil. And a lot of money. John read on. Nerno was just completing an environmental survey, but production would commence at the beginning of the second quarter.

John clicked onward and found an old news article about an oil spill in the Gulf of Mexico that Nerno was supposedly responsible for. One of Nerno's drills ruptured, sending thousands of gallons of oil into the sea and killing all marine life in the area. The article quoted several government sources that criticized how David Kahn had handled the disaster, but John couldn't find anything else that mentioned Ko Chang.

Next John found a picture of the Nerno senior leadership team on the last page of the report. David Kahn was a handsome man, in his mid-fifties John guessed, with swept-back grey hair. John looked over the executives, wondering if his caller was any of them, but there was only one woman in the group. Andrea Drashkov was the chief financial officer, the report said.

John searched Andrea Drashkov on the Internet and found a short article in *Business Weekly*. She was born in Calgary and graduated from Mount Royal College before getting a scholarship to Cornell. She worked for various companies including ExxonMobil and Chevron before forming Nerno Energy with David Kahn and George Hopkins.

John clicked on a YouTube link and found a speech Andrea Drashkov had given at some economics conference. She had a deep, distinct voice. She most definitely wasn't the woman he had spoken to on the phone.

John went back to the Nerno website and looked at other female employees—anybody mentioned in the literature—but he came up empty. Perhaps the woman he'd spoken to didn't work for Nerno at all.

He got up and walked over to the business section of the newsroom. He felt like he was passing through a wormhole of sorts. Reporters generally stuck with their own kind. Jocks with jocks, entertainment with entertainment. Home and garden had their own category, in John's humble opinion, right below the janitor.

The business section consisted of eleven reporters, and they were different from general assignment. For starters they were better dressed. Much better. They usually wore suits, sometimes with handkerchiefs that matched their ties and socks. Secondly, they usually looked down on the rest of the newsroom because they had master's degrees, and thirdly, they had more money than the average reporter.

Most of them had some experience working in the business world but had turned to journalism because it gave them some notoriety at cocktail parties.

John walked up to three reporters who were watching the business report on television. The handsome but bored anchor was talking about the stock market.

"The Dow Jones is up three points while the Nasdaq has lost four."

"Hey, can anybody tell me anything about David Kahn?" John asked.

Michael Chu looked up from his cubicle. He was in his mid-fifties, tall and broad-shouldered, with faded dark hair and a straight jaw line. He, like his colleagues, was wearing a suit and tie.

"Sure, I've interviewed him a couple of times. What do you want to know?"

"What he's like, for starters."

Michael shrugged. "He's charming, charismatic, a good talker like most CEOs."

"Smart?"

Michael laughed. "Most certainly. I wouldn't expect a man worth 3.4 billion dollars to be stupid."

"And how about cunning?"

"Why do you want to know? You doing a story on him?"

All eyes were on John now. He felt that they wanted to know why he was stepping on their turf and John, truthfully, had no idea apart from wanting to know why the mystery woman chose him.

"Possibly. I have to see how it shapes up."

"What's the angle?" Michael asked.

"No angle. Just looking at possible story ideas."

Michael paused thoughtfully. "I don't believe he's devious, if that's what you mean."

"So you believe what he tells you?"

"I suppose—I mean he puts spin on whatever he says. But if you're asking does he outright lie? I would say he's a pretty straight shooter."

John nodded. "Okay, thanks."

John turned to go but Michael stopped him. "You might want to watch out for the CFO. Her name is Andrea Drashkov. She's beautiful but evil."

"What do you mean?"

"I've only interviewed her once but there is something that's not right about her, that's cold and calculating. I didn't like her at all."

"I guess I'll keep an eye on her."

The Geologist

OLD TOM'S WAS AN ENGLISH pub on Dunbar Street. Pine trees lined the street and shaded the black and cream-coloured building.

John parked his car and went inside. The restaurant was dimly lit with stained wood floors with large booths. Soccer and cricket adorned the television sets. For a quiet Sunday morning, the restaurant bustled with people—mostly elderly Empire types, the men with white moustaches and the ladies with large silver brooches.

John looked around and spotted Charles in a corner booth. He walked over and collapsing into the seat opposite Charles. Charles, true to form, wore a suit, red tie on white shirt and a red handkerchief in his right breast pocket. He was already halfway through his breakfast, eggs benedict by the looks of it.

"How was Byron's birthday?" Charles asked.

John sighed. "I don't understand him. I guess I don't understand kids in general."

The attentive waitress came to the table and offered John a cup of coffee, which he accepted graciously.

"It'll get better," Charles said,

John wondered if that was actually true or not. If his own father hadn't died in a car accident how close would he be to him now? The stern Scot never exuded much warmth and John doubted he would have changed much with age. Without his own father's example, how was he expected to be a good father to Byron? It was a defence he had used with Hayden or several occasions. Mostly unsuccessfully.

"What about your family?" John asked, trying to change the subject.

"The same. They want me to retire, but I don't know what I would do. Take up golf or gardening?" Charles said, shaking his head. "I will not go gently into that good night."

John smiled and nodded, picking up the menu and pretending to peruse it. "I need a geologist."

"Based on what? The word of a woman you don't even know the name of."

"And I'm going to Calgary."

Charles stared incredulously at John over his reading glasses. "What? No you aren't."

"I've got vacation time. I'll get the union involved if necessary."

"You don't even believe this woman."

"I don't disbelieve her either. When did it become so terrible to follow up on a lead?"

"I never said that, but with today's technology you can do all that sitting in your own seat at the office. *The Economist*, for all its global perspective, manages to do it exceedingly well. I'm sure you can too."

"That's the Pommeroys talking."

The Pommeroys were the ancient family, originally from the middle of England, who owned a majority stake in the *Daily Globe*.

John knew it irked Charles more than anything to be compared to the aristocratic-aspiring family.

John came from lower class stock and couldn't have had less in common with the Pommeroys and couldn't have been more disdainful of their pompous ways, most of which consisted of having everyone call them "sir" or "duke" even if they had no claim to any such title.

"Just be thankful you don't have to sit in a budget meeting with them, John."

"I need to find this woman, and when I do I need to talk to her face-to-face."

Charles shook his head. "That just simply isn't going to happen. The reality is that we are forced to do more with less. And that means the geologist is out. When you find something more, we can talk."

John nodded. The waitress came back but John said he wasn't hungry. He insisted on paying for his coffee even when Charles offered.

"Don't want to break the paper's piggybank," John said bitterly, thrusting a couple of dollars on the table.

Charles eyed John stonily. "Just remember that they have an army of lawyers meticulously going through every word you put in print and if they see one misplaced 'a' then they will pounce on us and rip us to shreds."

"I think I've been doing this long enough," John said as he stood and walked out the door.

When John left Old Tom's restaurant, he drove to the office. Sunday traffic lackadaisically trickled through the city, as the sun peeked through the grey cloud that covered the sky like a coat of cement. Even though it was only October, it was a cold, frosty day.

John decided to park at his apartment and walk to work. It gave him time to think about Nerno Energy and his next move. But what if he was wrong? What if there wasn't a story? Charles would be right, and he would look like a fool.

John loved Sundays because he could do his work in peace without interruptions from editors or other journalists. He spent the whole day researching Nerno, looking at the thousands of works written about them. First he went through the newspaper's archives and then through all of the annual reports.

David Kahn had been working in the oil business for over thirty years, starting in marketing and then sales before founding his own company. Judging by the reports, before Nerno went public, Kahn raised equity mainly through Chinese channels. Nerno had acquired the rights to several profitable properties, including the Ko Chang project, which had shot the stock through the roof.

Around three o'clock, John shut down his computer. He had to get to his appointment with his psychiatrist. Just as John was grabbing his jacket his cell phone rang. He looked at the caller ID and found that it was a Calgary number.

John answered his phone a bit breathlessly. "Hello?"

There was a long pause and then the woman's voice again. "I'm sorry for phoning on a Sunday . . . I'm a bit paranoid."

"It's okay. I'm at the office anyway."

"Do you think you could help me?"

"That depends. What sort of help are you looking for?"

"I'm only trying to do the right thing."

"Of course you are," John reassured her. "You can trust me. You say don't print it, I won't. But I can't help you unless I know more about you."

There was another long pause. John could hear the static crack over the long distance connection.

"Well, what do you want to know?"

"Your name, for starters."

"Sheila McKinnon."

"Pleased to meet you, Sheila." John's job was to try and make Sheila as comfortable as possible.

"I'm the vice-president of marketing at Nerno."

John knew that he had to be careful with his next question. "In our previous conversation you said you did something. What did you mean by that?"

"I think David Kahn knows."

"What does he know?"

"That I read his email."

John looked up at the neon lights, already tired of coaxing information from Sheila, but he controlled the irritation in his voice. "What email are you talking about?"

"I found his password on a post-it note in his trash."

"What were you doing going through his trash?"

"I wasn't going through his trash. It was just lying on top," Sheila said, defensively.

John was always astonished that some of these large firms had such terrible security. "Okay, what did you find in his email?"

"His email said he didn't want investors to find out about Ko Chang before the sale."

"You mean to the Chinese?"

"Yes."

"What makes you think he knows?"

Sheila paused. "He's been acting kind of strange towards me."

"In what way?"

"I don't know. Giving me strange looks. Dropping into my office randomly."

"Has he confronted you?"

"No. At least, not yet."

"Okay, that's good," John said. "Tell me, did you already suspect something? Is that why you started snooping?"

"Yes."

"What was it?"

"It wasn't anything specific. Just the never ending delays and the lack of information."

"Okay, that's good. Can we meet in person?"

Sheila hesitated. "I don't think that's a good idea."

"I have to fly to Calgary anyway. We can meet for coffee and you can tell me what's going on."

"Somebody might see us."

"We will make sure it's discreet. Somewhere nobody would know you. Do you know a place like that?"

"There's this place by my parents called Coffee and Scream."

"Coffee and Scream?" John said, dubiously. "What sort of place is that?"

"I know, it sounds strange. It has this playpen for kids."

John wasn't about to question Sheila's choice. "That will be fine. There will be too many cute kids for anybody to take notice of us."

It was a lame attempt at a joke that fell flat with Sheila, who just seemed confused.

"Just give me the address," John said, quickly.

"North Mountain Drive and Chancellor Way. You think you can find it?"

"Yeah, no problem," John said, writing it down in his notebook. "When is good for you?"

"Well, when are you in town?"

"I fly out tomorrow morning. Can we meet in the evening?"

"That should be fine. I'll call you if I can't make it."

"Can you print a copy of the email?"

"I'm not sure. That means I have to go back into his email. What if he has changed the password? What if he has set up a Trojan?"

"A what?"

"A Trojan horse to track who has been into his account."

"Well, do what you're comfortable with. If you think the risk is too high then don't do it, but eventually we'll need some sort of proof. Especially if you decide not to come forward."

"Okay, I'll see what I can do."

Sheila hung up. John phoned Charles Dana right away.

"The woman called back. I'm meeting her tomorrow."

"What do you mean? I told you you're not flying there. It's not in the budget."

John couldn't believe what he was hearing. It was a conversation they wouldn't have had even two years ago, but things were changing so quickly. "She says she has an email that will corroborate her story," John said. "This could be a huge story and a big deal for the paper if this turns out to be true. I'm talking Pulitzer Prize winner."

There was a pause. "Okay. If you think so I'll talk to the Pommeroys."

"Boss . . . is it really that bad?"

"You don't know the half of it," Charles said, hanging up.

"Do you remember when you first came to me?" Doctor Kavita Nagi asked. She was East Indian, in her mid-fifties with hard, rubber skin and thick curly hair.

She had been John's psychiatrist for several years, ever since John had been shot by gangsters. Afterwards, the flashbacks became so debilitating that he couldn't hide it any longer.

John sighed, glancing up at the clock to see how much longer his session had to go. "Of course. Most of the time I was too drunk to even type my own name."

"And look how far you've come. You're healthier. Your relationship with your son is much better."

John thought about the time he had spent with Byron at the amusement park and felt a twang of guilt for cutting it short. But, still, he supposed it probably wouldn't have happened at all last birthday.

"I'm not abandoning you, if that's what you think," John said with a slight smile.

Doctor Nagi shook her head. "That's not what I mean. Your challenge now will be not to slide backwards, to hold strong."

"What makes you think I'll do that?"

"I'm just saying a lot of people think they are fine but they don't realize they are standing on thin ice. You're a compulsive person by nature. Always remember that."

The makeshift wooden crosses were dug into the brown sand looking out onto the dark blue water. The waves crashed onto the beach, slowly seeping up the land. John crouched down and looked at the three dozen or so crosses that peppered the landscape. In the foreground there was a large weatherworn sign that dedicated the memorial to the 132,000 civilians of Afghanistan and Iraq that had been killed by the allied occupation.

The lettering was fading now and John felt that he was fading with it, as if both the relevance of the sign and his own purpose were somehow joined through the cosmos. Would some strong wind pick the sign up and carry it out to sea? What would happen to him?

John was at Wreck Beach, the infamous nude beach at the tip of the university where hippies and pot smokers would dance and play music until nightfall. But there were no naked people walking around in the middle of a frigid October. In fact, there was nobody around at all except for a young couple kissing on the rocks in the distance.

Behind John, evergreens grew on the cliff. The wind coming off the water was cold and clammy but John didn't mind it as it hit his face and ran through his clothes and hair. Everything was serene and perfect. The Pacific Ocean stretched out to the horizon.

John usually visited the memorial a couple of times every year, in the winter when he knew he wouldn't have to face the herbal smell of marijuana or risk seeing unceremonious lumps of fat on display. He enjoyed the quietness so close to the bustling city. It was this pilgrimage—usually inspired after a particularly tough session with Doctor Nagi—that settled his mind and enabled him to face the world and its multilayered problems.

Nobody knew who had erected the memorial. It had just appeared overnight about a year ago. At the time, John had written a story about it, but was unsuccessful in finding its creators. The parks board had been reluctant to touch it, for fear of a negative reprisal during election season, and so the crosses and the sign had stayed.

Somewhere Amira is in there, John thought.

Amira was a woman, a girl really, who John had never spoken to. In fact, he had only seen her once and yet she somehow managed to linger singularly within John's mind. She had been the daughter of a restaurant owner in Baghdad and she had been tortured and killed by her kidnappers who wanted to make a quick buck.

John had seen a lot of people die needlessly. He had seen all their faces, heard their pleas for help, smelled the sizzle of burning flesh, but yet it was Amira who stood out somehow. She had symbolized everything that had gone wrong in Iraq and Afghanistan.

Sometimes John thought it was arrogant that so few crosses could represent so many deaths. John didn't think the human mind could really contemplate anything bigger than a thousand anyway.

Anything beyond that was just a non-quantitative number used only for statisticians and computers.

John thought about what Nagi had told him about slipping backwards. It wouldn't happen to him; he had worked so hard to put his life back together. Still, he had a bad feeling about the Nerno story. A feeling he couldn't shake. Perhaps it was Sheila's frightened voice on the phone that had made his shoulder muscles tighten up. He couldn't remember the last time a source had sounded so scared.

The couple had finished their makeout session and were climbing down the rocks. John watched the two distant figures make their way unsteadily down to the sand before he decided he too must turn and climb back through the forest, back to the road where he had parked his car and back to reality.

Calgary

JOHN WATCHED THROUGH THE AIRPLANE window as Vancouver slowly subsided into the distance. John loved his hometown, the familiar mass of the Fraser River and the boxy outlines of the buildings against the mountains. The plane banked, tipping the wing high into the air obstructing the view of the city. John felt that he was back on the rollercoaster with Byron and that if he shifted his gaze Byron would be sitting next to him, laughing and smiling.

John—always a restless traveller—loved the sky. He was a transient person and had always been so and the Boeing jet brought a new adventure, an excitement of things to come, and a sense that the mistakes of the past could be temporarily forgotten.

He thought of his meeting with Sheila in the evening. What would it yield? John felt that it would be good for his career, which had been in neutral since several of his articles had brought down a drug lord years ago.

As the plane rose above the clouds, his mind turned away from his failure with Hayden and Byron, turned away from the realization that he had escaped death twice—once in Afghanistan and once on the streets of Vancouver—and from the nagging feeling that he had entered into some hidden extra level of a computer game. A secret level that only soldiers and the dead knew. But with this feeling came a dull angst that he had done nothing with the added time.

The plane reached cruising altitude and the seatbelt sign duly dinged to tell the passengers that they could move around freely.

John read *Newsweek*, which he had bought from a news stand after the security check. There was a story about a school in Tanzania and it made John think about his first assignment, about an orphanage, also in Tanzania.

John had gotten on an airplane at sixteen, freshly scarred from his father's death and from the realization that school would never be for him. John Senior, who had grown up poor in Govan, a hard-up district of Glasgow, had always believed in education (his own dad was a ship builder who couldn't read) and would never have let John run away.

John was interrupted by the flight attendant who offered John something to drink.

"Just some orange juice," John said, returning to his magazine.

About an hour later, the plane started its descent. The wing flaps extended, causing the whole plane to tremble. The passengers shifted in their seats restless. John looked out the window at Calgary as the city came hurtling towards them. He could see the famous landmarks: the Saddledome, Calgary Tower, the Stampede grounds. Liquid red sunlight spilled into the snowy city scene giving everything a heightened intensity, as if every jagged edge, curvature and flat line was of extreme importance.

The plane touched down on the runway and taxied into the airport.

The captain announced their arrival over the loud speaker and everybody got up from their seats.

John collected his luggage and caught a taxi downtown. The air was sharp and cold. The sun was still low in the sky and cast ominous brown shadows across the concrete streets and sidewalk. There was a light film of snow dusting the city, making the horizon look like a Christmas ornament.

John looked out the window at the foreign landscape. Rows of stilted houses lined the street on each side. The blinds were all drawn. The lights were all off. The taxi turned onto a different road and several minutes later the houses turned into a large, gloomy industrial park. It had been years since John was last in Calgary and the street names were all unfamiliar. Eventually they reached the skyscrapers of downtown.

"Where to, boss?" the driver asked, glancing at John in the rear view mirror.

John checked the address for his hotel and gave it to the driver. "Edmonds Hotel."

"Got it," the driver said, turning onto 12th Avenue.

"You here on business?"

John nodded vaguely. He was feeling uncommunicative but the driver persisted. "Where are you from?"

"Just Vancouver."

"Hopefully you're not here too long."

John looked at the driver, his interest piqued. "Why?"

"Cold front coming in. Supposed to get to fifty below in the coming weeks."

John nodded. "Well, I shouldn't be here for too long."

"If I was you I would turn around and head someplace else. Someplace warm," the driver said, somewhat melodramatically.

Despite John's extensive travels, he had never been in any place with temperatures much below zero; anything like fifty below was a foreign concept.

John was staring out of the window when something on the radio caught his attention. He leaned forward and asked the driver to turn the station up.

"Rumours persist that the family that owns a majority stake in the famous *Daily Globe* newspaper is again looking for a buyer. Several unnamed sources say the Pommeroys are in talks with Cloud News Corporation."

John fell back in his seat, feeling sick. He didn't want to work for Cloud News, the third largest media conglomerate in the world, that epitomized everything that was wrong with journalism. The company that practiced modern day yellow journalism would have put Joseph Pulitzer and William Hearst to shame.

What am I going to do? John wondered.

They arrived at the Edmonds Hotel. It was an old fashioned building that was a faded brick colour. It had probably been grand

and majestic at one time but for whatever reason had grown dilapidated and a little neglected; moss and weeds filled the gaps between the bricks.

John paid the driver, collected his suitcase and walked through to the front entrance. The heat of the cavernous lobby hit him immediately, warming his whole body. Dim lights dangled from the ceiling.

John found a quiet nook in the lobby and called Charles.

"Why didn't you tell me?" John demanded when Charles picked up the phone.

"What are you talking about?"

"The Pommeroys are looking to sell to Cloud News."

Charles paused, slightly taken aback. "Who told you that?"

"I heard it on the news, Chuck. You should have told me."

"I'm doing everything in my power to prevent it but the family is tired of losing money. Every other paper is owned by some corporation or another. We are looking at the end of a dynasty."

"They can't sell," John said, stubbornly.

"And how are you going to stop them?"

"I don't know. I'll chain myself to the doors if I have to," John said, although he was already forming a plan, no matter how crazy it sounded, even to him. If he exposed Nerno then perhaps the story could be nominated for awards, and John knew that one thing endlessly rich people liked almost as much as money was accolades. It was a long shot but it might just work.

When John finished his conversation with Charles he lined up to check in. While in line he flipped through a promotional pamphlet showing pictures of Calgary with cloudless blue skies, a horizon that stretched infinitely on and on, golden brown wheat fields, bull riding, and clusters of people smiling brightly and wearing large cowboy hats. Written across the top of the pamphlet were the words WELCOME TO THE TEXAS OF THE NORTH!

John put the pamphlet back on the rack when the receptionist called him up to the desk.

Welcome to the Texas of the North indeed, John thought.

John paid a deposit and got a key. The elevator was out of order so he walked up to the third floor, expecting the worst. But John was pleasantly surprised by his room. It was clean and well furnished with a queen-sized bed and a flat screen television in the corner. John still hadn't sprung for a flat screen television for his own apartment in Gastown.

John placed his suitcase down next to the bed and went to draw back the grey curtains and look out at the downtown landscape. It was beginning to snow lightly again. He looked across the street. There was a small black Jetta parked next to a lamp post. He stared at the car for a moment. It was mostly unremarkable except that the bumper was dented. But John felt that he had seen the same car at the airport. Of course it was impossible that he was being followed. John hadn't told anybody what flight he was taking. Sheila knew that he was coming but John hadn't told her when he was arriving. Still, John was positive that he had seen the car before and he didn't take such feelings lightly, having had to rely on his wits in the Middle East and Afghanistan to track down sources and survive.

John wondered if his phone was bugged. But who had bugged it and when had they had the chance to do so? John had only learned about Nerno on the weekend.

John had a shower and got changed into a fresh set of clothes. He didn't have anything warm except for a pullover sweater and a light jacket. John chastised himself for not being more prepared. He had just been so focused on Nerno and Sheila.

John then went downstairs to the gift shop and bought a Calgary Flames baseball cap which he pulled down on his forehead. He then got the bellhop to hail him a cab. He told the driver to take him to the stampede grounds. It was the only Calgary landmark he could think of.

"Excuse me?" the driver asked, confused.

"You heard me."

The driver pulled away from the curb. The Jetta didn't move from its parking spot. John exhaled. Perhaps he was being a little jumpy after all. They drove for about fifteen minutes before John leaned forward in the car. "Perhaps you could let me out here."

"Right here?" the driver asked incredulously. "You'll freeze to death."

"I'll be fine. I just want to go for a short walk."

The driver frowned. "Suit yourself."

John paid and got out. The snow was beginning to come down in thick, dry flakes and it was hard for John to see more than ten or eleven feet in front of him. He was beginning to rethink the wisdom of his actions, but he had no choice now except to stuff his numb hands in his jean pockets and walk on. The snow stung John's face and neck and sloshed down his collar, chilling his chest and back. John crossed the road and walked down an alleyway and through the other side, looking for the Jetta, but nobody seemed to be paying much attention to the crazy man without a jacket or a scarf or gloves.

John waved down the next cab he saw and gave the driver the address of the Coffee and Scream shop. The heat was on full blast in the car and John's exposed red skin began to tingle with sensation.

The drive took thirty minutes. The coffee shop had a fairly unremarkable entrance with a maroon awning.

The perfect place for a clandestine meeting, John thought.

John opened the dusty glass door and was immediately hit by the thick odour of sweet cinnamon and oak. John ordered a straight black coffee and sat in the corner on a hard plastic seat. The shop was about half full. Nobody seemed to be in any particular hurry to brave the cold.

As Sheila had described on the phone, there was a substantial play area for the kids with large colourful toys. For the most part, the kids seemed to have been left to their own devices as their parents tried to gain a little freedom in their hot caramel macchiatos.

John knew he was a couple of hours early and so he booted up his laptop and answered a couple of emails that he hadn't had a chance to reply to before he'd left Vancouver. He then phoned Hayden but got her voicemail. He left her a brief message telling her to phone him back when she got a chance. John wondered what she had been so anxious to talk to him about, but doubted that he would find out anytime soon.

He next read a section of the newspaper that was discarded on the table next to him. After he was finished, he went back to his computer and Googled Sheila, hoping to find a picture of what she looked like so he could spot her when she entered, but he couldn't find one.

There was an old analogue clock on the wall, hanging above the play area. John watched the hands tick forward. He got a tickle in the back of his throat and he knew it was from the allure of a secretive meeting, the promise of some sensitive knowledge being revealed. What would she say? What was her story? Would her words be printed in thick block lettering across the front page of every edition of the *Daily Globe*? Would it be enough to save the paper from being sold to Cloud News?

John was always his most content just before he saw the pieces of the story fit together. The knowledge that he could cause a ripple in the universe, that his actions and writings mattered, even if it was for only a fleeting moment in time. This was, of course, the dream of every journalist since Watergate and before, perhaps stretching as far back as the story of David versus Goliath.

The clock seemed to inch forward in time. Six o'clock came and went and still there was no sign of Sheila. Had she gotten cold feet? Maybe she had been followed and she had gotten scared. Had she been kidnapped? John sighed. His imagination was getting hold of him.

John occupied himself by watching the kids, who aged from about four to eleven, shrieking and playing with antiquated toys. John remembered having a break from Afghanistan and being home with Hayden and Byron. One day he had taken Byron to the park. It had had been a cool blustery spring day. The ground had smelt like chocolate. The park was mostly empty except for a couple of mothers and their children.

John had pushed Byron on the swings until he had gotten bored and wanted to go play on the monkey bars. John smiled at the memory. Byron couldn't have been much more than five or six at the time. The troubles in Afghanistan—the murder, the rape, the destruction—had never seemed so distant or so frivolous as they had when John had been sitting on the cold wooden bench, watching Byron dangling himself so unselfconsciously, unconcerned with the bars.

Was that the secret of youth? John wondered. The lack of experience, lack of knowledge about things outside the five-foot playground?

A couple of years ago, John had stopped at the same playground and had found that the monkey bars had been dug up and replaced by some uninteresting log contraption. John had asked a mother why the playground didn't have the monkey bars anymore.

"It's not safe," the mother had replied. John nodded as if he understood, but the truth was that he didn't. Why did parents worry about something as trivial as a metal play structure when there were so many larger menaces in the world?

"Are you John Webster?"

John turned to find a woman in her mid-forties with short brown hair, bright red lipstick and doughy cheeks. She had probably once been very beautiful.

John forced a smile, but felt angry for being caught daydreaming. "Hi, how are you?"

"My name is Sheila McKinnon."

"I was beginning to think you weren't going to make it."

Sheila glanced down at her hands. "I wasn't going to come . . . the truth is I thought about turning around the whole drive over here."

"Well, I'm glad you made it. Can I buy you a coffee or something?"

"Yeah, sure. A latte. Well, no. I better not," Sheila said, smiling weakly, trying to laugh off her embarrassment. "Actually make it decaf."

John nodded and went up to the counter, hoping that Sheila wouldn't bolt while he was ordering her drink. But after John paid and returned to the table with the latte she was sitting at the table, her hands folded tightly together, the whites of her knuckles pressed against her skin.

John sat opposite her. "Thanks for agreeing to see me."

Sheila nodded but didn't say anything.

"What do you know about me?"

Sheila shrugged. "I know you are a journalist. You've been to Iraq, Afghanistan. You wrote a book called *African Hope*. I read it a couple of years ago and really enjoyed it."

John nodded. *African Hope* had been the first book he had written about his years reporting in the Congo, in Rwanda and other African nations. It was a collection of discarded human interest stories not really newsworthy enough to make the news, shuffled aside by presidential primaries, celebrity nipple slips or colossal tragedy in other parts of the world.

"You have a family, Sheila?"

Sheila stared stonily at John. "What does that have to do with anything?"

John was trying to put her at ease but it had obviously backfired. "Nothing . . . just making casual conversation. I have one son named Byron."

Sheila slumped in her seat. "I'm sorry. I didn't mean to sound like that."

"It's okay, I just want you to be comfortable."

"I have a husband named Matthew and one son. He's at university down in Whitewater on a baseball scholarship. He's studying business."

"You must be proud."

"The truth is I miss him." Sheila paused. "I don't know why I'm telling you this. I don't even know you."

"I think you just need somebody to talk to," John said.

At that, Sheila burst into tears. John was surprised by the sudden outpour of emotion. He stood up and got Sheila some napkins which she took gratefully.

"I'm sorry," she said. "I'm just a mess right now."

"It's okay. Take your time."

Sheila went to the washroom and when she returned she seemed more composed. "Okay, I'm ready," she said.

"Do you mind if I take notes?" John asked, taking a notepad out of his bag. For all the high tech gadgetry the world offered, John still felt most comfortable taking handwritten notes.

"Do you have to?"

"If it will make you nervous then I don't have to," John said, closing his notebook.

"I signed a confidentiality agreement. I could get into serious trouble."

John nodded. "I know."

Sheila looked at John as if she expected something more, perhaps a convincing argument as to why she should open herself up to such troubles, but when John offered none, she dug into her purse and handed John a folded piece of paper.

"This is the email I was talking to you about."

John opened the paper.

Sent: 23/08/2012 7:36pm
To: George Hopkins
From: David Kahn

George, don't worry about anything. I have it all under control. We just need to keep the lid on Ko Chang a little longer and then it won't matter.

David Kahn

Below on the page was a separate email.

Sent: 23/08/2012 5:48pm
To: David Kahn
From: George Hopkins

Why did you have to tell her? She just confronted me about it. She's going to ruin everything.

George Hopkins

John folded the paper back and looked up at Sheila. "What can you tell me about George Hopkins?"

"He's the chief science officer. I don't know. He was one of the founders with David Kahn."

"Who are they talking about in the email? Did you confront either of them about the Ko Chang Project?"

Sheila shook her head. "No. Somebody else must have found out."

"Who do you think it is?"

Sheila shrugged. "I have no idea."

"If you were to make a guess, who do you think it would be? Who is close to Kahn?"

Sheila hesitated, looking down at her coffee. "Andrea Drashkov."

"She's the chief financial officer? What do you know about her?"

"We're not close. She's tough. She's all business."

"Did you find any other emails?"

"No, nothing. But then I didn't search for very long. I was nervous about being caught."

John rubbed his face, deep in thought. It wasn't the smoking gun John was looking for. Even John knew that if he printed a story with just the email the Nerno lawyers would rip him to shreds.

"Can I keep this?" John asked, indicating the folded paper.

Sheila nodded. "I don't want it."

"You don't have a copy?"

"No."

"Do you want me to make you a copy? It might be a good idea, just in case."

Sheila shook her head adamantly. "No, I don't want to be caught with it."

John nodded. Secretly he was pleased. He now possessed the only copy of the email, which meant that Sheila wouldn't be able to take it to any other news outlet.

"Can you tell me when you first became suspicious of the Ko Chang Project?"

"It was about a year ago."

"That long?"

Sheila nodded. "Yeah. They had been inviting the press to view the oil field. David was talking about it in every meeting and then suddenly he just stopped. It stopped being so prominent in the quarterly earnings report. Whenever I talked to him about it he assured me everything was fine. That they were just finished promoting it and that was all. Once, when I pushed, he confided there had been a slight delay but things were back on track."

"You think anybody else became suspicious?"

Sheila shrugged. "I'm sure everybody was suspicious but nobody said anything. They were all too busy making shitloads of money from it. Why look too closely?"

"What made you, then?"

Sheila paused, thoughtfully. "I'm not sure. I just had to know, I guess."

"But you don't feel better about it now, do you?"

Sheila stared at John with large brown eyes. "I guess in the back of my mind I always thought I was wrong, you know." She paused. "I didn't know what to do. Should I contact the police? Should I confront David Kahn? I don't really have anybody I'm close to at work. I couldn't even tell Matt, my husband."

Sheila started to well up again, but this time John was prepared, and gave her some more napkins which she used to dab her eyes.

"Sheila?" John said. "Think about this for a moment. Is there anything else that you perhaps overheard that might be useful? Is there any other evidence you think you could gather?"

Sheila thought for a moment and then shook her head. "I don't know. I feel that I'm too deep in this already."

John needed more but he didn't want to push her. She might prove useful later on if John needed anything. "That's okay. I understand. I appreciate everything you've done and I'm sure everybody else will too." John hesitated, not sure if he wanted to bring up what he needed to say next, but felt he had no choice. "Sheila, you mentioned the police. You might want to consider notifying them. Tell them what you've told me. I will give them a copy of the email if you think that's best."

"No. No police. I can't have them asking questions."

Again, John was relieved. He could now pursue the story without any barriers. If the police got involved the story would be blown wide open and would spiral into uncertain directions which John wouldn't be able to control. Sometimes that was a good way to shake up a stale story, but not when John couldn't dictate the terms.

"You sure?"

Sheila nodded. "These guys are way too sophisticated. The police can't catch them."

"Okay, but keep it in mind. You might want to consider calling them later if things get dangerous," John said, recalling the Jetta that had been in front of his hotel room.

"Dangerous? What do you mean?" Sheila's voice was strange and high pitched. John could tell that she hadn't thought that what she was doing would be dangerous.

"Well, these guys are extremely smart. Real Type A personalities. They aren't going to take any of this lying down."

Sheila was silent. She looked like she wanted to say something but was unable to work her jaw properly.

John reached over the table and patted her on the wrist. "Don't worry, I'll protect you. I'll make sure nothing happens. Okay?"

Sheila nodded, uncertainly. She took a long sip from her coffee. "Tell me, what happens? You know, to people like me."

John knew that the history of whistleblowers wasn't very positive. Some of them went to jail, most suffered financial difficulty. Almost none of them came away unscathed but he didn't want to tell Sheila that, so instead he reassured her again. "Don't worry. Things will be fine."

"You planning on staying in Calgary for a while?"

John nodded. "As long as it takes."

Sheila looked to her left, towards the play area. She seemed to be digesting everything. "You might want to consider buying warmer clothes, probably some snow boots too. It's supposed to get real cold around here."

"So I hear," John said.

There was a long awkward silence between them.

"What are you going to do now?" John asked.

"Probably go home and cook dinner for my husband. He thinks I'm working late."

"No, I meant at work."

"Oh," Sheila said, embarrassed. "I don't know. I love my job. It really is my dream job. When I joined Nerno I didn't think I would ever leave. I just can't see myself working for anybody else."

"What's your son's name?"

"Kyle."

"Look Sheila, I know you haven't told him about any of this, but one day you will, and when you do he'll be proud of you. He'll know you did the right thing."

Sheila nodded and managed to choke out an "I know." She wiped her eyes with her left hand. John noticed the large diamond wedding ring on her finger. "But why is doing the right thing always so hard?" she asked.

John didn't answer right away. Sheila looked at him as if she genuinely expected a real answer.

Why was the right thing so hard? He thought back to the articles he had written about the people of Africa. Most of them he had scribbled out late at night under the cold star-filled sky. Back then it had all been about personal glory. About adventures. About a career. But that was before he had seen tragedy go unheeded, unpunished. Now, decades later, what was it about?

"Because there is no glamour in it," John said. "Unless you're the Dalai Lama."

Sheila laughed. Finally, John had succeeded in making her laugh.

They left separately. Sheila went back home to cook for her husband while John ordered another coffee and watched the children play for a while longer.

John looked up George Hopkins on his laptop. Unlike Sheila, George Hopkins had a huge profile online. He had grown up in Ottawa and graduated from the University of Toronto before forming Nerno with David Kahn.

John searched online for the number for Nerno's public relations division. He knew that they would be closed by now, but PR departments usually had an after-hours number that journalists could call in case of emergencies. John wasn't disappointed. The recorded message directed him to a man named Patrick Oswald, a PR man who worked for the New York firm Walker and Thompson. John knew the firm, as did most journalists.

John dialled the number even though he knew that it would be late in New York.

"Hi, is this Patrick Oswald?"

"Yes. Speaking. Who is this?"

"My name is John Webster. I'm from the *Daily Globe*. Sorry for phoning so late."

"It's okay. I'm still at the office. I thought you might phone."

John frowned. "What do you mean?"

"What is your story really about?" Patrick Oswald asked.

"I'm doing a profile about Nerno, about the sale to the Chinese."

"Charles Dana phoned me. He said you were doing research for CEO of the year."

"That must be for a different piece. I don't know anything about that."

"Mr. Kahn isn't currently doing any interviews."

"How about George Hopkins?"

There was a long silence. "Let me see what I can do. When is your deadline?"

"Tomorrow. Five p.m."

"Okay, I'll call you by then," Patrick said, ending the conversation.

John was furious at Charles. Why hadn't he told him that he had contacted Oswald?

He took a cab back to his hotel and decided to kill some time in the hotel bar. It had been a long time since he had visited any type of bar.

The room was dark and cheaply decorated to mimic a Victorian-era hotel. John supposed that it was intended to give the aura of class and civilization, a throwback to that chivalrous time where men took off their hats and lit slim cigarettes for the ladies. But instead the mantel looked cheap, the furniture old and the Persian carpet worn.

"What can I get for you?" the bartender asked.

John quickly scanned the selection of booze behind the bartender. What did he want? Strangely he didn't feel like a drink.

"Do you have virgin Long Island iced teas?" John asked, feeling slightly embarrassed.

The bartender nodded. He was either a good actor, or virgin Long Island iced teas weren't all that foreign to him.

Beside John two unshaven businessmen were sitting in a booth drinking martinis.

A television was playing in the corner. The sound was off but the closed captioning was scrolling across the bottom.

John suffered through several minutes of sports highlights before the news came on. Two anchors appeared behind a desk: one was a thin blonde woman and the other was an older man dressed in a crisp grey jacket. John recognized him as a well-known financial analyst.

"Nerno Energy has been slowly sinking in value in the past couple of months, but I really think it's time to buy now," he said, looking straight at the camera. "The CEO, David Kahn, is expected to announce a sale to China National Offshore Oil Company in the next couple of weeks, which will surely restore faith with Wall Street."

The bartender brought John his iced tea. It was in a tall glass and was filled mostly with ice and had a slice of lemon wedged into the rim of the glass. John took several hesitant sips, confirming his worst fears. He couldn't believe that anybody actually drank these. He glanced sideways at the two businessmen, wishing that he had ordered a martini instead.

But no, he would remain strong, he decided, recalling the words of his therapist, Doctor Nagi. He pushed the iced tea aside. He sighed, turning his attention back to the television screen. The picture had turned back to hockey.

John wondered if the Chinese knew what they were getting themselves into. Would they be left with a worthless company? Had they not done their research?

John's thoughts went back to Sheila and her position. He didn't envy her. Unable to speak out, yet unable to keep silent anymore.

What happens to people like me?

We will find out, John thought.

Nerno Energy

NERNO ENERGY'S HOME WAS ON 7th Avenue and Barclay Street, just across from the TD Tower. The Nerno building was made of glass and blue concrete support beams, giving it an airy environmental feel, and not that of the resource-sucking conglomerate that it was. The Nerno logo, a crisp blue and green swirl, was prominently displayed on top of the building.

The structure stood thirty storeys high and was an impressive piece of modern architecture. John watched as the decadent men and women entered and exited the building in small pods like herds of animals, venturing into the unknown.

But it wasn't the casual strides of the well-dressed that caught John's eye. He watched an old woman with a bulky red jacket push a rusty shopping cart past the Nerno building. The shopping cart was filled with clothes, a couple of tins of Spam, and an old ghetto blaster. John watched her shuffling through the snow, barely making a sound, and wondered where she was going, before he turned his attention back to the building.

John took a deep breath and decided to hold back and observe for a little longer, but watching the rich engrossed in their electronic devices was an exhausting exercise. Finally, John decided to make his move. He had no appointment. Patrick Oswald hadn't called him back. At the very least he could do some scouting and see if he could dig anything up.

The lobby was expansive. It had a flat marble floor, a ticker tape of stocks rotated overhead on a computer screen, and lots of natural light flooded in.

A bored-looking security guard, slouched behind his desk, stared dully at John. John, not in any sort of suit or tie, stood out from the building's other inhabitants and was easy to zone in on. John cursed himself for being so short-sighted. He really did need to go shopping and get more appropriate clothes. He hadn't even passed the first gatekeeper.

"Can I help you, sir?" the guard asked.

John thought for a moment on how to play it. "Yes, I have an appointment to see David Kahn."

The guard gave John a dubious look. "Your name, sir?"

"John Webster from the *Daily Globe*. I'm a reporter."

"Just a moment. Sir." The guard slowly picked up the telephone next to his desk and pressed a two digit extension.

"Ms. Lancroft? Yes, it's Ted down at front desk . . . listen . . . does Mr. Kahn have an appointment with a John Webster?" Ted the security guard tilted his head slightly as he listened. "Yes . . . okay. I see. Sorry to bother you."

Ted placed the phone back down on the receiver. "I'm sorry, but Ms. Lancroft says she doesn't have you down anywhere," Ted said, sounding not the least bit sorry.

John wasn't about to give up so easily, however. "There has been some sort of mistake. Please tell Ms. Lancroft I have an appointment."

Ted frowned and placed his palms flat on his desk and leaned towards him. John supposed that it was a gesture he had practiced in the mirror at home, dying to try it out one day. "Please, sir, don't embarrass yourself and make me phone the police."

John sighed and turned to leave the building. He was disappointed with his performance, but still it hadn't been a total failure. He had learned the name of the Nerno secretary.

Outside it was beginning to snow again and John couldn't help but think of the old homeless woman who had all her things in her shopping cart. What was she going to do when it reached minus fifty degrees?

John wrapped his coat tightly around his body and headed towards a coffee shop across the street. He ordered a black coffee and sat at the window, looking out at the Nerno building. From across the street the environmentally friendly building seemed a lot less welcoming and a lot more ominous.

John's phone started buzzing. It was Patrick Oswald phoning back.

"Mr. Webster?"

"Yes?"

"I'm sorry, but Mr. Hopkins isn't doing any interviews either."

"Is there anybody at the company willing to talk with me?"

"Ms. Drashkov said she would contact you shortly."

"How soon? I have a deadline to meet."

"She understands that. You just have to be patient. Good luck," Patrick said, hanging up.

John felt like throwing his phone out of the window, but instead he phoned the Nerno main line. He had to go through a couple of prompts before an actual person answered.

"Can you put me through to Ms. Lancroft, please?"

There was a pause and then another voice came on the phone. "David Kahn's office."

"Is this Ms. Lancroft?"

"Speaking."

"Hello, I work for a recruiting firm and your name was passed on by a client of mine who thinks your talents are being wasted."

There was hesitation on the other end. "Pardon?"

John repeated himself.

"What is your name?"

"Liam Plummer. My company is Next Recruitment. We are a boutique firm who only deal with select clientele."

"Who is the client?"

"I'm sorry, I'm not at liberty to say, but I think I have the perfect new job for you."

There was another hesitation. "Thank you, but I'm perfectly happy here. And besides, I don't think it's appropriate to be talking to me about this."

"Think for a moment. Your company is in financial trouble and in the process of being sold to the Chinese. How secure do you think your job is?"

"There is no financial trouble, Mr. Plummer. I don't know where you're getting your information from."

"You're the personal secretary to Mr. Kahn?"

"That's right."

"You think your position is secure? David Kahn wants to sell and retire to a warmer climate. He's not going to need you. What will you do then?"

"David wouldn't do that to me," Lancroft said, pitifully.

John watched the large, round chunks of snow fall outside. He felt slightly guilty about manipulating Lancroft, but he couldn't think of any alternative. He needed to talk to her and he needed to get her out of the office.

"At least have lunch with me. I will outline your options and if you don't like them there is no harm done. Our meeting will be totally confidential."

Lancroft hesitated. "Okay. Where?"

"How about lunch tomorrow? You can pick a restaurant that you would be comfortable with."

"There is a vegetarian restaurant called East Sixth that I like to go to sometimes."

"Perfect," John said. "See you then."

John called a cab to take him back to his hotel. While he was waiting his phone rang again. He looked at the caller ID and saw that it was a Calgary number. Sure that it was Sheila phoning him, he picked it up.

"Is this John Webster?" an unfamiliar voice asked.

"Yes, who is this?"

"My name is Andrea Drashkov. I'm the CFO of Nerno. I was told you want to do a profile of our company."

"Yes, that's right," John said, looking up at the Nerno building, feeling a strange and powerful presence, almost as if Andrea Drashkov was watching him through a window on top of her ivory tower.

"You're not a business reporter, are you?"

"I'm whatever reporter the job requires me to be," John replied.

"Yes, maybe. It's just strange that they wouldn't send somebody who I know. We have very good relationships with your newspaper."

John rubbed his forehead. He remembered his colleagues' warnings about her. Surely she suspected that he knew something, but she didn't know what it was, or who had told him, and that was his leverage.

"Well, the sale of Nerno to the Chinese National Offshore Oil Company is big news. I think they thought they needed somebody with an outside perspective."

"There are no talks between us and CNOOC. Those are just unfounded rumours."

"They must have come from somewhere."

"I get off work at seven. Perhaps you can meet me at my place at eight? Dinner? Make it a casual event. We can discuss these rumours at length."

"My deadline is at five, Ms. Drashkov."

"I'm sure a journalist of your esteem will be able to convince your editors to wait a day."

"Depends on what you give me."

"You'll just have to wait and find out," Drashkov said, giving John her address before hanging up.

John stared at his phone for several moments, wondering what sort of game she was playing. It all seemed too good to be true.

John spent the rest of the day making phone calls to Nerno employees, but nobody wanted to talk to him.

In the evening the temperature dropped even more and, for John, standing outside for even five minutes became an unbearable torture. The address Andrea Drashkov had given him wasn't too far from his hotel, but the thought of walking those ten blocks seemed impossible and so he retreated back inside and got the receptionist to call him a cab.

As John waited, watching the snow float slowly through the dark night, he thought about how the temperature was supposed to drop even more, and decided that tomorrow he would follow Sheila's suggestion and go buy some boots and some warmer clothes.

The cab came and John got in. They drove to Andrea's building where a gruff elderly doorman greeted him without even asking his name.

"Ms. Drashkov is expecting you."

The doorman took John to the elevator where he swiped his fob and hit the button to the penthouse. The doors closed and John travelled soundlessly up to the top of the building. He stood and watched as the lights blinked one after the other.

The doors opened into a small room with a door at the end. John walked across the floor and knocked on the door. No answer. He tried the knob and found it unlocked.

"Hello? Ms. Drashkov?" John called out.

But there was no answer.

He found himself in an expansive living room. The apartment smelled of vanilla incense. The walls were a bright white, matching the white couch, the loveseat and the carpet. Nothing seemed used and the whole place had a kind of showroom look. Beyond the pristine furniture and a polished table was a floor-to-ceiling window that overlooked the city. Skyscrapers outlined the night-time lights which glowed softly.

John walked over and cupped his hands on the glass to reduce the reflection, and looked beyond the buildings. In the distance, marked by a ghostly dusting of snow, he could see evergreens and family houses.

John pulled himself away from the magnificent view. Again he called out but there was no answer.

Was this some kind of trap? John wondered. Maybe she wasn't home.

John's eyes were caught by the paintings on the wall. They were all colourful, Impressionist paintings. He was drawn to one small painting in particular that hung over the couch. It was a thick oil canvas full of bright, swirling colours, seemingly of nothing at all. It seemed familiar, as if he had seen it in photographs or in a movie.

John stepped closer to inspect it.

"You like Monet?"

John's heart jumped in his chest, startled by the soft playful voice. He turned to see a short woman in her mid-forties leaning up against a door frame. Her wiry hair flowed across her shoulders against an oval, bloodless face. She wore a white strapless dress, accentuating her milky-coloured shoulders, which were round and slender. Her large unsupported breasts pressed against the thin white dress.

"Sorry, who?" John asked.

Andrea flicked a long thin wrist towards the painting. John noticed her grey nail polish. "The artist—Monet. This was painted in 1873 at the height of his brilliance. Not the original, of course, so don't get any ideas. I have the original locked up safe." Her large eyes moved from the painting and rested on John as if they were expecting something, an impressed murmur perhaps, an exclamation of sorts, but John was unsure what the protocol was when viewing really, really expensive brush strokes on a canvas.

"I didn't mean to snoop. I knocked but there was no answer so I let myself in."

"I was in the kitchen. I had the fan going so I didn't hear you. I cooked some salmon with sautéed vegetables. I hope that suits your taste," Andrea said, her gaze still squarely on John. John, who could usually read people, was unnerved by her stare. He had the feeling that she had intentionally left the door open as a sort of test. John wasn't sure if he had passed or failed.

Still, John managed a smile. "My tastes are bland British. My parents' fault."

Andrea tilted her head and gave a coy laugh. It seemed forced and unnatural. She moved off of the door frame and towards John. Her white dress moved with her, swaying at her white ankles.

"You don't know much about art, do you?"

John glanced back at the painting. "I know my son could probably do a better job."

Andrea smiled coldly. "The painting is worth more than you'll make in a lifetime."

John decided that he would have to be careful with her. "Well, now I know what to tell him to do so he can keep his old man in his old age."

Andrea stared at John before turning abruptly and walking out onto the balcony. John watched her for a moment before following her. The night was incredibly cold, and the wind took hold of Andrea's dress, and momentarily it seemed that it might slip off of her, but somehow it miraculously managed to stay pinned to her body.

John could barely stand the freezing temperature as it gnawed at his bare skin, but he knew this was a test of his will, and so he tried not to show any sign of weakness. Andrea, for her part, seemed not to feel the cold even though she was half naked.

She glanced at John as he walked up beside her. John clenched his jaw to prevent his teeth from chattering. Andrea smiled. "I was born here," she said. "But my parents immigrated from Russia. I don't think Russians feel the cold like most other people do."

John tried to concentrate on anything other than the cold. He concentrated on Andrea's perfume, a hint of vanilla, just like the penthouse. He concentrated on the streets below, tinted with a fluorescent orange from the street lamps. The noise of the city seemed like a living organism. He heard a yell, and the vibrating engines, and the hum of electricity. It was the heartbeat of the city, a city put together to control the whiskey and fur trades, but now oil served this town.

John looked towards the horizon. He could see the thick shadows of evergreens, and the Bow River rolling waywardly towards the west, past the city. The Rockies, which now glowed white, stood modestly like sleeping giants in the background.

John took it all in. He supposed that if he woke up every day to look across the city, then he might feel superior to everybody too.

"What do you think, Mr. Webster?"

"Please call me John."

Andrea twisted her shoulders and stared at John. He saw her out of his peripheral vision but didn't want to get into another staring match with her. She seemed to glow against the starless, dark sky. But perhaps that was just an illusion caused by her chalky-coloured form.

"I think you can tell a lot by what impresses a person, don't you think?" Andrea said.

"I don't know. I've never had anything that impressed anybody."

"You're a published author. That impresses people."

"You've done your research."

"Your biography lists you as an investigative journalist," Andrea said. "Tell me, what are you investigating at Nerno?

John wasn't ready to tell Andrea what he had just yet. "Is there something I should be investigating?"

Andrea turned to look back at the view. She still gave no indication of being cold, save perhaps the goose bumps that ran up her slender arms, and the two dark shadows that had appeared on her breasts that clearly outlined her nipples. "This doesn't impress you—I can tell."

"No, I am impressed. It's an amazing view."

Andrea shook her head. "No, I can see it in your eyes."

John tried to hide the annoyance he felt at being so transparent. "Okay, what impresses you? The woman who has everything?"

"What makes you think anything impresses me anymore?"

John was a bit taken aback by the melancholy and vulnerability in her voice. All of a sudden she seemed like such a lonely and disappointed person. Was it really that tragic having so much money? John, who never seemed to have more than a couple of thousand dollars in his bank account, couldn't possibly think so.

John's mind turned to the weather again. "I heard it's supposed to reach minus fifty degrees this winter."

Andrea nodded. "Is it too cold for you?"

"I'm just not used to it."

"While you're here you should take in some of the sights. We have good museums. You should spend some time at Fort Calgary."

"I'm not really a museum person."

"I'm on the board of the Glenbow Museum. I could get you a couple of tickets. I will show you around as an honoured guest."

"Do you show all journalists around museums?"

"Only the investigative kind," Andrea said, coyly.

There was a long pause as the echoes of the city wafted upwards. Finally Andrea suggested that they go inside. She ushered John through to the dining room where they sat at a long oak table, carefully laid out. At the centre of the table was a candle holder without a candle. John thought that it was an odd thing to forget, as everything else had been so meticulously organized and presented.

With much ceremony, Andrea brought out the salmon from the oven, laboriously describing the steps and care she had taken in preparing the fish.

"You enjoy wine?" Andrea asked, putting the salmon on the table. "I have a '91 French chardonnay that I haven't opened yet."

"I really shouldn't," John said. "My doctor told me to cut down."

Andrea tilted her head. "Really? You can't turn down a five-hundred-dollar bottle of wine. When will you ever get a chance to try one again?"

"It would only be wasted on me anyway."

"Come on, don't make me drink alone," Andrea said, getting up and disappearing into the kitchen. She returned with a bottle and two glasses and set them down on the table. She popped open the bottle and poured the wine. Reluctantly John took the glass and tasted the chardonnay. The liquid trickled down his throat and warmed the pit of his stomach. *It was good*, John decided. How long had it been since he had touched alcohol? He couldn't believe it had been so long and now he was sipping wine and, wow, how much he had missed it.

Andrea smiled. "You an alcoholic or something?"

John shook his head. "No. It's a blood pressure thing. It's just not good for me."

"My dad was an alcoholic. Drank this cheap vodka I can't remember the name of. So typical of a Russian man."

They started on dinner. John was surprised at how good the salmon was.

"I've got a special surprise for dessert too," Andrea said.

"How come you want to sell Nerno?" John asked.

"No business talk during dinner. I want to hear about Afghanistan."

John nodded. It seemed like everybody he met wanted to hear about his time in Afghanistan and Iraq. They looked on it as a kind of entertaining action movie. The trouble was that to John it wasn't entertaining, it wasn't action, and it certainly wasn't a movie.

"Let's not ruin a perfectly good dinner," John said.

Andrea leaned towards John in a conspiratorial manner. "Come on, I'm interested."

"You said no business. To me those countries are business. I made money watching people have their heads blown off."

This seemed to quell Andrea's desire, and so she ended up talking about her immigrant family fleeing the death grip of communism and ending up, through improbable circumstances, in an emerging city getting ready to enter greatness on the world stage.

Andrea's mother, John learned, had been a maid for rich Americans, while her father milled around ineffectually, occasionally getting work as a painter, a bike mechanic, a car mechanic, a mailman or any other part-time job he could find when he was sober enough to work. More often than not, he found refuge in bars across the city, or at the Russian Cultural Centre.

"The only steady job I remember my dad having was as a car mechanic for a shop called The Toy Shop," Andrea said, continuing her long narration. "I think it's still around some place. It serviced high-end cars like Porsches, Lamborghinis, Mercedes, Rolls Royces, Ferraris, that sort of thing. It strikes me now that those cars are all foreign—from places like Germany, Italy, Britain—but, at the time, they represented America." Andrea paused and stared up at John as if she expected a statement of some kind from him, but when he remained silent, she continued.

"My father would take me to the shop on weekends and show me all the beautiful cars. I remember him saying one day that I could drive one of those cars and it shocked me into thinking my destiny could be something different, something with a little grandeur in it."

Despite everything, Andrea's parents somehow managed to scrape together everything they had so Andrea could go to university. She spent one year at Cornell University, but even with a scholarship she couldn't make ends meet.

"It was the biggest disappointment of my life," she said. "I came back here and enrolled at Mount Royal."

"I never went to university," said John. "My father was killed in a car accident and suddenly I couldn't stand being in my house anymore. I joined Reuters and worked in Africa."

"You ever regret not finishing school?"

John shrugged. "Not really. I was a failure at school. My parents were extremely strict with me. They were both extremely smart but didn't have the money to go to university and couldn't understand why I, who had all the opportunity in the world, just threw it all away."

For dessert they had mousse cake and then Andrea cleaned the table and they went back to the living room. They had finished the French chardonnay, and Andrea brought another bottle, but John refused. He was feeling pleasantly numb but he knew that he needed to be sharp if he was going to find the truth about Nerno from Andrea. He wondered how she felt. Was this part of a plan that he had so easily fallen into? He decided he needed to heed his colleague's warning a little more. She hadn't risen to the high ranks of Nerno by being stupid.

"You want anything else?" Andrea asked.

"How about coffee?'

"Decaf?"

"Regular if you've got it."

"Of course," Andrea said, getting up from the couch. "It doesn't keep you up at night? Coffee makes me anxious."

"Not more than anything else," John replied.

Andrea disappeared to make the coffee. John took the time to wander around the room. There was a small bookshelf in the corner with books by Nietzsche, Chomsky and Camus. John didn't think Andrea was the type of person to read any of those books. One small book in the corner caught John's eye: *The Art of War* by Sun Tzu. He had heard that the book, although dedicated to war, was also used as a modern day business manual.

Andrea came back with the coffee. She poured herself a glass of rum and laid back and settled into the love seat. John sat down opposite her.

"You like my book collection?" Andrea asked.

"I was expecting more along the lines of *Ten Minute Manager*," John said.

Andrea smiled thinly. "Who can manage in only ten minutes?"

John brought his voice recorder out and placed it on the coffee table. "You don't mind, do you?" John asked.

Andrea shrugged, tucking her feet neatly under her body and putting one arm on the cushion. "Tell me first, what makes you so interested in Nerno? I mean, you're not one of the usual financial hacks that interview me. I bet you can't even balance your own bank account."

John smiled at this small slight, but decided it best to ignore it. "I was assigned to it. You'll have to ask my editor."

Andrea took a small sip of rum, cupping the glass like a hot cup of tea. "I thought a journalist of your pedigree and status would be able to pick and choose his stories."

"Pedigree?" John asked, raising his eyebrows some. "You think I have pedigree?"

Andrea leaned forward. "Oh, come on. Playing coy just doesn't suit you."

"I'm from a poor Scottish family. I grew up on meat and potatoes."

"You don't seem any worse off for it," Andrea said with a sly smile.

"all right, tell me about the Chinese sale."

"I can't officially comment on any negotiations."

"So Nerno is definitely for sale?"

"I didn't say that. We are always looking for new investors."

"Okay, how about background?" Background meant that John could use the information in his article, but couldn't attribute it to Drashkov.

"Do you want this interview to come to a swift conclusion?"

"Would be a shame after such a lavish dinner, wouldn't it?" John took a deep breath and decided to lay his cards on the table. "I have proof that your company is covering up the fact that the Ko Chang Project doesn't have any oil in it. I think you should come clean about it and I think you should come clean about it to me."

Andrea gave John a cold, dark stare. "I don't know where these rumours about Ko Chang came from, but I assure you they are completely false and damaging. If you so much as print one word about Ko Chang not having any oil then I will have our lawyers on you so fast you'll wish you stayed in Afghanistan."

"Your threats don't worry me," John said.

"They should. You have no idea what you're up against."

John stopped the voice recorder. "The story will run, Ms. Drashkov. It will accuse Nerno of corruption and fraud at the highest level. And that's just to start. I'm going to bring your entire company down if you don't cooperate."

"And if I say what you want you'll go easy on me, is that it?"

"It's your only alternative. I'm sure the police will look on you as being cooperative."

"I think it's time for you to leave now."

John nodded, stood up and gathered his things. "Thank you for dinner. I'm sorry it had to end like this."

John walked back to the elevator. Andrea trailed him a few paces behind. John pressed the button to go down. He then turned to face Andrea, whose face had softened a little. She no longer seemed the tough, domineering executive, but more just a middle-aged woman who didn't quite seem at ease surrounded by her lavish apartment.

"But I do intend to get to the bottom of Ko Chang," John said.

"John," Andrea said, fixing him with her deep, penetrating eyes. "I know you want a good story and a pat on the back from your bosses, but in the end you'll lose. There are just too many forces against you."

Joyce Lancroft

"**Y**OU UNDERSTAND, I GREW UP in a small town on the east coast called Georgetown," Joyce Lancroft said, playing with her Greek salad. "I've never been head-hunted before."

John smiled. He had ordered a tofu hamburger but it just wasn't the same as the real thing. Nevertheless, he ate it without complaint. He had tried to ply Lancroft with a cocktail or a glass of wine or some other alcoholic beverage, but she had refused all gestures.

"I can't go back to the office smelling of liquor," she had said.

Joyce Lancroft had a long, stalk-like neck, slender shoulders and redwood-coloured hair. She looked young too, maybe mid-twenties, and was dressed in a black pencil skirt and a blue blouse. She was pretty in a conventional, well-manicured way.

They were in a vegan restaurant on 6th Street in the East Village. She shifted uneasily in her seat, looking expectantly at John, but he didn't want to say too much at first. He thought it much better if he kept Lancroft uncomfortable and talking.

"Nerno is a good place to work. David is a good boss. So nice and understanding. I don't know if I want to leave. Of course I don't want to be a secretary forever. I want to go back to school for business administration—be a manager or something."

John just nodded and smiled. He could afford to take his time.

The restaurant was light and airy. The walls were splashed with primary colours. The young business crowd had just filtered in, mechanically ordering their lunch.

"I don't know what I'm going to do if David retires. I wish they would just tell us one way or the other, but they are so secretive."

John asked, "You believe what they are saying about Ko Chang?"

Lancroft shrugged. "I don't know. That Gates guy seems to think so."

"Gates guy? What are you talking about?"

"I don't know who he is."

"Is he a head-hunter?"

"No—at least I don't think so. He's some sort of stock analyst."

"What do you know about Ko Chang?" John asked, trying to breathe regularly.

"Why do you care about Ko Chang?"

"It's my business to know everything in the oil sector. I specialize in it. My clients ask about Nerno all the time. I don't want to recommend a company if it's been lying. It's my reputation on the line."

"I see," Lancroft said. "I try not to pay attention to those rumours. David is a fair and decent person."

"How can you be so sure?"

Lancroft put her fork down and stared at John. "Because I've worked for him for two years and I know him."

"Do you have stocks in the company?"

Lancroft nodded. "Yes, everybody in the company gets stocks as part of their benefits."

"And how much do you stand to make if the company is sold?"

Lancroft shrugged. "I have no idea. I guess it depends on what they are sold at."

"Joyce—you don't mind if I call you Joyce, do you?"

"No, not at all."

"I know you want to do the right thing. I have evidence that Ko Chang has no oil and that the top executives at your company are covering it up."

"That's preposterous. What evidence?"

"An email your boss sent to George Hopkins. But I need more. I want you to help me, Joyce."

"You want me to spy? Who are you?"

"I'm going to tell you but I want you to promise me you're not going to freak out."

Lancroft had her elbows on the table and was leaning forward, glaring at John. "That depends."

"I'm not a head-hunter. I work for the *Daily Globe*."

Lancroft sat back in her chair. "You're a reporter? You lied to me?" She got up, threw down her napkin and quickly put on her scarf and coat.

John also got up from his chair. "Joyce, please wait a second to hear me out."

"Get away from me, you scum," she screamed. "Things are bad enough without you snooping too."

Several restaurant patrons turned and glared at John. John tried to give them an appeasing smile before following Lancroft out the door. The cold hit his body immediately, stung his face and throat.

John caught up to Lancroft who was looking for a taxi. "You know the whole thing is going to blow up sooner rather than later," John said. "Whose side will you be on? You'll be out of a job whatever happens, but this way you can clear your conscience."

"And what happens if I spy for you and you're wrong? I would have betrayed David for nothing!"

"At least tell me about this Gates guy."

Lancroft gritted her teeth. "His name is Hank Gates. You've never heard of him?"

"I don't know. Maybe," John allowed.

"All I know about him is he runs some sort of investment company. He phoned up last week to ask a couple of questions about Ko Chang. Made a big scene about it. David seemed very concerned."

"Does he own shares?" The cold was almost unbearable but John wasn't able to move.

"I have no idea."

A taxi finally stopped and Lancroft got in. John thanked her and closed the door for her. He then waited for another taxi to stop. His phone started to ring, but his fingers were too cold to answer it, and so he let it go to voicemail.

I have to get myself some gloves, John thought.

Finally a taxi stopped and he got in. He spent the whole trip trying to warm his extremities. Once back at the hotel, he checked his messages and found it was a familiar number: Hayden. It was strange for Hayden to call him in the middle of the day. It was strange for her to phone him at all, in fact.

John dialled the voicemail but only got a short message to phone her back.

"Hayden?" John said when she picked up. "Everything okay?"

"Everything is great. How are things with you?"

"You know, slowly. I don't have enough to print yet."

"I didn't mean work," Hayden said. "I mean you, personally. How are you?"

"I'm good," John said, dumping his jacket on the bed and sitting next to it. "Is everything okay with Byron?"

"Yeah, he's the same."

"How's school? Is he still getting pushed around?" John asked. "I asked him about it on his birthday but he didn't really want to talk about it."

"Yes, he gets that trait from his father," Hayden said, sourly.

"That's not fair," John said. Had she phoned specifically to pick a fight?

"You're right. I'm sorry. I'm just anxious."

"Anxious? About what?"

"I'm sorry. This isn't a very good time to be telling you this. I should have told you sooner."

"Hayden, you're scaring me."

"I'm getting married again."

"Married?" John said, stunned.

"Yes . . ."

"Married? I didn't even know you were dating. Married? Who to?"

"His name is Paul. He works at my firm."

John suddenly became lightheaded. He was thankful that he was already sitting down, and he leaned his head down on the pillow. Paul? . . . Paul who? What was Paul like? If he was to hazard a guess he would be tall, with strong cheekbones and a deep voice. The type who'd wear a pin-striped suit to church once a year at Christmas.

John struggled to say something—anything—but his mind was like a car stuck amid gears. "You going to take his last name?"

Hayden paused. "I haven't thought about it yet."

"I guess congratulations are in order." John did his best to disguise any bitterness in his voice.

"You know you don't have to say it if you don't mean it."

"No, I mean it. I'm sorry—I'm just stunned, that's all."

"Yeah, it must be a bit of a shock. I meant to tell you earlier. It's just that I never found the right time."

John suddenly thought of Byron. A wave of guilt engulfed him because he knew that Byron should have been his first thought, not his own piteous feelings.

"And Byron? Have you spoken to him yet?"

"Of course. Byron loves Paul. They get along so well. You should see Paul play on the Nintendo with Byron. I wouldn't do it without Byron's consent."

John realized that he was holding his breath. He let it out slowly. Byron had known but hadn't told him? He suddenly felt an acute anger at both of them. Keeping him in the dark . . . that wasn't fair.

Byron should have given his father one last push for a come-from-behind victory. Wasn't that what Byron wanted? His parents to reunite? How could this Paul give her the things Hayden craved? The things she needed?

"How long have you been dating?" John asked.

"About eight months."

John let this sink in, trying to swallow eight months of moments in several seconds. "Eight months? You sure you want to do this?"

"John, I'm not having this conversation with you."

John quickly tried to make amends. "I'm sorry. I didn't mean it like that. I'm still in shock. I just wanted to know if you are in love with him."

"I'm sorry you had to hear this way," Hayden said. "I really have to go. I've got a house showing in thirty minutes."

"Yes . . . of course. Thanks for telling me."

John got up and stretched, and decided that he needed to go for a drink in the hotel bar. He ordered a double whiskey, straight. The bartender nodded his head approvingly before making the drink. John couldn't remember the last time he had drunk whiskey. The bartender put it down in front of him and he shot it straight back. He closed his eyes, feeling the intense sensation fill his throat and stomach.

"Another one?" the bartender asked.

John nodded and downed this one as well. This time the blood rushed to his head.

"Tough day?" the bartender asked, staring at John intently.

John looked at the bartender. He didn't like overly chatty servers. He just wanted to be alone with his thoughts and listen to the music play softly on the overhead speakers.

"You don't know the half of it," John replied, paying and going back to the elevator. A middle-aged husband and wife with their son got in with him. They smiled politely and John smiled politely back. The husband was wearing jeans and a wool vest, while his wife had on a fashionable purple dress. The wife leaned into the husband, who put a relaxed arm around her shoulders, looking perfectly content to be in the elevator at the Edmonds Hotel in snowy Calgary at that moment at that time. John envied them and wondered whether at any point in his life he had felt the same contentment.

He had always had the strange desire to be someplace else in life. As a young husband he had wanted to be documenting the world, but when he was out documenting the world he wanted to be back home, living a simple existence with his family. He supposed that it was in his nature to always be yearning in some form or another.

The family got off a floor below John. As the family was exiting the elevator, the boy looked up at John. "Have a good day, sir," he said in a tiny, high-pitched voice.

John was so surprised at the politeness of the boy that he was unable to respond. Would Byron be as polite?

The doors closed and John was alone with the hum of the elevator, feeling a little drunk and, although it wasn't late, a little tired. The day had seemed so agonizingly long.

Back in his room, John got on his laptop and searched for Gates Investments. He found a typical website that promoted Hank Gates as founder and CEO. It was a beautifully designed website but scant on actual details.

Gates was born in Houston and went to Johns Hopkins University. He got his legal degree before he founded Gates Investments. John read over several old press releases on the website, but they were vague and none pertained to Nerno.

The website told him that Gates Investments' head office was in Manhattan and it gave an email and phone number. John tried emailing first, and then phoned. The phone rang and clicked onto a generic message.

John then called Charles Dana to give him an update, but it also went to his voicemail, so John decided that he would get a cup of coffee. The mixture of the tofu burger from lunch and the two double whiskeys wasn't sitting well in his stomach.

He had noticed a coffee shop across the street earlier and decided that he would give it a try. It was decorated with a seventies disco awning and mustard-yellow walls.

There were only a few patrons scattered buckshot across the shop. Some sort of banjo was playing on the speakers.

John ordered a black coffee. As he sat down he remembered that the business reporters back at the office might know more about Hank Gates. He wanted to gather as much information as he could before he spoke with him. He picked Michael Chu again because he seemed like the best source of information.

Michael answered his phone on the third ring. "Michael Chu, *Daily Globe*," he answered.

"Michael, it's John Webster. I have some questions about a firm called Gates Investments. Have you heard of them?"

"Yeah. Is this for Nerno?"

John didn't want to give him too many details. He was always extremely cautious with other reporters but he had to concede that it was related to the Nerno story. "What do you know about them? Are they are a big investor in Nerno?"

Michael laughed at this. "No, not at all. They are known as giant killers that specialize in bringing down large companies."

"I don't understand."

"What Hank Gates does is investigate into companies that he thinks are lying to their shareholders or to the regulators. Then Gates short sells the stocks before releasing his findings."

"Michael, you have to go easy on me. What do you mean by short selling?"

"It's basically the practice of borrowing money, usually from a broker, who basically lends you the stock. You bet the stock will decrease in price, because when you actually buy the stock at the decreased price, the broker pays you the difference. If the stock increases in value you lose money because you need to pay the broker extra."

John closed his eyes. He could really feel the alcohol in his system. The coffee didn't seem to be helping. "As I see it, it's basically gambling."

"Unless," Michael said, "you know for a fact the stock will go down after you release a report saying the price has been artificially inflated. Gates Investments isn't technically an investment firm in the straight sense of the word. Gates has done this with a Brazilian forestry company and a mining company from Kenya. Both times Gates exposed corruption in the boardroom and both times the companies eventually went bankrupt."

No wonder David Kahn was so concerned, John thought. "So you think Hank Gates has been short selling Nerno?"

"If he's sniffing around Nerno, I would almost guarantee it."

"I don't get it. Is this even legal?" John asked.

"Well, the legality of it is definitely dubious. Financial law is murky at best. Morally I would say Gates is definitely in the wrong, but as Gordon Gekko said, 'Greed is good'."

"Who?"

"Have you never seen *Wall Street*?" Michael asked, astonished.

"No. Is it a movie?"

"Never mind."

"So nobody has tried to prosecute Hank Gates?"

"Not that I'm aware of. You have to remember it would be a vast and expensive endeavour that would surely fail."

"How much money do you think he makes?"

"Well, his firm is private, so he doesn't have to report earnings, but some reports have speculated in the millions of dollars."

John let out a low whistle. "Wow. Okay, thanks Michael. I appreciate your time."

John ate the rest of his panini and decided to call Charles Dana again. This time he picked up.

"I need a geologist and I need one today," John said. "I need to confirm my source's story."

"We've been over this. The answer is still no, especially with the paper's situation."

"There is something here. I can feel it."

"You need to get somebody else to corroborate and then we can run it."

"Charles, I don't have any time. Others are onto Nerno, and further ahead than I am. I will never catch up unless I get more resources. Tell the Pommeroys this will make the newspaper."

"Talk to the geologists who have been to the site. I'm sure I don't need to tell you how to do your job."

"Chuck, when did we become such penny pinchers?" John knew his boss hated to be called Chuck, and he usually did it just to annoy him.

"You know the answer to that one, John," Charles said, hanging up.

John looked at his phone and sighed. He exited the coffee shop and walked across the street back to his hotel.

How was he supposed to compete with an entire investment firm whose whole job was currently to bring down Nerno? Gates would have data and analysis. John just had the word of one Sheila McKinnon and an email that could be interpreted in any number of ways.

Hank Gates would call a press conference and everybody would have the same story—or worse, Gates would play favourites and only a select few publications like the *Wall Street Journal* and the *New York Times* would have it. And who was to say that other reporters weren't sniffing around?

John was so depressed and so sad he felt like going for another drink at the hotel bar, but decided that it would be best to go upstairs to his room. Next time he went travelling, John decided, he would choose a hotel without a bar.

Hank Gates

JOHN SPENT THE BETTER HALF of the next day making phone calls to different investment bankers, brokers and advisors in the city to see if any of them had a combination of information and loose lips. But John mostly got recorded messages, secretaries and hang-ups.

"It's a small town," one advisor said in a way that made it sound like a warning. John tried phoning Hank Gates again, but again he got his voicemail. John wondered if he was getting an office number or a cell phone. Either way, it seemed that Gates didn't have a big staff, and that cheered him up some. Maybe John still had a chance of getting the story before Gates did. Still . . . John never thought that he would be competing with an investment company.

At about eleven o'clock John phoned Joyce Lancroft at the Nerno office.

"You again?" Lancroft said quietly into the phone. "You're like a stray animal, you know. Looking for someone to take you in."

John had to laugh despite all the rejection and disappointment from the morning. "Is that a nice way of saying I'm a pest?"

"Something like that."

"Do you know where I can find Hank Gates? I tried phoning the number from his website but all I get is a recorded message."

"I shouldn't be talking to you."

"Why not?"

"If David finds out I could lose my job."

"All I want to know is the truth. Do you really want to work for someone who doesn't want the truth to get out?"

"Who knows what the truth is, John?"

"We pretend it is complicated because we don't want to hear it, but the truth is generally pretty simple," John pleaded.

"Goodbye, Mr. Webster," Lancroft said, hanging up.

John dialled her back without thinking. It rang once before Joyce Lancroft answered.

"Mr. Kahn's office."

"Joyce, don't hang up. I just want a phone number."

"I'm going to call the police. This is harassment."

"If what I told you isn't correct then I'll disappear like a ghost. You'll never hear from me again."

"I think you'll smear Nerno for a good headline."

"If that was the case I would have published what I have already. I'm not a tabloid writer, Joyce."

"Fine. I believe you. But I'm not giving you anything."

"Nobody will know where I got it. It's just a number."

"I don't have time for this."

"Then just give me the number and I'll disappear."

There was a pause. "All right. Hold on a moment while I find it."

John thought that she was going to hang up on him again, but instead she returned several moments later and gave him a phone number. It was a local Calgary number.

"Good luck," Lancroft said softly. "I hope you think of everybody who works here before you publish anything that will hurt us all."

"Joyce," John said. "Those are exactly the people I think about—every phone call, every interview, every word I write."

"I sure hope so," Lancroft said, hanging up.

John phoned the number that Joyce Lancroft had given him. A deep, lyrical voice answered, "Gates speaking."

"Mr. Gates? My name is John Webster. I'm a reporter for the *Daily Globe*."

"Yes, sorry, I've been meaning to get in contact with you. I've just been extremely busy lately as I'm sure you can understand."

"Do you think we can meet? I want to talk to you."

"Sure, how about dinner tonight? I know a great steak place called Ruth's Chris. It's on the second floor of the Calgary Tower. You can't deny a Texan his beef."

John smiled at his good luck. He stared at his phone, wondering who he should call next, and found himself dialling a Vancouver number almost by memory.

"Vanstone Realty," a voice answered.

"Yes . . . can I speak to Paul?"

"One moment please," the receptionist responded.

John held his breath while he heard the line being transferred. What was he going to say? *You bastard, you stole my wife?*

"Paul Vanstone speaking. How may I help you?"

Vanstone? His family owned the company?

"Hello? Who is this?"

John froze, unable to think of anything to say. He should have just hung up, but he was unable to. What was he doing?

"Is this John?" Paul asked.

John was able to let out a breathless "Yes."

"I see . . . Hayden said you might phone."

John rubbed his temples with his fingers. Of course Hayden would have predicted him phoning Paul . . . she knew him better than anybody else. Sometimes even better than he knew himself.

John suddenly felt incredibly stupid. "I'm sorry to have ambushed you like this. I'll let you get back to work."

"No, wait. I wanted to get together over lunch maybe. I think it's best if we start things off right. You know, for Hayden and Byron."

"Yes, well . . . I'm in Calgary right now on business. Perhaps when I get back?"

"Sure thing. Thanks for the phone call," Paul said, hanging up.

John sat at his desk, unable to comprehend what had just happened. Why did Paul want to have lunch with him? What was there to discuss?

John entered Paul Vanstone's name into a search engine and got a full profile of him. John felt foolish that he hadn't searched him before he had impulsively phoned. Vanstone Realty was at the top of the list and John clicked on the bio section. John studied the picture of Paul. He was a handsome older man with peppery grey hair, a thin face and large blue eyes. John read the description but it was just a basic profile of when Paul got his licence, how many years he had been in real estate, etcetera, etcetera.

As a precautionary measure, John entered Paul Vanstone's name into a database on law court proceedings to see if he had any criminal record, but nothing came up. John did find a civil case from 1997, where Paul had been sued over a land deal, but that was all the dirt that the investigative reporter could find.

How could it be that Paul was so unblemished? He looked like he was in his mid-fifties, and he had no battle scars? Nothing? John was careful of his suspicion, knowing that it was influenced by so many other feelings of jealousy, outrage, and resentment.

Ruth's Chris Steakhouse was a fancy diner with deep mahogany panels and white tablecloths. The curtains were a pale manila colour that complemented the subdued butterscotch tones of the restaurant.

John arrived early and, feeling a little bit underdressed, was seated by the window that looked down onto the street. He ordered a double whiskey and waited, grateful for the extra time to collect his thoughts.

He didn't have too much time to wait before Hank Gates arrived. He looked exactly like his photographs: in his mid-fifties, with faded blond hair, a long, suntanned face and chubby maroon-coloured neck, as if he had just stepped out from the Texan sun.

He was wearing a navy blue suit with a solid silver shirt and solid silver tie that only reinforced John's impression that he himself was underdressed in jeans and an old dress shirt.

"Don't you love this city?" Hank Gates asked, shaking John's hand. "It reminds me so much of home."

"I don't usually eat a lot of steak, personally."

"So this is the famous John Webster?" Gates asked, smiling broadly.

"Famous? I'm more infamous, I would say."

Gates sat down opposite John, spreading out his considerable body. "Drinking whiskey? I like you already."

He flicked his hand at the waiter and ordered a whiskey for himself. "You know you're not altogether unknown, even south of the border. I remember one of your books made quite a sensation."

"That's very kind of you to say," John said, not altogether convinced.

Gates leaned forward on the table, pressing both palms on the place mat and giving John an intense stare. "No, it's true. I'm a great admirer of your work."

"Well, I appreciate it, but I didn't want to meet you to discuss the past."

Gates smiled again, showing two sets of white teeth. "No, of course not. Journalists are all about the future."

"I want to know about Nerno."

Gates looked over the menu. The waiter came back and took their orders. Gates had the New York strip loin with extra mashed potatoes, while John had the salmon.

"Everything there is to know about the company is on their website," Hank Gates said. "Have you looked at it?"

"Don't play coy with me, Mr. Gates. I was just beginning to like you. I know you have information about Nerno, about Ko Chang."

Gates was suddenly in business mode. "I can't make any comment before all the information is gathered."

John knew that he had to be careful. He would have to try to bully Gates a bit, but he would have to strike a deal with him as well. "How much money do you think you'll make out of Nerno?"

"That remains to be seen. I have lots of costs I need to recuperate. All the research isn't free."

"Isn't what you're doing illegal?"

Gates shook his head. "Not at all, Mr. Webster. Frankly I'm a little bit disappointed with you coming in here, talking about money and calling me a criminal."

"Really? How much money did you make off the Kenyan and the Brazilian companies before you sent them into bankruptcy?"

"I don't do it for the money."

John scoffed incredulously. "Why then? If not for the money?"

"These people think they can get away with doing whatever they want. They lie and cheat and nobody stops them. They are common crooks, only they're smarter. I simply expose them for what they are. I thought you, of all people, would understand."

John stared at Gates in surprise. Gates actually seemed hurt by John's accusations.

"Let me tell you something, Mr. Webster," Gates continued. "My family is from Houston. We've been there for generations and generations. My father wasn't a sophisticated man like you; he fixed used cars for a living. It didn't make him rich but it earned him a decent income. He was frugal and always saved, putting money away into stocks, savings plans. Then, with the financial collapse of 2008, he lost most of his life savings. His accountant had advised him to put a large portion of his money into Lehman Brothers.

"The next day, my father took his hunting rifle and shot himself. He was seventy-six and he figured he had no way of recovering financially. A week later, the police came and kicked my mother out of the house they had been living in for forty-three years after she defaulted on the mortgage. A week later, she had a stroke and I had to put her in a nursing home. I was deeply angry and hurt but I did nothing.

"Then in 2010, a court-appointed examiner concluded, after a year-long investigation, that for years Lehman Brothers had been liquidating up to fifty million dollars into cash right before they published their financial statements making the company look a lot more stable than it actually was.

"This is, of course, fraudulent, and if proven conclusively could lead to jail time for many senior executives both at Lehman's and Ernst & Young, the firm that audited the company. But of course the burden of proof is a lot more complex than a straightforward court examination, and prosecutors have no stomach for that sort of thing.

"I read about it one day in my Dallas office and wondered how they could have gotten away with it for so long. Texans, more than any other Americans, believe in our founding fathers' promises, fed to us from our schools, our elders, and our literature. But where was the government, where was the fourth estate when my parents needed them? The answer was that everybody was too busy making too much fucking money."

John listened to Gates' story, not unmoved. "None of that makes what you do any better. In fact, you're just using the same financial practices as Lehman and the rest."

Gates frowned. "Yes, but it's all a means to a different end. The end result is what's important. I do the type of investigative reporting you can only dream of. I've hired more full time staff than your newspaper employs to look into Nerno. Something—I'm sure—you wish you could do."

John thought wistfully about the single geologist that he wanted to hire. "So you think of yourself as an investigative journalist?"

Gates' eyes grew large. "No, definitely not. I'm better than a journalist. I am a creature of the digital age. Our intentions are the same—we get the same results. The only difference is your business model is antiquated and unsustainable."

John took a slow sip of his whiskey, swirling the liquid in his glass. He didn't like what Gates was saying, but at the same time he had to see the logic in it. He thought about the Pommeroys selling their majority stake in the *Daily Globe*. About the massive number of layoffs and cutbacks. Perhaps his time was up. Perhaps it was time for businessmen like Gates to take over . . . but no. John didn't really believe that. Nobody could fully trust opportunistic Hank Gates, and there, perhaps, lay John's salvation (and perhaps, if John succeeded, the *Daily Globe*'s).

Gates smiled again, relaxing a little. "You remember Wikileaks? That's another organization doing your job for you. They are fulfilling the roles journalists can't anymore."

John shrugged. "You're just supplements. You would be nothing without us. You need us. Wikileaks partnered up with the *Guardian*. Why don't you partner with me?"

"Is that what this meeting is about?"

"Why not? Give me an exclusive and we'll pool our resources together."

"What do you have that I won't have in my report?"

"I have an inside source that could be persuaded to talk to you. In return, you give me what you've got."

"I have something better than a source. I have cold hard data. You can't beat that."

"Make me an offer then," John said.

The waiter brought the bill, as if on cue, and Gates made a big show of counting out his bills and laying them on the table.

"Do you know what David Kahn did last week?" Gates asked.

John shook his head. "No, what?"

"He had lunch with the President of the United States. You think you can touch a guy like that with your one source?"

"I've brought down more powerful and more dangerous people than David Kahn."

"You're talking about your Afghan warlords? Please," Gates said. "You have no idea what game you're playing. This is a whole different type of war, but no less dangerous."

They finished dinner. Gates paid the bill and they left the restaurant. At the door Gates shook John's hand.

"I do wish you the best of luck," Gates said.

"Look, Hank . . . what do you have to lose with a partnership?" John asked. "We both know timing matters a great deal, and neither of us wants to be a party spoiler. This way we can guarantee you get to sell your stock on time, and nobody beats me to the story."

Hank Gates stuck his hands in his pockets. "You're not a bad salesman after all, Mr. Webster. But the answer is still no."

John watched Gates walk across the street, braving the cold and darkness. John decided to walk the several blocks to his hotel, even though he hated the cold.

He stopped in the doorway of his room and instantly smelled lingering cigarette ash. He had quit smoking some years back and knew the sweet, seductive smell. It brought him back, like so many other things, to his time talking to the soldiers. But where was the smell coming from?

It couldn't have been the housekeeper. Was somebody lurking inside, waiting for him? He thought about the Jetta that he'd suspected was following him but had then disappeared. Was the driver inside his room, waiting for him?

He looked into the blue darkness for movement or unfamiliar shapes. Nothing seemed out of place or disturbed. He took a step in and closed the door silently, listening. Still nothing. His room wasn't large, and there were few places someone could hide. The queen-sized bed took up much of the room. In the corner, there was an oak desk where his laptop sat.

John searched for something he could use as a weapon. There weren't any objects that would be remotely effective. There was a mini fridge next to the open closet. On top of the fridge was an assortment of alcohol. John chose a six-ounce bottle of Jack Daniel's whiskey.

Not much but it would have to do, he decided.

John silently crept forward. He kicked the space underneath the bed, but his foot caught nothing but air. He bet down and looked, but there was nobody there. He straightened up, feeling slightly ridiculous.

Next John checked the bathroom. He imagined trying to smash an intruder over the head with a sample-size bottle of Jack's. Luckily the bathroom was empty as well.

John turned on the light, satisfied that he was alone. Was he just imagining the smell? No, it still lingered. It was real. He was certain somebody had been in his room. Was it the maid?

John walked over to the desk. Everything seemed to be in order. He opened up his laptop and checked his files. If anything had been touched, he couldn't tell. He closed his laptop and looked around again. That was when he realized that his notebook and voice recorder were both missing. He looked in all the desk drawers, certain that he hadn't placed them there, but fearing the alternative.

John tried to remember what he had on the voice recorder. He had a few interviews for a piece that he was doing about a real estate company, another about a politician—nothing really pertinent to Nerno except his interview with Andrea Drashkov.

Next he thought about his notebook. He remembered that he had taken notes when he had met with Sheila. Was there anything that could be traced back to her? He hadn't used her name but that didn't mean she was safe.

He felt he should phone her and tell her she might be in danger, but then he wasn't sure how she would react. Would she become uncooperative? He needed her. She was his only link and he didn't want to frighten her. But at the same time if she really was in danger he felt that he should warn her.

Then John remembered the copy of the email that Sheila had given him. He dug in his laptop bag, which was where he had hidden it, but to his distress he found that it was also missing. Now he had no physical evidence of any wrongdoing if he ever needed to prove it.

John sat on the lumpy bed and looked up at the blank television screen. He cursed his carelessness. He knew that it must have been somebody working for Nerno and he couldn't help but think that Andrea Drashkov and David Kahn were behind it.

John put on his heavy coat and went out into the cold to the nearest payphone. He paid close attention to his surroundings, making sure that nobody was following him. He dialled Sheila's cell phone number from memory. At least he was smart enough not to have written that down anywhere.

"Hello," Sheila answered on the third ring.

"Hi, it's me. I've got some bad news for you."

"What?" she asked, sounding panicked.

"Somebody broke into my hotel room and stole all my notes. Now I didn't name you specifically, but you never know what they will be able to deduce from what I wrote."

"My God," Sheila said, slowly. "What does that mean? Do they know who I am?"

"Like I said, I'm not sure, but they might be able to work it out. I can't guarantee you haven't been compromised. I'm sorry. I should have been more careful."

"You're sorry?" Sheila yelled into the phone. "Damn right you should have been more careful. I knew I shouldn't have trusted you."

"Look Sheila, if I had known they would be so desperate as to break into my hotel . . . let's look on the positive side. We now know they have something to hide, and they are desperate, which means they will make mistakes. Don't worry. It'll all work out in the end."

Sheila started yelling. "You say that, but you're not the one with your job and career on the line. Nobody will hire me if they find out I snooped into company records. I could go to jail, so forgive me if I am a little worried."

"Don't say that over the phone. You never know who's listening," John cautioned.

"I'm just pissed," Sheila said, more calmly now.

"I'm really sorry."

"I don't think you realize it. Billions of dollars are at stake here. These people will do anything to stop you."

"Right now, I don't think I'm their biggest worry."

"That's probably the only thing that is keeping you safe right now," Sheila said, hanging up.

The Geologist

GEORGE HOPKINS SORT OF WADDLED to his car, leather suitcase in hand. The light was dim in the underground garage, but John could see that Hopkins wore an expensive double-breasted suit that was wasted on his pedestrian looks. Hopkins put his suitcase in the back seat of his sun-yellow Lamborghini. Again, the sleek sexiness of the angular machine was at odds with the pudgy scientist.

John never understood cars or the appeal of really expensive models. Did Hopkins hope to appeal to girls half his age? Was it just a projected image, like makeup applied to something rotten?

John had decided to corner Hopkins, to get him away from his office, ambush him and bully him into giving some answers. Hopkins surely knew something about Ko Chang and John was intent on getting it from him.

He would be the weakest link, John decided.

John had rented a midsize Toyota for the occasion. He started his car in anticipation of Hopkins. The Lamborghini roared to life and exploded out of the parking stall. Hopkins swerved around the corner and up the ramp to ground level. John was already having a hard time keeping up with him.

Snow was coming down heavily and made visibility difficult. John felt like a piece of white paper was being held up several feet in front of his vision, blocking everything. John drove carefully, following the yellow blur as it accelerated down 4th Avenue.

John had forgotten to ask the rental shop if he had snow tires on his car, but he supposed that everybody drove with them in Calgary. His uncertainty and lack of knowledge embarrassed him.

He watched as the Lamborghini changed lanes and cut in front of a Nissan which had to apply its brakes. John followed Hopkins as he turned west onto Memorial Drive. The Lamborghini got further and further ahead.

John realized that if he remained at the same speed he would lose Hopkins. He could either disengage the pursuit or he could speed up and test his driving abilities. John tried to remember the last time he had driven in the snow. He lived close enough to downtown that he could either walk or take a cab if road conditions were too terrible.

John decided that he would slow down. It was not urgent for him to follow George Hopkins; after all, he could corner him another day, and there was no guarantee that he would learn anything worthwhile.

But then John thought back to the memory of Byron chiding him for not going on the rollercoaster. Was he getting too old for this job? Had he lost his nerve? He had once—not too long ago, it seemed—been in war zones, ducked bullets, evaded roadside bombs. Now he was afraid of speeding in a little snow.

Although it was a pointless exercise, John changed his mind, partly from foolhardiness and partly from determination, and decided to give chase. He pressed down hard on the gas pedal and he could feel the car lurch forward, the strain of the motor working. He weaved in and out of traffic, feeling the car skid on the freshly laid snow.

Up ahead, luckily, George Hopkins got caught behind an SUV that seemed bloody-minded in refusing to yield to the superiority of the Lamborghini, allowing John to catch up. He drove behind Hopkins along Memorial Drive for twenty minutes. The Lamborghini tried to weave in and out of traffic, but only with moderate success, which made it easy for John to stay with him. It was a beautiful drive. John looked out at the white blanket that engulfed the houses and the yards, and the downtown skyscrapers which disappeared behind them.

They turned off Memorial Drive onto Crowtrail Highway and headed north. The traffic got lighter, and so George put the Lamborghini into high gear, and John did the same in his Toyota. He pressed the accelerator harder, ninety miles an hour, then a hundred miles an hour. The tiny engine strained under him, rattling the entire car and it felt like the whole thing would fall apart under him. The tiny rental car was no match for George Hopkins' machine, and the gap between them widened.

The snow started to come down even thicker, and before long John could only make out the two red lights in the distance.

John was feeling increasingly nervous and uncertain of his car. His body was rigid, his knuckles were white from gripping the steering wheel so tightly, and his chest and neck were strained forward.

John didn't know how much longer they had to go. How long had he been driving for? Once again he thought about slowing down but something inside him—perhaps Byron's childish voice—stopped him.

The Lamborghini turned a corner and momentarily John lost it. When John turned the same corner, George Hopkins and his Lamborghini were nowhere in sight. John slowed to sixty to look around. There was another turn off to the right. *Hopkins must have gone there*, John decided.

He cut across a lane, ignoring an angry honk from behind, and got onto Citadel Boulevard. He was off the highway, and on each side of the street large modern stucco houses stood on large lawns with snow-covered spruce trees.

Finally John spotted Hopkins and his Lamborghini about fifty metres ahead, bombing around a corner. John pressed forward, his tires churning in the snow, trying to get a grip. There was nobody else around, no other cars, and the snow muffled any sound, so it seemed that John and Hopkins were the only two people left in this wintry world.

Hopkins slowed down, which John was grateful for, but now he had to be careful not to be noticed.

Hopkins turned onto Hamptons Boulevard and John did the same about thirty seconds later. The houses seemed to grow in size—big and blocky and gloomy in the street lamps. To John's right, hidden behind the blocks of houses he could see a luminous white park. It seemed so sublime and unreal.

John turned his attention back to the road just in time to see the Lamborghini swerve suddenly out of control and smash into a tree. The car crumpled like it was made of foil, and pieces flew everywhere.

John slammed on his brakes and pulled over. He jumped out and ran over to the wreckage. It was several moments before he even felt the bitter cold or the heavy snow fall on his hair and shoulders. The front of the car had been obliterated almost as if it had never existed. The windshield was cracked so badly it looked like a spider's web, and he could see George Hopkins lying unconscious in the driver's seat.

It took a moment for John to find the door handle because it was so streamlined into the body of the car, but it was jammed closed. John looked at the car; the entire body was warped from the collision.

By this time, people had started coming out of their houses to see what had happened. John yelled for somebody to call an ambulance.

John turned back to the car and called Hopkins' name and started to pound on the windshield, but to no avail. John studied Hopkins' body for any major injury—a gash or cut—but he couldn't see anything. The airbags had deployed and had probably saved Hopkins' life. He looked almost peaceful, as if he was sleeping deeply.

John looked around for something to smash through the window, found a medium-sized branch, and used it to break away the remains of the windshield. He then climbed through the hole to examine the geologist. He knew that without the proper training he could injure Hopkins even more severely if he moved him, but he wanted to see if he could at least help. John started by taking Hopkins' pulse. It was weak, but it was there. John examined the rest of the interior.

A middle-aged man in jeans and a T-shirt approached the side of the car. He seemed to be one of the neighbours. "You need a hand?" he asked.

"When will the paramedics get here?"

The man shrugged. "They said they were on their way."

George Hopkins' legs were crushed against the front of the car. There was no way to get him out without the jaws of life.

"Did you see what happened?" the neighbour asked.

John climbed out of the car. There was nothing he could do for Hopkins but wait. "I just saw him lose control. Probably hit a patch of black ice," he said, thinking about how fast they had been going and how lucky he had been not to lose control as well. He doubted that his rental car would be good in a crash.

"It's strange," the neighbour said. "I used to own a Spyder and it was great in the snow."

John stared at the neighbour, thinking of what the man had said. Was it possible that somebody had tampered with the Lamborghini? Had somebody tried to kill Hopkins? He thought back to what Sheila had said about how they would do anything to prevent the truth from coming out.

They stood there for a while, not saying anything, staring at the wreckage of the beautiful automobile and the unconscious man inside. John started to shiver and the neighbour standing next to him offered to go get a coat, but John said that he was okay.

He stared up at the immovable spruce tree that had halted the quarter-million-dollar machine, spread over the top of them like a canopy, seemingly unfazed by everything that was going on around it. As John surveyed the scene, everything seemed peaceful. He felt helpless and insignificant.

Then he heard the familiar wail of sirens, and a large fire truck turned the corner and stopped, and firemen jumped out. They walked over to the car, and after conferring for a while, began to cut George Hopkins out. Soon after, an ambulance appeared. The paramedics joined the firefighters, and after about fifteen minutes Hopkins was on a stretcher, being shepherded into the ambulance.

"Is he going to be all right?" John asked one of the firefighters.

The firefighter shrugged. "It's hard to say."

Two female officers were interviewing the neighbours. John hadn't seen them arrive. He had never had very good interactions with cops, and decided that it was time to leave, but before he could do so, one of the neighbours pointed him out.

The two officers were both short and stout—made more so by the bulletproof vests—so they seemed to waddle over to where John was standing.

"You're the driver of that vehicle?" one of the officers asked, pointing to the rental Toyota.

"That's right."

"You were driving behind the Lamborgini when it lost control?"

"That's right," John said. He did his best to describe what happened, leaving out the part that he was following George Hopkins.

"Where you from?"

"From Vancouver."

"What are you doing here?"

To John, it sounded like an accusation, but maybe that was just his imagination.

"I'm here on business," he said.

The officer who was taking notes looked up. "What type of business?"

John took a deep breath. "I work for the *Daily Globe*. I'm a reporter."

The two officers looked at each other and John could almost feel their backs stiffen. It wasn't an unusual reaction from police officers and it usually meant a little extra grilling from them. And this time there was no exception.

"Do you have a business card?"

John nodded and handed them one of his cards.

The officer taking notes studied the card. "What are you doing in Hampton?" she asked.

John thought quickly. "I'm doing a story about neighbourhoods across Canada and their American counterparts."

The two officers seemed intrigued. "You mean like the difference between the Hamptons in New York and here?"

John nodded, smiling. If he had learned anything about Canadians it was that they loved to be compared to Americans.

"Seems interesting," one of the officers said. "I'll look out for it."

"Anything you would like to add?" the other officer asked.

"I don't think so," John said. "You think he's going to pull through?"

"We aren't the people to ask," the officer said, closing her notebook.

John watched as the officers went off to interview more witnesses. John stayed around to watch the chaotic scene. He walked back to the Lamborghini. He remembered that George Hopkins had put a briefcase on the backseat and he wondered if it was still there.

The once beautiful vehicle was now no more than a mangled piece of metal, leather, rubber and glass. The firefighters had cut out a good portion of the side, like they were dissecting a cross section of a specimen they were studying. John looked around. Amazingly, nobody was paying him much attention.

John wiggled into the car and reached back and grabbed hold of the briefcase handle. It had fallen onto the floor and was wedged between two seats. With a clean jerk, John hoisted the briefcase out. He looked around to see if anybody had seen him, but the police were too busy interviewing the witnesses, and the firefighters were in a small circle conferring with each other.

John walked back to his car and placed the briefcase on the passenger's side. The briefcase was obviously well-worn, but equally obvious was its craftsmanship. It had a gold-plated lock next to the handle. John judged that it had probably cost a small fortune and probably had some sentimental value to George Hopkins. John fought the urge to try and open it up right in the middle of the street. Instead he did a U-turn and headed back to the city.

John didn't stop until he was back in his hotel room. After the break-in, he had requested the hotel to give him a new room, which they had begrudgingly done. John had made up the excuse that the bed was too lumpy and hurt his back.

The new room was on the north side of the building and, fittingly, John thought, he could see, masquerading behind several other office towers, the Nerno Energy building in its glass-panelled glory.

John put the briefcase on the bed. He went to the desk and took two large paperclips from a stack of notepaper. He bent one at a ninety degree angle and straightened the other one until he had a thin metal wire. He then inserted the two ends of the paperclips into the lock on the case. It took John a couple of minutes of jiggling the paperclips around in the lock before he heard the definitive click of the bolt, and the briefcase fell open.

There were several file folders and the remains of a sandwich. John wondered why a billionaire would pack his own lunch. John shook his head and threw out the sandwich and half eaten apple. He then flipped through the folders, but was disappointed at what he found. Everything was written in complex mathematical equations and John didn't understand anything he read. He opened the other folders but was equally disappointed. They were all beyond his comprehension and the Ko Chang Project wasn't mentioned anywhere—at least not that John could tell. The only other things that the files contained were a bunch of diagrams, and photos of places John didn't recognize.

He decided to call Charles Dana again and press for the money to hire a geologist who would be able break down the mathematics into layman's terms and so, at least, give him some perspective on the reports. John dialled Dana's direct line but only got an answering machine. He then tried Charles Dana's cell phone, but once again got a message.

John paced around his room, wondering what to do next. He thought about George Hopkins, unconscious, being taken to the hospital on a stretcher, away from the destroyed Lamborghini.

It could have been me, John thought. He had been speeding in imperfect conditions. All because he wanted to prove to himself that he wasn't an old man. Because Byron had taunted him about a rollercoaster.

Had the Lamborghini been tampered with? Had somebody tried to kill Hopkins to keep him silent?

John pushed these questions out of his mind, and decided on a whim to phone Hayden and see if he could find out more about Paul. He knew it was a bad idea, but it was like a craving in the deep pit of his stomach.

But Byron answered the phone.

"You want me to get Mom?"

"Yeah . . . actually no. How are things going?"

"What do you mean?"

"I just mean, how are you?"

"Why do you even ask, Dad?"

"Because I'm interested. That's why."

"When are you getting back?"

"I'm not sure. Not for a while."

John sighed. He wasn't sure what he was supposed to tell his son and, if he was honest with himself, he never had. Maybe that was part of the reason he had always been escaping; it created the delusion that it pardoned him from all parental responsibility.

John tried to think of what his own father had tried to tell him. The now dead theatre critic had taught John about literature and art and all the things John now hated. What did any man know anyway? Fathers were just ordinary men with ordinary knowledge of things like life, love, and death.

"Byron," John said. "Why didn't you tell me about your mom's boyfriend?"

"Because it's none of your business."

That really stung John, but the reality of that statement stung even more. "No, I guess it isn't."

"I'm going to go get Mom."

"Byron, hold on . . . when do you start driving?"

"You're going to teach me how to drive?" Byron replied, excitedly.

"What? No. Of course not," John said, suddenly feeling ridiculous and foolish. "Just . . . never mind."

"Okay," Byron said, a little confused. "I'm going to get Mom."

This time, John didn't stop him. He heard Byron and Hayden in the background. John sat down on the bed.

"Hello?" Hayden said. "What's going on?"

John sucked in a lungful of air and felt his head go dizzy, which always happened after he heard his ex-wife's voice. "Nothing, I just phoned to talk with Byron."

"How is the article coming along?"

"Not very well, to be honest." John thought about telling her about George Hopkins' car accident, but decided against it. He had spared her the gory details before, so why start now?

"I'm sorry to hear that but I'm sure you'll succeed. You always do."

"Not all the time."

"John . . . I'm putting a guest list together—for the wedding, I mean. And . . . well. Do you think you would want to come?"

"What? You're inviting me?"

"I know, it's stupid. I'm sorry."

"No, no. Of course I want to come," John said. "I'm just surprised, that's all."

The truth was that John couldn't think of any worse torture. He imagined himself as the stereotypical ex-husband standing by the bar and ordering drink after drink.

"You sure?" Hayden asked.

"Of course," John said, trying to sound as upbeat as possible, but to his own ears he just sounded ridiculously fake.

"That's good," Hayden said. "I was also thinking about inviting your mother. Is that weird?"

"I don't know," John responded. "Perhaps."

"It's just she's been such an important part of the family and I know Byron would love to have her." Hayden paused. "But if you don't want me to, I won't. I know the whole thing seems very strange."

"No, invite her. I'm sure she'll be delighted."

"I never wanted to get married again. I never imagined this would happen."

John didn't say anything. He didn't trust himself to say the correct thing. What was the correct thing? He knew what he wanted to say. He desperately wanted to persuade her not to do it, to convince her that it was a bad idea, but a small nagging part of himself said that maybe it would be the best for both of them.

Perhaps then he would stop pining for her. Maybe then he would stop comparing every single woman he dated to her. Maybe then he would stop hoping for one of those ridiculous Hollywood endings where the man runs through the airport to stop the woman from getting on the plane. That sort of ending was the reason John refused to go to the movies. The problem was that the film never showed what happened the next day, or the day after that, or the day after that.

Movies have warped everybody's minds, John thought. Hollywood had raised people's expectations of life. Happy endings weren't supposed to be, John had concluded long ago.

He again thought about his father and his love for stories, for escape from his lower class Scottish roots. That was why John had joined Reuters after dropping out of school and had never looked back. What did those teachers know except what Dickens and Dostoyevsky and Tolstoy told them anyway?

"John, are you still there?" Hayden asked.

"Yeah, sorry. I was just thinking of my mother and me at your wedding."

"I'm not worried about her. You, however . . ."

"I will be good. I promise."

"You and your promises."

"She always liked you better, you know."

"Come on, John."

"We both know it's true. If she had to choose between us she would pick you."

"What's wrong, John? Why are you talking like that?"

"I don't know, Hayden. I'm sorry. I should go."

"Okay. Call me when you get back," Hayden said, hanging up.

David Kahn

"**A**RE WE THE DEVIL?" DAVID Kahn asked. He was standing up on a podium and smiling with large white teeth at the crowd. His voice reverberated through the packed cavernous ballroom he had rented at the Fairmont.

"Do we tempt you to bite the apple?" David asked, seductively, pausing to look at the men and women from the Calgary Board of Trade. "In the media we are called the 'Dutch Disease'. A catchy name, I have to admit. We are portrayed as vultures, as hogs, as callous, as uncaring, just trying to squeeze a buck out of you. But the truth is we aren't as devilish as we're made out to be. We care deeply about the environment, about sustainability.

"Without us, civilization as we know it would cease to exist. We would still be travelling using horse-drawn carriages. There is nothing in this world that doesn't use oil, and to think otherwise is to bury our heads in the sand like ostriches. The world cannot yet run on solar energy or hydro power and I, like everybody in this room, look forward to the day when we can all use clean, renewable energy a hundred percent of the time, because Nerno will be there leading the charge. We already spend two-and-a-half-million dollars on wind and solar research. A fact I have not seen in one newspaper or television broadcast."

David paused to take a sip of water. So far the day had been stressful. In the morning he had gone to the hospital to visit George Hopkins, who was still in a coma. The doctors had told him that they were unsure if he would ever regain consciousness.

As a founding member of Nerno, George had been a vital part of their success. He had stuck by David's side all the way through, and the thought that he might not make it filled David with a grievous sense of loss. What would he do without him?

The police officer had phoned David and told him that the Lamborghini had slipped on a patch of ice and had lost control. David had just nodded, unable to say anything. He had wanted to believe it, tried to believe it, but the timing was just too suspicious. Of course he couldn't tell the police officer that. David wondered if Andrea Drashkov had had anything to do with George's accident. She had never liked him, even in the beginning, but would she be capable of engineering his accident? He didn't think so. Even she wasn't as callous or as calculating as to try and kill George. He was just being overly paranoid.

David regretted telling Andrea anything about the Ko Chang Project. But he needed to use her as a scapegoat if things went horribly wrong with the Chinese, and things were looking like they might. He didn't need the bad press, not now. Not with Hank Gates on his back and the reporter from the *Daily Globe* after him.

After the presentation, David drove back to his office in his Porsche, a little slower than he normally would have driven. He wanted to phone his secretary, Joyce Lancroft, and tell her to cancel everything for the next two or three days and take a long weekend, but there were two factors that prevented him: first, he knew George would want him to continue; and second, if he cancelled everything, it would only fuel the rumours more.

David fiddled with the radio, finding a news station that he listened to, until he heard the stock quotes. The market was generally on a downswing. David sighed. *At least it would make it easier to sell Nerno*, he thought. He couldn't wait to get rid of the headache.

David stopped at a red light and he could feel a sense of foreboding surrounding him, as if cold fingers were tightening around his throat. David concentrated on the radio. It was an appropriate song for a dreary winter day. The temperature gauge said that it was minus twenty degrees outside. The cold and the freezing temperatures always made David depressed. He usually took a vacation to the Bahamas for a month or two at this time of year. He already had his eye on this beautiful retirement villa where he would live out the rest of his life watching sunsets and sunrises and never see snow again.

David's cell phone rang. It was a member of the board of directors, who would offer his condolences, but was really calling to see what David would do without George Hopkins. David didn't have the energy to talk to him and so he let it go to voicemail. He had been dodging most people ever since he had heard the news about George, but he knew that couldn't last.

David's cell phone rang again. It was a project manager for Ko Chang. He put the manager on speaker phone.

"Have you got rid of the protesters yet?" David asked.

"Well . . . not yet."

"Then why are you phoning me? I told you to call the police."

"We did, but the police have refused to do anything about it."

"Goddamn it, what are we paying them for? Tear gas them or something. Blame it on the police. I don't care, just get rid of them. We can't afford more bad press, understand me?"

"I understand, but with all due respect, tear gas isn't going to improve the situation."

David let out a heavy sigh. He was agitated and having a hard time dealing with the esoteric details that his employees were pushing on him. "Call the police back again and tell them it is imperative—yes, tell them I said imperative—that they do something about the protesters, otherwise I'm going to phone the President and demand action. Got it?"

"Okay, will do," the project manager said, hanging up.

His phone rang again, and this time it was Andrea Drashkov. He didn't really want to talk to her either, but he was curious as to how she would react to the news about George, and maybe he could get a better sense of her involvement.

"My God, David, I just heard. That's awful," Andrea said, sounding genuinely distressed.

"It was just an accident. That's it," David said, although his voice sounded foreign even to himself.

"How can you be so sure? I'm scared, David."

David relaxed a little. Nobody was that good of an actor. "Don't worry. He'll pull through and soon we'll all be drinking down in Mexico, having a good laugh. I guarantee it."

"I don't think it was an accident. How can it be an accident? Things happen for a reason, for a purpose."

"Andrea, you sound hysterical. Are you okay?"

"No, of course I'm not okay. Why would I be okay?"

"You're right," David said. "But we'll pull through. We always do."

"I've got more bad news. That journalist John Webster has an inside source. He won't say who. I tried finding out but he gave me nothing."

"Well, keep at it. I'll get tech to start monitoring everyone's email and look into our phone records. Don't worry, we'll catch whoever it is."

"The damage might already have been done. If the Chinese get hold of this then everything will collapse."

"You worry about the journalist and let me worry about the Chinese."

"I'm just concerned, that's all."

"It'll be fine. Look, I'm just going underground and I'm going to lose you."

"Okay, I'll see you in a bit."

David hung up. He turned into the parking lot underneath the Nerno building and into his reserved spot next to the elevator. It was only eight o'clock but David felt like he had already completed a full day, he was so emotionally drained.

When he got to his office he asked Joyce Lancroft to make him some coffee. She returned several minutes later with a hot cup in her hand. David took it and thanked her.

"A journalist phoned this morning for you," Joyce said. "He keeps persisting."

David couldn't help but groan. Why did they never stop? What did they want from him? "Which one?"

"The one from the *Daily Globe*, I think. His name is John Webster."

David groaned again, deeper this time. It was the second time in less than an hour that he had heard that name and it was beginning to annoy him. "What does he want now?"

"I'm not sure. He didn't say."

"Notify Patrick Oswald over at Walker and Thompson. They should be the ones dealing with him."

"I already did. He said he already spoke with him."

David smiled. "You are amazing, you know that? I don't know what I would do without you."

Joyce smiled, but she seemed uncertain.

"What is it?" David asked.

"Oh, nothing," she said.

"You sure?"

"It's just . . . what's going to happen to all of us? I mean once the company is sold."

"Is that what's worrying you? Things will be fine. There will always be a job for you. I'll make sure of it."

Joyce smiled broadly. David always loved her smile, but it faded so quickly. "Oh David, you look so tired." She took a step closer to him and started rubbing his shoulders. David closed his eyes and leaned forward.

"Well, I didn't sleep very well. I was in the hospital for three hours."

"My God, what's wrong?"

David suddenly went rigid. He opened his eyes and looked up at Joyce, who also froze, a frown plastered on her face.

"You haven't heard?" David asked.

"Heard what?"

"George Hopkins had a car accident last night. He's in a coma."

Joyce covered her mouth with her hand and took a step back. "My God. I should send some flowers. Does the rest of the office know? Do you want me to make an official announcement?"

David looked down at his desk. He hadn't even thought of it. "Yes, that would probably be a good idea. Thank you."

Joyce nodded, turned and started walking to her desk.

"Wait," David said. His voice was low and urgent.

Joyce stopped and turned. "Yes?"

"Close the door and draw the blinds?"

"David, I don't think . . ."

"Please, Joyce," David said. He spoke quickly now, barely knowing what he was saying, as if it was a recording he had once heard of himself in some other lifetime. "You don't know how I feel. With George gone. I'm so confused. You are the only thing I have that is right."

Joyce paused for a moment, then nodded. "Okay, my love. I know how stressed you've been. You deserve to relax."

Joyce slipped her skirt off and took off her blouse. She dispensed with her underwear in an equally economical fashion until she stood naked, her hands rigid by her side. She had compact, upright breasts with small, hard nipples. Her stomach was slender, her hips jutted out like buttons.

David stared at her for a few moments, expecting something to stir in him, some sort of anticipation, but when nothing came he got up and slowly walked around his large desk, his eyes never leaving Joyce.

Mechanically he undid his pants and slid his boxers to his knees. Joyce bent over his desk like she had done a dozen times before. David felt like he was in a dull scene in a meaningless play. He caressed her bony back, then cupped her breasts with his hands. Joyce didn't say anything, not even when he entered her.

He concentrated on her body, her quivering muscles, her heavy breathing. When it was over, David quickly got dressed and told Joyce to do the same. Instead, she wrapped her arms around her body and crumpled to the floor and started crying.

David stood over her, not really sure what to do or say. He felt a sudden rush of guilt and shame, like a head rush from standing up too fast.

"Please, Joyce. Don't do that. Not now." David just wanted to be alone with his dark thoughts.

"He's going to be okay, right?"

"George? Honestly, I don't know."

"I can't believe it. He was here only yesterday. I spoke with him. I can't believe he's suddenly gone."

David straightened his tie and perched himself on the corner of his desk. His head was empty of everything, of thought and emotion. He just didn't have anything left. "Would you feel the same if I was in a coma?"

Joyce stopped crying and looked up at David. "Of course, my darling. Of course."

David knelt down beside Joyce and wrapped his arms around her. He didn't say anything. He just basked in the touch of her soft, warm skin. He felt small comfort that somebody in the world would feel something if he was gone. Would his wife of twenty years? Would his kids, whom he barely knew?

They stayed in this crouching position, not moving, for a long while. Time seemed to slow down. The office was quiet except for a mounted clock on the wall, but even that seemed distant and unimportant. After a while, Joyce got up and slowly put her clothes back on. David didn't watch her. He couldn't watch her. Instead he stared down at the dirty carpet. She didn't speak a word. David heard her soft footsteps as she pulled up the blinds and opened the door and walked through without closing it behind her.

"That was a great speech."

David was brought back to the here and now by the strong male voice. He turned to see a tall, middle-aged man standing in the corridor. He had on jeans and a cheap white dress shirt. His face was long with a strong, stubble-sprinkled jawline. Definitely not from the Calgary Board of Trade.

"You press?" David asked, wearily.

The man smiled and put out his hand to shake hands. He had a strong, business-like grip. His eyes were dark, large and lively, roving around so that they never seemed to miss anything. He was tall and a bit heavy. His jaw jutted but had loose flesh around the sides like flaps on an airplane. His whole body displayed a bit of world weariness, as if he didn't quite want to be there, or anywhere else for that matter.

The way the man smiled was tight, controlled, friendless, and contrived. David thought the man could be surrounded by a dozen harems ready to do his every bidding and he would still give the same strained smile.

"You were absolutely right about the press," the man said.

David nodded vaguely but looked around for an escape. David had come alone and now he was regretting the decision. He never liked to carry much of an entourage and now he had nobody to run interference for him. He said, "I only have a limited amount of time. I have another meeting in thirty minutes."

The man nodded. "I will walk you to your car then."

They started walking out of the ballroom. David gave his obligatory handshakes to the board members, smiling at them. A lot of them were investors after all. He had come to the Board of Trade with a mindset to conquer, and he felt that he had done a good job of that.

"You're a hard man to track down."

"I didn't catch your name," David said.

"John Webster."

David stopped walking and John was forced to stop alongside him. David said, "You're the one who has been hounding me. How did you know I was going to be here?"

John smiled wryly. "I want to talk to you about Nerno."

"What do you want to know?" David asked, although he already knew the answer to that question.

"Specifically, about the deal with the China National Offshore Oil Company."

"We are only in preliminary talks. Nothing has been finalized yet, and if that time comes, then I promise to tell you."

"Can you tell me about the accusation that you've been hiding reports that say there is no oil at Ko Chang?"

"First of all, the accusation is completely false, without merit and baseless. Second of all, I don't know who is making that accusation except irresponsible journalists who have nothing better to do than stir up controversy to sell newspapers." David had been taught that the best defence was always to go on the offence.

John shook his head. "You've pegged me wrong. I'm not here because I have some sort of axe to grind."

"Then why are you here?"

"I have a source that tells me you've been lying to the board, to the shareholders and everybody else about what you have in Ko Chang."

David glared at the journalist. In his younger days, David had been a pretty good card player, and John didn't seem like he was bluffing. Perhaps he really did have somebody on the inside. Was it George? No, he didn't have the guts to do something like that. Was it Andrea? She would be the type of person to do it. Was it a coincidence that this journalist showed up just after he had told her?

"That is ridiculous and if you print that I'll sue you into the ground," David said, but it was weak, and both of them knew it.

John smiled a knowing smile. "Is that really how you want to play it?"

"You only have words," David said with a scoff. He needed to regain the attack.

"Words are the most powerful weapon anybody has," John said, before turning and walking across the street.

When John left, David took out his phone and called Andrea Drashkov. "What are we going to do about this journalist?" he asked.

The Source

"**W**HEN WILL YOU KNOW?" JOHN was on his cell phone, talking to the media liaison officer for the Calgary police. John hated any media liaison folk but especially the police type. Their whole job was to prevent John from finding out the truth. They were doors to be unlocked. The trick was to find the special combination.

"Not for another week at least," the police officer said.

"Does it really take that long?"

"Well, there are a lot of complexities. It involves the investigators from the Alberta Motor Association. They will probably send it over to a collision forensic firm for analysis. They will sort through the wreckage, perhaps do some interviews, that sort of thing. I wish I could help more, but really, you'll have to be patient. These things cannot be rushed."

"Who is your supervisor? I believe the car may have been tampered with, and the case should be treated as an attempted homicide."

"What sort of information is that?"

"The owner, George Hopkins, is involved in a possible fraud conspiracy."

There was silence on the other end. Then the man said, "Do you have a case number?"

"Well, there is no official case, but perhaps you could get the investigation prioritized."

"Look, Mr. Webster, I have no time for fishing expeditions. We are doing all we can to expedite the process."

After John hung up, he phoned Charles Dana.

"I've got some good news," Charles said. "We've found a geologist for you."

"That's great. Who is it?"

"The company is a small one called Spring Research and they are right in downtown Calgary. The woman you'll be working with is named Mindy Rocher. She's expecting your call."

"Thanks so much. This will help a lot. I promise."

"It better, Webster. The Pommeroys are breathing down my neck on this one. Apparently they own a large stake in Nerno and aren't too keen on seeing you tear it down."

"Tell them to sell all their shares because I'm not going to stop."

Charles laughed. "That's actually what I told them you'd say."

"I need one more favour."

"Sure."

"I need somebody with contacts in the local police."

"Well, Vince Parkerson covers the crime beat there. Do you want me to get him to phone you?"

"That would be great. Thanks."

John knew Vince Parkerson by reputation. Vince had been working for the *Daily Globe* for what seemed like decades and so John had come in contact with him every so often at the odd work function or ceremony. They knew each other to nod a hello to, but that was about it.

Vince was an old school journalist much like John, but unlike John he had graduated college and had worked his way through student newspapers, then small dailies, until finally he reached the *Daily Globe*.

John hung up and phoned Mindy Rocher and they agreed to meet in about an hour.

"I've got some documents I want you to look over. Tell me what they mean."

"I've never worked for a journalist before," she said excitedly. "Is it kind of like spying?"

John smiled in spite of himself. "Sort of like that, yeah."

"Awesome. I can't wait to meet you!"

Next John found Vince Parkerson in his email directory and shot him a quick email to see if they could meet.

Several moments later John's phone rang. It was a local number.

"Hi John, it's Vince. I got your message and I think I have somebody who can help. The boss told me a little bit about the story and I think it's best we meet in person."

John liked Vince already. Some things were best done in person. "I agree. You know the town better than I do."

"There's a coffee shop called Confession in the East Village."

"Confession? Seriously?" John asked, realizing the irony of the name.

Vince chuckled. "I swear to God."

"Okay," John said. He calculated an hour to meet with Mindy Rocher and go over the contents of Hopkins' briefcase, and then about another hour to find the coffee shop. "How about three o'clock?"

"That should be fine," Vince said, hanging up.

John took the documents from Hopkins' briefcase and stuffed them into his laptop bag. He didn't want to be walking around with George Hopkins' briefcase; it was distinct enough to be recognizable, and John didn't want to take any chances. He looked outside, briefly wondering whether he should brave the elements or take a cab to Mindy Rocher's office.

In the end, he decided to try and walk it. He put on his new winter jacket and boots and took the elevator downstairs. The snow had stopped and settled onto the cement streets. The sun was already escaping the vast grey sky behind the row of skyscrapers. Mercedes, Jaguars and Porsches sped along the roads, leaving nothing but tire tracks and brown slush frozen in the gutters.

About a block into his walk, John was sorry that he ever attempted the trek. His entire face was exposed to the elements, and stung like needles prickling into his skin. He bent his head forward, trying to shield himself, but to no avail. He looked around for a cab that he could hail but there were none in sight.

He wondered what the temperature was exactly. He wished that he had checked at the front desk. Byron had shown him how to do it on his phone once but he had forgotten. Besides that, his fingers felt frozen in his pockets and he doubted that he could manipulate them the way that he wanted to.

John eventually made it to the correct address and was glad to get inside. He looked at the directory and found that Spring Research was on the fifth floor.

John took the elevator. The secretary took John to Mindy Rocher's office. She was a pretty woman in her mid-forties with cropped blonde hair and a round, serious face. She greeted John with a surprisingly firm handshake.

"I'm glad you could make it," she said, ushering John to a seat. "Coffee? Juice?'

"Coffee would be nice. Black."

The secretary nodded and disappeared. With her gone, Rocher took her seat and sat back, clasping her hands together. She had a large wedding ring on her left hand that sparkled as she rocked thoughtfully back and forth in her chair. "Now, I understand from your editor that you have some documents you need reviewing and, for lack of a better word, translated. Is that correct?"

"That is the start of it—yes," John said, unzipping his laptop case and giving Rocher the documents. Rocher took the folder and briefly flipped through them.

"Where did you get these? Or am I not allowed to know?"

"They were given to me by a source. That's all I can tell you."

Rocher paused at the logo on top of the page. "These are from Nerno Energy?"

"Yes, I'm doing a story on the Ko Chang Project."

Rocher nodded. "Yes, I'm familiar with it. I heard Nerno might be bought out by the China National Offshore Oil Company. Any truth to that?"

John gave Rocher a sly smile. "You know what they say. Never ask a journalist about the truth."

"Why is that, Mr. Webster?"

"Because we never let it get in the way of a good story."

Rocher laughed politely, but John got the impression that she didn't find it very funny. "You know, I lived in Beijing for several years, working for a surveying company. It's a completely different way of life. Different way of doing business."

"The story is that there may not be any oil at Ko Chang."

Rocher stared at John. "Really? You have any proof?"

"I do, but not enough. I was hoping you would be able to help me find some in those documents."

Rocher nodded. "Well, it'll take me a while to go through all this thoroughly. When do you need it by?"

John sighed. "Yesterday. How soon can it be done by?"

"Okay, give me a couple of uninterrupted hours and I'll see what I can dig up. I'll give you a call."

John stood up. "I appreciate it."

John turned to leave but Rocher called out to him. "Whatever I find in these documents won't make a difference."

John frowned. "Why do you say that?"

"Because they can afford the best lawyers in the country, and the best lawyers in the country can make anything go away."

"Nixon's lawyers couldn't make Watergate go away."

"Do all journalists cling to that one moment in time?"

John gave a weary smile. "Well, when it's all you have . . ."

"Must be a depressing profession."

That might be the case but John never liked to be told so—especially by someone who had so little contact with journalists personally. "Maybe, but we're invited to all the best parties," he retorted, somewhat pathetically. "We're the free entertainment. If we don't have a good story then we're sure to drink too much and do something really stupid."

"Well, I'm glad you serve some moral purpose."

"Tell me, what made you move back to Calgary?"

Rocher didn't answer right away, but instead looked down at the many stacks of paper on her desk. Eventually she looked back up at John. "Everybody says the future is China. But I disagree. I believe the future is right here in the Texas of the north."

John left Rocher's office. He smiled at the pretty secretary and took the elevator down to the ground level. The doors chimed closed and John was left alone with his thoughts. *Mindy Rocher is right*, he thought.

There was no way his newspaper would ever publish any story on Nerno, no matter how good it was. In the end, it all came down to who had the most money so they could buy the best lawyers, and in this case, as in most cases, the pitiful, unwanted step-child of a business, the *Daily Globe*, was outgunned.

Vince

CONFESSIONS CAFÉ WAS MOSTLY EMPTY except for a young, good-looking couple fondling each other in a desperate way, seemingly oblivious to the outside world, to the snow-swept streets in the windows, and to the glassy-eyed barista no doubt wishing that he was the one making out with the angular, long-haired beauty.

Do they not have any manners? John wondered, ordering a black coffee and tearing the barista away from the scene for a moment or two. John sat on the opposite side of the shop and tried to occupy himself with a free magazine, but it was so terribly written he felt that he would rather watch the couple.

John was depressed to think that Byron would soon be of the age where he would be interested in young women and that they would be interested in him. Had he taught Byron to respect women enough? Had he taught Byron at all? Things didn't seem so straightforward and uncomplicated as when he was unmarried and childless. Was that just life or was it the age they lived in? John looked at the couple and then over at the barista as if they would provide some sort of cosmic sign, but they went on obliviously living their own nonsensical lives.

The Animals' "When I was Young" came on over the sound system. John listened to them sing as he stared into his cup of coffee.

> My father was a soldier then
> And times were very hard
> When I was young.

John looked up and saw Vince Parkerson enter the shop. He smiled at John and slid into the seat across from him.

"It's been a while," Vince said. He was maybe fifteen years older than John. His brown hair and handlebar moustache were both tinged with grey. Vince looked like he could be a cop—the moustache especially could give off the feeling he was just one of the boys, that he could drink with the best of them and commiserate over a tough day. It was a trait most old school journalists knew—how to be a chameleon and fit in with one's surroundings. Not something the new blogging generation understood or cared to imitate. They preferred to wear glasses and plaid shirts, and dye their hair blonde.

John smiled. "Yes, it has. Murders still paying your bills?"

"It's been paying all our bills."

John thought about the *Daily Globe* being sold to some conglomerate that would more than likely dismantle it like a broken down car. He wondered how much Vince knew or suspected. "And hopefully it will keep doing so long after we are both gone," John said.

"Speaking of which, I think the last time I saw you was just after you had been shot," Vince said. "I remember that caused a bit of a sensation at the time."

John smiled. "Was that the first or second time?"

"Second time."

John didn't remember Vince, but his memory was foggy from that time, probably due to all the drugs he was taking.

"Was I conscious?"

"No. I just happened to be in town visiting my two daughters."

John struggled for facts, for a mental dossier on Vince Parkerson. He was divorced. He knew that. He was originally from Winnipeg. He also knew that also. "And how are they?" he asked.

"Fine, as far as I know. One is doing a double major in psychology and English, and the other is an accountant."

Perhaps Vince was listening to the lyrics of the Animals song as well.

My faith was so much stronger then,
I believed in fellow men.

"You want me to buy you a coffee?" John asked.

Vince laughed. "You owe me a lot more than coffee, I think."

"Yeah, you're probably right," John said. "Look, I'm trying to get access to a crash report. I think there may have been some foul play involved." John told Vince how he had witnessed George Hopkins' Lamborghini lose control.

"Okay, I have several contacts that might be able to help with that, but what makes you think it's foul play?"

"Nerno is most likely going to be sold to CNOOC, so there is a lot of money at stake. Sixteen billion or something like that."

Vince let out a low whistle. "Enough money to kill over, I suppose."

"I still remember when a gallon of gas was like twenty-five cents."

"We're dinosaurs, aren't we, you and I?" Vince asked, a bit wistfully, unknowingly echoing John's thoughts from a couple of hours before.

"I like to think we still have a little bit left in us."

"No, we're just in the way. Preventing some young, eager pups from making a good living chasing the bad guys."

"Those eager young pups—as you put it—still have their mothers wash their clothes for them. They don't grow up. They don't know tragedy like we do. My father was killed in a car crash when I was sixteen. Both my parents grew up in the slums of Glasgow. They treated me like they were treated by their parents. It wasn't very pleasant but it made me tough. So forgive me if I don't lay down for the cell phone generation."

Vince stared at John. His eyes narrowed thoughtfully. Neither said anything for a long time. Finally Vince shook his head. "You've got something else. I can see it. People don't just go around killing oil execs for no reason. If you want me to help you then you won't hold back."

"I'm not holding back. I think things are not as they appear. You didn't see the crash. It was as if the Lamborghini just stopped working."

"If that's the way you want to play it, I'm going to tell the boss my sources were uncooperative." Vince stood up and started to put on his coat.

"No, wait, Vince. Sit back down."

Vince smiled smugly and sat back down and waited.

"I have a source in Nerno. She has evidence that points— but not conclusively—to the CEO, David Kahn, lying to the stockholders about there being oil in one of their sites."

"That doesn't surprise me. Those oil guys are all a bunch of cocky assholes. They think they own the world." He paused in his rant. The features on his face relaxed as if he was contemplating what he had just said. He added, "I suppose in a way they do."

"Don't tell me you're thinking of getting into the oil business."

Vince laughed. "Only when I look at my retirement fund."

"You have a retirement fund? Wow," John said in mock incredulity.

"It seems I better sell my Nerno stock," Vince said, getting up again. "Let me know if there is anything else I can do to help."

"I appreciate it. When do you think you'll be able to find something out?"

"Give me a couple of hours or so."

John nodded. He would have liked to know a little sooner. He would give him a call in the evening and try to push the matter a little. "Thanks again."

"No sweat," Vince said, wrapping his scarf around his short neck. "I always thought you were the best of us, John. I mean it."

John watched as Vince exited the building and disappeared into the white world, wondering what he meant. *The best of what?*

John was surprised that Vince had not asked for a byline like a lot of younger reporters would, but, he reflected, when you got to a certain age, ambition seemed to matter less and less.

John went back to his hotel. He went back upstairs to his room and flipped to the business channel on the TV. He turned it to mute and started to make more phone calls to people who worked for Nerno, or who had done business with them, but nobody would talk to him.

"Mr. Kahn said we weren't to talk to you," one woman who worked in the accounting department said.

"Why not? Do you know something you shouldn't?"

"Of course not. That's ridiculous."

"Then what's the harm in talking to me if you've done nothing wrong?"

This caught the woman off guard. She stumbled over her words and then hung up. John immediately phoned her back.

"I demand an answer," he said.

"I don't have time for this, goodbye," she said, hanging up again.

John phoned her back but this time he just got her voicemail. He didn't bother to leave a message.

Next, John tried the police again but also without much luck. They kept making him run around in circles, calling this person or that person.

He put the phone down in frustration and glanced up at the television just in time to see the Nerno Energy logo flash across the screen. He reached for the remote and turned up the volume.

"The news of the takeover bid has sent the stock skyrocketing, gaining ten percent this week," the analyst said. "I see only more illustrious things from this company even if the takeover falls through. I put this stock in the buy category."

John shook his head in disgust and turned off the television. He had to get something on paper before Hank Gates beat him to it. John's phone rang. He saw that it was a local area code and expected it to be Mindy Rocher with her analysis of the documents.

"Have you been watching the stock exchange recently?" It was Hank Gates. *What was he doing phoning?* John wondered. He probably just wanted to gloat.

"I was just watching it."

"You see why these people have to be stopped?"

"I never disagreed with you on that," John said, sitting on the bed. "It was more the method you are using."

"But your method doesn't work. It never has. We're not talking about politicians who need popular support. These people make money for everybody and we all turn a blind eye as long as the stock price keeps going up and up and up."

"Did you phone just so you could lecture me?"

"I phoned to invite you for dinner."

"What do you have that we can't talk about on the phone?"

"Come on, we can trade war stories. Perhaps I can convince you to leave this journalism business all together and come work for me."

"Goodbye, Mr. Gates," John said, hanging up the phone.

John sat back on the bed and lay looking up at the stucco ceiling. He didn't feel like moving. Perhaps Gates was right. He should just retire and try to figure out something else to do, something that didn't involve lying and cheating his way to the truth. He was sure that there would always be a public relations job out there to get him by until retirement. He was tired. Perhaps he should leave the profession to the eager, the young, the unblemished. Did the old contribute anything to the world, or did they just coast along like a motorboat run out of fuel?

John pushed the phone conversation with Gates out of his head, and all his doubts as well. Instead he thought about Byron and how Hayden was getting married to some guy he had never met before. How did he know if he was good for her? How did he know if he would take care of her?

He closed his eyes. Static danced in front of him like a scrambled television set. He took deep breaths. He reminded himself that it wasn't his job to take care of her anymore. Besides, she had managed perfectly fine alone all of those years when he was far away in places that most had only seen on the Internet or on television.

John didn't hear the phone ring the first couple of times, but he eventually snapped out of it and answered.

"Hi, it's Mindy, I'm only about halfway through those documents you gave me."

"Anything about Ko Chang?"

"Well, there are actually a few interesting things about these documents. Apparently Nerno has recently acquired a drilling site in northern Canada that they hope to exploit using a new form of drill that is not yet in production. Now I don't know much about this new drill, except that it cost fifty-five million dollars to develop. The documents don't really go into much detail, but it goes much deeper than your average offshore variety."

"I don't understand," John said. "What is so interesting about it?"

"Why is a company that is about to be sold investing so heavily in research and development of a new drill?"

"It will probably add to the stock value."

"Only if they are successful. The drill isn't in production and CNOOC isn't likely to pay for an unproven drill."

"Okay, then what do you think is going on?"

"I'm not sure. It doesn't make sense. Perhaps this takeover bid is a decoy. Perhaps they don't intend to accept the offer at all."

"But why not?"

"That's your job. I just look at the data you gave me."

"Okay, thanks," John said, gloomily. He didn't want to know about any new drill, and he didn't particularly care about the takeover either. He needed information about Ko Chang. What he really needed was proof, because it seemed that his first impression was the correct one. The documents were valueless. "You'll tell me if you find anything else interesting."

"Yes. I probably won't get to the rest of it until tomorrow so I wanted to phone you," Mindy Rocher said, seemingly not understanding John's disappointment.

"Okay, thank you," John said, hanging up.

John put on a jacket again and braved the cold to find a payphone, where he phoned Sheila.

"You crazy? You can't phone me at work?"

"I'm sorry, but it's important."

"What is it?"

"I think it's best we meet somewhere?"

"Okay, can you come down to the Nerno parking garage in about an hour? I will get into my car and you can follow me."

John thought that she was taking this paranoia a little too far. "Fine, but where will you be taking me?"

"I'm not sure. Just follow me, okay?"

John hung up and went back to the hotel.

About an hour later he found himself in the parking lot in the catacombs of the Nerno building. He had bought a ticket from the machine just to gain access to the garage. John drove along trying to find a spot, passing BMWs, Mercedes, Escalades, Porsches and Ferraris. He quickly calculated that there were several million dollars' worth of cars in the lot. Even John's rented Nissan, which was new, clean and well-kept, looked shabby next to these curvy, sleek machines. Earlier in the day he had traded his rental car in for a different one to try and throw off anybody that might have been tracking him.

John found a handicapped spot next to the elevator that gave him a perfect vantage point to see Sheila. He listened to the local news as he waited, wondering if the cameras could spot him—or alternatively, if anybody was paying attention.

Now look who is paranoid, John told himself.

Thirty minutes passed, but there was still no sign of her. The long tube lighting flickered overhead. John began to worry. What was keeping her? What if somebody had heard them on the phone? He tried to quell his mind with the quiet drone of the radio, but the calm, even-keeled voices didn't help. If they found her, would they kill her?

A security guard sauntered over and tapped on the glass of the car. John almost jumped from fright, but he pulled himself together enough to roll down the window, already knowing what he was about to say.

"I'm sorry, but you're parked in the handicapped spot. I'm going to have to ask you to move."

"I'm just waiting for my wife. She should be out any moment."

"Well, you're going to have to wait someplace else."

John saw no point in arguing and escalating the situation and possibly getting found out. He started the engine and drove around the parking lot in a big loop. He looked out for the security guard before double parking in front of an eighty-thousand-dollar BMW. He hoped that he hadn't missed Sheila coming out. He didn't know what type of car she drove, and doubted that he would find her if she was in her car already.

Luckily, a couple of minutes later, Sheila appeared from the elevator with two other businessmen. The three of them dispersed into the parking lot. Sheila glanced at her watch and looked around anxiously. She was wearing a maroon suit and had a black leather suitcase in her hand. She walked quickly to her car, a silver Mercedes.

John followed her out of the parking lot and down 6th Avenue, turning left on 1st Southwest. The entire city was painted white and blue. John could almost see the crisp coldness in the air. On the corner were a pack of teenage girls wearing cut-off tops and identical pink boots. Two businessmen were coming out of a restaurant, chattering away animatedly. A dark-skinned man with a large coat and a handlebar moustache was wearing a cowboy hat, and John had thought that the hat was one of those stereotypes that you never actually saw.

The Calgary Tower was only a few blocks away and stood phallic-like between the skyscrapers. A bus passed John in the frozen slush. They drove across town for about twenty minutes. John fidgeted nervously in his seat at every red light. He wondered where she was taking him. Finally Sheila parked her Mercedes on the corner of a quiet narrow street.

John turned the corner and found a side street. He had no idea where he was, but he retraced his steps and found Sheila in a coffee shop. Sheila was waiting for him by the window. They found a secluded table in the corner.

"What's going on?" Sheila asked. Foundation poorly masked the bags under her eyes.

"I need your help."

"Doing what?"

"I need something more. My boss won't print unless I have something more concrete."

"I'm not doing any more spying."

"Then throw me something else. Somebody who might help me out."

Sheila said, "Do you know the terror I live in?"

John leaned forward, putting both elbows on the table. "Has anyone said anything?"

"No, but I feel I can't talk to anybody. People are conspiring against me. I have these dreams that everybody is pointing and laughing at me."

"I'm sorry," John said. "It'll all be over soon enough."

Sheila looked up at John and he thought that he saw hatred in her eyes. "Maybe for you, but I have to go on and live the next day and the day after that."

"And what would the consequence be if you did nothing?" John said, barely above a whisper. "All these people. The geologists, the stock brokers, the board tell themselves they had no choice. It wasn't their job. That's how they sleep at night. But everybody in your company has a choice, Sheila."

"Damned if I do and damned if I don't.

"Trust me, it will all work out in the end."

"I have to go to the bathroom," Sheila said, suddenly. "I'm not feeling very well."

Sheila got up and disappeared down the long hallway. As John waited he got a refill on his coffee. As he waited in line, he wondered if Sheila had snuck out the back door, never to return. But just as he was walking to his seat, Sheila appeared from around the corner. She looked better, more determined as she sat across from John.

"Okay, I'll see what I can do. I can't make any promises. My only condition is you never contact me again. If I find something I will phone you. You got it?"

John nodded. "Seems fair to me. I have one more question for you. Do you know about a new type of drill you guys are developing?"

Sheila shook her head. "No, nothing has come down my pipeline about that. Why?"

"I just heard something about it and it doesn't make any sense. Why would you be investing heavily into technology that you're just going to sell off?"

Sheila shrugged. "That's not my expertise. I just write colourful pamphlets."

"But don't you think it's strange?"

"I have no idea. Why don't you ask somebody on the production side?"

They left separately. John watched Sheila climb into her car and wondered if things really would turn out fine as he had promised. Would anybody hire Sheila if her name was discovered? John knew that he would feel the responsibility for the rest of his life. As he got into his car, he thought to himself, *it's not just you who has to live day after day after day.*

Polar Bears

OUTSIDE, IT WAS TOO COLD for snow. Icicles jaggedly lined the window sills. Ominous, super-long shadows from the buildings covered the streets and all their occupants. John had spent all day in his room, typing up everything he had on Nerno, and was beginning to feel a little cabin feverish. Perhaps it was the tawny light from the metallic desk lamp and the light blue walls.

The writing was slow and unrewarding. John got up from his computer, stretched and decided to call it quits.

He thought about going down to the bar and ordering a couple of drinks. Only a few, he told himself. Plenty of people do it without excess. He could be one of those people. Besides, there really wasn't anything else for him to do.

He had phoned everybody he could think of. Now he could only hope for a lucky break. Waiting was always the worst part of the job. Waiting in the Green Zone, waiting on the outskirts of Baghdad, in Kunar Province. Waiting for Vince or Rocher to get back to him.

Almost on command John's phone vibrated to life, but it wasn't anybody he knew. It was a blocked number. Briefly John allowed himself to fantasize before answering it.

"Hello?"

"Hi John, it's Andrea. You don't have any plans tonight, do you?"

"Nothing really."

"I need a date and I thought of you."

John frowned. Why would Andrea invite him of all people? "That's very generous of you. What for?"

Andrea laughed girlishly. It sounded strange coming from her. "Don't get any ideas. It's for the Polar Bear Foundation."

John thought of the oil project in northern Canada. "What's that?"

"It's a dinner auction. Nerno gives millions of dollars to the foundation. We are one of the largest donors. It's something both David and I feel very passionate about. Tonight we hope to raise at least a hundred thousand dollars. I hope to show you we aren't that evil corporation you think we are."

"I never thought you were evil. Who will be there?"

"All the top Nerno execs. David will make some sort of speech. But don't get any ideas about hijacking him. He told me you buttonholed him at the CBA."

"I asked him some basic questions. I wouldn't say I buttonholed him."

"So what do you say? Are you in?"

"Okay, what time?"

Andrea gave John an address, which John wrote down on his notepad. "Meet me at five p.m."

"Is this your place?"

"It's my house. The apartment is really my second home for when I have to work late."

"Okay, I'll see you then."

John ended the call and looked out the window, deep in thought. It was almost too good to be true: to have all the Nerno executives in one place at one time. What sort of game was Andrea Drashkov playing with him? What was the real reason for inviting him along?

John phoned Charles Dana to give him an update on his progress. He told him about the new deep sea drill.

"That's interesting, but what about Ko Chang?" Charles asked.

"Nothing new on that front, but it must be connected. I just don't know how yet."

"Okay, phone me when you have something soon."

"Chuck?"

"Please, Webster, don't call me that."

"What's going on with the sale?"

"John . . . perhaps you should just concentrate on finishing your article and not worry about that."

"Charles, I want to know if I have a job when I get back."

Charles paused on the phone, and with each moment of silence John became more concerned. Finally Charles said, "The Pommeroys are considering accepting an offer."

"An offer? From Cloud Media?"

"You can't tell anybody I told you."

"Of course not."

"The thing is, it's a company called Icelandic Media Corp."

"Never heard of it."

"Neither have I, and I know every media company in the world."

"So what do you think it is?"

"Well, I found through my sources that it was incorporated last month by a New York law firm called Goodwin and Keilberg. Basically it's a dummy company and we don't know who will be buying the *Daily Globe*."

"How can the Pommeroys do that to us?"

"Now, Webster, there is no use getting mad."

"Why not, Chuck? I think if there was ever a moment to get mad it's now."

"I'm using what influence I have but I think it's out of my hands now. We just have to sit tight and hold on." Charles Dana— always the calm influence.

After John hung up he decided that he would go down to the bar. He ordered a double whiskey and sat at the end of the bar staring down at his drink. Doctor Nagi was right, he was on thin ice. And the ice was breaking.

John finished his drink and ordered another one. He finished that one too and went back upstairs to get ready for the dinner party. He had a cold shower and shaved. He looked at his flabby body in the mirror, and the lines on his face. He looked so old all of a sudden. What had happened?

John stepped out of the shower. As he opened his suitcase he quickly came to the conclusion that he didn't have anything suitable for the evening. John wasn't a fancy suit person even at his best. He thought about going out and finding one to buy, but he didn't have the time or the funds.

He phoned down to the front desk. "Hi, is there some place close I can rent a tux for the night?"

"Hold on one moment, sir."

John was put on hold and was forced to listen to horrible elevator music until the man came back on the phone. "There is really nothing close. The nearest is a place on 4th Southwest."

"Okay, how far away is that?"

"About twelve blocks."

"That might be a little too far. Is there any place I could get a tie at least?"

"We could lend you one, if you want."

John went and collected a tie from the front desk. It was a plaid tie, probably previously owned by a ninety-year-old gentleman. He looked at himself in the mirror critically. He looked like a used car salesman, but there wasn't much that he could do about it now. He had to leave.

He drove in his rented car out to the address Andrea Drashkov had given him. It was in a neighbourhood called Upper Mount Royal. To John, it sounded posh, and he was right. The big brick houses sprawled across big estates, the hedges were trim, the fences immaculate.

John found himself slowing down, admiring the houses, and he hated himself for it. At one point he could have had a house in a neighbourhood such as this one.

John got to the address a few minutes before five, only getting lost once on a curved side road. Andrea's house sat back from the road, with dark masses of fir trees laden with snow surrounding it. There was a large stone fountain next to the walkway, now totally frozen.

John didn't like the look of the place, although he couldn't pinpoint why. It reminded him of the eerie, capacious mansions that eccentric millionaires lived in in the movies.

John parked his car at the front, and walked the long pathway up the marble steps and knocked on the large ornately carved doors. He expected a maid or a servant to answer, but instead the CFO herself opened the door and she took John's breath away.

She had a bright white smile on her face that seemed natural, and it lit up the rest of her hard face. She wore a blue strapless dress with a pearl necklace on her jutting neck. John, no expert, had no doubt that the pearls were real. Her thin brown hair was tied up in an intricate French pattern and her deep brown eyes juxtaposed against her colourless lips.

"Come in. We're still waiting for the limo to arrive," Andrea said, stepping out of the light. "I want you to see my house."

John refused to look embarrassed, and tried to stand stoically as Andrea's eyes critically went over his grey tweed jacket, his slightly battered grey pants.

"You look like a writer," she said, making it sound like a criticism.

"But I am a writer."

"Doesn't mean you have to look like one. You don't have anything better?"

"I wasn't expecting to go to any black tie event."

"You should have told me. I would have sent out for something."

"Well, you didn't give me much warning."

John stepped into a dark, cavernous room with oak flooring. A large crystal chandelier hung overhead, illuminating the room with sparkling columns of light. Beyond was a white staircase that went up to the second floor.

"You look so beautiful and I look so terrible," John said.

Andrea shrugged it off with a laugh and then said, "I bought this house from Baron Terrance Hapthorn. Of course he wasn't a real baron. He was American."

John waited for an explanation, but none was forthcoming. Instead, Andrea took John's jacket and gloves and hung them in the closet.

"Did you ever want to be American growing up?"

"Sure, I suppose. I think most non-Americans do."

"This whole neighbourhood used to be called American Hill because all the rich Americans used to live here. There still are a lot of them around. I will introduce you to some. I feel more comfortable around Americans. They always tell you what they are thinking. Don't hold too many secrets, Americans."

John agreed with her, although he wasn't really sure what he was agreeing with.

Andrea led John into the kitchen which was brightly lit and had smooth, rich marble counters.

"What are you drinking? Wine? I bet you're a beer drinker."

"Whiskey, actually."

Andrea smiled. "Well, it just goes to show there are a few surprises left in this world."

She reached into the cupboard and got out a whiskey bottle and poured it into glasses. "I might as well join you."

They went into the living room, which was just as beautiful and lavish as the rest of the house. John sat on a deep-green couch, and Andrea across from him. She flipped a switch turning on the electric fireplace.

"I desperately wanted to be American when I was growing up. My parents tried to teach me Russian but I refused to learn a word. I was pig-headed, even as a child. I watched all those old western movies."

John sipped his whiskey and watched as the flames danced in front of him. He sunk into the couch, feeling cozy and at ease. "My parents forced me to the theatre. My father wrote reviews."

Andrea smiled, as if imagining John Webster as a child being dragged along by his parents. "I bet you have so many secrets."

"Secrets? What makes you say that?"

"All these people who confess to you."

"I'm like a priest that way. Listen to everybody's sins."

"Would you like to hear my secrets?"

"Only if they involve Nerno Energy." John said.

"And who do you tell your secrets to? Do you pray to God?"

"I stash them in a secret place where not even you can reach them."

Andrea smiled. "I wouldn't be so sure."

John took a sip of his whiskey, unsure what to make of the woman. Was she threatening him? Michael Chu had said that she was beautiful but evil. Now he was beginning to understand what he had meant.

"I can help you," John said, "if you want to come clean. You can walk away the good guy in this."

"Out of the goodness of your heart?"

"Ms. Drashkov, listen closely. Hank Gates is going to publish his research and it's going to say there is no oil at Ko Chang. There's going to be a massive CSA investigation. The cards will fall. I can guarantee you that. The only question is who will come out on top. Is it going to be you?"

Andrea Drashkov crossed her legs casually, as if she had practiced the move a thousand times. "My parents, despite communism, were raised Orthodox. They taught me to fear God. But I don't fear God. I don't even fear the CSA."

"I know. A billion dollars can buy you a lot of pleasant dreams."

"There is one thing I do fear, though. You. I fear you."

John was taken aback. "You fear me?"

"Yes, you and your secrets that you won't share with anybody."

"Well if you think inviting me for fancy dinners and fancy parties will get you any closer, you are mistaken."

Andrea stood up. "I'm going to have another drink. You want one?"

"Sure."

Andrea got up and disappeared into the kitchen.

John felt restless and uneasy. He got up and walked over to the bookcase. His father had once told him that you could tell a lot about a person by the type of books they kept around. *David Copperfield, Ivanhoe, Tom Sawyer, Jane Eyre, Huckleberry Finn.* John picked up *The Decline and Fall of the Roman Empire*. The spine was new and seemed unbent.

John looked around for anything personal—a family picture, a sign of personality, but he didn't see anything. The whole room seemed void, lifeless, designed to convey a bland corporate feel.

"What do you think of me, John?"

John turned to see Andrea leaning up against the door frame. She had two glasses of whiskey in her hands. There was no telling how long she had stood there observing him.

"I really don't know you that well," John replied, sitting back down on the couch.

Andrea handed John a glass. John watched her as she moved so effortlessly, gliding across the floor. She folded her dress and sat next to him, holding her glass out from her, her elbow at a right angle. She smiled and leaned towards John conspiratorially and whispered. "But I'm sure you've heard of things."

"Just what I read about on the Internet," John said, cautiously, shifting in his seat.

"And do you believe it? The Internet?"

"I don't know. I'm sure it's not the whole truth."

"I did an interview with the *Wall Street Journal*. They called me the 'Black Queen.'"

Andrea tipped her head slightly and poured the whiskey down her throat while John stared at her white neck. She sounded like a bullied teenager looking for some validation. Perhaps that was all that she was looking for—some confirmation that the things around her were real.

John found himself in the strange role of comforter to the woman who was beautiful but evil. "I wouldn't worry about it too much," he said. "People are jealous of success. Especially journalists. Journalists are usually people who have failed at something else."

Andrea looked at John with large, melancholy eyes. "But I don't believe you're a failure. You've won awards, written books. You're different."

John thought of Hayden, Byron. "I've had my share of failures," he said politely, masking his face with a smile.

Andrea's house phone rang. She got up to answer it. She spoke briefly, and then turned to John. "The car is ready."

They braved the cold, hurrying down the marble steps and across a stone pathway. Andrea was several steps in front. John trailed, watching her as she bunched up her dress in her hands.

The driver opened the door to the stretch limousine. He must have been in his mid-sixties and was dressed in black with a fedora hat.

It seemed like some kind of dream. John was an eager teenager again, taking a beautiful girl to the prom. The prom he never had. Sometimes he missed having the usual little rites of passage.

John couldn't remember the last time that he had been in a limousine. Again he wondered why he was here. What sort of measure was he up against?

He looked across at Andrea, who had tucked one arm under her chin and was looking out at the world from behind the green-tinted windows. Her dress was creeping up her legs. Underneath it she wore white stockings.

"I always wanted to be American. Even when I was small," Andrea said, not turning around. Her eyes processed the wide streets and tall trees.

"Pardon?"

"I wanted my family to move to New York or Los Angeles. I always dreamed of moving there. I finally got my chance when I got a scholarship to Cornell University. It was everything I had hoped for in a university. Have you ever been to Ithaca?"

John shook his head. "I can't say I have."

"You want something to drink? The mini bar is stocked."

"I guess another whiskey wouldn't hurt."

"You can help yourself."

John shifted over, opened the door and took out a small bottle of whiskey.

Andrea said, "After I graduated I worked for ExxonMobil in the New York office for eight years, made a shitload of money before being recruited by David Kahn to help found Nerno."

"If you love America so much, why move back?"

For the first time during the ride Andrea shifted her head to look at John. "Many reasons, but I guess the biggest was I just missed home."

"Tell me about the new drill you are building."

Andrea's jaw dropped, but she quickly regained composure. "What do you mean?"

"I know about the R&D you've been putting into a new type of deep-sea drill."

"I don't know what you're talking about."

"Come on, I can tell by your face you know exactly what I'm talking about."

"You want me to kick you out right now? Make you hitchhike your way home?"

John leaned forward on the edge of his seat. "Threats aren't going to help you here and you know it. You're in a corner. All the money in the world couldn't save you from this. You need friends, and from where I'm sitting, you don't seem to have many."

Andrea's bottom lip quivered. Was this just an act, or had John actually hit on a sore point? "You don't know anything about the world I live in."

"I know you're taking me to this fundraiser and not some rich bachelor. That tells me quite a lot."

John thought that she was about to tell the driver to stop so that she could kick him out, but she just sat there in silence, not saying anything. Her face was an emotionless wall. John waited for her to say something, but the rest of the ride was silent, with only the occasional noise from the traffic outside the car.

They finally arrived at the Glenbow Museum. The driver opened the door for them. By then Andrea Drashkov seemed to have regained her composure, and smiled at the driver when he gave her his hand to help her out. She was just an actress, John reflected, playing the part that she had created for herself.

They walked towards the building. The museum was a large, characterless, grey building with a blocky red sign overhead.

Somebody opened the door for them and they were met with a blast of warm air that flowed over them. Peopled milled about, colourful cocktails in hand. The women were dressed in lengthy, bright dresses, the men were mostly in tuxedos. Again John wished that he'd had time to get something decent to wear. Instead he stuck out like a bruise. Even the waiters surfing the crowd with trays of pastries were better dressed.

Andrea grabbed John's hand and led him through the crowd of people and into a big yellow-lit hallway, where there were large photographs of polar bears hanging on the wall.

Andrea introduced John to several local politicians. John smiled and shook their hands diplomatically. A few of the politicians had read John's books or his articles and lavished him with false praise for his dedication to the truth, his bravery, his courage, and one grey-haired man even told John that he had valour. But John didn't believe in valour, courage, or bravery. And John had learned a long time ago, under the lonely African sun, that truth was simply the victor's prerogative.

John played his role just as those soldiers he'd covered did theirs. Some of them died while others won medals. All John did was watch and capture it for eternity on film and paper.

Andrea saved John from the politicians' frenzy and led him into the next room. It was a large show room with a makeshift bar set up at the end. It took a while to get anywhere, because at every step somebody would step in front of them and engage Andrea in conversation. They would ask Andrea everything, from which way the stock market was going, to how to prevent war in the Middle East. They would perhaps give a single, distasteful glance towards John, note his dishevelled appearance and decide that John wasn't worth an introduction. John liked these people better than the politicians, because at least they didn't try to hide their feelings.

Finally they made it to the bar, and Andrea ordered two whiskeys.

"I've never been much of a whiskey person myself," Andrea said.

"Then why don't you order something else?" John asked. "I'm sure they can fix you up anything you like. I heard your people like to drink vodka."

"I like to fit in," Andrea said, tipping the glass to her lips.

"My father used to drink whiskey. It reminds me of when he would come home smelling of the stuff. It was the happiest part of my day."

Andrea took John to a corner of the room where they weren't suffocated by people.

John looked around and saw David Kahn slipping through the crowd with a beautiful blonde in a purple ballroom gown. He stopped when he saw Andrea and went over to her and kissed her on the cheek.

"How are you, darling?" David asked, flashing a graceful, relaxed smile.

Darling? John thought. *Darling?*

Andrea shifted uncomfortably. "Hello David, hello Sophie. Can I introduce you to John Webster?"

Kahn turned and set his dark eyes on John, a confused frown on his face, as if to say, *what the hell is this idiot doing here?*

John smiled smugly and reached out to shake his hand. It lingered there in nothingness until Sophie, not Kahn, took it.

"I'm pleased to meet you," Sophie said. "I'm David's wife."

Kahn seemed to have recovered himself, and was giving John the same graceful smile that only moments ago seemed reserved for Andrea.

"Mr. Webster, a pleasure to see you. I hope you'll be bidding on some of the artwork for our Polar Bear Foundation."

John nodded solemnly, as if the idea was his all along. "Of course I will. Provided I get an interview with you."

David smiled smugly, almost as if to himself. "Bidding starts at thirty thousand dollars. Hope that's not out of your price range."

John tried to match Kahn's smile, but found it a difficult task. "That shouldn't be a problem. I'll just get on the phone to my agent and start the bidding for the rights to my next book."

Kahn kept his smile, which seemed so effortless, but his eyes shifted to Andrea for help. "Book? What book?"

John nodded. "The book I will be writing about corrupt oil execs. I think I'll start the bidding at a million dollars. I know for you it may not be much money, but I hope I'll be able to buy a couple of overpriced paintings."

At that moment, John thought that Kahn was going to punch him, but instead his wife touched him on the elbow. "Come on, dear. We don't have to listen to this."

Kahn nodded and then turned to John, leaning close to him. "You're a bully, Mr. Webster. My parents used to say, 'don't worry, they'll grow up', but the truth is bullies don't change. They grow older but as adults they are still the same old bullies. The only difference is I've now learned that underneath they are just cowards and should be treated as such."

John was too dumbfounded to answer. He had never been called a bully before.

Kahn took his wife and disappeared back into the crowd.

"What the fuck was that?" Andrea whispered once they were alone. "I brought you here. Don't you ever embarrass me like that again."

"What did you expect? You think I was just going to shower him with praise like all these other flunkeys?"

"I was hoping you would keep the gloves on for at least a night."

"What are you two conspiring at?"

"Conspiring? We're not conspiring at anything."

"Tell me about Ko Chang. Tell me about this new drill you're designing."

"Like you said, it's a deep-sea drill, designed to go deeper than anything else on the market."

"Why now?"

Andrea sighed loudly. "Because it's possible. Because it gives us a competitive advantage. Why do you think?"

"How much money went into its development?"

"I can't remember the numbers off the top of my head."

"You're going to sell the technology to the Chinese?"

"Possibly. If they will pay for it."

"You think they will pay what it's worth?"

"All this business talk is making me tired. I'm going to get another drink." Andrea turned and walked quickly through the crowd. John watched her go, taking another sip of his whiskey.

"You seem to be a little out of place," said a woman with a British accent.

John turned and was surprised to see a beautiful Asian woman dressed in grey with a white blouse. She had a lanyard around her neck with the word "Press" clearly identifying her.

"Well, you've clearly talked your way in here as well."

The woman smiled. "My name is Madeline Xiao. I work for the *Beijing Star*."

They shook hands. "John Webster. You're a long way from home."

"I'm here covering the CNOOC deal. I'm guessing you don't work for Nerno Energy. Otherwise you would be a little better dressed."

John laughed despite himself. "Sadly, no."

"Okay, I give up," Madeline said. "What are you doing here?"

"I'm deeply committed to polar bears."

"WWF? Non-profit?" Madeline said, not catching John's sarcasm. "Don't you think it's strange, a bunch of oil blokes standing around moaning about global warming?"

"Not until you mentioned it."

"Well, you should think about it."

"You want a drink?"

"Sorry, I'm on the job."

John smiled and held up his empty glass. "Technically, so am I."

Madeline unzipped her purse and rummaged around until her thin hand appeared again with a card. "This is my card. The bottom has my local number. If you hear anything, give me a call."

"Hear anything? About what?'

"About anything important to the great People's Republic of China."

John took the card and studied it.

"Great talking to you. I've got to start mingling some more. I'm sure I'll see you in a bit."

Madeline walked off, leaving John alone. John surveyed the crowd for Andrea but instead saw David Kahn among a large circle of people. John couldn't see if David's wife, Sophie, was with him. Kahn was talking to them with his large smile, apparently amusing them, as every couple of sentences were punctuated by laughter.

John finished his drink and put it on the tray of a passing waiter and made his way over to Kahn.

"Can I have a moment of your time?" John asked, putting a hand on Kahn's shoulder.

David frowned deeply. "Please tell me your mother taught you better manners than that."

There was another round of laughter, probably because it was David Kahn talking.

John just nodded. "You're right. She would be deeply disappointed with my behaviour, but then again, she usually is."

"I have nothing to say to you."

"I actually disagree. I think you have plenty of explaining to do." John looked around at the crowd of people. "How many of you fine young gentlemen are stockholders of the proud company, Nerno Energy?"

The crowd hesitated, looking around at each other.

"Well?" John prompted.

Kahn interjected. "I don't think this is necessary."

"I want an answer," John said, smiling at the CEO. He found great pleasure in watching Kahn lose composure.

John looked around at the men and women. A few raised their hands. Then a few more. John waited several more moments until eventually everybody in the group had raised their hands.

"Now, wouldn't you want to know how your money was being spent?" John asked.

"We trust Mr. Kahn do the right thing. After all, it's mostly his money," somebody said, and there was a murmur of agreement.

"Have you heard the rumour that there is no oil at Ko Chang? Have you heard that's the reason he's selling the company?"

"That's ridiculous," Kahn said.

"Have any of you asked him why he's selling the company?"

"Because it's going to make us a shitload of money," Kahn said. He had regained his smile. John supposed that talking about money made most rich men smile.

"And what about your new drill?" John asked.

Suddenly a hand took John's elbow and roughly pulled him away from the crowd. John yanked violently but the grip was strong. John looked and saw a handsome man, probably in his mid-sixties, with thick peppery-grey hair and a stony glare on his hard, Germanic face. He looked familiar, but John couldn't place him.

"John, what are you doing sniffing around Mr. Kahn?"

"Who are you?"

"Never mind who I am. Answer the damn question."

"It's none of your business."

The man leaned in close to John. "Suddenly it's nobody's business? I thought you just said it was everybody's fucking business. You need to make up your mind."

"Look—" John said, but the man cut him off.

"A word of advice: don't go near him. Don't touch the subject. You have no idea what you're dealing with."

John took a deep breath. "Now look here, I don't care who you think you are, but nobody tells me what I can or can't do."

The man shook his head. "You journalists are all the same, sticking your noses into places they don't belong. You don't know what they can do to you."

"Is that a threat?"

"No, Mr. Webster. A promise." And with that, the man turned and walked away. John stared after him. Where had he seen him before?

Alone again, John looked around the room for Andrea, but he couldn't see her among the mass of white and black dresses. He wandered through the room. The large paintings on the walls caught his eye. He stopped at one moody portrait. Below, on a plaque, in small script, it read that the painting was a portrait of the Earl of Chatham circa 1850. John looked up and wondered if this guy was a self-styled earl, like the baron who had owned Andrea's house.

John moved on to the next painting, a watercolour of the French countryside, when he heard a familiar Texan voice.

"I didn't know you were an art connoisseur, Mr. Webster."

John turned to see Hank Gates grinning at him. He was wearing a tuxedo and had a glass of wine in his hand.

John, apparently, was considerably less pleased to see him than Gates was to see John. "What are you doing here?" John asked.

"The same thing you are, I imagine," Gates said with a wink. "Trying to gain some inside information."

"What sort of information? I thought you knew everything?" John asked. Was it possible that Gates was bluffing about how much he knew?

"Almost everything, Mr. Webster."

"If we are truly going to be adversaries, I think we better start calling each other by our first names."

John looked past Gates and saw Sheila McKinnon in a white gown with elbow-length white gloves, giving her a slightly bridal appearance. Next to her was a handsome man with a closely cropped haircut and a scruffy beard. He must be Matt, Sheila's husband. They were deeply engaged in conversation with another couple.

Sheila looked over at John but quickly averted her gaze, giving no indication that she knew who he was. *Of course she would be here*, John thought. Why wouldn't she be? He shouldn't have come. He should have stayed away. But now it was too late.

He wanted to walk through the crowd and talk to her . . . and say what exactly? To say hello? To say *sorry, things might not work out the way you wanted, and I'm culpable*? He didn't know. Perhaps it was just to escape Hank Gates.

Sheila and Matt laughed at something that was said and leaned in towards each other. He couldn't actually hear them across the cavernous room. It was more a pantomime of happiness, of a perfectly content couple.

"You see somebody you know?" Gates asked.

John shook his head. "No, I was just staring at the paintings. The truth is I don't even know the difference between Romantic and Impressionist."

Gates smiled, as if he was talking to a small child. "It's actually Romantic period," he said. "And I doubt you would care if I explained it to you anyway."

John shrugged, struggling to seem natural. Had Gates seen Sheila? Had he guessed that she was his source? "You're probably right," he said.

"I saw you making a scene there. Did you learn anything useful?"

"If I did, I certainly wouldn't tell you."

Gates smiled and leaned forward. "Come on, give me a preview of what I'm going to read in tomorrow's paper. I'm intrigued. Or did you just make a fool of yourself?"

John didn't rise to the bait. "You'll just have to be patient like the rest of my readers."

"You are such a tease," Gates said, good-naturedly.

"Okay, one thing. Do you know about the new drill Nerno is developing?"

Gates frowned, and John knew that he had gotten something that Gates didn't know. "What does that have to do with Ko Chang?"

"Maybe nothing."

"You're clutching at straws, John."

A man passed close by. He was the same man who had warned John to stay away from David Kahn. John pointed to him. "Who is that guy?"

Gates followed John's finger. "You mean Jerry Gottler? He's the Minister of Energy. I'm surprised you don't know him."

John suddenly felt embarrassed and foolish in front of Gates. But what was the Minister of Energy doing getting involved with the Nerno deal?

Gates seemed to be reading John's mind. "What? You didn't think there was a political element in all this?"

John wasn't looking at Gates but at Sheila, who was smiling. Her husband was at her side, one arm around her waist. John marvelled at how natural they looked. How comfortable they seemed. John wanted to take her away, to grab her hand and pull her to safety. Save her from what? From the greed surrounding her?

Gates put a hand on John's shoulder, and shook him out of his trance with a laugh. "How is it possible you haven't thought of this? What do you think 'national' stands for in the China National Offshore Oil Company? Kahn would be basically selling Nerno to the Chinese government."

"Gottler wants this to happen?"

"You have to remember this is all about money."

"Does he know about Ko Chang?"

Gates shrugged noncommittally. "By the way, I'm going to send you a press release about my press conference. It's on for tomorrow."

John felt his stomach fall. He felt like punching Gates in the mouth. He didn't care if it was right in the middle of the show room and he was surrounded by people.

But John managed to smile. "That won't be necessary. I already know exactly what you're going to say."

"Do you, I wonder?" Gates said, almost to himself.

John watched as Gates strode off to talk to somebody else. John had a hard time thinking. Everybody seemed to be shouting, drowning out his thoughts. He heard the sound of footsteps on the carpeted floor, the sound of glasses clinking, the sound of bodies moving. Everything but his own thoughts.

Soon the news would be all over the place. His story would be inconsequential, yesterday's news.

He looked at his watch. He still had two hours until deadline. Could he put something together that would be acceptable to Legal? He didn't know, but he knew that he had to try. He had to beat Hank Gates.

"There you are," Andrea said, appearing from the crowd with two whiskeys in her hand. She gave one to John.

"Do you think you can stop Hank Gates?" John asked her.

Andrea took a long sip. "I doubt we can stop him from spouting his stupid mouth, if that's what you mean."

"I'm sorry, I have to make a phone call," John said, excusing himself.

He made his way through the crowd, pushing his way to the entrance. He suddenly felt suffocated by all the tuxedos and exposed cleavage and the smell of hot, stale breath. He looked around him and saw Madeline leaning into Gottler. He had his large hand around her narrow waist. They seemed to be having a very intense conversation. What were they talking about? John wasn't close enough to hear.

He had to get out. He had stepped through a circle of people when he saw a face he recognized in among the throng: Vince Parkerson. *But what would Vince Parkerson be doing here?* John wondered.

John changed directions and pushed his way through until he was in Vince's wake, but no sooner had he done that than Vince had disappeared and John couldn't find him.

Maybe I'm imagining everything, John thought. *He wouldn't be here.*

John found an empty hallway, away from everybody, and dialled Charles Dana. However, as the phone rang, the thought of seeing Vince in the crowd was bugging him. Why hadn't Vince phoned back? John's imagination was beginning to get the better of him. Maybe something had happened to him? But what? Had Kahn gotten to him? Did Gates have something to do with his disappearance? Was he in a coma like George Hopkins?

John's thoughts were cut off when Charles Dana answered the phone.

"Chuck, the story is going to break. We need to run something tomorrow," John said breathlessly into the phone.

"John? Calm yourself and tell me what's going on."

John explained how Hank Gates was going to release his report on Nerno.

There was a long silence on the phone. "Okay, tell me what you have."

"I have my source and I have the documents about the new drill."

"I don't care about the drill. Focus on Ko Chang. You need more than one source. Nobody else is willing to go on the record?"

"Not yet."

"You need to be more persuasive. Tell them the story is going to break either way."

John gripped the phone hard. What was he doing wasting time arguing with Charles? And why was Charles telling him how to do his job? "You don't think I've been doing that?"

"John, the paper is on the brink of being sold. If Nerno sues us, it will destroy us. They will tie us up in court forever."

John suddenly had an idea. "Nobody will want to buy us then. Maybe that's your way out."

There was a long silence, and John could feel that Charles was thinking about it. "When I was a young journalist, before I worked for the *Wall Street Journal*, I worked for a small paper called the *New York Leader*. We did journalism that would now be coined new journalism, gonzo journalism in the sixties and seventies. I remember we were so cavalier. We had the weight of the world on our shoulders but not a care in the world."

Charles Dana paused, and John waited for him to continue, unsure of what was happening.

"Back then we were ready to burn down the house," Charles continued. "Rebuilding seemed so easy. But if I make this paper unsellable, who will be here to take our place? To pick up the pieces?"

John waited, but he suspected that Charles wanted him to answer. "Won't that Icelandic corporation just break us up into pieces anyway? If we're going to go down, why not go down in a fight?"

"Don't worry. I will make sure that doesn't happen."

"How, exactly? You don't seem to have much of a game plan."

"Let me worry about the paper. You worry about the article."

"It's the wrong decision, Chuck."

Charles paused. His voice was calm as usual. John always marvelled at how he could argue his point coherently without raising his voice. "Do you know anybody in the Gates camp? If he has all the information then why not look at that angle? I think that would be acceptable as a second source."

John hadn't thought about that. Why hadn't he talked to any of Gates' researchers? Hopefully he had time. At the very least he would be able to get his article online before Gates' press conference. "Okay," John said. "Let me see what I can do." John hesitated. "One more thing, Chuck."

"Yes?"

"Has anybody managed to get hold of Vince Parkerson?" John asked.

"Yeah, of course. I phoned him this morning. He said he left you a message on your phone."

"That's strange. I never got it."

"You were never very good with technology, John," Dana said.

"Okay, I'll give him another call."

John ended his conversation with Charles. He checked his phone, but there were no new messages. He then phoned Vince, but his call went straight to voicemail. John looked up Vince's home phone number online and phoned his house. A woman picked up.

"Yes, I'm looking for Vince. Is he around?"

"No. Can I take a message?"

"My name is John Webster. I'm a colleague of Vince's. Do you know when he will be home?"

"He said he would be late. Have you tried his cell phone?"

"Yes, it's not on. There's no other number?"

"No, I'm sorry. I'll tell him you phoned."

"Do you know where he is? It's really important I get hold of him before deadline."

"He said he was meeting a source. I'm not sure where. He doesn't really tell me much."

"Okay, thanks. Get him to phone me as soon as he comes in."

Frustrated, John knew that there wasn't much he could do but wait.

The Two Reporters

AFTER THE PARTY, ANDREA DROPPED John off at his hotel. He went upstairs and had a warm shower. He dried himself off and folded his clothes and placed them neatly on the bed. John took his wallet from his pocket and placed it on the nightstand. With the wallet was Madeline Xiao's card which he slipped out and held up to the light. He dialled her Calgary number. It rang five times before Madeline answered sleepily.

"It's John Webster. We met at the party tonight."

"The fundraiser? Yes, I remember."

"I need your help."

"Help with what?"

"Can we meet tonight?"

"Sure. Where?"

"I'm staying at the Edmonds Hotel. Can you meet me there?"

"Okay, see you in about thirty minutes."

John got dressed and went downstairs to the bar. The place was as dark and quiet as before. A soft piano was playing on the speakers. John ordered a whiskey and sat at the bar. He felt defeated. He was a chess player who had run out of moves. Check and mate. Hank Gates would have his press conference and would get all the glory, and John would be left with nothing. It didn't seem fair. Just because Hank Gates had more money.

Madeline entered the bar. She wore the same suit that she had worn at the party. She spotted John and sat next to him, crossing her left leg over her right knee and placed a bony elbow on the counter and stared at John with large, deep eyes.

"What's the score?" she asked.

"Pardon?"

Madeline indicated the television, which had a hockey game on.

"Oh, I don't watch sports," he said.

"I thought all Canadians were obsessed with hockey."

"I thought all Chinese were communists," John retorted.

Madeline smiled openly and John, despite his dark mood, felt himself relax around her and her British accent. "I confess I don't understand the sport. What's with the sticks and the ice? And you guys actually cheer when there is a fight?"

"It's the only sport we can play outside for most of the year."

Madeline saw that John had finished his drink. "Can I buy you another one?"

"If you like," John said, shrugging.

Madeline waved at the bartender and ordered another whiskey, and a Bellini for herself. "So," Madeline said, incredulously. "You're not a fundraiser, are you?"

John looked down at his empty drink. "I never said that."

"Really? Because you sure gave that impression, but after you called I looked you up on the web, and do you know what I saw?"

John glanced at Madeline, who was giving John a suggestive smile. "I can only guess."

"I saw a mug of your beautiful face and underneath it read investigative journalist for the *Daily Globe*. Fundraiser my arse." Madeline slapped John playfully on the shoulder. "Why didn't you tell me?"

"Because I'm wary of other reporters."

Madeline seemed to accept that answer, settling down in her seat. "I guess for good reason."

The bartender put the drinks on the table. Madeline opened her black purse and slid a credit card across the table with two fingers. "Can we start a tab?" She then turned and smiled at John. "I think this might be a late night."

John clinked glasses with Madeline. "So how did you come to work for the *Beijing Star*? Were you born in China?"

"Born and bred in a city called Harbin, in the northeast of China."

"Who taught you English? It's very good."

"I studied in the U.K. for three years, then moved to Beijing for work."

"How are you finding the weather here? A little cold for your liking?"

Madeline laughed. "Believe it or not, I'm used to the cold. Harbin is sometimes nicknamed the Ice City. In the winter we often build these large ice sculptures. It's a very beautiful city. You should visit some time."

"If you give me an invitation, I will."

Madeline laughed again, and John found that he enjoyed her laugh. It was easy and spontaneous.

"So, what is it like being a journalist in China?"

"I feel like I'm being interrogated."

"I'm sorry, but I'm just curious."

Madeline paused, as though wondering how much she should tell John. "We on the record here?"

John held up his hands. "No, not at all. Personal interest only."

"It's difficult for sure. There are a lot of censorship issues we have to deal with. A lot of topics we are forbidden to write about, and we're always threatened with being shut down." Madeline shrugged. "But we just learn to deal with it."

"Why study in England?" John asked.

"I have family that immigrated there after my father was executed for writing something against the government."

"Madeline, I'm sorry," John said, reaching over and putting his hand on hers. Madeline just shrugged, taking a sip of her drink. "It was a long time ago. I barely remember him."

"My own father was killed when I was sixteen. It doesn't seem that long ago, but I find my memories of him are fading."

Madeline tried to smile, leaning towards John. "I presume you didn't phone me to talk about our fathers."

John tried to match Madeline's forced smile with one of his own. "I phoned because I need your help with something."

"You need my help?" Madeline asked. "I thought you were going to help me."

"I need some information on Nerno."

"Why?"

"Do you know a man named Hank Gates?"

Madeline shook her head. "Who is he?"

"He's an investor of sorts. He short sells companies he knows are lying and earns millions of dollars."

Madeline stared at John intently. "How do you know this?"

"He has a proven track record. Search Gates Investing online and you'll find it all there."

"And he's mixed up in Nerno."

"Yes, your government is about to buy a very overpriced company."

Madeline didn't seem surprised. "You can prove it?"

"That's where you come in. I need your help."

Madeline didn't say anything for a while. "And if I help you what do I get in return?"

John was incredulous. "You get a story. What more do you want?"

"I can get the story by myself, thanks."

"Not the story I can give you. You've never even heard of Hank Gates. You're too far behind in the race. You can't catch up before Gates makes everything public."

"And what would that be?"

"I have a source inside Nerno with good information. I can't tell you who, but we might be able to come to some kind of arrangement. We're not competitors."

"Why should I believe you?"

"I have no reason to lie to you."

Madeline thought for a moment. "Okay. What should we do?"

"You know the CNOOC players?"

"Of course."

"Can you get me an interview with one of the CNOOC execs? You could translate for me."

Madeline stared down at her drink. "I don't know. They usually don't like meddling from journalists."

"Why not? You both work for the Chinese government. Isn't there anybody you can call?"

Madeline looked up and frowned. "I don't work for the bloody government. My newspaper is independent."

Sure it is, John thought. But instead he said, "Can you at least try? I want to start pressing them about Hank Gates, about Ko Chang."

"Okay, but I want you to go back to your source and ask if he'll meet with me."

John nodded. "That's fair."

Madeline paid for the bill and got up to leave. "Let's talk tomorrow and see where we are."

"Okay, phone me in the morning. Hopefully we're not too late."

The New York Times

For John, the morning was an unwelcome sight. The sunlight trickled through the curtains, hitting the carpeted floor. John jolted awake, with shivers and goose bumps covering his arms and legs. He brought the sheets up to his chin to try and shield himself, but it was a useless gesture.

He rolled over, facing the unbroken pillow next to him. The bed was queen-sized and John seemed to sink within it. John hated large unfilled beds. They made him feel lonely and restless. He didn't move for what seemed like a long time, but whenever he closed his eyes, mocking images of Hayden and Byron appeared.

Finally he sat up and rubbed his face. His head was spinning. When was the last time he had drank so much? A year?

Your challenge now will be not to slide backwards, Doctor Nagi had told him. She had been right. What had happened? Was it the stress? Was he just unable to cope with life? He felt that he was back to where he had begun: downing homemade alcohol in small unmapped African towns and sipping from flasks in Iraq.

John stumbled over to the washroom without turning on the light and peed into the toilet, the stream trickling against the water. He felt awful. He turned the faucet above the sink and drank deeply. Afterwards he collapsed back onto the bed and turned on the television, flipping it to the news.

On screen a woman anchor in a pretty red blouse was speaking into the camera.

John went over to his suitcase and looked at what fresh clothes he had. He needed to do laundry. He was digging through his shirts when something from the television caught his attention.

". . . A stunning article in the *New York Times* claiming the Calgary company Nerno Energy has falsified its earnings, specifically referring to one of its major oil fields, which isn't producing as many barrels as reported."

John's head began to spin faster, but he was unable to take his eyes off of the television. He gripped the edge of the screen with his large fingers, pressing his fingertips into the hot metal. He couldn't understand what the anchor was saying. When she went on to the next story, John stumbled to his computer and logged onto the *New York Times* website, and sure enough, the front page had a story about Nerno. He clicked on the story. It took him a while to digest the story. It was written by Vince Parkerson. At first he didn't trust his own eyesight. Then he thought *no, Vince doesn't work for the* New York Times.

John was stunned. How had this happened? How had Vince Parkerson betrayed him? Now it was very clear why Vince hadn't returned any of his phone calls, and it was clear that the bastard had taken the knowledge that John had given him, and turned around and sold it to the *New York Times*. But the *Times* would have had to promise him more than a couple thousand dollars for an article; they would have had to promise him a job. Was that possible? It seemed unlikely. Perhaps Vince had wanted to retire and go out with a bang.

John fell back onto the bed and looked up at the ceiling, trying to collect his thoughts. The hum of the lights seemed overly loud and distracting.

There were a couple of things that John didn't understand. He was positive that he hadn't told Vince about Sheila McKinnon, so how had he known about his source? And just as pertinent, why had Sheila betrayed him? Was it because Vince had told her that he worked for the *New York Times*? Those seductive words loosened a lot of tongues.

Another thing that John didn't understand was how Vince Parkerson had convinced the *New York Times* to publish his story with so few facts, unless, of course, he had managed to get some information from somebody that John hadn't spoken to. John didn't know which was more frightening.

Either way, he had been outmanoeuvred, albeit a little underhandedly, but outmanoeuvred nonetheless. It didn't happen often, but when it did, John never took it well.

With great effort, John got up and went back to his computer. He thoroughly reread the *Times* story and wrote down every source that Vince had used. Most of the story was attributed to an unnamed source—probably Sheila. The article mentioned George Hopkins' crash, and a police source that said that there was no foul play suspected, but that the investigation was ongoing.

When John read about Hopkins he clenched his jaw until his muscles hurt. He couldn't understand how somebody could do something so low, so cowardly. Even for a journalist, a profession known for its thievery and low morals, John couldn't believe it.

John grabbed his phone and called Sheila, not taking his usual precaution to phone her from a payphone.

"You sold me out," John said when she answered.

"What? What are you talking about?"

"I'm talking about the *New York Times* article. It's front page."

"What phone are you using? Didn't I tell you not to contact me directly?"

"But you lied to me," John shouted. He felt his neck tighten and his chest swell with rage.

"I honestly don't know what you're talking about."

"What, I'm supposed to believe that the reporter, who up to recently worked for my newspaper, got another whistleblower to talk? Forgive me if I find that too hard to swallow."

"What do you want me to say?"

"I want you to tell me the truth."

"Fine. You took too long. What was I going to do? Wait around forever until you decided on what to do?"

That was all the admission that John needed. He hung up on her, fearing that he would say something he would regret. Instead he threw the phone on the bed and buried his face in his hands. He couldn't remember the last time that he had felt so enraged, so betrayed by so many different people. Vince, Sheila and even Charles Dana. Yes, Chuck was supposed to be on his side.

John got up slowly and had a shower, hoping that it would calm him down. He turned the nozzle on full blast and let the water fall down his face. The warm water felt good on his body. He felt his limbs loosen and some of the tension drain away.

He closed his eyes, and for the first time wondered what he was going to do now. His entire story was blown. He had nothing. He thought that perhaps he could catch the next flight to Vancouver, head home to Byron and the next story. But there was some resilience deep inside that told him that he had to stay and fight. He could do a follow up, find a better angle than the one Vince got, but he knew that the first one out of the gate was the winner.

John got out of the shower, and as he was drying off he heard his phone ring. He wrapped the towel around his body and picked up his phone from the table.

"Webster? It's Charles."

John took a deep breath. "Hi boss."

Charles Dana seemed almost at a loss for words, a rarity for him. "Parkerson really got us. I can't believe it."

I told you so, John thought. He felt vindictive, but there was no point in rubbing it in now. Charles was probably beating himself up enough already. Instead, John said, "He somehow found out my source. I don't know how. I never told him."

"He was always a moral reporter. I don't understand it." Charles said.

"What do you want me to do?"

"You think you could do a follow up?"

John swallowed. It seemed unfair doing a follow up now. "Well, I'm going to go to Hank Gates' press conference this afternoon. Besides that I don't have much except what I've already told you."

"Okay, keep hitting the pavement."

John swallowed, still tasting last night's alcohol. "I intend to. Do you think you'll take any legal action?"

Charles sighed. "I don't know. I'll talk to the board and to Mack but I think I know what they will say." Mack Carrigton was the newspaper's legal counsel.

"Chuck, you have to fight this. You can't let the *New York Times* just poach whoever they want."

"Don't worry, we'll do something. It may not be legal, but we have other weapons."

John felt deeply saddened. In the past, Charles would have fought to the very last deposition, but things had changed. John said goodbye and hung up.

He dried himself off, shaved and got dressed. He looked at himself critically in the mirror. The stress of the last couple of days seemed to show in the redness of his eyes.

John phoned the police media hotline. When he identified himself he was put on hold. *They would be busy for the next couple of weeks,* John thought. He paced around the room for the next ten minutes, keeping himself amused by flipping through the channels on the television. Eventually he decided that he was hungry and that he needed some caffeine, and so he hung up. He doubted that the PR guys would be able to tell him anything that Vince's article hadn't already told him about George Hopkins' crash.

He took the elevator down to the lobby and got in the queue for the breakfast buffet. The smell of grease was permeating the air and it made John feel nauseous, and he wondered if it was from last night's alcohol, or from knowing that he had been betrayed.

John filled the coffee to the brim, but despite his previous hunger, he looked at the sausages, the pancakes and the hash browns without much desire. Instead he took a couple of pieces of fruit and headed for a corner table.

It seemed that everybody was talking about the Nerno scandal and it made John's stomach tighten into further knots.

All of the overhead televisions were tuned into the business station, where handsome men and handsome women were smiling for the camera while delivering the most dire of news. Underneath the talking heads the screen read in blocky letters: IS THIS THE END OF NERNO ENERGY?

John's phone rang. John contemplated not answering it, but he would be getting a lot of calls today, he figured. It was Hank Gates.

"This is your doing, isn't it?" Gates shouted. "You just didn't want me to be the first one to announce it."

"No, I wish I could say I was that smart, but we were both outmanoeuvred," John replied.

"You're lying to me. You thought that if at least another reporter got the story then it would prove journalism wasn't completely dead yet."

John felt himself beginning to get annoyed. "Gates, think about what you're saying. Why would I give the scoop to another reporter, to another newspaper even? I honestly don't care about winning a petty ego battle with you that much."

"You're an asshole," Gates said, hanging up.

John sighed and returned to his breakfast, which he picked at slowly. The fruit was making him feel better. An elderly couple at the next table over were reading the *New York Times*, and began discussing Vince Parkerson's article loudly with each other.

John hadn't finished his fruit or his coffee, but decided that he couldn't take it any longer and that it was time to leave. He got up, deciding that he would leave his breakfast but take the rest of his coffee back to the room. He squeezed between the tables towards the hallway when a tubby, elderly Chinese man leaned back in his chair and knocked John's coffee. The hot liquid spilled on John's wrist and on the floor. Luckily nobody else was burned.

The Chinese man quickly got up and started to apologize in a deep, thickly-accented voice. The man must have been in his mid-sixties, with round chin and cheeks, but he seemed agile enough.

"No, it okay, really," John said, as the man examined the red flesh on John's wrist.

The man's wife also got up and said something to the man in Chinese. John didn't understand, but she appeared to be scolding her husband, who looked sheepishly towards her, then back at John, as if appealing for his help.

John obliged, turning to the woman, who was equally old as her husband, telling her that he was okay, that his burn would be fine in a couple of hours.

The woman, however, didn't understand John, or ignored him, as she started to soak up the coffee from the floor with a napkin. John felt it necessary to help the old woman, who was now down on her hands and knees.

Eventually one of the hotel staff came over to quell the chaotic scene.

"I'll go get a mop bucket," the staffer said. "Everybody please just enjoy your breakfast."

This seemed to satisfy the wife, who evidently understood the staffer, despite giving no previous indication of understanding English. She sat back down and continued to eat her breakfast.

The Chinese man was still standing and kept repeating, "I'm very sorry."

"It's okay," John said. "Enjoy your stay."

"You as well, sir." He smiled brightly and tilted his head, as if he and John shared some secret. John decided that he would get some more coffee later and went back to his room, pushing the incident with the old Chinese couple out his mind.

When John arrived back in his room, he instinctively looked around to see if anything had been disturbed. He found that he was still angry over the break-in, not so much because he had had his voice recorder and notebook stolen, but because the invasion of privacy really bothered him.

John booted up his computer. He thought about phoning the media hotline again, but decided that it would be a waste of time, and so he decided to try phoning the Nerno building again, although he knew that by this time it would be swarming with reporters and would be in lockdown mode. He would have a small chance of seeing anybody. That, too, would probably be a waste of time.

He phoned using the local hotel line but, as suspected, he got a busy signal. He wondered how many lines were jammed up with reporters calling and requesting interviews.

John decided to drive to the Nerno building and see what he could do in person. As he turned from the hotel parking lot and out onto the road, John decided that he would try and give Andrea Drashkov a call on her cell phone. She was probably avoiding everybody as well, but it was worth a try. John dug into his pocket, but didn't find his phone. He must have left it back in his hotel room, and he cursed himself for his carelessness. He shook his head. Usually he was pretty good at keeping his phone on his person, but he guessed that with everything that had happened in the morning, he had simply forgotten.

The drive to the Nerno building took only a few minutes, and didn't give John time to prepare for the chaos that he saw. The entrance was swarming with reporters with video cameras, with microphones and digital recorders. News trucks were double parked, blocking the road, their satellite dishes pointing towards the heavens. People were running around, frantic, like they were in a war zone. Every single Nerno employee that came and went was instantly surrounded like lions on a sick zebra.

Energy was vibrating in the air. Buzzing from the people, from the commotion. John could feel the static rising on the back of his neck. It was what John loved about his job, and what kept him coming back, like a drug that he knew was bad for him but kept him on a high.

John got out, braving the weather with everybody else. The coldness hit his face full blast and seemed to spread down his spine like a liquid. John wondered what the temperature was. It was unlike anything John had ever experienced before. He could feel his skin burn, even under his multiple layers. His eyes began to water.

John looked for a police presence, and was surprised when he didn't see any blue uniforms anywhere. They usually kept an eye on the fourth estate, appearing as soon as they did anything unruly. John did, however, spot another reporter he knew named Arthur

Ransome. He was standing on the curb of the sidewalk, his hands in the pockets of his big Tiga jacket. Around his neck he had a small digital camera. He was wearing large snow boots.

John walked over to him. The last time that they had met, Arthur had been working for the *Vancouver Times*.

Arthur instantly recognized John and smiled at him.

"Art, what are you doing here?"

"Got laid off," he said, shrugging. "What are you going to do?"

"Who are you working for now?" John asked.

"I'm freelancing, trying to make some money selling video to blogs."

John smiled sympathetically, thinking of the *Daily Globe*'s own financial problems. Even if the newspaper survived, how long would he be working there? The new owner, whoever that was going to be, would probably want to hire young journalism graduates and fire the old reporters with the larger salaries.

What if this is my last story for the newspaper? John wondered. *What if I can't find work anywhere else?* He tried to shake his worries.

John shook his head. "Tough gig."

Arthur smiled. "Tell me about it. I make about half of what I did before and I'm busting my ass twice as hard. I have a wife and kids. They don't understand why I don't do something else. It's depressing."

John thought about what Hank Gates had said about the new journalist. Was that really what it was coming to? Would there be any true reporters left in ten years' time?

"Maybe it's time we all apply for work as janitors. That's about the only other thing I'm qualified for."

Arthur shook his head sadly. "I'm afraid you'll have to pry the microphone out of my cold dead hands."

John shivered, although he wasn't sure if it was from the cold or not. "What's going on here? Anything?"

"Employees have been coming and going, but so far nobody has commented on the *Times* story." Arthur glanced at John with large interested eyes. "Didn't Vince Parkerson work for the *Globe*? I don't remember him switching."

"Yeah, I think he did."

"How do you think he got the scoop?"

John tried to hold back a grimace, but he was sure that it was detected by Arthur. "I've got a pretty good idea."

Arthur frowned, waiting for John to continue, but when John didn't, he seemed to decide not to push it.

John decided to change the topic. "You know about the press conference this afternoon?"

Arthur shook his head. "I don't think Nerno has announced a press conference. They haven't responded yet. They're looking pretty bad in this whole thing." Arthur paused for a moment and then said thoughtfully, "Maybe I should go into PR."

"No, it isn't Nerno. It's a lawyer named Hank Gates." John explained what he had learned about Gates, his company and his history.

Afterwards, Arthur just shook his head. "I wish I was smart enough to do something like that."

John couldn't think of anything to say to that. He just stood in silence next to Arthur, waiting for something to happen in the Nerno building, but all that John could see was the security guard pacing back and forth nervously, looking out at the swarm of reporters. Evidently he was worried that everybody would just decide to charge and storm the building, demanding quotes and sound bites.

John tried to move his fingers and toes to try and keep them warm. His face started to sting savagely. He glanced at Arthur, who was also trying to stay warm.

After a while John decided that he didn't want to wait around in the cold anymore. He told Arthur that he would be back, and found a payphone. He dialled Andrea Drashkov's cell phone. Not surprisingly she didn't pick up, but he left a somewhat disjointed message saying that he didn't have his phone on him, but that she could email him if she wanted to get hold of him.

John waited around a little longer, but it was no use. He wasn't going to get anywhere standing with dozens of other reporters in the elements.

John turned to Arthur. "You want to come with me to the press conference? It will get you out of the cold at least."

Arthur looked back to the entrance of the Nerno building and seemed to come to the same conclusion.

"Sure," he said. "I'll drive, if you want."

"Okay, but let me get my computer. I left it in the car."

They walked to John's rental and then to Arthur's car, which was parked only a couple of blocks away.

Arthur drove an old Nissan. The seats were all torn and there were candy wrappers on the floor. Both cup holders had half empty coffee cups in them.

"Sorry about the mess," Arthur said. "I feel like I live in this car more than at home."

"No problem," John said, brushing some crumbs off of the seat before sitting down.

Hank Gates had rented a room at the convention centre for the event, which was not far away, on 9th Avenue. It was a great glass structure with lots of slopes and curves, and in the noon light the glass panels reflected the blurry image of the Calgary Tower and the surrounding skyscrapers.

Arthur parked in the underground parking lot.

"So, you think this will be any good?" Arthur asked as he turned off the engine.

John shrugged. "It will be a show, if nothing else."

"You think you can split parking with me?"

John nodded. "The life of a blogger, huh?"

"I don't have a newspaper that I can expense."

John thought about how he had used Air Miles for his trip to Calgary. "Why are you so sure I do?"

They took the elevator up to the main floor. He couldn't remember the last time that he had gone to a press conference. Maybe in Kabul, Afghanistan? Press conferences were usually over-hyped affairs, high on glitz and glamour and low on substance.

John and Arthur were early, which was good. John always liked to be early for events, because not only did it assure the best seat, but sometimes also the best information, spilling out before anything got started.

As John and Arthur took their seats, John spotted Hank Gates standing below the podium. He was dressed in a dark suit and a deep pink tie. His hair was so oiled it reflected the powerful overhead lights. He looked suave except for his face, which was a mask of anxiety.

John ducked his head, but he was too late, as Gates spotted him and made his way over.

"John, good to see you. I didn't think you would come," Gates said, his anxiety all but melted from his face, replaced by the seducing smile.

John returned Gates' smile and motioned towards Arthur. "Hank, this is Arthur Ransome, he's assisting me."

Gates and Arthur shook hands.

"It's good to see you got some help," Gates said, turning back to John.

"I hope you'll make it worth our time."

"I will," Gates said, almost absently. "I'm going to put on quite the show."

Gates left, and both John and Arthur set up their computers and placed their voice recorders on the table.

"How come you told him I was assisting you?" Arthur asked, sounding slightly annoyed.

John shrugged. "Using a little psychological warfare on him."

Soon other reporters—some from big networks—filed into the room, carrying cameras and sound equipment. It was a pretty big turnout for a story that had already been leaked.

As John waited, he connected up to the wi-fi and saw that Andrea Drashkov had emailed him. John opened the message up.

Meet me at Turno's at 4pm.

John hit the reply button and wrote that he would be there. He looked up at the clock and saw that he had more than three hours before he had to be there; plenty of time to find the place.

John spotted Madeline just as she walked in. She had a camera and a laptop slung over her shoulder, and she wore sunglasses. She seemed only marginally more put together than John, and somewhere inside of him John felt a smug sense of satisfaction.

"Excuse me," John said to Arthur. "I need to talk to someone. Can you keep an eye on my laptop?"

"Sure," Arthur said, although he was deeply engrossed with his own email.

John walked over to Madeline, who had found a table to sit at and was making herself comfortable.

"I thought you were going to phone me," John said.

"I did phone you. Your phone was off."

John suddenly remembered that he had left his phone at the hotel. "You got anything?" he asked.

Madeline shrugged. "I hope this press conference won't be a waste of time."

John looked around. "Me too."

"How's your friend?" Madeline asked. She seemed irritated, or perhaps hung over. Or both.

John frowned, confused. "My friend?"

"Yes, Andrea Drashkov."

"She's not my friend."

"You were with her at the fundraiser, weren't you?"

"She invited me, yes, but I wasn't with her."

"Have you spoken with her today?"

John didn't want to tell her about the email correspondence. He had already been burned once by someone he trusted. "No, she's in hiding. I can't get hold of her. How about your end of the bargain? Did you get in contact with anybody from the oil company?"

"It doesn't work like that, John. I put in my request and it may take months before I get a response."

John bent down close to her ear and whispered angrily, "We don't have months, Madeline. Don't you see that?"

Madeline straightened her back and stared up at John. "I'm sorry I bloody well can't be of service to your needs."

John wanted to say something to get back at her, but, afraid of what it would do, he bit his bottom lip and went to sit back down by Arthur.

When one o'clock came, Hank Gates stepped up to the podium. Behind him, there was a big projector screen which displayed the logo for Gates Investing. Gates knew that he was on primetime television.

Gates slowly looked around the room, seemingly taking everything in. His nerves seemed to have dissipated. Now he was the showman. The actor. The presenter.

"Nerno first bought the drilling rights to an area just off Ko Chang Island in 2007 after much extensive mapping of the area. Ko Chang is the third largest island in Thailand and is located in the Gulf of Thailand."

Gates clicked through several slides; one was a map of Ko Chang, another of beautiful forests, the next of beautiful, serene beaches. Gates turned around to face the crowd. "It is a lush area with lots of wildlife and many natural resources. Oil, however, is not one of them. At least, not in the area Nerno Energy has bought."

Gates then clicked to a slide showing an info graph that John didn't understand.

"I had my team of scientists do a seismic survey of the Ko Chang area. Now for those who don't know, these types of surveys are done to detect oil reservoirs. Here, on my graph, I can show you my findings."

The presentation lasted forty minutes and John, despite himself, couldn't help but be impressed with the depth of Gates' research. Gates concluded with a final slide. It was a picture of David Kahn, George Hopkins and Andrea Drashkov.

"These three people are the architects of this criminal deceit. George Hopkins lies in a coma as we speak after his Lamborghini lost control. I think the police need to do something fast before other employees of Nerno Energy are hurt. Thank you. Any questions?"

Arms began to shoot up. Gates picked somebody from the front row. "That's a very impressive presentation. You accuse those three Nerno founders of intentionally misleading the stockholders and public, but you don't offer any proof. Do you have anything that would prove your allegations?"

Gates smiled and nodded. "It's true, I can't back up my claims with concrete evidence, but once the police open up an investigation I am confident they will prove I'm correct."

John took a couple more photos with his phone and walked back to the elevator with Arthur Ransome. He looked around for Madeline but he couldn't see her.

"Thanks for telling me about that," Arthur said, as they got into the car. "I think I got some great stuff."

John smiled, but he was already thinking about his upcoming meeting with Andrea Drashkov. He knew that she would be distraught, and that she would want somebody to comfort her. John wouldn't bring out his notepad or recorder. Perhaps he could lure her into saying something she wouldn't otherwise say in her distraught state.

Arthur dropped John off at his car. There was still a large contingent of reporters milling about the Nerno building. He supposed they were hoping that David Kahn would pop his head out at some point.

John decided that he couldn't live without his phone any longer, and so he drove back to the Edmonds hotel. He looked around his tiny room and finally found it on the floor next to the television. He picked it up and scrolled through his missed calls. There was one from a number that he didn't recognize.

John didn't remember leaving his phone by the television. Usually he kept it charged by his bed. *Maybe in a drunken stupor I dropped it,* John thought.

John dialled the number back. It rang twice before a man answered it. "Andy Coburn, Nerno Energy marketing department."

John thought fast. "Hi Andy . . . my name is Liam Plummer. I got a call from this number."

"Liam Plummer? I'm sorry, I don't think remember calling you. Is this with regard to advertisement?"

"Perhaps I was mistaken. Sorry. Have a good day," John said, hanging up. He knew that marketing was Sheila McKinnon's department. Had she tried to get hold of him using Andy Coburn's phone? Had he caused Coburn to be suspicious? At this point he didn't really care. She had betrayed him. What did she have to say? Nothing except endless *I'm sorry . . . I'm sorry . . . I'm sorry.*

John didn't want to hear it. He had to concentrate on his meeting with Andrea. It might be his one last chance to turn this disaster around and get something good from it.

John went downstairs and asked the receptionist where Turno's was.

"Is it a restaurant?" the receptionist asked.

John thought for a moment. "I'm not sure. A friend of mine just said to meet me there."

The receptionist looked it up on her computer. It turned out that Turno's was a café on the east side of the city, just past the outskirts of downtown.

John thanked the receptionist and went to his car. His phone rang and, without looking at the caller ID, he answered it.

"John . . . it's Sheila."

"What do you want?"

"John, I'm scared. I don't know what to do."

John felt anger swell up. "Sheila, I don't have time to play these games with you. You got yourself into this mess. I'm sure you can get yourself out of it."

"I need your help. You promised you would protect me."

"I can't protect you from yourself," John said, hanging up. His phone started ringing again, but this time he ignored it.

John had driven for several minutes when his head began to spin and he began to feel nauseous. He looked at his phone, which was on the seat next to him. It was blinking with a new voice message. John wasn't thinking clearly. He needed to focus.

He looked up at the sign posts, icicles dripping from them, and realized that he was going in the wrong direction.

John turned around and headed east on 12th Avenue. He proceeded slowly. His nausea slowly disappeared, and he decided to turn on the news, but he already knew that everybody would be talking about Nerno. He wasn't disappointed.

One caller suggested that the police lay criminal charges. Another proposed that the stockholders should sue. John flipped to another station, where another host reported that Nerno had lost nearly half of its value on the stock market. A lynch mob was slowly developing across the city.

John found Turno's without too much trouble. He parked and put two hours in the meter.

Turno's had a wide blue awning, making it look quaint and foreign. The inside was well-lit and lively with people trying to stay out of the cold.

John looked at his phone and realized that he was twenty minutes early. He was going to order himself a coffee and wait, but then he saw a woman in the corner. She had on large sunglasses and a North Face jacket with the hood pulled up.

John walked over to her and peered down. The woman looked up at him, unsmiling.

"Andrea?" John asked.

"Sit down," she said.

"Let me order some coffee. You okay? You look terrible."

Andrea gave a half-hearted smile. "Have you ever lost twenty million dollars in one day?"

John nodded. "Good point."

John ordered himself a black coffee and sat down opposite Andrea.

"Is it true what they say?" Andrea asked. "Is there really no oil at Ko Chang?"

John studied Andrea closely. "Don't play that game with me. It doesn't suit you."

Andrea took a sip of her coffee but didn't say anything.

"Well, what are you going to do now?" John asked. "You're kind of stuck between a rock and a hard place, aren't you?"

Andrea still didn't look up at John. "Do you ever wish you were somebody else?"

John was momentarily confused. "What do you mean?"

"I don't know . . . it seems like we are always trying to be other people."

John thought about it. "I guess we all try and fulfill the roles we give ourselves. I don't know if that's what you mean."

Andrea looked up. Her face was stern and rigid. "You didn't answer my question."

John stared into her face, his own reflected in her dark sunglasses. He reminded himself of somebody he barely knew, except as a domineering presence in his childhood. "Yes . . . I suppose . . . I always wanted to be my father. He wrote reviews of musicals and stage plays."

"You want to be a critic?" Andrea asked, surprised.

"No, not exactly. You know how sometimes you're in love with the idea more than the thing itself?"

"Sure."

"Well, that's how I feel about my dad."

John didn't know why he was telling Andrea this. Perhaps it was the vulnerability in her voice.

She's beautiful but evil.

Maybe Michael Chu had it wrong. Maybe she was a porcupine, displaying her spikes to the world, but inside she was a different creature.

"Andrea, I just came from a news conference that accused you of lying about the oil at Ko Chang. You need to respond. You need to tell me what to write."

Andrea's jaw dropped, and for a moment John thought that she was going to shout or scream, but instead she just looked around the room in disbelief.

"I don't understand why everybody is against me. I did nothing wrong."

"What did you do exactly?"

"It's all a ploy—that Hank Gates is using you, don't you see it?"

"So you're saying all those reports he has are false?"

"Yes—I don't know where he got them."

John leaned back in his seat, and took a sip of coffee to give him time to think about what he wanted to say next. "I believe you, but I don't think many other people will."

Andrea nodded. "I need your help."

John shrugged. Sheila had asked for his help too. Now everybody suddenly wanted his help. What did he, John Webster, have to offer anyway? What did he have? "I don't know what I can do unless you tell me everything you know from the beginning."

"I only found out a month ago that there was no oil at Ko Chang. David Kahn phoned me on vacation."

John stared at Andrea without saying anything. With her glasses on, it was hard to read her, so he watched her mouth.

"I didn't know what to do or where to turn. For the first time since I was fourteen . . . I felt helpless."

"So you just waited, hoping the Chinese would buy your company and it would be somebody else's problem. Is that it?"

Andrea nodded. "What was I to do? Nobody would have believed me."

John nodded as if he agreed, but he had heard that excuse so often before, it made him sick. *Nobody would believe me that he raped that woman . . . Nobody would believe me he killed that kid . . . Nobody would believe me they tortured him. Nobody ever believes me.* John always believed that it was a weak excuse.

John took a deep breath and said, "Okay, let's back up a bit. You never questioned George Hopkins or anybody else when there were delays in production?"

Andrea shrugged. "Why would I? They were the experts. They knew what to look for, and besides, everybody was calling for our blood anyway. It was my job to defend George, to protect him from the negative press."

John felt emotionally exhausted when he got into the car. He started the engine and pulled the car onto the road, trying to keep his eyes open.

He found himself on the way to the hospital. He thought about what Andrea had said about George Hopkins. Why he felt the need to go, John didn't know, only somewhere deep down in his soul he knew was in his nature, perhaps it was the journalists instinct to bare witness, no matter how unpleasant.

John parked in the parking lot, paid his ticket and took the elevator up to the third floor to the ICU. The walls of the hospital were featureless and painted in mild pastel colours.

John stopped a young nurse who told him where he could find George. John walked down a long hallway. He passed an old woman pushing an even older woman in a wheelchair.

John wondered again what he was doing. What was he going to do? Give him flowers? He had never even spoken to George Hopkins, yet deep inside of him he somehow felt responsible for his condition. If he hadn't followed him home . . . what? He wouldn't have crashed his Lamborghini? It seemed stupid thinking about it, yet he couldn't shake the feeling.

John found the room and just as he entered a doctor came out. He looked startled to see John.

"How is he?" John asked. "George Hopkins?"

The doctor looked behind him before saying, "Oh, no changes.

The doctor was young, mid-thirties. He was thin, pale-looking with wispy reddish hair and wore a blue lab coat. A stethoscope hung around his neck.

Perhaps he is a resident, John thought. That would explain his jumpiness.

"Thank you, doctor."

The doctor gave a weak smile and slipped past John who watched him go before turning and entering the room. The room had three beds in it, separated by a curtain. It smelt musty and stale as death lingered close. George Hopkins was in the bed closest to the window which looked out towards a park. John tried to open the window but it was bolted shut.

John sat down beside the bed and looked across at Hopkins. Immediately he saw something was wrong. His monitor had been turned off and the many machines going into Hopkins body didn't seem to be working.

John put an ear to Hopkins' chest but couldn't hear a beat. He tried to take Hopkins' pulse but there was nothing.

John ran to the hallway shouting for help. A nurse rushed towards him.

"He's not breathing. You have to help him," John said, pointing at the room.

The nurse ran into the room. John turned and ran down the hallway. He had to find the doctor.

No . . . he hadn't been a doctor, John realized. *He was sent to kill Hopkins*. The sudden certainty of that statement gripped John and wouldn't let go.

John ran towards the elevator but he didn't find the man in the lab coat. John found the emergency exit and took the stairs. Out of breath, he pushed the door to the lobby open. Several people mingled in the waiting room. A couple of nurses passed, not even glancing in John's direction.

He ran towards the entrance. There were two paramedics talking by the vending machine.

"Hey, did you guys see a doctor with red hair pass here?" John asked.

The paramedics looked at each other before shaking their heads.

John ran out into the parking lot but he didn't see the man in the lab coat. John bent over onto his knees and coughed. He watched for a vehicle leaving quickly, some sort of sign. But the parking lot was quiet. John realized it was a futile effort. The man in the lab coat could be anywhere.

John took the elevator back up to the ICU, leaning against the elevator door. He found the nurse in the hallway, rubbing her hands together, her eyes darting to the floor.

"How is he?" John asked.

The nurse shook her head. "I'm afraid he's gone."

"There was a man dressed up as a doctor. He was coming out just as I entered."

"Dressed as a doctor?" the nurse said. "I don't understand."

"I think he was murdered," John said. His head was spinning and his mouth felt dry.

"I'm sure you're just upset," the nurse said. "I'll get you some water."

"I don't want any water," John snapped. "I want you to phone the police."

The nurse shrugged, as if to say suit yourself. John followed her to the nurse's station where he watched the nurse call the police. He then sat down and waited.

Moments later a doctor came to speak with John. He was much older than the man John had come across in Hopkins' room. His hair was thin and white and his complexion was of thin wax paper.

"I'm sorry for your loss," he said.

"I didn't know him," John said.

The doctor looked surprised and took a moment to compose himself. "Surely we don't need to get the police involved," he said.

"You're just worried about being sued."

"Well there is that," the doctor admitted. "But to say he was . . . well . . . murdered. That's a little absurd, now isn't it?"

"We will see when the police get here," John said.

The doctor sighed heavily. He stared at John as if at a loss for words before he shook his head and walked away.

About thirty minutes passed before two uniformed officers arrived, a man and a woman. The man took John's statement while the woman went to question the nurse.

"What makes you think he was murdered?" the officer asked.

"He was a witness to a conspiracy," John said. He explained what he could about Nerno while the officer listened patiently.

The officer asked a couple more questions before he nodded. "Thank you. I'm going to confer with my partner and we'll be back to talk to you.

John waited patiently until the police officers approached him again.

"Well?" John asked.

The male officer looked down at his notes. "The nurse said it was probably just a resident you saw. She said your description could match several of the residents who are currently doing rotations now."

"Are you going to question them?" John asked.

The police officers put away their notepads. "We'll make our report and let homicide follow it up if they have any further questions."

"And what about the machines that were turned off?"

"She said everything was working perfectly when she went in to check on him."

"That's it?" John asked.

The police officers nodded and headed towards the hallway. John watched them go. At the end of the hallway, the male officer turned and said, "Personally, I think you've been watching too many movies."

The Wedding

S HE APPEARED IN THE DOORWAY in white, just as before. Her
dark, rich skin was the colour of coffee. She smiled radiantly,
and John felt his entire chest expand as he watched her slow,
careful progression up the aisle. She seemed to be walking painfully
slowly, but perhaps John's perception of time had disappeared.

John had known that seeing Hayden in a long white dress
would affect him, but he wasn't ready for the strong swell of
nostalgia that lodged in his throat. Her chin was extended,
emphasizing her long neck and her deep cleavage.

Her dress was more practical this time around, showing less
skin—John had always thought that it was her best asset. But it
was more than just sex appeal. He sensed that the dress was more
mature, more seasoned, more sophisticated. She was a mother now,
an ex-wife, soon to be a bride. She knew what life had to offer, and
it wasn't all romance. There was a lot of heartbreak in there too.
She had learned that well.

The church was hot and stuffy. People crowded in. They still
came to see Hayden do it a second time around. Earlier John
was surprised to see William Russell, his old colleague from
Afghanistan, who was filming documentaries now. John hadn't
been aware that Hayden was still in touch with him, and although
John smiled and they shook hands, he felt betrayed. William had
filmed their wedding, and sent all the guests copies, so what was
he doing here? What was anybody doing here? Didn't they know
that this wasn't a real wedding? This was just a pale imitation of

the one that had come before. Why was everybody participating in this hoax? Why wasn't anybody saying anything?

John spotted Byron in the front row. He was sitting between an elderly couple, who John figured were the groom's parents, and that was the thing that hurt the most. John figured that they were his new family now. But how could a family be broken and remolded so easily?

John had to admit that Paul looked handsome in his tuxedo. His grey hair shone lustrously in the light. He shifted his weight from one foot to the other, displaying none of the confidence that his online profile picture had oozed. He was shorter than John had imagined him.

John reached to his side and squeezed his mother's hand. She looked over and gave him a pitying, sympathetic look that told John that she knew what he was going through. But nobody knew his torture.

Hayden grabbed her white dress in her hands and climbed the three steps to the altar where Paul was standing, and for the first time in a long while, John wished that his father was still alive to dispense his impeccable advice, whatever the situation.

What would John Webster Senior say now? How would he comfort his son? No doubt he would tell John to be stoic, to bear the situation like a man. But how much could one man bear? When was too much, too much?

The priest was a short flabby individual dressed in a white robe, looking very noble and very pious as he joined Paul and Hayden's hands together. They said their vows, repeating after the priest. Each word, each syllable agonizingly poked at John's conscience, and he held his mother's hand tightly to stop himself from crying out, from making a fool of himself in front of Byron.

John's wedding—their wedding—had been in a better church, more grandiose, with stained glass windows that splintered the sunlight onto the pews, colouring the ground with an array of rainbows. They had white roses lining the aisle. Hayden loved white roses, and it had been the only thing that she had insisted on.

John remembered it like a daydream; her soft touch, her large lips, her slender shoulders, her sweet smile.

The priest put the rings on Paul and Hayden, and for a moment John felt a strange tingling sensation on his left hand, as if the priest had put a ring on his finger too.

They had both been much younger of course, back then, but she was no less beautiful now. Paul was a lucky guy. John remembered how they had been more inclined to rashness and indiscretion, as youths were so often prone to be, eating spicy food, skinny dipping in the park. Those were memories that nobody— not even Paul—could take away from him.

After the ceremony, John went for a walk in the church gardens with his mother. Mary didn't walk very well anymore and she shuffled along, barely lifting her feet, but she had prescribed herself at least an hour of exercise a day, and she doggedly stuck to it as people from old working class Scottish families generally did.

It had been raining earlier, which had washed away all the unpleasant odours that had built up in the city streets. Pools of water collected in the crevasses of the garden pathway, and the leaves had large dewdrops which refracted the sunlight as it came out from behind grey clouds.

John couldn't help but feel a little vindicated: his own summer wedding day had been perfect and sublime with sunshine.

"It's cold out here," Mary said, hooking her thin arm around his. John smiled down at his mother, patting her hand. He had a feeling that she wasn't actually that cold; it was just an excuse to be close to her son.

"Why did you come today?" John asked his mother, when they had paused so Mary could catch her breath.

"I should be asking you the same thing," she said, in her thinly accented Scottish brogue.

"I don't really know." John hesitated, struggling to voice his feelings. "I just had to be here."

"You think a writer would be able to explain himself better."

John laughed despite himself. "Always know how to put me in my place, don't you?"

"I think you came for the same reason you became a journalist and ran away to Africa when you were sixteen."

John frowned, confused. "I don't understand."

"You are a witness, John, even if you don't like it. Maybe because you don't like it."

John thought for a moment. "Maybe you're right."

Mary smiled; her teeth were sunken in her gums. "Of course I'm right. I'm your mother."

John laughed. "And only you and my boss get away with talking to me like that."

John's phone started to vibrate in his pocket. He had remembered to turn it to vibrate mode for the wedding. He glanced at the caller ID and saw that it was an Albertan number. He didn't recognize it, so he put it back in his pocket and let it go to voicemail.

John had been avoiding Calgary ever since he had returned. He had written two articles since his last meeting with Andrea Drashkov. One had been about George Hopkins' death, and the other had been a piece about Andrea. John had questioned the hospital staff about the red-haired man who had pretended to be a doctor but he had gotten nowhere. One of the nurses had called security on him and threatened a restraining order. John hadn't gone back after that. The whole experience had left a bitter taste in his mouth, and he was happy to move on to other stories.

Despite trying his best to ignore Nerno, he learned that the police had opened an investigation into fraud allegations, but John knew from experience that those investigations were complex and could take months, and sometimes years, to complete. He wasn't very hopeful that anything would come of it, but he knew what damage the investigation would have on the public perception of Nerno, and John was surprised that the company hadn't filed for bankruptcy yet. David Kahn wasn't going to give up on his company, that was for sure.

John supposed that he could have stuck around and collected enough material to write a book, but he was tired of the whole production, tired of the players who all seemed fake, each in his or her own little way, trying to spin the truth to their advantage.

Charles Dana had told John that Vince Parkerson had been offered a part-time job at the *New York Times*, without benefits. It didn't have much glamour or glitz associated with it, but, John supposed, it was better to end your career working for the *Times* than in Calgary.

For some time, John had tried actively hating Vince, but in the end he just felt that it was too much work. John, like Charles and like Vince, was drawn to the excitement of news like an alcoholic to booze, and none of them could resist a big story.

John, who had never worked in New York, but who went there whenever he could, felt the kinetic energy as soon as he stepped off of the plane at JFK Airport. He ultimately understood Vince being drawn there, to the magnetism, the myth, the magnitude, the magic of the Big Apple.

In the end, the board of directors had decided not to pursue any legal suits against Parkerson. Charles said that it would have been too expensive, with no positive outcome. John had responded to the news by telling Charles that the board had lost its teeth. Charles had just shrugged and said that everybody was scared for the future of the paper.

As for the potential sale of the newspaper, Charles wasn't saying anything. John had tried every source that he could think of, but nobody was biting. The uncertainty was killing John, and he wished that he was more in the loop.

John and his mother got to the end of the garden, where they stumbled on a small line of gravestones, half hidden among the shrubbery. John and Mary stood silently looking down at the names, reading them one after another, and John thought of his trek out to Wreck Beach and the graves that stood there.

At times like these, John supposed, most people would wonder what sort of people the dead had been: good, happy, ordinary, depressed, indifferent, but John had seen too many graves in his lifetime to be able to think much more of them than as bodies and lost souls.

John turned to his mother, ready to go back, but there was something in the old woman's intense gaze that prevented him from disturbing her thoughts. What was she thinking about? Her own oncoming demise? Or was she thinking about how she had lost a husband and nearly her only son, twice, to bullets?

Eventually John prodded his mother, and they turned and shuffled in slow steps back to the doorway of the church.

They had several hours to kill before the reception at the Portuguese Club located on Commercial Drive, and so they decided to go for high tea at the Georgia Hotel. John and his mother usually followed this tradition once a year for Mary's birthday, but Mary had suggested it as an extra treat. John, who preferred coffee to tea any time of the day, relented.

As they were driving, John's phone rang again. It was the same Albertan number as before. Somebody wanted to talk to him badly. He glanced at it before shoving it back into his pocket.

"You want to answer that?" Mary asked.

"It's against the law to talk on your cell phone and drive," John said.

Mary looked out the window, distracted. "I always figured this day would come."

"What do you mean? What day?"

"The day Hayden got married again. She's too beautiful to stay single."

"There are lots of beautiful women out there who choose to be single."

Mary made a clucking sound with the tip of her tongue. "No woman chooses to be single. That's just something they say to pretend they are happy."

"Don't be so old fashioned, Mother."

Neither of them said anything for a while. John decided to turn on the radio, and they listened to the news, but the words seemed to garble together. Mary was staring out of the window, watching the stucco houses go by.

They arrived at the hotel and were seated in the corner by a tall Japanese waiter who moved in the sharp, definitive movements of somebody who was proficient in his job.

They ordered the tea, and some cake to go with it.

"You look well," Mary remarked suddenly. "You've lost some weight."

"I've been trying to exercise more," John said.

"How's that going?"

"Slowly," John admitted. He had been restricting his alcohol intake ever since he had gotten back from Calgary, and he knew that that probably had something to do with his weight loss.

John had called the Calgary Police several times to see if they had opened an investigation into George Hopkins' death but each time he had been rebuffed. The police refused to believe it was a homicide.

The waiter brought the tea and the cake with much pomp. John drank his tea black while Mary poured cream and some honey into hers. She then dipped the cake into her drink and took a bite, sitting back, fully satisfied.

Mary talked about her friends at the bingo hall and the politics at her church. John only half listened, his mind wandering to the mysterious caller. He guessed that it was Andrea Drashkov trying to lure him with an unknown number, trying to persuade him to write another positive article about her. John stubbornly refused to check his messages.

John went to the washroom, and when he was walking back to the table his phone rang for a third time. This time he decided to answer it, but there was no answer on the other side.

"Who is this?" John asked, getting annoyed. "Hello?" He thought that he heard the sound of choked sobs.

"What's going on?" John asked, now alarmed.

Finally a voice managed to say something, but it was raspy and unclear.

"I'm sorry, I didn't understand."

"I said she's . . . gone."

"What do you mean gone?"

"I mean she's dead."

"Dead? Who is dead?"

"Sheila. She's gone."

John's heart stopped and his back stiffened. He couldn't speak for what seemed like an eternity. "You mean Sheila McKinnon?"

"Yes."

John was suddenly back in his old family living room with the ugly yellow curtains and the brown suede rug. His mother was sobbing deeply, her face buried into the cushions of their couch. John had been so shocked that he just stood in the doorway, unable to move, every part of his body numb.

He had never in his life seen the tough Scottish woman cry. When she finally realized that he was standing there, she raised her body, as if by superhuman will, and looked straight into his large eyes and told him that his father had just died.

Everything after that changed.

John was called back to the present by the voice on the other side of the phone.

"Hello?"

John shifted the phone to his left hand. "Sorry . . . who is this?"

"Mathew McKinnon."

"How did it happen?"

"Carbon monoxide."

John leaned his back against the wall. He couldn't believe it. It couldn't be true. He felt that his jaw was stuck together.

A woman in a blue dress jostled John slightly as she made her way to the bathroom. She didn't look back at John or make an apology, and John felt like yelling at her. How could she be so insensitive? But instead he controlled himself and tried to focus.

"Carbon monoxide? What do you mean?" John asked.

"She killed herself . . . in her car."

John thought back to the last conversation he had had with her, how he had ignored her pleas for help. Could he have done something to prevent it? Could he have been a little more understanding?

His head was beginning to throb. He buried his face in his hands. "Any note or anything like that?" he asked.

There was a long pause. "No, no note. She just hadn't been herself since she lost her job and then Nerno threatened legal action and it just became a huge mess."

"Wait a moment. She lost her job? What sort of legal action?"

"Oh, I don't know. Something about 'proprietary information'. Of course it was all bullshit. They wanted to make her life as miserable as hell. After several meetings with lawyers she grew really depressed, and for long periods of time she wouldn't come out of her room."

"I'm so sorry, Matt." His apology seemed to waken some feeling inside Matt, who had seemed, up to now, dulled of any emotion. "You're sorry? You bet you're sorry! You did this to her. You fucking abandoned her!"

"Abandoned her? How did I abandon her? She made her own choices. We had an agreement, which she broke."

"Fuck you," Matt said, hanging up.

John stood staring at his phone for a moment before he decided to phone Andrea Drashkov. He thought that he had better call her before he became too angry to talk to her.

"What a pleasant surprise," Andrea said, when she picked up. "I thought you had forgotten about us over here."

"Why did you fire Sheila?"

There was a pause on the other side of the phone. "Because she wasn't doing her job," Andrea said. Her light, flirty tone had disappeared, and was replaced by the cold business voice.

John bit his lip, struggling to remain calm. "You know she killed herself?"

"Yes, so I heard. Tragic. Seems like a waste of life." Her voice had changed again into a mixture of remorse and resilience.

John took a deep breath. "You knew she was leaking information to me. That's why you fired her."

"No, you're wrong. I had no idea she was doing that. She made a series of bad judgments. That is why she was fired."

"Then why sue her? Firing her wasn't enough revenge?"

"John, you have the wrong idea. It was David's idea, not mine. I shouldn't be telling you this, but I was against it. Apparently she stole some documents before she left, and threatened to give them to Chevron if she didn't get a larger severance package."

"I don't believe you. You're lying," John said. He looked around, realizing that some of the restaurant patrons were giving him strange looks, but he just stared defiantly back at them, daring them to say something. Nobody challenged him. Not even the waiters.

"No, I don't think so," Andrea said. "She made the bed and she laid in it."

"I'm not going to let you get away with this," John said, his voice trembling with anger.

"Get away with what? You can't prove anything. The police won't be able to either. We'll dig our heels in, just as we've always done."

John hung up. He struggled to keep upright. His legs felt invisible. Sheila's death was beginning to sink in. It was his fault and he knew it.

John, I'm scared. I don't know what to do, she had told him.

What had he done? Nothing. He had left her unprotected. A deep penetrating sense of shame overwhelmed him, and he knew that it would be with him for the rest of his life.

Somehow David Kahn and Andrea Drashkov had figured out that Sheila was his source and had fired her. Perhaps Vince Parkerson had told Nerno about Sheila.

"There you are."

John looked up and saw his mother standing there. He had completely forgotten about her. She was supporting herself with one hand on an empty chair. "I thought you had walked out on me," she said. "I know you don't like tea much but surely you can bear it for one afternoon."

"No, Mom. I'm still here."

"Is everything all right?" Mary asked.

John rubbed his eyelids. "No, it's not at all."

The Nightmares

T HE RED AND BLACK COLUMNS of thick, dark smoke rose from the fire and bloomed over the dark, starless night. The smell of ash and burning flesh filled the stifling air. John looked around, not understanding what was happening, not recognizing where he was. He saw sandy-coloured, shabbily built houses lined up on a narrow dusty path, not really even a road.

John suddenly noticed about twenty yards away that there was a flipped-over Lamborghini. Had it always been there? John couldn't tell. He suddenly realized that the smoke was coming from the car. Was there anybody in there? Was somebody in danger?

John ran towards the car, but there was nobody inside. It was empty. Where had the driver gone? And why had the Lamborghini flipped? John searched his mind. He had the sensation that it was on the tip of his tongue. He knew the answer somewhere in his brain. He just couldn't retrieve it.

He paused to wipe the sweat away from his forehead and neck. He then went in search of the driver to see if he or she was all right. He circled around the car, but there were no clues as to the whereabouts of the driver. As he turned, a woman appeared before him. She hadn't been there before, John was certain.

Her clothes were all tattered and blackened. Her blouse had disintegrated and her heavy breasts hung out, exposed, yet she didn't even seem to notice or care. She had long dark hair matted to her dark angular face, obscuring her features, but even so, John recognized her immediately.

It was Amira, the teenage girl who had been gang-raped and killed in Iraq. A girl from the past. A girl he had never really known.

John ran to her and took her by her bare shoulders.

"What happened?" he asked.

"You killed her," she replied, in thickly accented English.

"What do you mean? Killed who?" John asked.

"You killed her," she said again.

She didn't seem to feel any pain from her burns.

"But Amira, I didn't kill anybody," John said, holding her close to him. He could feel her breath against his neck. Her heart against his chest. *You're alive*, he wanted to say. *I've saved you!*

"You should have protected her. You had a duty, as a journalist."

She made her bed and she laid in it, Andrea had told him.

"I know," he cried. "I know, I know."

John woke up in a sweat. He looked around his Gastown apartment. The heavy shadows cut across the room like thick brushstrokes.

He put his feet on the cold hardwood floor and went to the bathroom. His urine hit the side of the bowl and trickled down. He flushed the toilet and washed his hands. He flipped on the light, wincing at the sudden brightness.

He stared at himself in the mirror, trying to remember the last time that he had dreamed of Amira. It must have been a couple of years at least.

As John looked at himself, the details of last night's debacle came back to him. Foolishly he had gone back to the reception, where he had proceeded to get incredibly drunk. It ended with a big climactic scene and Hayden yelling at him.

"You're ruining my wedding. Take a taxi home," she said.

"What about Mother?" John asked. "How will she get home?"

Paul stepped up beside Hayden, as if materializing from nowhere, and put an arm around Hayden's waist. He smiling warmly, but John thought that he detected something menacing in his demeanour. John wanted to point at him and yell at everyone—but Hayden most of all: *See? He's not as nice as he pretends to be.*

He's human like the rest of us. John knew that he should have felt somewhat victorious, revealing Paul as a mere mortal then, but he didn't. Not even close.

"Don't worry," Paul said. "I'll make sure she gets home safely."

John wanted to punch him. But he didn't. Instead he nodded and got the valet to hail him a cab. Ashamed and alone, he got in and watched the Portuguese Club disappear in the rear window as they pulled away, and with it, everything he loved.

The phone rang and John picked it up on the first ring. He was at work, searching the *New York Times* for Vince Parkerson's contact info. He wasn't surprised when he didn't find it. He had tried the Calgary number that Vince had given him, but it had been disconnected. He wasn't surprised about that either.

Eventually he emailed the general inquiry email address from a fake account. He wrote to say he had a story that Vince would be interested in and wondered if he could contact him directly.

"Is this John Webster?"

"Yes."

"My name is Lyle Ojagh. I'm returning your call."

John, who was only half listening, focused. The name sounded vaguely familiar but he couldn't place it.

"I'm sorry, who are you?"

"I'm from Lynne Mechanical Forensics," Ojagh said. There was another pause and then Ojagh added: "I'm in charge of the crash involving George Hopkins."

John remembered phoning and leaving a message, but that was a couple of weeks ago. He didn't actually expect a call back. "Yes, excuse me."

"No problem," Ojagh said. "I realize it has taken me a while to get back to you. I'm sorry."

John shifted in his seat, taking out his notepad. "No, don't be sorry. I'm glad you called."

"Yes, well . . . by coincidence I had just finished reading your book about Thomas Ronkin over Christmas."

John smiled to himself. Thomas Ronkin was a Vancouver serial killer that John had written about earlier in his career. Books didn't only provide him with a much needed secondary income, but could also add a little more credibility.

"Have you found the cause of the crash?"

"Well, not exactly. It was probably the result of a combination of black ice, speed, and the front airbags failing to deploy, resulting in Mr. Hopkins suffering severe head trauma," Ojagh said, his voice taking on an official tone.

"How come the airbags didn't deploy?"

"The side airbags came out, but the front one failed to. It looks like there was a manufacturing defect with the crash sensor. It didn't detect the impact. We will know more once Lamborghini does their own tests."

"Could the sensor have been disabled?"

John could hear Ojagh sigh. "Not easily, and not without a great understanding of Lamborghini manufacturing. I know what you're thinking. I read the newspapers, Mr. Webster, but what you are suggesting is highly improbable. I don't believe the safety mechanisms were tampered with. Lamborghinis are highly specialized machines, unlike most other cars, and not a lot of mechanics service them."

John frowned. He didn't want to antagonize the only man who'd had the decency to call him back. "I'm just trying to cover all the basics. I didn't mean to offend you. It's just my job, you understand."

"Of course. I didn't mean to rant like that," Ojagh said, actually sounding remorseful.

John searched his notes frantically, but couldn't think of a good question to ask—his head still hurt from last night's drinking—so instead he said, "What else can you tell me about the crash? What speed was Mr. Hopkins going at?"

"It's very hard to tell speed before impact because the variable snow and ice made it impossible to come up with a reliable co-efficient of friction."

"Co-efficient? What's that?"

"It's a number given to a certain substance. For example, in the snow we chose .20 but I'm not really happy with that. We also had trouble selecting and measuring the skid.

"The crush profile studies, which we use to estimate speed of impact, suggest a pre-impact speed of seventy miles an hour, but none of our studies have involved Lamborghinis before. In the end, all I have is a guess, I'm afraid."

"You examined the brakes?"

"Yes. We did tests on them and they were working well within the safety code."

"Do you think Lamborghini will do a recall?"

"It's not really my place to say, Mr. Webster. I'm sure Lamborghini will make up their minds once they do their own tests."

"But don't you make recommendations?"

"Sure, but we have no power to enforce any recalls."

"I really appreciate your information, Mr. Ojagh. Would it be possible to send me a copy of your report?"

"I'm sorry but it's confidential. I really can't."

"It will be for background information purposes only, I promise. I just want to make sure everything I write is accurate. It will be very damaging if people believe something false, don't you agree?"

Ojagh hesitated. "I don't know."

"I promise nobody will know I have it," John said.

You promised you would protect me, Sheila had said. Her voice echoed from the back of his mind.

"Okay. I'll email it to you as long as it doesn't get back to me."

"It won't. One last question. Do you still have the car or have you sent it back to Lamborghini already?"

"We have it until the end of the week and then we're shipping it back. Why?"

"I don't know, just in case I have a few more questions," John replied. He knew that once Lamborghini got the car he would never get any answers.

John gave Lyle Ojagh his email and ended the call. He waited until the email came through about a minute later, and then printed the report out. It was twelve pages long and didn't shed much illumination on the subject matter. John read the paragraph about the airbag twice, but the report was just cold, hard facts and didn't speculate on why the airbags didn't deploy.

The last couple of pages were pictures of Hopkins' Lamborghini. John studied them closely. The high-tech car had been reduced to a small metallic box.

Another photo showed the inside of the car. The windshield was broken, bits and pieces scattered across the dashboard and seat. As Ojagh had said, the side airbag had deployed, but not the front one. There was a close up shot of the steering wheel.

John filed the report away with a sigh. He was beginning to doubt himself. Perhaps he had just seen a resident coming from George Hopkins' hospital room. Perhaps he was just too embarrassed to report Hopkins' death and he left him for one of the nurses to find.

John opened up his fake email address and saw that the *New York Times* had emailed him back with a Yahoo email account for Vince Parkerson. John sent him a carefully worded email asking if he knew that Sheila was dead, and asked how Nerno had figured out that Sheila was their source.

As he was typing the email, his cell phone rang, but he decided to ignore it and continue with his email. He finished typing and sent the message off, hoping that Vince would help him.

John's phone rang again in his pocket and this time he answered it. The caller ID said that it was Hayden phoning, but why would she be phoning him?

"Where are you?" Byron demanded as he answered.

"What do you mean?"

"You forgot, didn't you?"

A moment of panic seized John, as only a dressing-down from your child could do. "What was I supposed to do?"

"Mom's away on her honeymoon, remember? You're supposed to drive me to school."

John remembered vaguely promising Hayden to take Byron to school, but they had never confirmed a time. Or had they? Why hadn't she phoned to remind him? Was she still angry at him for his behaviour at the reception?

"Okay, I'll be there in fifteen minutes," John said,.

"Forget it. I'll be late. I'll get Belinda to drive me."

John didn't want to miss an opportunity to spend some time with his son. "Belinda? Who's Belinda?"

"She's Paul's mother. She's staying at the house while Mom and Paul are gone."

Why was Paul's mother looking after Byron? What did he know of this woman? "No, I'll be there soon," John said.

Byron hesitated. "Fine. I only have P.E. first block anyway."

"Great, see you soon," John said, hanging up.

John collected his jacket and shut down his computer. He felt that Hayden had done it on purpose, to drive a wedge between him and his son.

Flora, the blonde receptionist, looked up and smiled as John passed her by. She was in her late forties and had large black-rimmed glasses. She had been with the newspaper for twenty-five years.

"Hot story?" she asked, as John impatiently waited for the elevator.

"No, just going to go pick up my son."

"You have a son? I didn't know that."

John stared at her, unsure of how he should respond. Luckily he was saved from making any sort of comment by the opening of the elevator doors.

John met Byron outside of their old house. It was a beautiful olive-green colour, with hedges surrounding it, and an ornate stone walkway.

Byron plonked his small body into the passenger seat, putting his backpack on his lap. He didn't greet John with a smile or a hello.

"When are you going to get a new car, Dad?"

John forced a smile. "When I get a raise."

"And when will that be?"

John thought about the negotiations to sell the newspaper off. "Tell me about Belinda," he said.

"I think you need a new job."

"How long is Mom gone for?"

"Two weeks."

"Am I driving you to school every day?"

"Look, you don't have to. I'm perfectly capable of taking the bus, or Belinda can drive me."

"I didn't mean it like that. I'm sorry."

"It's fine, Dad. Thanks for picking me up."

John glanced over at Byron. He was still staring straight ahead at the road, refusing to look at his father.

"How's school going?"

Byron sighed and he shifted in his seat, relaxing a little. "I don't know."

"What do you mean you don't know?"

"I just don't see the point. It's all bullshit."

"Don't swear, Byron."

"Why not? Everybody else does."

"Only people who can't express themselves properly swear," John said, suddenly realizing that he sounded more and more like his own father. How often had John Senior lectured him on swearing and the proper usage of the English language?

Byron leaned over and turned the radio to a hip-hop station. "Why do you always listen to the news anyway? Don't you ever get bored of it?"

"What do you want to be when you grow up, Byron?"

"Really, Dad?"

John frowned. "Really what?"

"We're having this conversation now?"

"Why not? Is there a better time?"

"I want to be a writer, okay? When I turn sixteen I'm dropping out."

"You can't drop out. What would your mother say? She would kill both of us. You need an education."

"You've said yourself education is useless. On numerous occasions."

John bit his bottom lip. He didn't think that his words would be used against him. He should learn to keep his opinions to himself around Hayden and Byron.

"What are you going to be? A journalist?"

"I don't know. Maybe."

"There won't be any jobs by the time you graduate."

"If you're trying to persuade me not to drop out it's not going to work. I've made up my mind."

They arrived at the school. John pulled into the driveway and Byron pulled on the handle to get out, but John put an arm on his shoulder.

"Wait a moment, Byron. I want you to seriously consider your education. The world is changing fast and an education is the only way to keep up."

Byron stared at John with hard eyes, his lips pursed in an intimidating frown, making John think that he would make a good journalist after all.

"I have to go, Dad, I'm late."

"Okay, but think about it."

John watched Byron hop out of the car and saunter in his pre-teen walk up the cement stairs to the school, and disappear behind the large brown doors. The school was big and boxy, built in the Victorian style, John supposed, to give it some authority in the modern cyber world.

John leaned his head against the head rest, staring out at the landscape, feeling groggy and ill-equipped for domestication. It was hard to keep the self-loathing at bay.

The road leading up to the school was peaceful and quiet. John could hear traffic far away. The gloomy sky was an overcast grey. The playground was empty and littered with wrappers and other garbage. Nobody was around, and to John it seemed a little melancholy. Schools were supposed to be surrounded by carefree children laughing and running and playing. A hive of the most innocent minds, unbothered by the noisy, troublesome world that lurked just beyond the school's borders.

John turned and looked next door. There was an after-school daycare building, a shack really, that looked like it had been built by early Quakers. A small, lush park stood adjacent. It was empty except for a lone dog walker throwing a tennis ball for a jumpy brown Lab.

It was a good place to sit and think, John realized. He imagined himself being a stay-at-home dad. Driving Byron to school every day. Other dads did it, why couldn't he?

John remembered when Byron was six or seven and he'd asked, "Why do you take care of people?"

John had been taken aback. "What do you mean?"

"Well, in your stories you always write about people who need to be taken care of."

John had laughed because he didn't know what to say. He'd picked Byron up and tickled him, distracting him enough to forget his many questions about life and purpose.

John started the car. The engine rippled to life and brought John back to the present.

He slowly made his way back to the office, parking in the underground parking lot.

Was it his job to look after people? Should he have looked after Sheila more? Did he have to look after her family? Was he nothing but a glorified babysitter?

He sat back at his computer and opened the file that he had on Nerno. As he was doing so, he saw a group email sent to the entire office from Charles Dana, saying there would be a meeting at four o'clock. Attendance was mandatory, it stated.

Charles Dana never sent emails to all the staff. John knew that it could only mean one thing: that the newspaper had been sold. He wondered what it would mean to his future. Would he still have a job? The first thing the new owners would do would be to eliminate the high-salaried positions.

John felt almost nothing at all. No remorse, no sorrow, no loss. His destiny, it seemed, was out of his control. So instead of dwelling on it, John reviewed all the information that he had about Nerno, to see if he had missed anything. He knew that he had a good story about George Hopkins' Lamborghini and his death at the hospital, but he wanted something more, something that could put David Kahn and Andrea Drashkov in prison.

John had learned to keep all his notes very organized over the years. In the Nerno file, he had subfolders with the names of the people he had interviewed as either an mp3 file or a Word document, with a couple of notes which he had transcribed from his notepad.

John had typed the letter "x" for Sheila's file but now replaced it with "Sheila McKinnon" since there was no need to keep her name secret anymore.

Downloading an mp3 onto his computer was a new thing for him, and usually he had to get one of the interns to do it for him.

John didn't find anything helpful in the files, but he wasn't surprised.

He checked the email account that he had messaged Vince Parkerson from, but he hadn't replied. John realized that he would distance himself as much as possible from the *Daily Globe*.

Next John searched the Internet for information about Nerno, and he found an article in the *New York Times* by Vince Parkerson. The headline read:

> "Despite worthlessness of Nerno stock,
> CNOOC is still interested in purchase."

John read the article, but by the end the question, still, was why the China National Offshore Oil Company would want to buy what was, essentially, a worthless company. John looked at the stocks and confirmed Nerno's stock price: a pathetic seventy-two cents.

He grabbed his phone and called up Mindy Rocher, the geologist consultant. The secretary put her through.

"Mr. Webster, you've come across some more interesting documents, I assume?"

"No, Ms. Rocher, I need some help understanding something."

"I will do my best."

"Why does CNOOC still want to buy Nerno?"

Rocher laughed. "Are you asking my opinion or do you just want me to confirm your own?"

"I think CNOOC wants that drill technology."

"I wouldn't think they would be willing to pay eighteen billion for it, but they might pay a couple of million."

"Is that possible?"

"Sure," Rocher said.

"You spent some time in China. What do you think CNOOC is doing?"

"I don't know. I don't presume to know what the executives are thinking."

John pressed on. "If I was putting a gun to your head."

"Well," Rocher hesitated. "I would assume CNOOC wants the technology. You must remember CNOOC is owned by the Chinese government, so if this technology is as ground-breaking as Nerno claims, then the buyout wouldn't just give CNOOC a significant competitive advantage, it would give the entire country of China one for the next fifty years or so. If you think about it, this buyout might secure China's spot as the world's next superpower."

"Thanks, Ms. Rocher. You have been most helpful."

That night John had the same nightmare that he had dreamt the previous night. He played it out like a stage actor working his way through his nightly performance. He woke around two-thirty in the morning, knowing that more sleep was out of the question and so he turned on the television instead.

CNN, his nightly drug of choice, was covering an election down in Texas. John watched for a while, but he started to crave a drink, something to numb his overactive mind. He hadn't kept any alcohol in his apartment for months, and was thankful that he had dumped everything out.

After a couple of hours, John took some sleeping pills and went back to bed. He stared up at the jagged shadows on the wood-slatted ceiling, which seemed to take on mysterious forms. He folded his hands tightly together and waited for the pills to take effect, but he felt no drowsiness.

He thought of the colourful images on CNN, and the shadows and the apartment lights around him all took on the shape of Sheila McKinnon. It came as no surprise to John that Sheila would visit him in the shadows, in the state of half sleep and half wakefulness.

She was just one in a long line of women that he had failed. Hayden, Amira, Michelle . . . there were others without names, only faces. Ghosts upon the walls.

Was there no escape from them? No peace? John always thought it was strange that when he was in the middle of war the nightmares ceased to exist, as if his psyche made a deal with itself—a living hell instead of a night-time one. What sort of defence mechanism was that?

Sheila had asked him once why the right thing was so hard to do.

Because the people who do the right thing get punished for it, John should have told her.

But the people who abandon the righteous get punished too. She had called him, asking for his help, and he had ignored her. Yes, the living were punished too.

John knew that there was really only one recourse. The instruction manual was clear. John thought that it was strange how the future could be so carefully laid out.

John had tried to escape once, but his conscience hadn't let him. It had beaten him again and again into submission. It was once again reacting, telling him to stop running, stop hiding.

This time he could do something. He could take the plunge and not drown. In the deep, he knew what would be there waiting for him.

Sheila's ghost staring back at him.

Calgary Again

JOHN LOOKED OUT OF THE window as Calgary came into view through the white clouds. (*Who is now taking Byron to school?* John thought to himself). The Bow River meandered through the centre of the town, and the great buildings huddled close together like frozen statues. The city was colourless, stoic-looking and icy. John had checked the forecast, determined to be better prepared this time. The cold front was still hovering around Calgary like a cloud of locusts.

The roar of the engine reverberated through the cabin. John enjoyed some coffee and a sandwich while he read several magazine articles he had picked up about China. One was about the emerging economic power of the country, and the other was about how human rights abuses were being unchecked by Western powers.

In the morning, John had knocked on Charles Dana's office and told him that he was going back to Calgary.

"I'm glad you're going back," Charles said. "I think it's the right thing to do."

John let out his breath, unaware that he was holding it. "I was afraid you would be against it."

"You know if they decide to break up this paper it will be kind of like having a death in the family. I'm not sure I'll be able to survive it."

"What will you do?"

"Oh, I don't know. Matilda has been bugging me to move back to New York. I'm sure somebody would hire me."

"You don't ever think of retiring, do you?"

Charles shook his head. "No. I don't like sports and I don't know anything about plants."

John just nodded. "It's funny. It makes you think, doesn't it? I sort of decided last night I would go back to Afghanistan if I got laid off."

Charles sat back in his chair and looked over at John, trying to mask his surprise. "Really?"

"I know I swore I would never go back but . . . I don't know. I keep thinking why not? I don't really have anything to lose, and I want to see if things have changed over there. If things have got better or worse."

"You should be concentrating on Calgary first. Who knows what is going to happen?"

John stuck his hand out awkwardly, and after a moment Charles took it. "If this is it," John said, "I just want to thank you for everything."

Charles nodded. "My pleasure."

John left Charles' office and decided to stop by Michael Chu's desk. Michael was wearing a light blue suit, looking dapper and at ease in his large body. He was intently studying the stock market on his computer when John approached.

"You heard anything new on Nerno?" John asked.

Michael shook his head. "The police are looking into charges, but nobody seems overly optimistic."

"You have any contacts I could speak to? Know anybody in the Calgary police?"

Michael shook his head. "No, sorry."

"No distant cousin, long lost relative?"

Michael smiled. "I'm from Toronto, remember?"

John sighed. He thought as much. "Thanks anyway."

"So what do you think of this sale?"

John was tired of talking about it. "You're the financial guy. You figure it out."

Michael nodded, not really paying attention. "I feel like an idiot," he said.

John had no time to comfort Michael Chu, or anybody else for that matter. Michael could always find a job. He was intelligent, rich, smart and good with money. The world needed people like him to deal with their bank accounts. Nobody, on the other hand, needed a burnt out war correspondent.

Michael, however, didn't seem to catch onto John's disinterest and continued. "All those favourable interviews I gave those bastards and all the while they were lying through their teeth. Just a month ago I gave Nerno a buy rating."

John didn't say anything. Part of him wanted to tell Michael that everybody had gotten it wrong, but part of him also didn't want to let him off the hook so easily. Next time Michael interviewed somebody, hopefully he would do his due diligence first. The experience would make him a better journalist and less of a banker.

"I should have known, John. I should have known," Michael said, shaking his head, his voice shaking with emotion.

John looked up at him. "I shouldn't have been beaten to the story. We all screw up."

"I heard about that. It wasn't your fault."

"Whether it was my fault or not it happened."

"So what are you going to do now?"

"I'm flying back to Calgary this afternoon."

"Let me come with you. I can help you."

John paused. Michael Chu probably knew his way around the business world better than he did, but still his instincts still told him no. Aside from the fact that he had been betrayed by Vince Parkerson and felt distrustful, when John had been in the Middle East a lot of freelance reporters had wanted to tag along with him, the surly veteran. Most of the time he had said no then, as well. One time, in Iraq, he had given in to a jaunty kid with big knees and elbows. In the first hour, he had been shot in the stomach. John had rushed him to the hospital. The doctor saved the kid's life, but he would never be so jaunty again.

"Well, I'm on my way to the airport right now," John said, collecting his notepad and standing up.

"That's fine. I'll just catch a later flight."

"Don't you have other assignments?"

"Of course I do, but Nerno is a big story and nobody knows them like I do."

"I know they have a few reporters working on it already. I'm not sure if they need another."

"If you don't want me working with you, just say so."

"It's just the thing with Vince and . . . it's been a long time since I worked with a partner."

His last partner had been William Russell, back when he had worked in television. That had been a long time ago.

"Maybe it's time to try it again."

John put a hand on Michael's shoulder. "I'm sorry Michael, but at heart I'm a lone wolf."

John took a taxi to the airport. He had phoned Belinda and asked her if she would drive Byron to school for the next couple of weeks. She seemed delighted by the prospect.

John checked in and went through security. He remembered when it had been less of a chaotic production. Now airports had gigantic X-ray machines and other large scanners, operated by unsmiling guards who were either taught to be as gruff and as rude as possible, or just hated their jobs and, by extension, their lives so much that they couldn't possibly ruffle up a moment of politeness for the travellers who were going on to new and exciting adventures.

John longed for the days before 9/11, when the world was innocent, naive and unaware. John had grown up with the vague knowledge of nuclear weapons, and that those weapons were in the hands of the disintegrating enemy, but the threat of nuclear winter had seemed to fade and be forgotten by the next generation, and even John forgot about the fear and the bomb shelters in his friend's yard and the school drills he had been forced to participate in.

Before 9/11, it seemed that the possibility of mass death and destruction was still just a notion pushed back into the collective consciousness. It took the concentrated efforts of one crazed Al-Qaeda leader and his cohorts to push the possibility into actuality.

Would this phase pass too? Would fear again morph into a new threat, yet unseen in this increasingly complex, competitive world?

A security guard asked John for his passport, and he was aroused from his daydream. The world of John's youth had disintegrated, and with it John's own unsophisticated, sophomoric view of it.

John passed through all of the checkpoints without trouble and got to the gate. There he watched through the window as planes took off and landed, going to all parts of the world. The sky was cloudless and formless, and if he concentrated enough he almost felt like that little boy going on his first adventure.

"Hi Madeline, you still in town?" John asked. He was waiting at the baggage claim, watching the carousel trot suitcases around in a circle. He had phoned Madeline on a whim, not really expecting her to be there.

"Yes, I'm still here," she replied. "What happened to you? You just disappeared and then I heard you'd gone back to Vancouver."

"Yes, sorry, but I'm back. I just landed, actually, and was wondering if you have time to go for coffee?"

"I have an even better solution. Why don't I come pick you up from the airport? I didn't have any lunch and so I'm starving. We can have dinner together."

"That sounds fantastic, but I can meet you somewhere if it's too much trouble."

"No, it's okay. I've filed my story, and blogged, so I don't have much to do this evening anyway."

Madeline arrived in a Chevrolet. She was dressed in a red jacket and white capris, a colourful scarf wrapped around her neck. Her thick hair was braided down her back. They hugged, and John soon found himself telling her about Hayden's wedding. He felt better telling somebody about it.

"What do you feel like eating?" Madeline asked.

"I don't mind. I had a snack on the plane so I'm not all that hungry."

"It will be a surprise then." Madeline glanced at John, smiling briefly.

"Madeline, I need somebody inside the investigation. You know anybody?"

Madeline smiled. "Can we talk business over dinner? We have plenty of time."

Madeline took John to a placed called Emerald Garden Restaurant on 16th Avenue.

"I come here sometimes when I have a little bit of extra time," Madeline said, as they were seated.

"It reminds you of home?" John asked, smiling.

"No, not really, but if I squint and pretend, it's good enough."

They both laughed, and John remembered how he had enjoyed her laugh.

The waiter came and John let Madeline order two glasses of whiskey. She then briefly looked at the menu and ordered a couple of dishes.

As she handed the waiter the menus, she said, "I hope you don't mind sharing. It's not often that I actually get to eat with anybody."

"Don't you have some colleagues over here or something?"

Madeline shrugged, staring intently at her knuckles. "Not really. Mostly I'm by myself."

John decided to change the subject. "So I gather if you are still here covering the story then the China National Offshore Oil Company is still interested in purchasing Nerno."

"They seem to be, yes," Madeline said, cautiously.

"Why?"

"I'm not too sure, to be completely honest with you."

John studied Madeline closely, and instinctively he knew that she was holding back, but he didn't want to push it.

"Why are you back in town?" Madeline asked.

"You still want to work with me?" John asked, thinking of Michael Chu.

"Sure, if I can, but you have to help me out too."

"I want to talk to somebody with the Calgary police. You know anybody willing to go on the record?"

Madeline shook her head. "Sorry, John. I can't help you out there."

"Can't or won't?"

Madeline stuck her tongue to her top lip for a moment. "John, I would love to help you out but they have closed the bloody gates. I'm sorry."

John nodded and sat back. "My source committed suicide. Somehow Nerno found out who I was speaking to, and blackballed her. I suspect it was one of my former colleagues, Vince Parkerson, who told them."

"You want revenge? To even the score?"

John leaned forward, putting his elbows on the table. His thoughts were interrupted when the waiter put down two glasses of whiskey. The waiter smiled and left.

"I'm not too sure," he said finally. "It's kind of hard to explain."

"Try me," Madeline suggested.

"I guess I feel responsible."

"But you yourself said it was your former colleague who told Nerno. It was not your fault," Madeline said.

"Have you ever had a source commit suicide?"

Madeline shook her head. She seemed to want to say something, but instead she just stared into her glass of whiskey. John waited, wondering what she was imagining.

When she remained silent, John continued. "It's not revenge I want. It's justice. It's for the world to show me there is some sort of karma that eventually sets things right."

The waiter arrived with dinner. Madeline ate most of the food, while John just picked at it. Over dinner they talked about other things. John found himself talking about his time in Iraq and Afghanistan more openly than he had in a long time. He found that it was good talking about it to somebody who seemed to understand. She didn't interrupt, or ask him what it felt like to watch a head explode, and for that, John was grateful.

After they had finished dinner, they ordered more drinks.

"I don't think I've met a woman who holds her liquor as well as you do," John said, after about their fourth drink.

Madeline smiled. "I don't know whether I should be flattered or offended."

"It was meant to be a compliment."

"And you, John. You must get tired of all this travel."

John laughed. "I suppose. But I'm not so far away from home as you."

"Yes, I do miss it sometimes. It's only natural."

"When I was young, to be honest with you, I didn't miss it. Of course I told everybody how much I missed them and how I wanted to be home, but looking back on it, I think it was all lies."

"You're a liar?" Madeline exclaimed in mock surprise.

John smiled. "All the time."

Madeline laughed. "This whole industry seems like such a fraud sometimes."

John was too drunk to argue, so he just nodded. "Tell me . . . do you honestly not know why CNOOC is interested in Nerno?"

Madeline shrugged. "China is a large country. We have a big need for oil. Nerno has other assets that CNOOC is willing to pay for."

"Like what?"

"I don't know the details. But why are we talking about this now? You think getting me drunk will loosen my lips? You think I'm bloody holding out on you?"

"I'm just making conversation," John said, flashing his most innocent smile.

They spoke for another forty minutes, and at the end, Madeline insisted on paying the bill. "It's compliments of the great country of China," she said, smiling wryly.

"I think we should catch a cab," John said. "I don't think either of us are able to drive."

Madeline nodded. "Do you have a hotel booked?"

"No, I was just going to check into the Edmonds again."

"Well no need to waste money. I have a place at the Marriott. Why don't we share one?"

John hesitated. "Well . . . I don't know."

"Come on. Don't argue with me," Madeline said, taking John by the arm and walking with him to the front desk, where they got the hostess to call them a cab.

John looked out at the snow layered on the ground, and the icicles frozen to the tree branches like long glass tentacles. It had a Narnia-like beauty about it.

"How cold do you think it is outside?" John asked.

"It's minus fucking freezing," Madeline replied, laughing at her own joke.

The elevator doors closed, and Madeline pushed the button to take them to the sixth floor. They watched the lights ascend for a while and listened to the mechanical clinking of the elevator as it pulled them upward. Then Madeline turned towards John, not looking up into his eyes; he was grateful because he was scared of what he might find in them. She was breathing heavily and she smelled of whiskey.

John took a step towards her and put an arm around her waist. Madeline pulled him close and tilted her head back to be kissed. John pressed his lips against her, feeling her warmth and softness.

They parted briefly, but then Madeline pulled John against her, resting her head against his chest.

"You know, I'm not the person who you think I am," she mumbled into his armpit.

John laughed, because he couldn't think of anything else to do. "Are you Madeline Xiao for the *Beijing Star*?"

Madeline raised her head and looked into John's eyes for the first time since they had entered the elevator. "Yes, I am."

"Then what else is there to know?"

The doors opened and Madeline led John to her room. She unlocked the door and they stumbled into the darkness of the bedroom.

Madeline quickly disrobed. She had a miniature frame with small arms and legs. She wore plain cotton panties, and a white cotton bra that had been laundered one too many times. She smiled shyly at John, straightening up as if presenting herself for his inspection.

John felt embarrassed, so he kissed her and pushed her down on the bed. He took off his shirt. Madeline watched him intently, a small smile on the corner of her lips. He then hooked his forefingers into her panties, slid them down her smooth legs, and then buried his head in her crotch. He was suddenly overwhelmed by a cocktail of melancholy and grief, excitement and anticipation, longing and disgust. He didn't want to move from the warmth of her legs, the smell of her sweat.

"You sure this is okay?" John asked. "I mean . . ." His voice trailed off.

She looked up at him tenderly, running her hands through his hair, and seemed to read his mind. "Don't think about it," she whispered.

She ran her fingers enticingly over his body until she reached his pants.

They laid down on the bed together, grasping at each other. John kissed her stomach, her chest and neck. She moaned softly. John shifted his body on top of her. His movements were slow and tender, filled with an alcoholic haze. She smiled up at him, urging him on. Her thick dark hair spread out under her head like a flower against the white crispness of the pillow, and her nubby breasts cast small dark shadows on the rest of her body.

After they finished, John put his head down on the pillow. They didn't move or speak for a long time. The night was silent except for the sound of Madeline's soft breathing, her heart against his body.

John was suddenly exhausted. He closed his eyes, feeling the darkness collapse against his eyelids.

The Boardroom Meeting

ANDREA GLANCED AROUND THE ROOM and saw John sitting in the corner, sipping his coffee from a paper cup. He gave her a kind of half smile. He looked tired and dishevelled. His eyes were bloodshot and he was unshaven, his hair was like weeds sprouting out of his head at unnatural angles.

Andrea paused to look around the coffee shop. She was confused by the children's playpen in the corner where several kids were yelling and screaming, and several mothers were huddled, heads close together, probably telling each other motherly secrets.

"My God, were you run over by a dump truck on your way here?" Andrea said. She didn't move to sit down, and John didn't get up to greet her, so there was an awkward distance between them.

"I just need some coffee and I'll be okay," John said, wearily.

Andrea had been reluctant to meet John in the first place, but she needed an ally in the media, where she was taking a good thumbing. She needed to find out what he knew. However, she was already regretting having agreed to the meeting.

"I don't like this place," Andrea said. "Why did you insist we meet here?"

John responded with a shrug, but didn't say anything. Reluctantly Andrea slid into the seat opposite John, and then asked the question that had been bugging her since John had called her. "I don't understand. Why did you come back?"

"You saying I shouldn't have?"

"I don't have long. Can you buy a poor girl some coffee?"

"You can't be that poor."

"I sold my boat. I couldn't afford it anymore."

"Have the police questioned you?"

"Sure. A couple of times. They asked me all sorts of crazy questions."

"Did they ask you about Hopkins?"

"What does he have to do with anything?"

"He was murdered."

"You're being paranoid," Andrea said, glancing around the coffee shop.

"What did the police ask you?"

"They asked what I knew about Ko Chang. They subpoenaed my work files."

"I had nothing to do with it. The police won't find anything. The whole thing will be dropped. My predictions."

"My predictions are both you and David Kahn will be found guilty and go to jail."

Andrea stared hard at John. She could tell from his eyes that he didn't really believe it. Andrea decided to play it as though she had been intolerably wronged.

"I don't have to listen to this," she said, getting up from the table. John followed her.

"You know why I wanted to bring you here?"

This gave Andrea pause. She stopped and looked back at John. A kid screamed in the background. "What's so special about this place?"

"This was the first place Sheila and I met. This was the first time she gave me proof that there had been a cover up."

"If you have evidence of a cover up go take it to the police," Andrea said. "I'm tired of your games."

"I want you to see Sheila as something more than just an obstacle in your path. I want you to see her as a person"

Andrea pushed the door open. The cold air immediately hit her face, stinging her flesh. She had parked her Lamborghini directly out front. It sparkled in the October sunlight like the many faces of a diamond. She always loved the gawks she got, but lately, with the unwanted media attention, she got more dirty looks then envious ones. She might have to sell it and drive her truck, and the thought made her sad.

Andrea stopped walking and looked at John. She could tell that he was freezing, and she took great pleasure in watching him try to keep warm.

"Sheila McKinnon was the author of her own demise. I'm not going to take blame for something that wasn't my fault."

Andrea opened the car door and climbed in. John got in the passenger seat beside her.

"What do you think you're doing?" Andrea demanded.

"I'm getting a ride with you."

"No you're not. Get out of my car. Don't you have your own car?"

"This is the same car Hopkins had," John said, looking around the interior.

"Yes, very observant. We got them as a bonus one year. Now get out. I have a meeting I need to go to."

"You'll just have to let me tag along," John said.

Andrea tried to calm herself. *I brought this on myself,* she thought.

"Fine," she said, pressing the button to start the engine, causing the whole car to erupt with vibration. "You ever driven in a Lamborghini before?"

"You sure this is safe?" John asked. "You're not worried?"

"You can get out anytime," Andrea said, releasing the brake and backing up.

"Tell me about Sheila's firing."

Andrea shrugged. "David came to me one day and said he had proof she was meeting with Chevron executives behind his back. I told him to fire her and he did. End of story."

"Does he usually do what you tell him?"

"No. He was already angry. He asked me what I thought he should do. We had to let a whole bunch of the staff go. She was either going to be fired or let go. We chose to make a statement."

"Did Kahn ever tell you how he knew she was meeting Chevron executives?"

"No, and I never asked. But what does that matter?"

"Are you still going to sell the company to the Chinese?"

Andrea shrugged again. "I don't know. We are still negotiating but we're keeping our options open."

John felt desperate and nowhere nearer the truth, so he asked, "Tell me about the new drill you've developed."

"When did you become so boring?"

"You think that is why the Chinese still want to buy Nerno?"

Andrea stared hard at John. "Why are you so certain George was murdered?"

"Somebody pretending to be a doctor walked in and took him off life support."

"That's crazy. The police would have told me if that was true."

Andrea pressed the gas pedal. The car sped up through the intersection. The world outside became a blur of colours. Another car let out a loud, prolonged honk. Andrea gave a girlish laugh and looked over at John. He was sitting with his back straight, his arms grabbing his knees. This only made Andrea laugh harder. She clutched the wheel harder and looked at the speedometer. They were going ninety kilometres an hour. Then, just as everything was disappearing behind them, things started to slow down in front of her. There was an almost superhuman clarity. She saw everything laid out. The pedestrians on the sidewalks, the cars driving by, the lampposts covered with frozen snow.

Before the next intersection she hit the brakes. The car skidded for a few seconds, there was a loud screech, and then the brakes kicked in and abruptly they came to a halt.

"See?" she said, letting out her breath. She looked over at John who, for once, seemed at a loss. She gave him her best smile. "What's the matter? Mr. War Correspondent can't handle a little speed?"

"What was the point in that?" John asked.

"To teach you a lesson."

John stared at her with his large, dark eyes. "How did Sheila take her firing?"

Andrea bit her lip, struggling not to show any emotion on her face. She knew that he had asked the question to throw her off, and it had worked well.

"Where do you want me to drop you off?"

"You still haven't answered my question."

"If you don't answer mine I'm just going to leave you right here."

"I'm staying at the Edmonds."

"I never spoke to Sheila after she was fired, but who takes firing well?"

"Do you know if she was hired anywhere else afterwards?"

"Look, John, I'm sorry for what happened to her, but if I had to make the same decision again I would do exactly the same thing. I had no idea you had been talking to her, and she had been leaking information to you, but it just reaffirms the initial decision."

"I can help you with your legal troubles."

Andrea turned to him. "How?"

"We don't need to be on opposite sides in this."

"John, you're a journalist. I'm a businesswoman. We're always going to be on opposite sides."

They arrived at the Edmonds Hotel and Andrea pulled up to the curb. For a moment Andrea didn't think that John would get out. He sat there and just glared at her. But a moment later he climbed out onto the sidewalk. She watched as he walked in the front entrance and then she sped to the office.

"Look, I don't think we should accept the offer. We still have a sizable field off in northern Canada. We already know it could be very lucrative," Andrea said.

She was sitting across from seven other board members on the top floor of the Nerno building. David Kahn was leaning back in his chair, his legs crossed. He seemed uncharacteristically nervous, and Andrea thought of how John had looked that morning.

This ordeal is taking its toll on everybody, Andrea thought.

"But profits are years away. We're not going to be able to sustain this company for that long. We have to sell, and the longer we wait, the lower the price will drop."

"No, we need more time to develop the prototype drill." Andrea leaned forward, staring at each board member in turn. "This was the Chinese plan from the beginning. They never wanted Ko Chang. They were always after the fields in the Mackenzie Valley and the prototype."

David Kahn seemed to be having small spasms. "What does it matter? This is the position we are in now. I don't know how I can make myself more clear; we don't have the capital to finish the year, let alone build the prototype."

"We will find it," Andrea said.

"How?" David exclaimed, rising slightly from his seat. "Nobody will touch us with a fifty-foot pole."

"Then let me buy out your stake. Two million and a half."

David snorted, sitting back down. "The Chinese are offering five. Why should I settle for half?"

"Because this way we still control the company. This is only a temporary setback. The oil up north is the future. China National Offshore Oil Company knows it. Why can't I convince you?"

"Andrea, I have a family I need to support. Kids who are in university."

"David, you need to trust me on this."

David didn't say anything for a while. He looked around at the other board members, who had remained silent. "What do you guys think?"

"We'll follow whatever you think, David," Ed Hurnbert said. He was the CEO of Cube Electronics and a close friend of David's. The other board members nodded in agreement.

Andrea tried to conceal her frustration. As long as David was leading the company, she had no hope of convincing them.

Andrea closed her eyes, wishing that the world would just go away and leave her in peace. Her head was buzzing with a mixture of alcohol and sleepiness. She was really drunk, she realized. How many glasses of wine had she had? A bottle's worth? More? She looked around for evidence, but there was only an empty glass on the coffee table.

She forced herself to rise ever so slightly, supporting her frame with one elbow, and looked out the window into the dark sky, the city lights in the distance like hundreds of fireflies. Andrea looked for the moon, but couldn't see it behind the clouds.

John had said George Hopkins had been murdered.

Whatever John printed would only further damage her reputation and that of the company. She had to protect herself.

Andrea sighed and looked around her apartment. She loved her home. It was so peaceful. She loved how she felt utterly secluded, yet was surrounded by an entire population. She felt like nothing could touch her, but she also knew that it was an illusion. She was very vulnerable.

She thought of the time that she had brought John up here. She had thought that she could use him, mold him, but now circumstances had changed. He was beginning to become a nuisance. She had other, bigger issues to deal with.

She reached for her phone and scrolled through her contacts until she found the number that she was looking for. She pressed the dial button and waited for the phone to ring.

A sleepy Patrick Oswald answered. It was almost 3 a.m. in the city that never slept, but Patrick knew to answer his phone when Andrea phoned. The amount of money that Nerno gave to Walker and Thompson excused any behaviour.

"Patrick, it's Andrea."

"What can I do for you, Ms. Draskhov?"

Andrea hesitated, realizing that her hands were moist with sweat. Was that from the alcohol or from nerves? Her mind went back to speeding in her car with John. She had felt nothing then. Why now?

"David said . . . you offer a special service."

There was a long pause on the other end. "Hold on," Patrick said.

Andrea could hear soft footsteps and the closing of a door. "Okay. What type of special service are you talking about?'

"David said the type you do for your special clients."

"I think I know what you mean," Patrick said. "Have you talked to David about this?"

"Yes, he's in the loop. Can you do it?"

"It requires an additional fee. This is not covered in your package."

"Understood. How much? I'll wire you the money first thing tomorrow."

Patrick told Andrea how much it would cost, but then hesitated. "You sure about this?"

Andrea sat up. The blood rushed to her head, and she began to see black spots in her vision, but they soon dissipated. "We've made the call. That's all you need to know."

"You'll need to wire it to another company. Three instalments. You got a pen?"

Andrea went to the kitchen. On the counter were two empty bottles of wine. At least that mystery was solved. She grabbed a pen and paper. Oswald gave her a numbered account listed in the Virgin Islands.

"Okay, who's the target?"

"A journalist named John Webster."

"You'll hear from us in a week," Oswald said, clicking off.

Andrea stood in the kitchen, not moving for a long time. Again the silence was the only thing present, but now, instead of being a source of comfort, Andrea dreaded it. All she could think was, *what have I done? What have I done? What have I done?*

Over and over again.

The Household

A N ELECTRIC FIRE WAS GOING in the other room, and it would have given the place a homely feel if it wasn't for the oppressive sorrow that hung over the entire household, sucking in the air like a large vacuum.

The dark mood tainted everything. It was evident from when John first stepped onto the porch. It was evident from the first hollow knock that resonated across the white yard. It was evident from John's first glance at Sheila's husband, Mathew McKinnon, who answered the door, from his dead eyes, from the "For Sale" sign hammered deep into the frozen ground.

"Yes? Can I help you?" Mathew asked.

It was the first time that John had seen Mathew up close. He was a man firmly settled into middle age; his blond hair was thin and wavy, and he had a ring of fat forming around his stomach. He had the large features of the ordinary suburban man who cared for little more than his job, his family, and having a few drinks on the weekend while watching football.

"My name is John Webster. I was wondering if I could have a couple of moments of your time?"

John hadn't phoned in advance, or even told anybody from the McKinnon family that he would be in Calgary, and he was nervous about the type of reception that he would get. But he never liked to give his interview subjects too much time to think about what they were going to say.

Mathew blinked and frowned. He probably thought that John was some sort of mirage, a phantom of his imagination. They stared at each other awkwardly. Neither one said anything.

The house was in the middle of the suburbs, along a flat road with large stucco housing on each side. It was a wealthy neighbourhood, with huge ash trees covered with frost and ice, and picket fencing surrounding each yard.

Everything was still and silent, and John couldn't see a living thing in the neighbourhood, but something lingered, only John wasn't sure what. Perhaps it was the lingering presence of the dead, so close to him, urging him forward. But it wasn't just Sheila, John somehow knew. It was George Hopkins and other ghosts too that John felt, souls from other assignments, other worlds and other times.

John couldn't help but feel that there were more deaths still to come, and he wondered who would be next and what would happen. The only way to know for sure would be to continue.

"You've caught me at a bad time, Mr. Webster," Mathew said. "I don't have time to talk."

"I won't take more than a moment of your time," John said. "Do you mind letting me in? I'm not used to the cold, and I'm freezing."

John didn't think that Mathew would relent, but he finally stepped aside, and without saying anything, led John into the kitchen.

John was surprised to find a group of people sitting around the kitchen table. They were slumped over like large sacks of potatoes. By the fridge a tall, strong man was leaning against the counter. He resembled Sheila so much that John knew he must be her son. He struggled to remember his name but couldn't. He looked so much like Sheila that John had a hard time meeting his eye.

Everybody turned to look at John as he entered. He struggled to smile at everybody and he found it a hollow attempt.

"Hi, my name is John Webster," he said.

"Who are you?" asked an elderly woman sitting at the table. She was small, her skin was dried and flaky.

"I'm a friend of Sheila's."

John never saw the boy coming. He took several athletic steps and within seconds was a foot away. He brought his fist back and punched John like a club brawler. He remembered then that the boy had won a scholarship for baseball. Only the slight turn of his head at the last moment prevented him from being knocked out cold.

The boy's fist landed hard on his cheek. The second punch smashed into John's jaw and he fell to his knees. John struggled to look up at the boy, his vision blurred, and he felt a warm liquid run down his chin.

"You son of a bitch," the boy cried.

John didn't move. Instead of the boy he saw Sheila. Instead of the boy's strong masculine tones, he heard Sheila's soft feminine voice.

"You son of a bitch." She was standing over him. Her small mouth frowned at him.

He didn't flinch as the third punch landed on his forehead with a loud crack. John fell to the floor, bracing his body with his hands.

"Son of a bitch."

John looked up at the lights and realized that he was lying back on a leather couch. He slowly shifted his body and looked around the room. Mathew was staring at him with a concerned look.

"You want me to drive you to the hospital? You want me to phone an ambulance?"

John felt his face with the tips of his fingers. It was already swelling. "I think I'm okay." He sat up. He was in a living room. Across from him was a television.

Mathew gave John a glass of water, which he took, but drinking it was painful. "I'm sorry about Kyle. He's taken his mother's death extremely hard."

"Do you mind if I use the bathroom?"

Mathew nodded, but then he looked uncertain. "You're not going to press charges or anything? I mean he's just a boy. He has his school . . ."

John got up. "It depends on how cooperative you are."

Mathew frowned, and John could see the disgust in his face, but he quickly covered it up. "Of course. I'll do anything you ask."

"I just want the same thing you want, Mathew." John's voice felt croaky and distant.

John went to the bathroom. He turned on the lights and looked at himself in the mirror. The lights hurt his eyes, and he closed them until they adjusted to the persistent rays of light.

His face looked terrible. Both of his eyes were black, and he had dried blood surrounding his mouth and smeared on his chin.

John let the tap run until it was cool. He then gently splashed his face and dried himself with the hand towel, not caring that he was getting blood on it. He put the towel back and gently felt his jaw. It hurt, but he didn't think that it was dislocated.

John went back to the living room. Mathew was sitting on the couch waiting for him. John slowly sat in a chair opposite him. Each exchanged uncomfortable glances with the other.

Mathew was the first to speak. "You sold my wife out. She wanted you to do something, but instead you turned her over to Kahn."

John raised his hands. "I never told anybody about your wife except my editor, and he didn't tell anybody. You're blaming the wrong person."

"How did they know then?" Mathew seemed to have regained some of his anger now that he knew that John wasn't demanding to go to the hospital or press charges.

"Mathew, I'm trying to find out. You either help me or stand out of my way."

Mathew frowned and sat back. He obviously wasn't expecting John to respond like that. "Why didn't you defend yourself?" he asked, a little quieter. "You just knelt there, not moving."

John didn't answer for a long time. Should he tell him about Sheila's mirage? How he felt that Sheila was giving him the punches that she had been refused in life?

"He just needed to let his anger out. I know you're all probably really angry at me. You're right. She wanted me to act and I didn't. She asked me for help but I didn't give it to her. Just believe me when I tell you that I never told anybody from Nerno she was my source."

Mathew nodded slowly, seeming to accept John's response. "Did you write her name down anywhere? Was there any way somebody could have figured it out?"

John shook his head. He thought of the Jetta that he had seen at the airport and at the hotel.

"The only way was if Sheila was followed. I took every precaution you can think of. I've done this many times before."

"What about the story in the *New York Times*?"

"I don't know. I always thought Sheila had talked to them. The author of that article used to work for the *Daily Globe*. He must have retraced my steps somehow."

"She said she didn't speak with anybody other than you. She always thought you had told Kahn out of some sort of spite."

"Why don't you start at the moment when Sheila got fired?" John took out his notepad and a pen.

"Why should I trust you?"

The question made John look up from his notepad. "Because I'm going to help you."

"How is this going to help me? Is this going to bring Sheila back?"

"No, but it will bring closure. It will help people understand what actually happened."

Mathew looked down at the floor, as if gathering his thoughts. John waited, knowing that some people needed time. Finally he looked back up, took a deep breath, and started his narrative.

"Two weeks ago, I had come home from work. I'm a car mechanic for a Nissan dealership. This particular night I found Sheila on the couch crying with the lights off. Sheila told me she had been fired; David Kahn knew she had been talking to a reporter."

John stopped Mathew. "Did she use my name specifically?"

Mathew thought for a moment, and then shook his head. "No, not then. But she had told me about you before. Said you were some war correspondent."

"Did she ever mention anybody named Vince Parkerson?"

"Are you calling my wife a liar?"

"No, just making sure I have all the facts straight."

"She used your name specifically. She never talked about another reporter. Why do you think I called you?"

John took a deep breath. "Okay, let's move on. What happened after she was fired?"

"She became seriously depressed. She lost all her stock options—which were worthless anyway. We lost our extended medical plan. But worst of all, we struggled to keep Kyle in school."

"I thought he was on a scholarship."

"On a partial scholarship. It doesn't cover housing or food or other expenses. She begged me not to tell him she had lost her job. She was worried he would lose focus."

"Wait, so Kyle never knew his mother had lost her job?"

"Not until I called to tell him his mother had died."

John didn't say anything. Parents paying for their children's school was a completely foreign concept to him. He knew vaguely that Hayden had put some money away for Byron's university. But John had only just started to pay child support to her. He couldn't imagine paying for Byron's university tuition. His own parents had been working class and had made John pay for everything. When other kids were getting allowances, he was doing a paper route that his father had gotten for him.

Mathew continued. "I kept telling her she could find something else, something better but she kept saying Nerno had blackballed her. Nobody would talk to her."

John looked up from his notepad. "Do you think this was true?"

Mathew remained silent for a while. "I'm not sure. I know she tried applying to a couple of accounting firms, but they never called back."

"Had anything like this happened before?"

"What do you mean?"

"Had she shown any suicidal tendencies before?"

"No, never." Mathew paused, his mouth open. "Her aunt committed suicide, but that was a long time ago."

John shifted uncomfortably in his seat. "I'm sorry, but I need to ask this next question. Are you absolutely sure it was suicide?"

Mathew closed his eyes and seemed to lose himself. It appeared that he had not thought of another alternative. "What do you mean?" he asked, his eyes still closed.

"I'm just thinking of other scenarios. I don't know."

"You think somebody from Nerno did this? You think . . ." But Mathew couldn't finish the sentence. Instead, he left it hanging, as if he didn't quite have the energy to close it.

"I'm not sure," John said, slowly. "Can you think of anything that might suggest murder?"

"She was depressed," Mathew said quietly. He seemed to be using every ounce of strength to speak. "But I never thought she had it in her to do something like that."

"Did she leave a note or anything like that?"

Mathew shook her head. "No. Not that I could find."

"What about the autopsy? Did they do a toxicology test?"

"What's that?"

"A test to see if there were any alcohol or drugs in her system."

"Sheila didn't do drugs."

"I know. I'm just saying perhaps she was drugged."

"I'm not sure. I'm sure they would have said something."

"I'm sorry . . . were you the one to find her?"

Mathew gave a quick nod, and then looked down at the carpet. John waited to see if Mathew would say anything more.

"I came home after work around six. I opened the garage. I thought it strange that the lights in her car were still on. I thought maybe she had forgotten to turn them off. I pulled up beside her car and that's when I saw her in the driver's seat."

Mathew stopped, and began to sob uncontrollably. John got up and handed him a box of Kleenex. John knew that he couldn't hurry Mathew, and so he sat back down and waited until the sobs dissipated. He tried not to look at the pathetic, grieving man, but instead retreated into his own recesses of memory. He thought, as he did so often, of Byron and Hayden. After a while, John looked up and saw that Mathew was silent.

"I'm sorry," Mathew said, putting the box of Kleenex on the coffee table. His hands were unsteady.

"It's okay. I shouldn't have asked."

John scribbled a note in his pad reminding him to find out if an autopsy had been done. "Now, I was wondering if I could see the garage."

"What do you want to see that for?"

"Like I said, I want to cover everything. You want to find out what happened?"

"The police have already been through it."

"I know, but it doesn't hurt to double check."

Mathew nodded and stood up. He led John through the hallway.

"The police impounded the car. I don't know when we get it back. I don't know if we're supposed to call."

"Maybe give them a call and check," John suggested.

"But who?"

"Did the police leave you a number?"

"I'm not sure. Maybe."

John patted Mathew on the shoulder, and as soon as he touched him he knew that it was a mistake. Mathew recoiled as if he had been bitten. John tried to cover up the awkwardness with a smile. "I'll find out for you. Let me handle it."

Mathew nodded like a frightened animal. "Okay. Thanks."

They stopped at the end of the hallway. Mathew pointed at the door in front of them. "That leads to the garage. I can't go in. I'll be in the kitchen."

Mathew then spun around and walked away. John watched him go, and then turned and twisted the knob. The door creaked open and John felt a cold, musty draft.

John flicked on the light, which flickered and hummed. The floor was made of cold cement, and in the corner there was an oak work bench with a set of power tools hanging above. Everything seemed normal, except for the police tape that was still stuck to the garage door.

John felt Sheila's presence in the air. He remembered the first time that they had spoken on the phone. He was with Byron at the Pacific National Exhibition, eating candy and trying to avoid the crowds of people. How long ago the memory seemed now. He remembered that his phone rang, bringing the two of them together, and that the moment he answered their destinies collided.

Standing alone in the gloomy garage, John wondered why he had wanted to see it. What did he hope to learn?

Was it possible that somebody had knocked her unconscious somehow, and left her in the car with a pipe running to the window? It would be impossible to know without an autopsy.

Satisfied that he had learned all he could from the garage, John retreated back to the warmth of the hallway, where it was bright and inviting.

He found Mathew alone in the kitchen, bent over the sink, his back towards John. John wondered where Mathew's family had gone. Maybe after the fight they had decided to leave.

Mathew turned, and John could tell that he had been crying. He quickly wiped his eyes and tried to smile. "Sorry . . . is there anything else I can do? I think I should be alone for a while if you don't mind."

John was sympathetic, but he wasn't done, and he didn't know if Mathew would ever let him into the house again. "There is one more thing. Did Sheila keep any work here or is it all at the office?"

"No, she had a home office. The police have already been through, it though."

"Did they take anything?"

Mathew shook his head. "They just towed the car."

"Do you mind if I see the room?"

"Sure."

Mathew once again led John down the hallway, but they turned to the right and Mathew indicated the door. "I haven't been in there since it happened."

Mathew left and John opened the door. It was a small room, about the size of a regular bathroom. There was a white desk, and a computer monitor that took up much of the space. Everything was neatly organized into folders. Underneath the desk was a file cabinet, which John opened. The files were filled with marketing strategies on how to strengthen the Nerno brand. There was nothing on Ko Chang.

Next, John turned on the laptop, but it was password protected. John got up to find Mathew to see if he knew the password, but he wasn't in the kitchen or the living room.

"Mathew?" John called out, but his voice just echoed through the hallway.

John tentatively searched the entire first floor, afraid that he might run into Kyle again, but the house was empty.

In the hallway, John stopped to look at a photograph of the McKinnon family. John judged that the photograph was about ten or eleven years old. The snapshot appeared to have been taken at the beach, the ocean spanning out infinitely towards the horizon, the red sunlight soaking the entire frame.

A brown bath towel was sprawled out underneath them. Kyle was a disjointed teenager in a bathing suit, a giant mop of brown hair covering his eyes. He was grinning mischievously for the camera. Mathew and Sheila were both slimmer, handsomer in their youth, smiling lazily for the unknown photographer. It seemed to speak of a happy time that could never be reclaimed.

John dusted the frame off with his fingers and decided to climb the stairs to the second floor. Again he called out Mathew's name, but there was no answer.

John knocked on several doors, opening them, before he found Mathew in the bedroom, standing with his back towards him, staring out the window at the snow plateau as if mesmerized by the landscape.

"Mathew?"

"You a religious man?" Mathew asked, without turning around.

John took a deep breath and decided to answer honestly. "No, not really."

"Not really?"

"Well, in my experience God hasn't helped anyone."

"There was a story I learned a long time ago in church," Mathew said. He still had his back towards John, and it felt strange entering the bedroom without Mathew's permission. He had invaded the McKinnons' privacy already, but the bedroom was too much.

"I was named after Matthew, the prophet who wrote about Jesus fasting in the desert for forty days and forty nights. Perhaps you've heard about it. When Jesus gets tempted by the devil?"

John nodded. "Yes, Jesus goes out into the desert and the devil tells Jesus he will give him everything if Jesus will bow down and worship him."

Mathew turned and stared at John. He crossed his arms tightly against his chest as if he was cold. To John, he looked like a morose statue against the backlight from the window. "You ever feel like these oil guys are just worshipping the devil?"

John didn't know what to say. "I suppose so. I don't really know."

"You think people will understand after your article?"

John shrugged. "I hope so. It doesn't always work as well as I want it to."

"You think anybody will ever pay for what they did to my wife?"

John shrugged. "The police are looking into it, but the law is kind of hazy. It's really hard to prove."

Mathew leaned his large frame against the window. "I guess you are all I have, then."

John nodded as if he felt confident in himself. "I was wondering if you knew Sheila's password for her computer. I wanted to take a look at what's on there."

Mathew stared blankly at John. "It's probably written on a piece of paper somewhere."

"You know where?"

Mathew shrugged. "I generally stayed away from her office."

John went back downstairs to the office. He looked everywhere for a password, but couldn't find one. He tried simple ones like "Nerno", "Kyle" and "Mathew" but none of them worked.

He went back upstairs. Mathew was sitting on the edge of the bed, looking lost and bewildered. John felt sorry for him.

"Do you mind if I borrow your wife's computer?"

Mathew shook his head. "No, I have no use for it anymore."

The Detectives

"**S**O YOU ARE SAYING YOUR father forgot the password and you want us to break into it?" the clerk asked, giving John a dubious look. John's black eyes probably didn't help either. He knew that he looked like a boxer who had been on the wrong end of a title fight.

John was in a small electronics store in Pacific Place Mall on 36th Northeast Street. The store was small and cramped, with computer boxes piled almost to the ceiling. John had chosen this store because he figured that they wouldn't ask too many questions, but he was already having second thoughts.

"Yeah, my father is really forgetful these days. He said he wrote it down somewhere but he seems to have misplaced the piece of paper as well. I told him I didn't think he needed a password in the first place, but he's getting more and more paranoid. I wish I could get him to see a doctor, but he won't hear of it."

John hoped that the story was enough, and the clerk seemed to accept it.

"Yeah, we can probably do it."

John gave the clerk his credit card, wondering if he could write it off as a business expense. The clerk said that it would take a day and that John should come back then.

"Thanks, I really appreciate it."

"Maybe your father should make the password something easy."

John drove to a restaurant, where he had a meeting with Detective Orlando Corea, who was the head of the Calgary unit of the Market Enforcement Team, sometimes abbreviated to IMET.

After visiting the McKinnon house, John had gone back to his hotel to write up an article which would be titled "The Last Days of a Whistleblower."

The article appeared in the newspaper that morning and had already caused a stir. Charles Dana had called to congratulate him. So had Michael Chu. But the most important call was from Orlando Corea, who asked if John was available for lunch. John said that he was, and they set on a place called The Knight's Tale. John learned that it wasn't too far from the old police headquarters in downtown Calgary.

Before John had gone to the meeting, he had done some research on IMET, and had learned that the Calgary IMET team was one of ten that worked across the country, and one of two that was based in Calgary. IMET consisted of Royal Canadian Mounted Police investigators, security regulators, Calgary police officers, forensic accountants and various support staff. The IMET units worked closely with the Securities and Exchange Commission, as well as other U.S. law enforcement agencies, to help catch white collar criminals.

John learned that Corea had been head of one of the Calgary units for three years, and had been a part of IMET since its inception in 2003, when Enron and Worldcom were making unwelcome headlines across the world. Before IMET, Orlando had worked in the Commercial Crime Section.

John's cell phone rang, and he figured that it was Corea telling him he wouldn't be able to make it, but instead it was Madeline.

"I haven't heard from you for a while. You have anything for me?"

"I'm just about to meet the head investigator of Nerno. I'll let you know."

"How about you tell me over dinner?"

John hesitated. He wasn't sure that he wanted to see Madeline so soon. He still felt slightly embarrassed. "I don't know. I might have to meet some colleagues tonight."

"You can't cancel? I would really like to see you."

"I might," John allowed.

"Come on," Madeline said, playfully. "I have something I want to tell you."

"What?"

"Not over the phone. I'll see you tonight?"

"Okay, it's a date," John said.

John met Corea in the waiting area of the pub. John had met many police officers in his lifetime, and they usually had certain gruff, macho mannerisms that he could pick out. But Corea was a short, soft-spoken man with dark skin. He was wearing a flashy grey suit that was incongruous with the police stereotype.

They shook hands and made introductions. John noticed that Corea had dark circles under his eyes.

"Thanks for meeting me today," John said as they took a booth in the corner, near the emergency exit and washrooms.

"I don't usually meet with reporters," Corea said, after they ordered ginger ales. John desperately wanted a beer, but he thought that it was wise to refrain from drinking in front of the detective.

"Why meet with me then?" John asked.

"I read your article this morning. It was very good. I didn't realize you were in Calgary before the whole thing happened."

John nodded but didn't say anything.

The waitress returned with their ginger ales.

"And I thought you might have some information that might be helpful to the investigation."

John hesitated, debating over how he wanted to play it. "I will be as cooperative as I can. But I want what you have in return."

Corea frowned. He was obviously not used to bargaining with reporters. "I can give you some background information for context, but that's it."

"That's not good enough."

"You know I can force you to cooperate?"

John shrugged. "Perhaps, but I hold the cards. You either take my offer or leave it."

"I can't give you privileged information about the investigation. It could seriously jeopardize the whole thing. You have to be reasonable."

"How about I hold off until the investigation is complete?"

"Until after the trial?"

"You really think it will ever come to that?"

Corea took a sip of ginger ale. "Are we on or off the record?"

"Off. I just want a general impression of how strong your case is."

"Right now we have a lot of circumstantial information that adds up to dick all."

All of a sudden John realized the whole reason for the meeting. "You didn't even know about Sheila McKinnon before this morning, did you?"

Corea looked down at his place mat. He didn't say anything for a long time. "I just pulled her file this morning. I didn't see the connection."

"Okay, I give you everything I know about Nerno in exchange for full access."

"I will have to clear it with my boss, but I think we can work with that."

"Did you ever talk to Vince Parkerson?"

"Yes, we interviewed him soon after his article came out, but he wasn't very helpful. He wouldn't reveal his sources even after we threatened to subpoena him."

John shuddered at his own experience at the wrong end of a subpoena. "Did you look at Sheila McKinnon's autopsy?"

Corea bit his bottom lip. "Yes we did . . . but I can't comment further."

John frowned. "Full access means full access."

"There are privacy concerns. I won't have you print gory details."

"If I can get next of kin to sign off, will you get me the report?"

"Again, that depends on my boss," Corea said. "I don't have access to the report. It's not my case."

The waitress came back and took their orders. Corea had a cheeseburger and John decided to try the BLT.

John waited until the waitress was out of earshot before continuing. "Okay, theoretically, if everything falls into place, you can get me the report?"

Corea shrugged. "Maybe. That's the best I can do right now."

"If this is going to work, you have to be a little more open with me. You can at least tell me if you found any red flags."

"I'm not the officer in charge. I don't know anything."

John played a hunch. "After you read my article about her you were curious, weren't you?"

Corea gave John a guilty half-smile that showed John that he had been correct.

"Who is the detective in charge of the case?"

"Detectives Dennis Crow and Evander Katt," Corea said.

"What did they tell you?"

"Everything was consistent with carbon monoxide poisoning. They did a full toxicology report and found nothing in her system, not even a trace of alcohol or drugs."

"Is that normal?"

"In suicide cases there is no normal."

John stared thoughtfully out the window. The harsh midday light cut across the restaurant. "Modern cars have catalytic converters. Is it still possible to kill yourself with carbon monoxide?" he asked.

Corea nodded. "Sure. It's a lot harder than it used to be, but Sheila McKinnon managed to produce the right conditions. It's still a very common method."

John thought quickly. He was on a roll. "I want to switch back to Nerno for a moment. How far are you into the investigation?"

"It's my turn to ask questions."

John shook his head. "No. You need more than I need you. You want me to walk right now?"

Corea sighed. "We have interviewed as many people as possible. We have seized Nerno's records and are slowly making our way through emails, memos and other documents, looking for irregularities, but as you can imagine, it's slow going."

John thought about Sheila's computer. Should he tell Corea about it? No, he decided. He didn't even know if there was anything useful on it, and if he gave it over to the police, he would most likely never see it again. If he found something, he could always turn it over later.

"Have you looked through David Kahn's email yet?" John asked. "There is an email Sheila gave to me from Kahn to Hopkins, basically telling him to keep his mouth shut and everything would work out. Unfortunately the copy I had was stolen from me, otherwise I would give it to you."

Corea stared at John. "Stolen? I have a hard time believing that."

"It's the truth. Stolen from my hotel room. I don't know who, but I suspect it was either somebody from Nerno, or Hank Gates."

Corea looked thoughtful for a moment. "Would you be willing to testify to all this?"

"I don't see why not. My source is dead."

John leaned in close to Corea. "I still believe George Hopkins was somehow murdered. I don't have any proof, but the timing is just so strange."

"And what about Sheila McKinnon?"

John dropped his shoulders. "I don't know . . . my gut tells me suicide but . . . two deaths in a month?"

"The investigators ruled it an accident. I looked into that one too. It's pretty hard to tamper with a Lamborghini and make it look like an accident."

"So I've been told," John said. "So you're not going to investigate further?"

Corea shook his head, a little annoyed. "No, it's been closed. Our resources are stretched as it is."

"What if I told you I have good reason to believe it wasn't an accident?"

Corea looked at John wearily, his lips pursed. "What's that?"

John told Corea about the fake doctor he had encountered in Hopkins' room.

"And what did the hospital said?"

"They said it was one of their interns but I wasn't convinced."

"I'll check it out," Corea said, but John could tell he wasn't convinced.

"Off the record again: what do you think of the probability of arrests?"

Corea sighed heavily again. "I'm sure you know our track record."

When John had researched Corea, he found out that during their ten year history, IMET had been responsible for about fifty convictions—which, by anybody's count, was a dismal record. Although, unlike many others, John thought that it was unjust to lay the blame squarely on IMET. The laws were complicated, the cases complex, and the funding inadequate.

"It's one of the most complex cases I've ever seen," Corea said. "I think we would be lucky to make any sort of arrest—let alone a conviction."

"So Kahn, Drashkov and the rest will get away with it?" John said it more for his own benefit than for Corea's.

"Well, maybe with the publicity somebody will come forward. It's worked before."

They finished their meals and John gave the waitress his credit card to pay.

"Thanks for lunch," Corea said. "And if I see any of this in the paper I'll string you up before a judge before you know what hit you."

John nodded. "I understand."

A few moments later, the waitress came back and said that his credit card had been declined.

"That's strange," John said. He had just made a payment and he would have had plenty of credit. "Could you try it again?"

The waitress smiled and nodded, but again she returned. "I'm sorry, sir. Do you have another form of payment?"

Corea asked, "Did you tell your credit card company you were travelling? Sometimes they don't approve charges in other cities unless you tell them you are going there."

"No, I never phoned them," John admitted, feeling extremely embarrassed. All that work of trying to retain the upper hand had instantly been wiped out.

"Don't worry, I've got it," Corea said, pulling out his credit card. His worked, and John left the lunch frustrated; now he owed Corea a favour.

John went back to his hotel intent on making some more phone calls, but as soon as he entered the lobby he saw a familiar figure walking towards him. It took a couple of moments to realize that it was Michael Chu. He was wearing an expensive-looking dark business suit with a red silk tie, and was carrying a small leather briefcase. He looked like he had just stepped out of some executive meeting.

Michael stopped in front of John, smiling as wide as a cat burglar.

After they shook hands, John said, "I'm a little surprised to see you here."

"I thought you would be. I got assigned to Nerno."

"You got assigned to Nerno?" John asked, incredulously. "The boss would have told me."

"How do you think I found you?"

"Okay, but if you think I'm going to help you, you've got it all wrong."

Michael's frown disappeared. "Please, John. You could use a little help."

"Forgive me, but the last time I got help from a fellow reporter my story ended up in the *New York Times*."

"Let me buy you a drink, at least," Michael said. "I've flown all this way."

"The boss doesn't even know you're here, does he?"

"Of course he does," Michael protested, a little too readily.

"Look me straight in the eyes and tell me that."

John waited for an answer, but Michael didn't say anything. His mouth hung open as if it was a broken cog.

John just stared at him, his eyebrows raised. "I can buy my own drinks," he said, and turned and walked to the elevator. He pushed the button, but something made him turn and stare at Michael. He still stood in the middle of the lobby, not moving, his head lowered. A sad, pathetic figure. People passed him by, not even glancing at him.

The elevator door opened and an elderly couple got out. John hesitated.

I'm going to regret this, he thought to himself.

He turned back to Michael and took a deep breath. The elevator doors closed and John slowly walked back to Michael, who looked up at John with large, rueful eyes.

"Yesterday I got a call from someone who invested thirty thousand dollars in Nerno based on one of my articles," Michael said. "He blamed me. He didn't yell or anything. He spoke in a real soft, sad voice. I think that made it worse. Last night I couldn't sleep. This morning, instead of driving to work, I drove to the airport. Before I knew it, I bought a plane ticket and I ended up here."

"Come on, let's go get that drink," John said.

They went to the bar, where several business people were enjoying an afternoon cocktail. John ordered two whiskeys.

"Can you get me an interview with David Kahn?" John asked, once the bartender had brought the drinks.

Michael nodded. "I think so. I know these guys. I know how they operate."

"You know, we're all to blame. Don't get all weepy just because one guy is frustrated he lost money."

"It's personal for you, too. Don't deny it isn't."

"That's different."

Michael took a sip of his drink. "Yeah, how so?"

It was John's turn to be silent. "Okay," he said. "But I've been doing this much longer than you. I don't want your help."

"I've been doing finance a lot longer than you. Why not work together?"

"If you get me an interview, then we can work together."

Michael nodded. "Okay, I accept."

"And I want you to ask everybody you know about Nerno. I mean everybody."

Michael nodded agreeably.

"Tell me, Michael. Isn't journalism a little pedestrian compared to high-stakes finance?"

Michael smiled vaguely. "I'm sure you've heard all the rumours and gossip."

John nodded. Reporters were the worst kind of gossips, and when they worked in such close proximity to each other, it was impossible to keep a secret. "Of course, but I want to hear it from you."

"You know defection isn't that uncommon."

"Perhaps," John said. "But to a newspaper that pays you about a third of your former salary, it is. You think once the paper is transferred over you'll go back to finance?"

Michael smiled again. "You might not believe this . . . but I actually wanted to be a poet when I was a teenager. Live in Paris . . . I never told anybody, of course, especially not my parents. I grew up in a very strict Chinese household, so any career that didn't make a ton of money was out of the question."

John tried to imagine the serious, straight-laced Michael Chu as a teenager spouting poetry to passing girls.

"What's so funny?" Michael asked.

"Nothing, go on."

"I worked as a special advisor on a deal for this Japanese cell phone company, to buy a Californian electronics company that made microchips. Both sides were compulsive dealmakers and they would phone me at all hours of the night. At the time, I was still working for an investment banking firm, so my stress level was through the roof. And then, one day, my heart just gave out on me and I found myself in the hospital.

"I had a lot of time to think about what's important. My family came to visit me, and it struck me that it was the first time we had all been together in about two months. Anyway, I finished the deal and made enough money to retire on, and did. My family was very supportive. But I soon found myself restless in retirement, and so I started writing a weekly column suggesting stocks to sell or buy. For the first time in forty years I found myself enjoying writing again."

They finished their drinks and Michael moved on to a martini.

"Okay, what I don't understand is, I'm sure you've made bad investments before. Why do you feel guilty about this one?"

Michael thought a while before answering. "I guess before, I always worked with multinational corporations and huge firms that owned most of the world . . . they were so far removed from actual people, I guess. I had to deal with pissed off CEOs, but they could afford to lose a few million. The people who lost money on Nerno are more tangible. They struggle to pay their mortgages."

"Michael Chu for the people, is that it?"

Michael frowned, clearly hurt. "No, it's not like that."

"I'm sorry. I shouldn't have said that. It's very noble of you."

But Michael didn't seem to accept the apology. "No, it's no more noble than anything else."

"You think if you can help prove David Kahn and the rest are guilty of fraud, then it will be better?"

"I hope so."

John sighed. "I have bad news for you, then. It never gets any better."

"Never?"

"When I came back from Afghanistan I thought I could just shove everything in the trunk and forget about it, but sometimes the trunk just accidently gets popped open. Nothing ever leaves us."

"What did Detective Orlando Corea say?" Madeline asked. She wore a sleek black dress that showed off her slender arms and small white knees. She looked stunning, and John again felt acutely embarrassed for wearing a faded pair of jeans and an old collared shirt.

John shrugged. "Not much."

Madeline was still smiling, but showed a hint of irritation in her voice. "He must have said something."

"The investigation is going poorly and he doubts he'll be able to gather enough evidence against anybody from Nerno."

The waiter sauntered over, giving a perplexed, woeful smile. John ordered a whiskey and Madeline had a Bellini.

"We don't have Bellinis in China," Madeline said.

"I think you're beginning to be corrupted by the evil Westerners."

"That's not funny, John."

"I'm sorry," John said, beginning to think that the whole dinner was a mistake. "In all seriousness, do you ever get to go home much or are you always travelling around the world?"

"No, this is my first foreign assignment."

"Please don't take this the wrong way, but I'm surprised you're still here."

"As long as CNOOC is interested, I will be here."

"That's another thing I don't understand. What value do they still see in Nerno?"

Madeline tilted her head and smiled. "You should be happy. We still get to play together."

"But then you go back to China and I never see you again?"

Madeline shrugged. "I go where my master bids me." She then leaned over the table and kissed him. John closed his eyes and reached around her back. They parted and he took a deep breath in.

"Come on, John. Why not just have some fun while we still can?"

"I'm sorry, Madeline, but I don't think that's a good idea."

"Why not?"

John had no answer. *Why not?* Because he didn't want to get emotionally attached. Because he didn't want his heart broken. But those weren't reasons he could give to Madeline.

"I just don't think it's a good idea, that's all."

"What are you afraid of, John?"

"Everything . . . I'm afraid of everything." John was stunned by his own admission. Was it the truth? He didn't know. There were days he felt afraid of everything. There were days he felt he was afraid of nothing.

Madeline frowned. "The war correspondent who has faced down terrorists, gangsters, criminals is afraid of everything?"

"Just because I've been shot doesn't make me any less afraid."

"You're a coward, John," Madeline said, leaning forward. "An emotional coward."

John didn't refute it. How could he? She was right.

They hid awkwardly behind menus for a few minutes, pretending to study the entrées. Madeline seemed to desperately look around for the waiter, but he was busy taking orders from another table.

Madeline ordered a chicken salad and John decided on the roast beef. He folded his menu and put it down on the tablecloth. He looked over at Madeline who was staring unhappily at her Bellini.

He thought of things to say, of conversations he could use to make her smile but he came up empty and so he gave up and began to think of Nerno and CNOOC and different scenarios involving the two.

Then John had an idea that filled his entire chest with cold dread. He suddenly knew why CNOOC was interested in Nerno.

You don't think there is a political element in all this? Hank Gates had told him.

"Excuse me a moment," John said. "I need to go to the washroom."

John got up and walked to the washroom. He closed the door to the stall and listened. Satisfied that Madeline hadn't followed him, he took out his cell phone and phoned Mindy Rocher.

John was afraid that she had gone home for the night, but luckily she answered.

"Mindy? It's John Webster. I need a favour from you."

"Of course, John. What can I do?"

"Remember when you said Nerno has a site in northern Canada?"

"Sure."

"Do you remember exactly where it is?"

"I don't know off the top of my head, but if you give me a moment, I can find out."

"Okay," John said, hoping that it wouldn't take too long. He didn't want Madeline to get suspicious.

Rocher came back on the line a couple of minutes later. "I found an interesting article online about northern Canada. Apparently Nerno is the fifth largest investor in the Northwest Territories."

"The fifth?"

"That's what it says. Nerno owns two thousand square kilometres in the Mackenzie Valley."

"Can you forward the article to me?"

"Of course."

"Thanks," John said. "I really appreciate it."

John went back to Madeline and sat down opposite her.

"It's not the drill prototype you guys are interested in, is it?" John asked.

"What are you talking about?"

"I'm talking about the oil fields in northern Canada."

"I'm not bloody interested in any of it," Madeline said. "You think just because we have a communist government, we're all the same."

"You know what I mean. Your government isn't interested in the prototype, is it?"

"Why do you think that?"

"I thought it was the technology, but it isn't. It's all about the politics."

"What are you talking about? Politics?"

"You want control over the oil in northern Canada."

Madeline scoffed. "Oh please! You Canadians always think you're more important than you are."

"I'm not talking about CNOOC. I'm talking about the Chinese government."

"Pardon my expression, but that's just Cold War bullshit," Madeline said, getting up from the table.

"Where are you going?"

"I'm going home. I'm tired of listening to your conspiracy theories."

"You know more than you're telling me."

"You're unbelievable, John."

Madeline hovered as if she was expecting John to stop her, but when he didn't she had to follow through on her threat. John watched as her dress swayed with her quick steps. She pushed the door open and she was gone from the restaurant.

John paid and went to his car. While he waited it to warm up, he thought about Madeline and how beautiful she looked in her black dress and he wondered why he had the instinct to drive everybody in his life away from him.

He put the car in drive and headed back to the hotel. He drove slowly fearing the ice on the road. He turned on the radio and listened to the news which kept him company. The anchor's deep voice cut deep across the vast nighttime sky and seemed to echo off the thin trees and the grey buildings like the word of God.

John glanced in his rear view mirror and saw the car behind him was riding his tail. It was a black Jetta, the same type that had been following him earlier from the airport. The Jetta turned on its high beams, momentarily blinding John.

John covered his eyes and flipped the rear view mirror away from him so the light didn't shine into his eyes.

He heard the powerful motor behind him and the muffled sound of tires on snow. He was worried he couldn't see what the Jetta was doing without fully turning his head. John increased his speed, trying to get away, the tiny engine groaning under his foot.

John gripped the steering wheel hard, his knuckles turned milky white and perspiration ran down the side of his face and along his neck.

He felt a bump as the car jolted forward as if something had hit him. John tried looking back but the power of the high beams was too much.

John pressed the gas, speeding up some more. The speedometer passed sixty. He felt something hit his car again and his head snapped forward.

The Jetta must be ramming me, he thought. The Jetta would run him off the road and he would die like George Hopkins.

For a moment his thoughts went to the back of his mind where Sheila was waiting for him. Would he see Sheila again in death? Would he then be able to get on his hands and knees and beg forgiveness?

John straightened his back, letting out a loud compression of air. His heart was racing as he forced himself to concentrate on the road ahead. The buildings and trees became a blur. He didn't want to think about what would happen if he didn't shake the Jetta.

The Jetta changed lanes and came up beside John. He could hear the car approaching. It seemed to speed up effortlessly as if John wasn't even moving. John tried to see who was in the driver's seat but he could only make out a black outline of a figure.

The Jetta then slammed into John's car, knocking him off the road. John struggled to correct his steering but skidded and spun out of control. The car hit the ditch and rolled. His stomach lurched forward as if was at the top of the rollercoaster again. There was silence. The sound of the motor, of the wheels, of the radio just ceased to exist. Had time stopped as well? Eventually there was a loud thud, knocking John sideways and the car came to a stop, miraculously upright.

John didn't move for a long time. His arms and legs felt frozen, but whether it was from fear or something else, he didn't know. He was breathing heavy and he tried to calm himself down.

He was alive.

His windshield was cracked. He tried to see through the breaks in the glass for the Jetta. The street lights gave off a soft orange glow but he couldn't see any other cars. The road was empty.

Was the Jetta gone? Was he safe?

John did a mental check of his body, searching for pain. He knew for experience shock came first and then pain later. But as the numbness wore off everything felt fine. He started to slowly move his arms and legs. Still no pain. He let out a huge breath of air.

He unbuckled his seatbelt and tried to open his car door but it was jammed shut. He reached over and tried the other side but it was equally as stuck.

No need to panic, John told himself.

He looked around, thinking of options. He sat back in his seat, raised his legs and started to kick at the broken windshield. On the fourth try the pieces shattered and John was able to crawl out.

The cold air stung him savagely and he began to shiver uncontrollably. He tried to use his cellphone but he couldn't work his fingers work the buttons. His eyelids began to stick together. He thought about going back to the wreckage but he would not be able to stay warm there.

John walked down the road, hoping to keep the blood flowing in his joints.

A car appeared on the road and for a horrible moment John thought it was the Jetta returning to finish him off but it was a truck. Its large oval headlights pierced the darkness.

John stepped into the middle of the road and waved his arms frantically, hoping the truck wouldn't run him over.

The truck slowed to a stop and John ran to the window which the driver reluctantly pulled down. The driver looked to be about in his mid-fifties and had on a black cowboy hat.

"Yes?" he asked, suspiciously.

"I've just had an accident," John said, pointing to his car. "I need your help. Can you drive me to the hospital?"

"My God, you okay?" the driver said. "Get in. I'll drive you."

Empty

JOHN WOKE UP, THE TELEVISION still on. Some grey-suited man on CNN was blaring incisively away, but about what, John couldn't comprehend. He groped for the remote to turn it off. The television faded away, blending into the rest of the darkness.

John rubbed his eyes and glanced over at the clock. It was only 6:34am. He couldn't have been asleep for more than four hours. He rolled over, but found it impossible to fall back asleep. His neck and back were beginning to stiffen up.

He had spent three hours in the hospital waiting room. The doctor examined him, did some x-ray tests and declared nothing wrong with him.

John spoke with the police who took down a description of the Jetta and all of his information and said they would be in touch if they found anything. John was doubtful they would

John got up and went to his computer. He searched the address that he had written down on the piece of paper and was surprised to find an old realtor's video footage of the entire property, including the inside, but couldn't find anything about the owner of the house.

John went and had a hot shower. The heat rejuvenated him, relaxed his back muscles and as he got out and towelled himself off, he felt ready to face another day. He looked at himself in the foggy mirror and thought—perhaps through a trick of condensation— that he looked younger, more vigorous. He could not see the wrinkles that he knew were beginning to form on his face and neck, or the dark circles that seemed to be a permanent feature around his eyes.

John wrapped the towel around his waist and went to his cell phone. He dialled Charles Dana's number.

"I got run off the road," John said. He then explained how the Jetta had rammed him and forced him off the road. "I'm okay," John said. "Just a little rattled, that's all."

"You told the police?"

"I doubt they will ever find that car. I don't know what I'm going to tell the rental company."

"Don't worry about that. I'll have the newspaper take care of that," Charles said. "And if they don't I will."

"Thank you, boss. I appreciate it."

There was a long pause but Charles eventually broke it, clearing his throat. "Webster, I have to tell you. I got a call yesterday from a lawyer representing Icelandic Media Corp. I'm going to make an official announcement today, but I might as well tell you . . . I think it's going around anyway."

"Yes? What?" John said, holding his breath.

"We're being shut down. A skeleton crew will be kept on to manage the online division, but everyone else is going."

John felt dizzy and had to sit down on the bed. "What? You sure?"

"I know it's hard to take in, and I'm sorry for telling you like this. The last print edition will be in two weeks. The building will be sold."

"Boss, we can't let this happen."

"What are we going to do? You know no one loves the paper as much as I do. If there was anything I could do, I would."

"Can't we fight it in court? Illegal takeover or something?"

"I'm sorry, John. I know this is as much of a shock for you as it is for me."

"You have to convince the Pommeroys to buy it back."

"John, they're done with the newspaper business. Believe me, I've tried everything."

John hung up the phone. The room was still spinning. He laid down and stared up at the ceiling. His stomach was churning uneasily and something was buzzing in his ear.

He remembered the day that he had first met Charles for a job. He was married and had a new son. The Second Gulf War had had a promising start: images of Saddam Hussein's statue being toppled, and American flags whipping in the desert wind, played out on television. The whole world seemed to be regaining a sense of optimism, and hope for an end to the bloodshed. John would just smile and agree whenever somebody told him that the war would soon end.

Charles and John had hit it off instantly. Charles had been courting John practically from the moment that Charles had left the *Wall Street Journal* and got hired for the *Daily Globe*. John wasn't sure if he wanted to leave Reuters, but Hayden was pressuring him to get a local job, one where he would be home more often.

Charles had become nostalgic, and gave John a tour of the building. He'd showed him some old photographs taken by long-gone *Daily Globe* photographers, and an old printing press in the basement that had last been used in the sixties.

John got up and went to the mini bar, where he cracked open a bottle of whiskey. When the whiskey didn't put him to sleep he moved on to the Scotch.

The liquid burned his throat and stomach. He felt so utterly alone, as if everybody had abandoned him.

What would he do now? Who would have him? Maybe he could go back to Reuters. He knew that many colleagues his age were jumping ship and going into public relations, but John would never survive as a corporate hack, spinning stories to whomever would listen.

Maybe he would go back to Afghanistan. It was such a beautiful country, with rolling hills and sharp mountains.

Maybe. Maybe. Maybe.

"I'm sorry, but your credit card was declined," the clerk said. John was at the computer shop, trying to retrieve Sheila McKinnon's computer.

John sighed. He was feeling sick from the alcohol that he had drank in the morning, and with everything that was going on, he had forgotten to phone the credit card company after his lunch with Detective Corea.

What was he going to do? He wondered if he had enough money in his bank account to cover it. He quickly calculated, and decided that he should have several hundred dollars in his chequing account.

He handed his debit card to the clerk, who inserted it into the machine. The clerk smiled as John entered his PIN number. The machine beeped and a "declined" message appeared on the screen.

"I'm sorry, sir," the clerk said, giving him a dubious look.

John tried his debit again, but he knew that it wouldn't work. Had he forgotten to transfer some money into his account?

The debit beeped cheerfully. Declined again.

"I'll be back," John assured the clerk, giving him a weak smile.

He put his card back in his wallet and walked out the door. He had spotted a coffee shop up the street. He would grab a coffee and debate what to do next.

John hunched over and walked quickly. The cold was almost unbearable. He found the coffee shop and pushed the doors open. He was happy to be inside again.

He lined up and ordered a black coffee, hoping that it would warm him up. He gave the barista his debit card.

"I'm sorry, but it didn't go through. Could you try again?" the barista said, giving John the same awkward look that the computer clerk had given him.

John frowned. Now he was becoming really concerned. He tried again, but with the same result.

"That's strange. I'm sure I have enough money to cover a coffee," John said.

"Do you have another form of payment?"

"No. My Visa isn't working either."

"Then don't worry, sir. The coffee is on us."

John sat down in the corner with his coffee. He sipped at it slowly. After getting drunk, he had corralled his spirits some, and managed to meet Michael Chu for breakfast. John didn't feel like eating, but he managed to swallow half an omelette.

Over breakfast John had relayed his conversation with Charles to Michael, who seemed less perturbed than John had been.

"You can always go back into finance, but I've got nothing else," John said, bitterly.

"Oh don't worry, I'm sure somebody will hire you," Michael said.

But John wasn't so sure. Nobody had hired Arthur Ransome after he had been laid off from his job at the *Vancouver Times*.

John set down his coffee, took out his phone and called his bank. When he finally got through to someone he explained his problem.

John could hear the woman on the phone type in his information.

"I'm afraid you are overdrawn on your account," the woman said.

"That's impossible. I should have at least two hundred and fifty dollars in there."

There was a pause while the woman checked on her computer. "I'm sorry, sir, but your account has no money in it."

John felt his headache intensify as he tried to concentrate. "Can you at least tell me my last transaction?"

"Of course. You withdrew three hundred and fifty-six dollars yesterday."

"What? No, I didn't."

"I'm sorry, sir, but that's what our records say."

"Does it say where I withdrew the money from?"

"Let me see," the woman said. "It says here that you withdrew the money from a debit machine at 6th and 1st."

John shook his head in frustration. "No, that's not right. I didn't withdraw any money."

"You're saying you didn't take out the money?" the woman asked.

"That's exactly what I'm saying," John shouted into the phone. Several people turned their heads and glared at him, and John was immediately sorry for raising his voice.

"Look, I apologize. I'm just stressed out. Do you think you could transfer some money from my savings account? I don't carry a bank card for it."

"Let me see," the woman said. John gave her the account number and he could hear her typing again. The woman made a clucking noise with her tongue.

"Is everything all right?" John asked, beginning to panic.

"You sure you gave me the right account number?"

John had used the same account since his divorce. "Yes, I'm sure. What's going on?"

"You didn't make any withdrawals?"

"I'm positive. I haven't withdrawn from that account in ten years."

"Let me get my supervisor," the woman said.

"Please, at least tell me there is some money in there."

"Before I proceed I'm going to get my supervisor."

John was put on hold, and had to listen to annoying elevator music while he waited. What was going on? Had somebody hacked into his account? If so, who, and why? John had many enemies, some, he supposed, who had enough power to hack his account.

The longer John waited, the more anxious he became. He looked around at the people in the coffee shop talking and laughing with each other, seemingly totally oblivious to his anxiety.

As John waited, he got a beep from the other line. He looked at the number, but didn't recognize it, and let it go to voicemail. The area code was unfamiliar as well, and John wondered what the call was about.

Finally a man came on the line. "I'm sorry for your wait. What can I do for you?"

John patiently explained the situation again.

"It seems you transferred all your money into your chequing account on Sunday and then took it all out in small sums over the day."

"But it wasn't me. Somebody must have stolen it." John was shocked. He had heard about people hacking into bank accounts and wiping them clean, but he never imagined that it would happen to him.

He heard the supervisor ask him something, but he felt like his head was underwater. His brain starved, crying out for oxygen.

"Pardon?"

"I said does anybody else know your password?"

John gripped the phone, trying to remain calm. "You're not listening to me. Somebody hacked into my account."

"Our security is very tight. Are you sure you didn't leave your account open on an unsecured computer?"

John felt like yelling at the supervisor, but he needed him on his side if he was ever going to resolve the problem.

"I'm positive. I don't ever do any online banking. I don't even know how."

"All right. I'll alert our security team, but it will take a couple of days to investigate."

"And what am I going to do in the meantime?"

"I'm sorry, sir, but there is nothing I can do until we fully investigate."

"I need to talk to your supervisor. You guys lost my money. Can I at least borrow some money until then?"

"I will be happy to put you in touch with one of our lending specialists."

"No, I want you to fix this."

"Like I said, there isn't much I can do."

"Then let me talk to your supervisor."

John was placed on hold again, and again had to listen to "calming" music. As he listened, he vowed that if he recovered his money, he would take it all out and put it under his mattress.

A woman came on and told John exactly the same thing that the supervisor had told him. John sighed and hung up.

John felt like throwing his phone against the window when it rang. It was Michael Chu, but he had no real desire to talk to him, so he let it go to voicemail.

Next he called the credit card company, but got similar results.

"Our records say you transferred your balance over to another credit card and then cancelled it," the operator informed John.

John spent several, painstaking minutes explaining to the operator that he didn't cancel his credit card, and that somebody had hacked his account.

"But I don't understand," the operator said, with a tone of incredulity in his voice. "Why would they want to cancel your card? Usually they run up charges, not cancel the card."

John didn't want to explain his theories to the operator, so instead he just said, "I have no idea. That's your department. Not mine."

"You want me to mail you a new one?"

"That would be really helpful, except I'm stuck in Calgary without any way of getting home."

John had no return ticket, since he hadn't had an idea of when he would return to Vancouver.

John listened to his messages. The first call was from a man named Gerard Levitt on behalf of the Icelandic Media Corporation, who said he would very much like to speak with John. John deleted the message without bothering to call him back. The second message, left by Michael, asked John if he had heard from Levitt.

Apparently Gerard Levitt was making the rounds.

John called Michael back.

"I just got laid off," Michael said, when he picked up. He spoke in a very calm, collected tone. He sounded either as if he was in shock or had accepted his fate.

"What?"

"I got a call from this guy named Gerard Levitt representing the Icelandic Media Corporation. He said effective immediately, my position at the *Daily Globe* has been eliminated."

"Yeah, I got a call too but I didn't answer. He left me a message."

"What are you going to do? Are you going to phone him back?"

"Phone him back so he can fire me? I don't think so," John said.

"What are you going to do?"

"I'm not going to let this story go to waste. I'm going to submit it as usual."

"You know, as a freelancer, you would be able to get a good price for the story out on the open market."

"No, Michael. This story belongs to the *Daily Globe*."

"But why? You don't owe them anything. In fact, they've probably already cut you loose."

"I know you're a finance guy and loyalty doesn't make much sense to you but the boss . . . well, he's the boss."

"They've probably fired him too. Are you going to be loyal to the Icelandic Media Corp? I say fuck them and go give it to the *New York Times*."

"Just like Vince did?"

"No, of course not. This is different."

"Not to me, it isn't." John said. "I've worked for the *Daily Globe* for a long time. I owe them this, even if it's not really the *Daily Globe* anymore."

"Okay. If you say so."

"Michael, I'm calling because I need a favour. Can you meet me at a computer store?"

"Uh . . . sure. Why?"

"Somebody hacked into my bank account, stole all my money and cancelled my credit cards."

"My God, that's awful. Have you told the police?"

"No, not yet. I just got through dealing with the bank."

"Okay, I'll come meet you. What's the address?"

John gave Michael the address and then hung up. He wanted to get another cup of coffee while he waited, and debated whether he could convince the barista to give him another one. He decided to try it. The barista gave him a funny look, but gave him a fresh cup anyway.

John sat down again. He found a discarded *Calgary Herald* and read it, hoping to take his mind off of his imminent demise at the *Daily Globe*. He read an article about rental space in New York and it made him think about Charles Dana.

John suddenly remembered when he and the boss had gone down to the Palace Bar, the local joint that John frequented. It was such a rarity to get Charles away from the office, especially into a bar.

They slid into a booth in the corner, eighties rock playing on the stereo. John ordered a double whiskey and Charles a Diet Coke—he had given up drinking long ago.

"Webster, Smyllie is going on vacation for two weeks. I want you to take over for him while he's away." Robert Smyllie was the city editor, and this would mean John overseeing the department while he was on vacation.

John, who was at best envied and at worst hated, didn't see how he would be able to cajole ten or fifteen stories from as many reporters.

"I'm flattered, but why me?"

"Because I think you're the right man for the job," Charles had said. "You're questioning my decision?"

John shrugged. Rarely did anybody question Charles' decision. John, in fact, was usually the only one. "I'm happy where I am. You want me to mentor the newbies, then just say it."

Charles took a sip of his Diet Coke, swirling the ice with the straw. "No, Webster, I want them to mentor you."

"I don't understand."

"Smyllie, Duncan . . . even I won't be around forever. Before I go, I want to leave the paper in good hands. Pass the torch on, so to speak."

John shook his head. He now understood why Charles had decided to join him at the bar. He didn't believe that Charles would ever retire. He was the hub around which everything else pivoted.

He had never imagined a world where Charles wasn't there to guide and question him.

"You know boss, I always thought you were immortal."

Charles laughed. "Think about it."

"Well, I guess I can do it for two weeks. I can't screw it up that badly now, can I?"

"No, I don't mean that. I mean further down the line."

John rubbed his chin. "You want me to take over the paper?"

"You understand the sacred trust more than anybody else I know. You understand the responsibility and the burden. Why not you?"

Because I'm a hopeless alcoholic, John thought, but did not say. *Why don't you choose somebody more stable?*

Things hadn't turned out at all like Charles had planned. They were taking his baby away from him, gutting it like a fat animal.

The Computer

ICHAEL AND JOHN DROVE BACK to the hotel using Michael's car.

On the way back, John phoned Detective Orlando Corea and told him that he had been hacked.

"You should call the fraud department. That isn't my area," Corea said.

"But Detective, this is all related to Nerno. Somebody is trying to stop me from finding out the truth."

"You sure it's not just some guy out of Nigeria?"

"I'm positive. It's not a coincidence."

Corea paused. "Okay, I'll get in touch with somebody at ITCU and I'll get back to you."

"Thank you. I appreciate it."

They parked in the underground parking lot and went up to John's room with Sheila's computer. They placed it on the desk and plugged it in. The technician had reset the password to 1234, and when John keyed in the numbers, the home screen appeared.

"Okay," Michael said, turning towards the door. "You want to meet for dinner? I have an early flight."

"What do you mean?" John said, straightening up.

"Well . . . I've been fired. I no longer have a job. I have no reason to be here."

"But don't you want to see this thing through with me?"

"Of course I do," Michael said. "But Levitt told me to catch the earliest flight available."

"You're going to let some hack tell you what to do?"

Michael was silent. He seemed to be thinking deeply. He finally looked over at John with a strange smile on his face. "I guess I've always let some hack tell me what to do."

"What about the people who were screwed by Nerno? You still want to get justice for them?"

"You just need me to be your banker."

John felt guilty, because partially, Michael was right. "I'm sorry, Michael. But you can't blame me for being cautious after what happened."

"Are you really going to give this story to the Icelandic Media Corp?" Michael asked.

"As far as I know, I'm still employed by them."

"Is this some sort of attempt to save yourself from being fired?"

John looked up at Michael. "Of course not."

John's phone rang, and he looked at the caller ID. It was Gerard Levitt's number. John showed Michael the phone.

"Speaking of which . . . it's that Levitt guy trying to fire me," John said.

"Interesting. It's a 212 area code."

"Why? What area code is 212?" John asked.

"It's Manhattan. I've dealt with enough Wall Street guys to know."

John's phone stopped ringing, and beeped to announce that there was a voicemail.

"I'm going to find out who this Gerard Levitt works for," Michael said, turning on John's laptop.

As Michael did that, John searched Sheila's computer. He found her work files neatly organized into the different projects that she had been working on. He opened them up one by one, but they were fairly dry reports on marketing strategies and media campaigns. Nothing on Ko Chang.

Michael called John over to his screen. "So, Gerard Levitt works for a big human resources firm called Excel Human Resources."

Michael then did a search for Excel Human Resources and got their webpage. He clicked on the "Clients" tab, which took them to a page naming some of the bigger companies that Excel worked for. But there was no mention of Icelandic Media Corp, so John told Michael to go back and click on the "About Us" tab.

Together, John and Michael read through the history of the company.

"In 2005, Excel was bought out by Walker and Thompson," Michael read out loud.

"Walker and Thompson?" John asked. "That name sounds familiar."

Michael went back to Google and typed in "Walker and Thompson + Nerno". "If I'm not mistaken, Nerno also employs Walker and Thompson," he said.

A few minutes later, Michael's suspicion was confirmed. "Interesting that Nerno and the Icelandic Media Corp use the same company . . ."

John smiled. "I thought I was the one with the crazy theories."

"Well, we don't know who owns Icelandic Media, and this Levitt guy is the only way we can trace them. I have a feeling there is a connection."

"I don't know. As I recall, Walker and Thompson is a big company and has lots of clients," John said.

He went back to Sheila's computer and connected to the hotel wi-fi, and her Outlook email popped up.

"If somebody is willing to hack into your bank account and cancel your credit card, then maybe they bought the *Daily Globe* with a shell company just so they could fire all of us," Michael said.

But John wasn't paying attention. Strangely enough, Sheila had received a new email into her account. The email was labeled "Ko Chang" and embedded within it was a compressed audio file, which John downloaded.

"I think I've got something," John said.

Once the file finished downloading, it played automatically. John recognized David Kahn's distinct voice. "You know our Ko Chang Project?"

"Of course," Andrea Drashkov said.

"There seems to have been a mistake," Kahn's digital voice replied.

"For fuck's sake, David. Just tell me."

"There's no oil. At all."

"What do you mean?"

"I mean we're dry."

"Nothing at all? Shit, David," Andrea said. "Who fucked this one up? I mean how could we be so wrong?"

John could feel static electricity climb up his body as he listened. This was it. This was what he had been searching for. He felt a sense of relief that he hadn't been chasing a ghost after all.

"Okay, David, I'll see you when I get back."

"That's a good girl," Kahn said.

Neither Michael nor John said anything for a long time. They just stared at the computer. Michael was the first to sum it up: "Holy shit!"

John clicked on the person who had sent the file. It was another Hotmail account, Ko-ChangProject@hotmail.com.

"It seems to be an account set up just to send this file," Michael said.

"What do you think will happen if we email them back?" John asked.

Michael shrugged. "I'm guessing they will probably want to remain anonymous."

"I'm going to try it anyway," John said, typing a reply and hitting "send".

Moments later he got a reply from Hotmail saying that his message could not be delivered.

"It seems," Michael said, reading the email, "the account has already been closed. The police might be able to trace it. I don't know."

John nodded. He wasn't ready to give the file over to the police quite yet. "It's kind of strange. The email was sent yesterday morning."

John shook his head. By the time Sheila's email account had received the message, she had already committed suicide. What did this mean?

"I think the file was actually meant for you," Michael said. "Whoever sent it knew you had the computer."

John turned and looked up at Michael. "Now you're thinking like an investigative journalist."

Michael gave John a slightly embarrassed smile. "Thank you."

"The only person who knew that we have the computer is Mathew McKinnon, Sheila's husband," John said, thoughtfully.

"You think he sent you the file?"

John shook his head. "I don't think so. I think it has to be somebody inside of Nerno. Perhaps a friend of Sheila's."

"But whoever had the file, why would they hold onto it for so long?"

"It doesn't matter. We have it now. Can you burn the audio clip to a disc for me and make several copies? I don't want somebody stealing it this time and leaving me empty handed."

John dug his phone from his pocket and dialled the Nerno office.

"David Kahn's office."

"Joyce, it's John Webster."

"What can I do for you, Mr. Webster?" Joyce Lancroft asked. Her voice instantly changed from polite and perky to cold and hostile.

John felt slightly giddy from his good fortune. "I would like a Pulitzer Prize. You think you could get me one?"

"I'm in no mood for jokes, Mr. Webster."

"Then do you think you could get me your boss?"

"I'm afraid he's unavailable at the moment."

"Joyce, he will want to talk to me."

Lancroft let out a frustrated sigh. "And why is that?"

"Because I'm going with a story tomorrow saying that he knew all about the lack of oil at Ko Chang."

"Goodbye, John."

"Joyce, don't hang up on me. I have a recording. Let me play it for you."

John put his phone up to the speakers of Sheila's computer and played the audio file for Lancroft.

After the recording was over, Lancroft said, "Let me go see if he's in his office."

John waited about six or seven minutes until he heard the phone transfer lines. "David Kahn here."

"Mr. Kahn, it's John Webster here. I'm writing a story saying you knew about the lack of oil at Ko Chang, and willingly misled investors to drive up the stock value of your company. Do you have any comment?"

There was a long pause. John wasn't aware of anything else except the silent phone. John looked over at Michael, who was staring intently at him, and John smiled back at him. It was these moments that John lived for. The long pauses, the stunned silences, the checkmate moment when the indestructible broke down like an old, rusty engine.

"I don't comment on shit, Webster," Kahn said, finally.

"Really?" John said. He once again held his phone to the computer and replayed the clip. When he got back on the phone there was another period of silence that lasted so long, John was afraid that Kahn had hung up.

"Hello?"

"John . . . what do you want?"

John was confused by the question. He hadn't expected Kahn to react so calmly. "What I want is a comment I can put in my newspaper."

"Let me put it another way. How much would it take for that recording to simply disappear?"

"I don't think you know me very well, Mr. Kahn. The recording isn't going anywhere."

"Everybody has a price, John. What's yours?"

"Is this how you do business, Mr. Kahn? Because, if so, I'm not surprised you are in your predicament."

"A million dollars? Ten million dollars?"

"How about you put the money you stole from me back into my bank account? Then we call it even."

"Sorry? What bank account? Name any account and I'll deposit the money."

"Just give me a comment so I can write it in the paper."

"Congratulations, Mr. Webster. You've proven you're not a coward after all," Kahn said, before hanging up.

John put his phone slowly back into his pocket.

"What did he say?" Michael asked.

John looked thoughtfully up at Michael. "He really didn't know what I was talking about when I told him to put my money back into my bank account."

"You don't think he was the one that did it, then?"

John shook his head. If it wasn't David Kahn, then who was it?

John took about an hour to write the article. Michael reread it after he was done and suggested a couple of changes, which John added to his copy. John stared at the words on the page. He was having mixed feelings about the story. Would it be the last one that he ever wrote for the *Daily Globe*? If so, he was happy that it would be one of his best. He hadn't written a story this good since he had followed the Heart Gang in Vancouver.

"You sure this thing is authentic?" Michael said.

"As sure as I can be without professional equipment."

"You don't want to hold off on the story until we get the file checked out, or at least find out who sent it?"

John shook his head. "The *Daily Globe* doesn't have that luxury."

"You still want to give it to them. I know some business magazines that will pay you top dollar for this."

John stood up and stretched. Was he letting his emotions get the better of practicality? Perhaps, but he didn't care. "Let's just call it my swan song to the paper," John said.

Michael seemed to accept this, and they emailed the article off under the byline John Webster and Michael Chu. The byline felt strange, although not wholly wrong. Years ago he would have fought for the sole credit, but now he was being laid off. Soon he wouldn't have a job. Things changed. He couldn't remember the last time that he had shared a byline with anybody.

It must have been back in Afghanistan, he thought. *Maybe Iraq.*

Michael suggested that they celebrate, and so they went downstairs to the bar. They sat in a booth while jazz piano played sombrely on the speakers overhead. John listened to the song for a while, sitting back in his seat and letting the sound seep through his entire body. The notes were slow and melancholy, as if the piano player was crying as he played, and John felt an overwhelming sense of sadness for the unknown composer. Eventually the piano was joined by a slow, gravelly voice that crooned about love, loss and life.

A waitress came over and Michael ordered a bottle of champagne.

"I'm not really a big champagne drinker," John said. The last time he had drank champagne was at his wedding. "Maybe I'll just stick to whiskey."

"No, this is a momentous occasion. We need to mark it. Don't worry, I'll buy it."

The waitress came over with two glasses and the bottle of champagne. She set the two glasses down and showed Michael the bottle, and he surveyed it critically.

"Yes, that's good," he said, nodding towards the waitress. The waitress poured the colourless, fizzy liquid into the glasses, and they toasted.

"To us and the future," Michael said. "You know, maybe I'll start up an online magazine. You want to help me? You could be my first hire."

"I don't know," John said. The loss of the *Daily Globe* was too great. Too fresh in his mind.

"Are you going to give the recording to the police?" Michael asked.

John shrugged. "I will give them a copy, sure. Perhaps they'll arrest David Kahn. Perhaps they'll even get a conviction."

John took another sip of champagne. Looking at the glass, he wondered why it always marked the milestones in people's lives.

He remembered finishing off the last of the champagne in the hotel suite that he and Hayden had rented, looking out at the dark water and beyond, at the multitude of sparkling lights. She was still in her white satin dress, slumped over the couch, smiling lazily up at John.

He was still in his tuxedo. His body had been muscular and slim back then. He had once been handsome.

He had leaned down to kiss Hayden. Her lips were sticky and moist, a mixture of lipstick and perspiration. He had loved those lips then, but now they belonged to somebody else. Now Hayden had somebody else to get drunk with.

Michael and John ordered some food and finished the champagne. They ordered more drinks.

The bar eventually closed and they were kicked out, and they decided to go back to their rooms. They were feeling giddy and lightheaded as they slowly criss-crossed their way to the elevator.

They laughed, not knowing exactly what they were laughing at, as the elevator made its way skyward.

They parted at their respective doorways. It took John several moments to locate his wallet and find his key card.

"John?" Michael called from down the hallway.

"What? Keep your voice down."

Michael took several drunken steps towards him. "Does it bother you that we don't know who sent Sheila that file?"

John paused to consider it. His brain felt like a bunch of cross wires, scrambled and unable to make a decent connection. "It bothers me, but not greatly. It happens sometimes. People just don't want to be identified."

Michael shook his head. "I don't know . . . to me it just feels like we are being coerced into some plan we can't see."

Devastation

JOHN WAS AWOKEN BY A sound in the hallway, the soft shuffle of somebody making their way to the elevator. He sat up and rubbed his forehead. He had a seething headache from the alcohol. He got up and went to the washroom, where he took two painkillers.

He looked at himself in the mirror. He thought that he would have slept soundly after vindicating so many ghosts, but the ghosts didn't seem placated by David Kahn's fall. He still felt Sheila McKinnon lingering around. Why didn't she leave him alone? What was he missing? Did she want him to send Kahn to jail? Then would she be happy?

He had dreamed the same dream, only slightly varied. The Lamborghini still crashed and sent funnels of smoke rising, but instead of Amira standing there, it was Sheila, accusing him.

"You hear the wind?" Sheila asked, cupping her hand to her ear. They were standing in the middle of a deserted road. Silence permeated the street.

John stood and listened, but he couldn't hear anything. "What are you talking about, Sheila?"

"The wind is calling your name, John. Listen to it."

John woke up at that moment. Or at least, he couldn't remember anything more.

He stepped into the shower and turned the nozzle until it was icy cold. He stood underneath until he started to shiver, and then he turned the water off. He now felt awake, aware and alive.

He stepped out of the tub and dried himself off. He checked his phone and found that he had two missed calls. One was from Charles Dana, and the other was from Gerard Levitt. They were both probably phoning to tell him that he was no longer employed, and so he ignored both the calls.

You hear the wind? Sheila had said.

Before John got dressed, he stopped and listened, but the sounds were all the usual sounds associated with the morning routine of a hotel. Out in the hallway a cart was being pushed and a maid was knocking on doors, and John thought that he heard a television being switched on. Outside, he could hear the quiet hum of cars travelling along the highway.

Sheila had told him to listen to the wind, but he could no more hear the wind in his hotel room than in his dream. Hadn't he done what she'd wanted him to do? Sure it had cost, but what in life didn't?

John shook off the presence of Sheila and put on some clothes. His phone made a helpful buzz, reminding him of his messages, but instead of listening to them, he knocked on Michael's door to see if he wanted to get some breakfast, but there was no answer. He was either already downstairs or was passed out in his room.

John found a copy of the *Daily Globe* and went to the lobby for breakfast. He looked around for Michael, but he couldn't see him, and so he sat down and ordered a cup of coffee and some bacon, eggs and French toast.

Maybe the grease would soak up the remaining alcohol that still lingered in his system, John thought.

He looked at the front page. The top article was written by Charles Dana, about it being the last print edition of the *Daily Globe*. John was always amazed at how brilliant a writer the boss was. Charles wrote about the changing landscape of journalism, and the storied history that the *Daily Globe* had achieved since it was founded in 1844.

Below was John's article. He read it over several times, as was his custom, and was pleased to find that the copy editor hadn't changed much.

John's phone buzzed again. He looked at the caller ID, and saw that it was Charles Dana again. John was in the middle of a mouthful of eggs, and decided that he would call back later. Was it possible that Charles was phoning about something else? John put his phone away. He would deal with it after breakfast.

An older couple sat down at the table adjacent to John's. They were already talking about his article, and David Kahn.

"It's too bad the paper couldn't be saved," the man said to the woman. "I always enjoyed reading it."

John finished his breakfast and walked back to his room. He was about to phone Charles when he was interrupted by a man calling his name. John turned and saw Detective Orlando Corea and another man, presumably Corea's partner, walking towards him.

"Webster, what the fuck?"

"Good morning, detectives," John said, forcing a smile on his face.

"What the hell is this about a recording?"

John took an aggressive step forward, deciding that the best way to hold his ground was to start his own attack. "Weren't you supposed to phone me with an update about my bank account?"

"I told you ITCU is working on it."

"How can I make myself clearer? I have no money. My bank account is empty."

"They are trying to find out how your account was cracked into. They are hoping that way will lead to some clues on whoever did it. But so far it seems like the hackers were experts. Tell me about this recording. Where did you get it?"

"I found it on Sheila McKinnon's personal computer. I will send you a copy once I'm done with it."

Corea shook his head. "No, you'll hand it over now." Corea took a step up to John so that they were no more than a couple of inches from each other. John could smell his breath.

"All right, I'll just make sure I have a copy."

"And we want the computer."

John shook his head. "I'm sorry, but I'm not finished with it. I'll drive it over personally, I promise."

"How did you get the computer in the first place? Did you steal it?"

"Her husband gave it to me. Talk to him if you don't believe me."

Corea and his partner exchanged glances. There seemed to be some sort of unspoken communication between them. "John, we don't want to get a search warrant if we can help it. Perhaps we can make a trade."

"What do you propose?'

"You give us the computer and I give you an exclusive interview."

John shook his head. "No, I want full access."

"Full access? We've been over this," Corea yelled. "We don't even know if there is anything on the computer."

"Well, you have the audio clip and I bet you'll find something else useful. I just haven't had a chance to fully explore it."

"How do we know you're telling the truth?"

John shrugged. "You don't. But I have no reason to lie. I want David Kahn to go to jail as much as you guys."

Corea looked back at his partner.

"All right, give us a moment."

Corea and his partner walked several feet down the hallway and talked quietly with each other. John tried to listen in, but they were too quiet and they had their backs turned. John's phone rang again and he looked at the caller ID. It was Charles Dana phoning him again. John figured that it must be urgent if he would phone three times in an hour.

John debated whether to answer it, but before he could make up his mind, Corea and his partner walked back towards him, forcing him to put his phone back into his pocket.

"Okay, it's a deal," Corea said.

John nodded, pleased at the leverage that he had used. The truth was that Sheila's computer probably wasn't very useful to him, and that it would be much better to turn it over to a team of forensic scientists, who would be able to do a much better job than John would.

"Follow me," John said.

John took them to his room, but just as John turned the door knob, Corea's cell phone started ringing.

He looked down at the number and said, "Sorry, I have to take this."

Corea answered the call and started walking away from his partner and John.

John looked at Corea's partner. He looked slightly younger than Corea, and darker skinned.

"I'm sorry, but we haven't actually formally met," John said.

"Detective D'Hereaux."

John nodded and offered his hand to D'Hereaux, who took it as if he was touching a limp dog toy.

"How do you spell your name? Just in case I need to use you in my article."

D'Hereaux frowned deeply, which was just the reaction that John wanted. D'Hereaux reluctantly pulled a business card from his coat pocket and handed it to John.

"Let's hope it doesn't come to that," D'Hereaux said.

John glanced down the hallway, where Corea was still on the phone. "Shall we wait for your partner?"

"Let's just get this over with."

John went into his room and D'Hereaux followed him. Sheila's computer was still on the desk, so John unplugged it and gave it to D'Hereaux. Corea opened the door and looked frantically at his partner. "Come on, we have to go."

"Why?" John asked. "What's going on?"

Corea didn't answer, but motioned D'Hereaux to hurry.

"We have a deal," John said, indignantly, following the two detectives down the hallway.

"This is something else," Corea replied, not looking back at John.

They entered the elevator, and John motioned to follow, but Corea blocked the doorway with his arm. "You're not coming with us."

John held the door open. "Why not? You've obviously got something important."

"I told you, this is something different."

The elevator started to wail in its electronic voice as the door struggled to close. "Stop blocking the door," Corea said.

"Not until you tell me what's going on."

"You want me to arrest you for obstruction of justice?"

"Just tell me what's so important."

Corea moved swiftly, grabbing John's wrist and twisting it behind his back. John barely registered what had happened until he was facing the opposite direction. Corea then gently and with great finesse shifted John about a foot back, clearing the door so that the elevator could close. Corea then stepped back into the elevator.

John turned—rubbing his wrist, which wasn't really hurt—but he was too late. The elevator doors had closed, leaving him alone in the corridor.

But John wasn't about to let a good lead get away, and decided that he would take the stairs. About halfway down, John found himself breathing hard, and he had to stop for a minute. A cramp was beginning to form on the side of his stomach, but he pressed on, and made it to the main lobby just in time to see Corea and D'Hereaux exit the main entrance.

John cursed that his car was in the underground parking lot and would take too much time to retrieve, so instead of wasting time, he got the bellboy to call him a cab. John jumped into the back and told the driver to follow the unmarked police car, which was speeding away.

"You're kidding, right?" the driver said. "I'm not chasing anybody."

"I'll double your fare," John said, suddenly remembering that he had no money in his account to even pay the standard fare.

"Give me a destination, otherwise please get out of my cab right now."

"Please, they're disappearing."

"Who are you anyway?" the driver asked. "You think you're in some kind of movie?"

John just shook his head and got out of the cab. He wasn't wearing a jacket, and the cold bit at his arms and face. He quickly retreated inside, where it was warmer. He took out his phone and called Corea, but as he suspected, there was no answer. He wondered if he should bother getting his rental car, but decided that it was a futile effort. Corea and D'Hereaux were gone.

As John waited for the elevator to take him back to his room, his phone rang again. It was Charles Dana, and this time John answered.

"Webster, I'm so glad you answered. David Kahn committed suicide late last night. I need you to go over to the Nerno office and see what's going on."

"What?" John stood, stunned. The elevator doors opened and then closed.

"I tried getting hold of Chu, but he's not answering his phone."

John felt a rush of blood to his head. "I just talked to him. Are you sure?"

It was a stupid question to ask, but John couldn't think of anything else to say.

"I'm positive," Charles said. "Now get over there."

"How did you learn this before I did?"

"You know me. I have sources everywhere."

"Does this mean I'm still employed?"

"Did you talk to Levitt yet?"

"No, not yet."

"I'm supposed to refer all questions over to him. Anyway, this is my last day. I'm not sure who they are going to appoint to replace me, but I guess you'll be answerable to them."

"Boss?" John took in a deep breath of air.

"Yes?"

"Thanks . . . thanks for everything, for hiring me. Thanks for believing in me."

"It's okay. I'm glad to have worked with you."

"What are you going to do?"

"I don't know. Take a vacation, I guess." Charles paused, but he sounded as if he wanted to say something more. "You know," he continued. "I never did any of the tourist stuff before, so I guess now is my chance. I think I'll go ski Whistler first."

John couldn't help but laugh. He had a hard time picturing the lanky body of Charles Dana on a pair of skis, looking down a ski slope.

"Okay, have fun."

"And remember, John . . . it's not the stars that hold our destiny, but ourselves," Charles said, and before John could guess where the quote was from, Charles had hung up.

John put the phone back in his pocket. He knew that he should get to the Nerno office as quickly as possible. He realized that that was probably where Corea and D'Hereaux were heading, but he needed a moment to think, to collect his nerves. Did Kahn commit suicide right after John had spoken to him? Was he responsible?

John took the elevator back to his room. He knocked on Michael Chu's door, and this time a weary voice answered.

"Michael? It's John. Can you open up?"

It took a while for Michael to open the door. He was still in his boxers, and his hair was a scraggly mess. His hangover seemed to have been worse than John's, or maybe he just wasn't used to them.

"What?" Michael asked.

"David Kahn committed suicide last night. We need to go over there."

Michael nodded. "Okay, just let me go to the bathroom and get dressed."

"Okay, but hurry up. We don't have much time."

Ten minutes later they were in the car. John was driving. It was the beginning of the morning rush hour, and John had to contend with a lot of traffic.

"You think we'll be able to get in?" Michael asked.

"I hope so. Detective Corea just promised me an exclusive."

Michael leaned his head against the window. He looked pale and sick. "I wish I had brought some water," he said.

"We'll stop for some water on the way back," John promised.

They arrived at the building, but were unable to find a parking space anywhere. Although the police hadn't blocked off the street, there were about five police cars and two Crime Scene Unit vans parked along 7th Avenue. There were also two media vans. John decided to turn onto Barclay Street and park several blocks down.

By the time John and Michael got to the entrance of the Nerno building, John estimated that Kahn had been dead for about twelve hours. John wondered why the police would still be at the scene of a suicide. Perhaps it was because David Kahn was so high profile that they wanted to make sure they did a thorough job.

At the door, a security guard stopped them. He was wearing a light blue uniform and his name tag said Wright. The cold air was beginning to seep through John's jacket and into his bones.

"Who are you?"

John looked at Michael, but decided that the truth was the best option. "We are reporters from the *Daily Globe*."

"I'm sorry, but you can't enter."

"Don't worry, Mr. Wright. We have been authorized by Detective Corea."

But the security guard wasn't about to be fooled so easily. "I'm sorry, sir, but I still can't let you in."

John smiled. "I understand, but if you could call Detective Corea or Detective D'Hereaux, they would be able to confirm I am authorized to enter."

Wright frowned. "Does it look like I'm employed by the Calgary Police Service?"

John, who was freezing, was beginning to lose his patience. "Then who do you report to? Get them on the phone so we can go upstairs."

John thought that Wright was going to tell them to get off the property, but instead he told them to wait, and he disappeared inside.

"That was brilliant," Michael said, although he still looked like he was about to pass out. "Absolutely brilliant."

For some reason the praise bothered John. He turned to Michael and said, "It will be brilliant if we get upstairs."

Wright returned several minutes later. "I'm sorry, but I was told you're not allowed to enter."

"Did you talk to Detective Corea?"

"Yes I did, and he said he doesn't know you, and not to let you enter."

"That's impossible. Phone him back. Let me talk to him."

"I'm afraid that's not going to happen. I suggest you help your friend. He doesn't look so well."

John scowled and looked over at Michael, who appeared to be on the verge of toppling over. John pulled Michael back to the street. John took out his phone to try to call Corea, but he found that his fingers were too cold to use it.

"What do we do now?" Michael asked.

"Follow me," John said. They walked to the Canadian Broadcasting Corporation van and knocked on the window. Two men were sitting in the front seat, looking bored, and reluctant to roll down the window. John tapped again and this time the driver pressed the button, opening the window only a crack.

"Yes?"

John didn't recognize either the driver or the passenger.

"My name is John Webster. I'm a reporter for the *Daily Globe*. You got anything?"

"John Webster?" the driver asked. "Yes, of course. I know you."

"Is there some place we could talk?"

"There is a coffee shop just around the corner."

The driver and the man in the passenger seat, obviously the reporter, judging by the bright blue suit and the red tie he had on, and the glossy haircut, conferred with each other. John wasn't able to hear what they said, but eventually the driver got out.

"My name is Lenny Brockington." He shook hands with John and Michael.

"How long have you guys been here?" John asked.

"About two hours. We got a tip from a Nerno employee."

Although John was curious to know, he knew that he couldn't ask who the employee was. Brockington would never tell him.

"Anything happen this morning?"

Brockington shook his head. "We got some good B roll but that's about it. Haven't been able to interview anybody yet."

They arrived at the coffee shop. John ordered three coffees and then made Michael pay for them. Michael scowled at John, but then handed over his credit card.

"My bank account was tampered with," John explained to Brockington.

"Really? I had that happen a few years ago. Scary, isn't it?"

John agreed, but didn't want to get into it. "I think we can be helpful to each other. What do you say we exchange information?"

Brockington nodded. "I read your article this morning. You think it was what triggered the suicide?"

"Okay, for starters, who is calling it a suicide?"

Brockington shrugged. "I heard a self-inflicted gun wound. The police haven't confirmed anything yet."

"Where did you hear that?"

Brockington shook his head. "I can't say . . . plus, exposure of a major fraud would indicate suicide. I mean, it makes sense. You actually got a recording of Kahn admitting to it?"

John nodded. "I'll get you a copy if you can help with sources."

"Exclusive?"

John nodded. He knew that Charles wanted a copy for the *Daily Globe* website, but if he made a trade, it might be worth holding off the website for a bit. He knew that Charles might not think so, but he would chance it.

Brockington lapsed into silence. He also had a major decision to make. Usually sources were gold, and selfishly protected, but playing an audio clip on television was far more powerful than it would be reading about it in the newspaper. "Let me talk to my source and I'll see if I can pass the name along."

John nodded, noting how Brockington had avoided using gender in his sentence. John wondered if that meant that his source was a female. In the male dominated business world of oil companies, John assumed that Brockington would have felt it okay to use "he" but not "she". "She" might just have limited the possibilities too much. Then again, John wondered if he was reading too much into it.

John nodded. "Okay, it's a deal."

Brockington said that he would have to get back to the van. After he left, Michael asked if they were going too, but John shook his head. "No, let's wait for a while. I want to call Corea."

Corea answered after what seemed like an eternity of ringing. "John, if you ever pull anything like that again there will be serious consequences."

"We had a deal, detective. Full access."

"Well, this isn't my investigation."

"Don't split hairs with me, detective."

"Regardless, I can't let you into a crime scene."

"The crime scene is about twelve hours old. I doubt we could do any harm. What are you doing there still?"

"I'm not going to comment."

"Can you confirm some facts for me at least?" John said, taking a pen and small notepad out of his pocket.

"Only off the record."

"No, that's not going to fly. I'll do it on background."

"All right. It's a deal."

"Is it a murder or suicide?"

"David Kahn undoubtedly took his own life," Corea said, sounding uneasy.

"Did he leave a note?"

"No, no note has been found, yet."

"Well, if you haven't found a note after twelve hours, isn't it safe to say there isn't one?" John asked, feeling a little testy.

"I think it's a little premature to rule anything out. He could have emailed it to his wife or a colleague. He could have left it someplace else."

"How did he die?"

"He was killed with at P-32 semi-automatic, sometimes referred to as a mousegun."

"A mousegun?" John said. He had never heard the term before.

"It's a small gun designed for self-defence."

"Did anybody know he owned a gun? His wife, secretary?"

"No, nobody knew anything about a gun."

"So wouldn't that be a reason to suspect murder?"

"His secretary was outside his office the entire time. She said nobody went in or out during the time she was there."

"Unless she was lying," John pointed out.

"I don't think she's lying. She was the one who called 911."

John sighed. Did he just want it to be murder because he felt guilty? Was his judgment compromised? He didn't like to think of the possibility.

"Okay, thanks for the info, detective."

"And remember: keep my name out of it."

"Okay, no problem," John said, and hung up. He looked across the table at Michael, who was looking at him intently.

"What next?" Michael asked.

"I need to make a phone call."

"To who?"

John hesitated. "She's a fellow reporter. I promised to help her if I got a scoop."

Madeline picked up on the second ring. "It's good to hear from you," she said, cheerfully. "I was afraid I mucked everything up."

"I've got something for you."

"Even better."

John told Madeline about David Kahn's suicide, and about the weapon that he had killed himself with.

"John?" Madeline said, after John had finished explaining.

"Yes?"

"I'm sorry I walked out of the restaurant."

"It's okay."

"So we're still friends?"

How had the Jetta known where to find him? Did Madeline have anything to do with it? John was beginning to see conspiracies everywhere.

"Sure," he said.

After John got off the phone, he turned to Michael. "Well, we've got some good information to go on. Let's go write a story."

"But who are we going to give it to?" Michael asked with a frown.

John considered this for a moment. "Maybe we do it your way and auction it off to the highest bidder."

The Press Conference

ANDREA DRASKHOV TOOK THE STAGE, the big Nerno logo on a banner draped behind her. The cameras were already flashing, creating spasms of light. She tried to look calm and composed. This was her time. She was stepping up to the plate. She had chosen her outfit with the greatest care: a grey suit with a tube skirt and a purple blouse. Her fingernails matched her blouse. Her usual wire-thin hair was permed and glossy.

She stepped up to the microphone and adjusted it needlessly. She had already adjusted it eleven or twelve times in the hours leading up to the press conference, but it was a habit that calmed her. She looked out into the sea of reporters gathered in the small conference room that she had rented at the Hyatt, a couple of streets down from the Nerno building.

The press conference had been hastily convened, but as Andrea had predicted, there was no shortage of interest.

"Ladies and gentlemen," she started, just as she had in the morning. "I am here today because our CEO and chairman of the board, David Kahn, died tragically yesterday. I can only offer condolences to his wife and children. He recruited me personally to work at Nerno. We worked many long hours together over the years. He was a good man and I will miss him greatly." Andrea paused for effect, again looking around at the reporters. She looked for John Webster, but couldn't see him anywhere. She hadn't spoken to him since he had written the article about the audio file on Sheila McKinnon's computer.

"But I am also here for another reason," Andrea said. "The board of directors convened early this morning, and it has appointed me acting CEO of Nerno Energy. I am going to take this company in a radical new direction, one that will build a new future for the employees, customers and shareholders of this great corporation. I look forward to the new challenge. I will take a few questions before ending this press conference."

About three dozen hands shot up. Andrea chose a reporter, Josh McGuire, who worked for the *Calgary Herald*, and with whom Andrea had established a good working relationship over the years.

"You said you are going to take the company in a new direction. Can you expand on that?"

"Certainly," Andrea said. "Although I can't go into specifics, I can say that we will close Ko Chang and that horrible chapter in this company's history, and search for new reserves both here in North America and across the globe. Secondly, we are going to discontinue talks with the China National Offshore Oil Company. We have no interest in selling at this time."

There was a murmur that went through the crowd. More hands shot up. Andrea chose a young reporter in the front row. "You said acting CEO. Does that mean you'll be looking for a replacement? And secondly, as acting CEO, do you feel you are qualified to make such large decisions?"

Andrea smiled brightly, as if she had been expecting those questions all along (which she had, since she had promised the young reporter an exclusive). "The board has assured me they will not be looking for another CEO anytime soon. As for your second question, I feel like I must make the best possible decisions for the company while I have this responsibility, and as such, I feel we need a new start." Andrea paused. "Thank you, everyone, for being here."

Andrea drove home in her Lamborghini. The sky was a soft pink colour, with pink clouds like cotton candy. She felt that the news conference had gone well, although she didn't know if she should have had it so soon after David's death. She hadn't had time to properly digest his death. Everything had been so fast and spontaneous. She kept thinking that the sadness and the grief would appear suddenly and pour out of her, but so far nothing had come, and she felt only a robotic numbness.

She listened to the news reports on the radio and they were mostly positive, praising her leadership in troubled time, and saying that the stock exchange would react favourably to this new direction.

Let's hope so, Andrea thought. The company could use a price increase. And the instant that she thought about the stock price, she cursed herself for being insensitive, but that was what the board was thinking about too. Why else would they have convened in the morning to appoint her CEO?

Her cell phone rang, and even without glancing at the screen she knew instinctively who it would be. And she was right. She smiled as she answered the phone.

"John Webster, I didn't see you at my press conference. I put on a glorious show."

"Yes, I'm sure you were perfect."

"Yes, I was perfect," she said. "I was sad when I didn't see you. Why didn't you show up?"

"I don't do press conferences."

"Oh, I forgot, you are above press conferences. They are for inferior journalists."

"No, I just don't think there is much use in getting the same information as everybody else. I call that public relations, not journalism," he said.

"I hate it when you get on your high horse, John. It doesn't suit you."

There was a pause on the phone.

"I guess I owe you an apology," John said.

"I guess you do, but why don't you make up for it by coming over for dinner tonight? You can apologize in person."

John hesitated. "I really shouldn't."

"Why not? Don't like fraternizing with the enemy? I thought we'd signed a peace treaty."

"All right . . . what time?"

"I expect you at seven. Don't be late," Andrea said, ending the call and throwing her phone down on the seat beside her. She smiled at herself in the mirror. It was beginning to turn into a great day.

Andrea parked her Lamborghini and went over to the elevator. She got in and swiped her card, pressing the button for the penthouse. She watched the television as the elevator quickly took her to her destination. She hated elevators; the cramped metallic quarters made her feel claustrophobic, and she was relieved when she got out.

She took off her high heels, which hurt her feet, and went over to the window. She stared out at the traffic below. The city was glowing with lights, and if she had been closer and a little less insulated, she would have been able to hear the sounds of engines, of horns honking, of people yelling. She crossed her arms and looked up at the white Rockies, standing like mirages in the distance.

Her phone rang, but she didn't answer it, letting it go to voicemail instead. She suspected that lots of people would want to get hold of her: journalists, the board, her staff. She had to decide what to do with Joyce Lancroft. So many decisions . . . but they could all wait.

Andrea had a shower, plucked her eyebrows and did her nails. Her phone was ringing constantly. She looked at the missed call list and did not see a single number that she recognized. She decided to turn her phone off and not think about her duties for one day.

Tomorrow she had two important television interviews lined up, and then a day full of meetings.

Andrea went to her closet to decide what to wear, when her intercom crackled to life.

"Sorry to disturb you, Madame," the doorman said. "But I have two police officers here who would like to speak with you."

Andrea sighed. She wanted to put off talking to the police, but it seemed that it wasn't possible. She would have to deal with them now.

She pressed the intercom. "Okay, thanks. Send them up."

Andrea slipped a light dress on and waited for the elevator door to open. Two men dressed in cheap suits stepped into the penthouse. They looked around with stupid expressions on their faces. Andrea was used to people looking around in bewilderment at her apartment, and at first she had liked it, felt flattered even, but the feeling quickly wore off and she just felt impatient, especially since the two detectives were unwelcome intruders. However, she didn't let any of that show as she smiled and shook hands with the two detectives.

"Detectives D'Hereaux and Corea."

"Yes, I remember," Andrea said.

"We were wondering if we could ask a few questions." They were both dark-skinned with short, slim builds, and moved economically, as detectives were apt to do.

"Of course. Can I get you anything?" Andrea led the two detectives into the living room, where they sat on the couch. They seemed like an odd couple. They didn't have the brashness that she usually associated with police officers.

"What can I do for you?"

"Well, we are helping out with the Kahn investigation," Corea said.

"Wait a minute . . . investigation?"

Corea looked down at his sweat-stained cuffs. "Yes. We just want to cover all our bases."

"You don't think it was suicide? Is that what you're trying to tell me?"

"No, we are pretty certain it was suicide. We just want to interview everyone who is involved. Cover our bases, like I said."

Andrea put on her best smile. "Sorry, detectives. It's just the whole thing is very shocking."

The detectives nodded. "We understand. We won't take up much of your time, we promise," Corea said.

"Did David Kahn seem depressed?" D'Hereaux asked.

"No, of course not," Andrea said. "He was under a lot of pressure, for sure, but he definitely wasn't depressed."

"Did he receive any death threats?"

Andrea looked from one detective to the other. "You probably know better than I do. You guys have his computer."

The two detectives gave each other a knowing look that Andrea interpreted easily. "He did have death threats," Andrea said.

The two detectives nodded. "That's partly why we wanted to follow up."

"What sort of death threats? Do you know from who?"

Corea shook his head. "No. We haven't been able to determine the source yet."

Andrea studied him. *He's lying*, she thought. *Why is he lying to me? It must be somebody within the company, but who?* Andrea tried to give her best dainty smile. Business required so much acting.

"Were there any other indications he didn't commit suicide?"

"We already told you, we're certain it's suicide."

"Well, you can't be too certain if you're asking me about death threats." Andrea was aware that she was raising her voice, but she was unable to control it.

Detective Corea leaned forward. "This case is highly sensitive. Very political. I'm sure you understand."

Andrea stood up suddenly and started pacing, her mind churning like broken machinery. Outside the sky was flat and gloomy, and seemed to stretch into eternity. The sun was blotted out by bilious cloud cover, and it gave the city a sad, mournful colour. "I'm sorry. This is all very troubling."

"We are very sorry. So David never told you about any of the death threats?"

"He never said he was particularly worried about anybody. I don't think he could have been very bothered by them . . . at least he didn't seem to be." Andrea wrapped her arms around her shoulders. Although her penthouse was perfectly regulated, she suddenly felt cold.

"Well, we won't take up any more of your time," Corea said. "We'll see our own way out."

After the two detectives left, Andrea went into the kitchen and took a bottle of wine from her wine fridge. She uncorked it and poured, but her hands started to shake so violently that she had to stop halfway through. She put the bottle down on the kitchen counter and took a couple of deep breaths.

Where was David when she needed him? He wouldn't be rattled by this, he wouldn't be rattled by anything. For a brief moment Andrea thought that she had been wrong to take the CEO job, but her self-doubt quickly dissipated. It had been what she wanted, what she had been dreaming about.

She went and sat down in the living room, but got up again. Her eyes glanced restlessly over the apartment. It all looked wrong somehow. The coffee table was the wrong colour. The lamp was in the wrong place. The walls needed painting. Even the Monet seemed off somehow. Maybe she should sell the place and move. To where, she didn't know.

The intercom buzzed again, and Andrea gasped.

"Sorry to bother you, Ms. Drashkov, but I have a John Webster here to see you."

Could it be that time? Andrea wondered. But when she glanced at her Cartier watch she realized it that was seven o'clock already.

"Send him up," she said, hoping that her voice sounded natural.

When John arrived, Andrea took his winter layers. Underneath he was dressed in a washed pair of jeans and a striped shirt. His hair was glossy and he smelt fresh, inviting.

"What type of cologne are you wearing?"

John smiled, looking embarrassed. "I don't know. Something I found in the hotel."

"Would you like a drink?"

"Of course."

They clinked glasses and drank. John sipped. Andrea took a liberal gulp.

"You okay?" John asked.

"Yeah, of course. Why?"

"I don't know."

"I mean the police were just here."

"Oh?" John tilted his head.

"It was nothing. Just routine. They wanted to know if David had received any death threats."

"And had he?"

Andrea collapsed on the couch, her skirt riding up her thigh. She didn't bother to straighten it. "Why am I talking to a journalist? I think I should just stop talking."

John sat next to her. She could feel the heaviness of his breathing, and the smell of alcohol on his breath. "Well, for the moment you're talking to an unemployed journalist. What sort of death threats?"

"I don't know. The police didn't go into any specifics. David never told me about them."

"Why do you think he never mentioned it?"

"Let's forget it. Let's talk about something else."

"Sure, Andrea, we can talk about anything you like," he said, soothingly.

She suddenly found herself resting her head against his chest. His heart was pumping fast. She closed her eyes, listening to the soothing rhythm of his body. She didn't move. She wasn't aware of anything until he put his arms on her neck. His fingertips felt warm and moist. She looked at up at him and kissed him, slow and tentative at first, but then with force and passion.

She pulled him into her bedroom, and he somehow meekly followed. They shed their clothes quickly, and in the smooth darkness they explored each other's nakedness. She found the large scar on his leg and recoiled her hand, and then felt suddenly acutely embarrassed.

"It's okay," John whispered. "It's okay."

When he entered her, she let out a low gasp. She found that men liked it when she did that, as if she was having sex for the first time.

John supported his weight with his arms, his body crashing against hers like ocean waves. She felt his chest, the crevasse in his shoulder, no longer frightened by his chewed up body. She moved her hands down his abdomen, and to his sharp hips.

In truth, she felt nothing. No pleasure. No pain. She closed her eyes and let a calm warm feeling swell inside her chest. Nothing came to her mind, and that was how she wanted it. An elixir for her life's burden.

Then she felt something close around her neck. She opened her eyes and found that John had his right hand around her. She smiled up at him, knowing that he didn't have the guts to do it, even if he wanted to.

"Harder," she said.

John squeezed harder. His large, warm body compressed hers. She felt her airway close, her chest expanding as she gasped for air. But no, he wasn't in control. He thought that he could kill her anytime he wanted, but they both knew that he had reached his maximum, his emotional tipping point. He could go no further. Andrea looked up at John, knowing this, even as his face was emotionless, half obscured by the darkness.

"Harder," she gasped, taunting him, feeling her tongue in the back of her throat, her eyes wide.

How far would he go? No matter, she would go further, to show him who the boss was.

John released his grip and Andrea felt a rush of oxygen to her head, and—no matter what she told herself—relief.

After they were done, they just lay in bed, neither moving for a while. Andrea heard John's deep breathing, and in the distance the hum of the fridge, reminding her of the outside world.

"I think I need another drink," John said, after the prolonged silence.

Andrea rolled over. "Okay, I'll fix you one. What do you want?"

"I think I'll get it myself, if that's okay?"

Andrea smiled. "Why don't you relax a bit?"

But John was already sitting up. The sheets fell from his body. He put on his pants and slipped his shirt on over his head, and went in search of his own way to destroy his body.

Andrea rubbed her head and sighed. Her bedroom suddenly seemed large and cold and vacant. Why did men always have to have guilt afterwards?

She suddenly missed David Kahn and his large, confident smile. He used to be a great bedroom talker. Could probably have talked a nun into sleeping with him. But the best thing about him was that he never felt guilty about anything. He took responsibility for his actions, even to the end.

Why did things turn out as they did? she wondered.

Andrea got up and slipped on a white dress, and went in search of John. She found him in the kitchen, sitting on a stool, his broad back hunched over. He had taken a bottle of whiskey from the cupboard and had already made a sizable dent in it.

Andrea got a glass and some ice from the freezer, and sat across from John.

"You always like this with women?" Andrea asked.

John didn't answer. He took another sip of the whiskey.

"You okay? You seem, I don't know . . . distracted."

"I should go," John said, standing up.

"Are you worried about your job, is that it?"

John turned, his expression unreadable, extinguished in the darkness.

"What do you know about my job status?"

"You told me you were unemployed."

"You don't seem too curious. What is the Icelandic Media Corporation?"

Andrea sighed. "I don't know what you're talking about."

"You bought the *Daily Globe*, didn't you? You shut it down to stop me writing about you."

"Oh, come on. Now you're just sounding paranoid."

"Am I?" John said. He advanced towards Andrea. His eyes were wide and his mouth taut.

Andrea backed up until she was against the wall, and waited, but John just stood there, poised.

"Come on, John. Do what you want to do to me. Don't hold back."

John let out a gust of air, relaxing his body. "Just tell me this: did you create the Icelandic Media Corporation just so you could buy the *Daily Globe*?"

"I was trying to protect everybody," Andrea said. "Now look what you've done. David is dead. The company is on the brink of ruin. All because of your fucking article."

"Why would you do that? You've destroyed everything I've worked so hard for."

"It's my duty to protect my company. I won't let you harm it."

John bit his bottom lip. Andrea tried to remain calm. Her breathing steady.

John reached back, and for a moment Andrea thought that he was going to punch her, but instead he flung the whiskey bottle against the wall. The bottle smashed, whiskey running down the wall. Glass was everywhere, and the stinging smell of alcohol hung in the air.

John grabbed his jacket. "I'm not going to let you get away with this."

"It's all perfectly legal," Andrea said. "You can waste your time hiring lawyers, but I dotted every 'i' and crossed every 't'."

John pushed the button, recalling the elevator. Andrea watched him go, the elevator doors closing, leaving her alone once again.

The Detective's Story

THE HEAT WAS ON FULL blast but John was still cold. When he closed his eyes he felt like he was on the top of a building in the middle of Kabul in Afghanistan, stretching out his arms and spreading his fingers open, the frigid night wind blowing across his body.

John would sometimes escape onto the top of a building to be utterly alone, the city chaos below him. There he felt a sense of peacefulness, as if nothing could touch him, as if time stood silent, unmoving.

You hear the wind? Sheila asked.

John got up and went to his suitcase to put on a sweater. He then went back to the bathroom and fumbled in the darkness for more sleeping pills. He took a gulp of water and downed two more.

John climbed back into bed, and pulled the covers over his shoulders and closed his eyes. He listened for a moment or two to the traffic that crawled along in the night-time hours.

Why did you abandon me? Sheila asked. Her short, blonde hair was matted inexplicably with maroon blood.

John opened his eyes and went to get his bottle of whiskey, which he had put on the coffee table. He unscrewed the cap and took a swig. He felt the liquid settle in his body.

Hours went by slowly. John didn't move. He finished the bottle, and still he wasn't able to disappear into a stupor. John began to feel an intolerable rage build up in the pit of his stomach, rumbling through his limbs. He threw the empty bottle against the wall and it smashed, making a loud crashing sound that seemed to echo even louder.

John walked over to his bed and crawled under it. His nose was filled with the smell of dust and decay. Sheila wouldn't be able to reach him under here, he figured. There was no room. He closed his eyes. He remembered some breathing exercises that his shrink had given to him. Deep breath in . . . deep breath out . . . deep breath in . . .

John opened his eyes, and at first he didn't realize where he was. He saw a bunch of spring coils just inches from his face, and it took several moments for him to situate himself. He climbed out from underneath his bed and brushed the dust off of his pants and sweatshirt. He looked at the digital clock, which read 10:15 a.m.

John checked his cell phone, but the battery was dead, so he fumbled for the charger in his suitcase. He eventually found it and plugged it into the wall.

He managed to make it to the shower, and turned on the hot water tap. He held his face up to the water, letting it douse his body. He stepped out and had a big drink from the sink faucet.

John got dressed and phoned Detective Corea, half surprised that his phone was still connected.

"It's been a while. I was beginning to miss you, Webster."

"And I you, detective. I want to meet and discuss our arrangement."

"What arrangement?"

"Come on," John said. "Don't act like that now that you've got what you want."

"Why should I cooperate with you?"

"Besides it being the honourable thing to do?"

"The honourable thing to do is to protect the interests of this investigation."

John sat at the edge of the bed. "So it's still an investigation?"

"I don't know. Like I said, that's not my department."

"Can you meet me in about an hour?"

"I can't be seen with you."

"I have some information you might find handy."

"What?"

"You think after what I got from our last negotiation I will just hand it over to you?"

Corea fell silent, and John waited while Corea decided on the best angle to play. "Okay, there's a Thai place on 8th Avenue. Can you meet me there at noon?"

"Sure, I'll find it. Don't bring your partner."

John expected that Corea would object, but he didn't, and John hung up.

John was about to go into the hallway to find Michael Chu, but remembered that he had already flown home. He'd wanted to borrow some more money from him, but he supposed that he would just have to make do with the money that he had.

The restaurant on 8th Avenue was called the Rose Garden Thai. John had a little difficulty finding it because 8th Avenue inexplicably turned into Stephen Avenue. The Rose Garden had an ugly pink and green awning which was covered with icicles. John opened the door and stepped inside. It was long and narrow and had mirrors on the walls, to make it look bigger, John supposed.

Orlando Corea wasn't there, so John sat in the corner, his back to the wall. An old habit that he had formed in Iraq and had kept with him, along with the nightmares and all of the funny quirks that most people didn't understand.

The waitress, wearing an old pink dress, poured him some lukewarm tea. John tried it, but decided that he would order a coffee instead. The waitress came back with a pot. As John suspected, it wasn't very good, but he drank it anyway.

John waited, reading the newspaper. After a while, he looked at the clock on his phone. It was quarter past twelve, and he had begun to think that he was going to get stood up, when Detective Corea sauntered in the door. He was alone. He slid into the booth across from John.

"What do you have for me?" Corea asked.

"Not so fast. I want the case file for Sheila and Kahn."

"It's not mine to give."

"You can get me Sheila's."

Corea shrugged, as if he didn't want to commit either way.

John leaned in close to Corea. "Two suicides and one accidental death. At what point do you believe there is a pattern?"

"When we find a pattern?" Corea said. "One was a car accident, one was carbon dioxide poisoning, the other was a gunshot to the head. You see a pattern?"

"They all knew something about Nerno. Somebody is trying to cover up their tracks."

"Who?"

"Somebody who has lots of connections and is very powerful."

Corea sat back, slapping his hands on the table. "And who is on your list of suspects now?"

"I'm not sure, and I won't know until I have a look at Sheila's car."

"We both know that's not going to happen."

"Did the CSU find anything to indicate murder?"

"You know, even if they did, I wouldn't tell you."

John nodded. It was about what he had expected. "How about we make a trade? My files for yours?"

Corea cracked his knuckles. Giving a reporter an active police file could get him put on desk duty indefinitely, but on the other hand, if the file John traded him could crack the case he would come away looking like a hero and, if John had guessed correctly, possibly have an out from IMET. Nobody wanted to stay in IMET forever. It was a dead-end job with little possibility for promotion.

"Why would I want your files, especially when I could just subpoena you?"

"You know, even if you subpoena me, I won't hand them over."

"What do they contain?"

"All my notes on Nerno."

"And what good would they do me?"

"I have information you don't have. They may be helpful. They may not. It's a risk you'll have to take."

"Okay, you give me your file for one of mine," Corea said.

"No, I want all the files you have on Hopkins, McKinnon and Kahn."

Corea shook his head. "Why would I trade all three for your one? You have to choose."

John thought hard. He knew that the older ones would be potentially more useful because there would be more information in them, but Kahn's case was the most interesting, and would be potentially the most newsworthy.

"I will go with Kahn."

Corea nodded, and then, as if he was reading John's thoughts, he said, "But it's only for background. No direct quoting from the file. Otherwise they'll know somebody gave it to you."

John nodded. "Deal."

Corea stood up. "I don't know what you're looking for, but you're wasting your time, man. He killed himself, pure and simple."

"Where are you going?" John asked.

"It's in my car. I'll be right back."

"You had it all along?" John asked.

Corea smiled. "Just as backup. In case."

"You have the other files too?"

Corea smiled wider but didn't say anything. He returned a while later with the file. It was in a thin brown folder with no marking on it. John could tell that it wasn't the original.

"You photocopied it?"

Corea nodded. "Send me what you've got."

"I'll do it as soon as I get back to my hotel."

"No, do it now. I know you've got it on your phone."

John smiled and nodded. He took out his phone and forwarded it to Corea's email address.

Corea smiled. "Okay, I'll leave you to your dinner."

"You're not going to eat with me?"

"No, I think you have a lot of reading to do."

Detective Corea turned and walked out the door. After John ordered, he opened up the folder and spread the pages across the table. Instantly he knew that the file was incomplete. It was missing the crime scene photos, but that was to be expected. Corea had probably just photocopied the important statements, and didn't want to risk having the photos end up in the newspaper; the temptation to use them for a front page byline might have proven too much. But then John also had to consider what else was missing.

John read the first witness statement.

Witness stated she was at her desk from about 12:50pm to 4:00pm when she had to go to the washroom. She returned several minutes later and continued to work on her computer. David Kahn had about sixteen calls between 4pm and about 5pm, mostly from media. The witness only put two calls through, one from a man named Jerry Gottler, the Minister of Energy, at approx 4:20pm and Todd McGuinny at approx 4:45pm. During this time David Kahn had no visitors.

The witness worked past her usual home time of 5:15pm. At approx 5:40pm the witness heard a loud unidentified bang from Mr. Kahn's office. She knocked on the door and when Mr. Kahn didn't answer she opened the door. She found Mr. Kahn with his head tilted back, a gunshot in the bottom of his chin. There was no one else in the room. Mr. Kahn appeared to be deceased.

The witness did not step further into the room but ran to her desk to call the police. After she finished she went to the washroom to vomit. She then went downstairs to direct the police who arrived at approx 5:50pm.

The witness stated that the period from the time of the gunshot to the time she entered Mr. Kahn's office was about thirty seconds and not enough time for somebody to have exited the room without her knowledge. Also, the only way somebody could have come or gone from the room was through the hallway where the witness was present.

John put the witness statement down. He found it interesting that Gottler had phoned Kahn about an hour before he was killed. Did Gottler say something that made Kahn shoot himself? It was a possibility. John didn't recognize the name Todd McGuinny, and wrote down a note to check him out. Next John pulled out the forensic report. It was short and to the point.

The vic was killed by a Kel-Tec P-32 semi-automatic gun, which was found at the crime scene. The serial number had been filed off, suggesting the gun has been used for illegal activity. The slug and bullet both match the P-32. The gun had the vics thumb and index finger print on it. No other prints were found. The entrance wound was on the bottom of the chin and was approx 1cm in diameter. It was a black-greyish colour from gunpowder burn and was also rimmed with cordite. The exit wound, at the top of the skull, was approx 2cm in diameter.

The vics desk and chair were dusted for prints. There were prints from the vic all over the desk but there were also several unidentified partial prints on the top of the desk and on the knobs of the desk drawers.

I also examined the blood splatter found on the wall, chair and desk. I have concluded, judging by the trajectory of travel, that the vic was sitting upright at his desk when the bullet entered the vics skull.

My conclusion is that the gun was fired at approx 5 mm from the vics jaw and, based on forensic evidence, was likely self-inflicted.

John put the forensic report to one side and reviewed the remaining statements. The detectives had interviewed many Nerno employees, and Kahn's family and friends. They asked many of the same questions: what was Kahn's state of mind? Did he have any enemies? Most of the answers were the same. Kahn was distraught over the allegations of fraud. He had taken to going on long walks at night. The answers about whether Kahn had enemies were a little more interesting. There were a variety of answers, from environmental groups to former colleagues, and even John's own name was thrown in there.

John put down the report. There was nothing that indicated that Kahn was murdered. John's food came, and he put the folder away and ate in silence.

He gave the waitress some of the money that Michael Chu had given him, and he realized that he didn't have much left, and hadn't yet heard back from the bank, so he gave them a call.

He dialled the number on the back of his now useless credit card, and after ten minutes of listening to elevator music he finally got a man on the phone.

John explained the situation to the operator, and how the bank was supposed to have phoned him back.

"Let me just pull your file, sir," the operator said.

John waited again, listening to the typing of a keyboard.

"It seems you phoned back and said the problem was resolved."

"Pardon?" John exclaimed.

"It says here you phoned yesterday and said your problem had been fixed."

"That wasn't me. The problem wasn't fixed," John said. "Do you have a record of the call?"

The operator hesitated. "I'm not sure. He gave your password, date of birth, everything . . . the problem hasn't been fixed?"

"No, it hasn't been fixed," John said. "I'm going to phone the police right now and get you to turn over those tapes." John hung up on the operator.

Next, John called Detective Corea.

"The hacker is still at it," John said. "I need you to get the tape recording from my bank."

Corea let out a long sigh. "We're working on it, Webster. You just have to be patient."

"In the meantime, I have no money."

"I will let you know as soon as I hear anything. You finished your reading yet, Webster?"

"What can you tell me about the Kel-Tec P-32 Kahn used? Can you trace it?"

"I don't know. It's proven difficult."

"It can't be that common on the street."

"No, in fact I've never seen anything like it before. We are trying to match it to previous crimes, but so far we haven't got anything."

"Which would be consistent with the suicide theory."

"Exactly. We have interviewed all of Kahn's close friends, employees and family, and none of them know where he got the gun from."

"Okay, thanks," John said. He got up from his seat and exited the restaurant. As he was doing so, he bumped into a man who was just entering.

"Sorry," the man said, smiling at John.

John just nodded and let the man pass. He looked familiar, but John couldn't place him.

John looked up Joyce Lancroft's address, which was in Corea's file and typed it into his phone on Google Maps.

John took 70th Avenue Southeast until 26th Street where he turned south. He passed a country club and travelled along the Bow River, which twisted and curved in snake-like fashion. It was frozen solid and glittered purplish in the midday light.

John arrived at Dover Mews after about twenty minutes. It was a row of duplexes lined with snow-covered spruce trees.

John parked and braved the weather once again. He found Lancroft's door and knocked. His hand made a hollow sound against the wood. John waited, rubbing his hands, which were beginning to burn from the cold. He knocked again and looked through the window, but the inside was dark.

John was just about to give up when Lancroft opened the door. She was wearing a white housecoat, and her hair was a tangled mess. Around her neck was a set of pearls—John couldn't tell if they were real or fake, but nevertheless, they were a weird accessory for a housecoat.

"You again? What do you want?" she demanded, hostilely.

"Just a couple moments of your time."

"Goodbye, Mr. Webster."

But before Lancroft could close the door, John stuck his foot in it to prevent it from shutting. Pain shot up through his leg.

"Please, Joyce."

"If you don't remove your foot, I'm calling the cops."

"I don't think Mr. Kahn committed suicide."

Lancroft stood there not saying anything for a while, looking almost dumbfounded. "It was so strange. He was never a quitter but it couldn't have been . . ."

"Of course he wasn't a quitter. Suicide doesn't make sense."

Lancroft opened the door wider. "Do you have any proof?"

"Will you let me in?" John asked. "It's freezing out here."

Lancroft nodded, and stepped back so that John could enter.

"Just let me go upstairs and change," Lancroft said. "Make yourself comfortable."

John couldn't help but peek around, but there wasn't much for him to see. He looked around the living room and the kitchen. Usually John could tell a lot from a person's home, but by the end of his search, Joyce Lancroft was as much of a mystery to him as before. Eventually he sat down in the only chair that he could find.

Lancroft came down wearing a pair of frayed jeans and a black turtleneck sweater. She had taken off the pearls.

If it was possible, she looked even younger and more innocent than the first time that they had met for lunch. How long ago that seemed, John thought.

"You don't have much company?"

Lancroft gave an embarrassed smile. "No, I usually go out."

"Well don't let me take the only chair." John got up, but Lancroft shook her head and disappeared again. She returned with a bar stool, which she sat on.

"That picture was taken from your home?" John asked, nodding towards the photograph on the wall.

Lancroft nodded. "How did you know?"

"Lucky guess." John said. "Why were you wearing pearls? Were they real?"

Lancroft blushed. "No, they are fake. They're just a keepsake, that's all."

"From a boyfriend?"

Lancroft's face reddened even more. "Nobody special. So what do you want from me? A story, I suppose . . . I've been avoiding calls all day. Nobody has come knocking demanding money, though."

John laughed. "I have a couple of questions, if you don't mind."

"What if I do mind? What if I don't want to answer your questions?"

"Then you are perfectly right not to, but I'm sure you have some questions of your own, don't you?"

"I suppose I do."

"Then let me help you find answers. What would you say Mr. Kahn's state of mind was over the last few days?"

"Well, he was obviously very upset."

"Did Mr. Kahn own a gun?"

"No, of course not."

"What makes you so sure?"

"He hated guns. He said on more than one occasion that anybody who owned one was a redneck."

"Then where did the gun come from?"

Lancroft shrugged. "Perhaps somebody gave it to him."

"Somebody who hasn't come forward? You don't think that is a bit suspicious?"

Lancroft thought about it. "I suppose so."

"So do I. Until I get a satisfactory answer to that question I'm going to treat it as a homicide, even if the police don't."

Lancroft shook her head. "But it's impossible. I was there the whole time."

"In your statement to the police, you say you went to the washroom. Is it possible somebody snuck in while you weren't there?"

Lancroft shrugged. "I suppose, but I would have heard something. And I went into his office right after the shot was fired. There was no escape."

John nodded. "Yes, that is a problem, but maybe the killer climbed out the window. Maybe that's the way he entered too."

"But who do you think wanted to kill him?"

"I think this stock conspiracy is larger than just Kahn and Hopkins. I think it goes deeper than that, and whoever killed those two is covering it up. Can you think of anybody? You filtered Kahn's phone calls. Who do you think could be involved?"

"I don't know. David got calls from a lot of different people."

"If I was to suggest Jerry Gottler . . . he phoned your boss about an hour before his death."

Lancroft shrugged. "I know he was friends with David. They phoned each other a couple of times a month."

"Do you think it's possible he wanted to kill your boss?" John pushed.

Lancroft got up from her stool. "I don't know. I told you, I didn't know him very well."

"He phoned about an hour before Kahn supposedly killed himself. Do you think it's possible he phoned to check to see if he was in the office?"

Lancroft frowned. "Anything's possible, I suppose."

"But you don't agree with my theory?"

"I've played it over and over in my mind and there is no way somebody killed him. It's just not possible."

Theories

"That's because you haven't paid for your last three nights," the desk clerk told John.

"No, there must be some misunderstanding. My company is paying for it. They should have picked up the bill," John said, although he knew as soon as he said it that the *Daily Globe* had cut him off. It was all part of Andrea Drashkov's plan.

"Well, our records show that you still owe us two hundred and sixty-eight dollars," the clerk said with a smile.

John shook his head. "Is it okay if I phone my boss and get back to you?"

"Of course, Mr. Webster."

John stepped away from the desk and dialled Charles Dana's cell phone number, but it was disconnected. He decided to phone the main switchboard, hoping to get one of the receptionists that he knew, but instead a gruff, unfriendly voice answered.

"Who is this?" John demanded.

"This is Gerard Levitt. Who is this?"

John thought about hanging up, but he was too angry to move. "What are you doing there?"

"Let me guess, this is John Webster."

"Where is Charles?"

"He is no longer employed here. The building is property of the Icelandic Media Corporation and we are preparing to put it on the market. Have you been avoiding my phone calls, Mr. Webster?"

"You're not going to get rid of me that easily," John said, walking further away from the hotel's front desk.

"I'm sorry, Mr. Webster, but you didn't make the cut. I will email you the details of your compensation package. I hope you find it adequate."

John hung up, feeling the rage swell up inside him. He walked back to the front desk.

"I'm afraid there has been an accounting mistake. It should get sorted out soon, though."

"Let me go ask my manager," the clerk said. He disappeared into a back room. John waited for what seemed like an agonizingly long time until he returned. "I'm sorry, but my manager said you were already warned, and had ample opportunity to remedy the situation."

"Fine. Is there a place I can store my things while this gets sorted out?" John asked.

John went upstairs to pack his suitcase, put away his notes and shut down his laptop. He looked around at the room one last time before he went back down to the lobby. The clerk showed him the storage area.

"We can only store your things here for six hours. Then you have to make other arrangements."

John nodded. "I understand. No problem. Thanks for your patience."

After John had locked up his belongings he sat on the couch in the lobby and looked up at the vaulted ceiling. He switched on his laptop and connected to the free wi-fi to see if the money had transferred back into his account. He wasn't surprised to find that it hadn't. He was now homeless and without any money.

John phoned Charles at home, but nobody answered. He then tried Michael, but he didn't pick up either.

John sighed and closed his laptop. He desperately wanted to get a drink at the bar, but he didn't have enough money. He rubbed his face, feeling utterly alone. What was he going to do?

John looked up to see a Chinese couple staring at him. They were young and handsome, and looked like they were on their way to a fancy dinner party.

"Pardon?" John said.

"I asked if anybody was sitting next to you."

"No, sorry. Go ahead."

The couple sat down and started talking, but John didn't listen. He suddenly remembered where he had seen the Chinese man at the Thai restaurant: he had been in the breakfast room at the hotel with his wife. John put his laptop away and rushed back to the breakfast room. He remembered how he had collided with John then, too.

But why? Had he been trying to steal something? Take his wallet, maybe?

More importantly, who was the man working for? The Chinese National Offshore Oil Company was his first thought. But why would they be following him?

John called Madeline.

"Madeline, I need to borrow some money."

"Money? Why?"

John explained again how his bank account had been hacked.

"Of course. I will be glad to help. How much do you need?"

"I don't know. Maybe you can meet me at the hotel?"

"Sure, of course."

"Also, I think I found a lead," John said, excitedly.

"What sort of lead?" Madeline said.

"I think the CNOOC has been following me. Perhaps even trying to kill me."

"That's crazy. Why would they want to kill you?"

"I'm not sure, but perhaps they are the ones who hacked into my bank account."

The breakfast room was deserted except for an old man reading the newspaper. He looked up at the intruder, but John didn't pay him much attention; he was too busy looking up at the ceiling for security cameras, but he couldn't see any.

"If anything, they would be helping you, not hindering you," Madeline said.

"Maybe. Just meet me at the hotel."

"Okay," she said, hanging up.

John backed out into the hallway, where he spotted a dark glass dome on the ceiling: a telltale sign of a security camera lurking quietly, observing everything that passed by. The Chinese man and his wife would have had to come down the hallway to get to the breakfast room, and would have been caught on tape.

I've got you, John thought. Unless, of course, the footage had been erased already.

John didn't bother with the front desk. He doubted that they would be helpful, so instead he phoned Corea.

"I think I've got the hacker. He was here at the hotel with his wife when I was staying here the first time."

"Are you sure?"

"No, not certain," John said. "I knew I had seen him before. Can you get the hotel to give you the security tapes?"

Orlando Corea was silent for a while. "Yeah, I'll look into it. Meanwhile, I've also got the recording from the bank. Whoever phoned in, it definitely wasn't you. The voice is a lot more high-pitched, with a bit of an accent. We're putting it through analysis, but if you want to come down, maybe you can identify it."

John's spirits rose. Finally, some good news. "Okay, I'll do that now, but I have a question: how did he manage to convince the operator he was me?"

"The man had all your information: birthday, your social insurance number, and even your password. I'm not sure how he got those things, but he was convincing."

"I guess that's the peril of living in a modern age."

John thanked Corea and closed his phone.

John waited for Madeline and together they drove to the police headquarters. The police building was a modern design, with sloping glass panels and faux brick siding. John found Orlando Corea's office, which was on the ground floor, down a long hallway filled with photographs and other police memorabilia. John knocked on Corea's door. His gruff voice called to John and Madeline to enter. John shook hands with Corea and D'Hereaux, who sat opposite his partner. John introduced Madeline to the two detectives.

"Madeline works for the *Beijing Star*."

"Pleased to meet you," Corea said.

D'Hereaux, however, just offered a deep frown. Apparently D'Hereaux was still not over the fact that he was left out of the deal brokered between John and Corea.

Corea offered John and Madeline a seat.

"We get shoved here because we don't report to anybody here," Corea explained, expanding his hands to indicate their cramped, dark office.

John nodded. "You generally report to the RCMP?"

Corea nodded. D'Hereaux had turned back to his computer and was ignoring their conversation.

"Our work usually doesn't fit into any particular jurisdiction, and as a result, we are punished. They don't want us to feel superior to them in any way, I suppose."

John nodded. It was good information, and he filed it away in the back of his memory. Corea, without knowing it, was giving John leverage—psychological ammunition he could use to get Corea to bend to his will.

Corea made a couple of clicks on his computer to bring up the voice recording. He played it for John. An operator asked what he could do, and the hacker answered that his name was John Webster. As Corea had said, the doppelganger gave the operator all the right verifying information. He then told the operator that the matter with the missing money had been resolved. He had remembered that he had transferred the money to another account, and that there was no need for an investigation.

John felt strange listening to the recording of his doppelganger pretending to be himself, almost like he was staring at himself in a mirror, yet not quite.

Corea stopped the recording, and turned his chair to face John. "So? Do you recognize the voice?"

John shook his head. "You have any leads?"

Corea played the recording again, and this time John listened more to the sound of the words, rather than to what was being spoken.

Again he shook his head. He was certain that he had never heard the voice before. John sighed and looked ruefully at the detective. Finding this guy would be next to impossible. The voice on the phone probably wasn't even the hacker, but rather somebody who didn't even know what he was doing.

"I'm sorry I couldn't be any more help."

"Let's try one more time," Corea said. "When you phoned me and told me about the Chinese guy who bumped into you, I found it very interesting."

"Why?"

"Just listen," Corea said.

On the computer, John's imitator said, "I phoned earlier about my account. There was a problem with it, but it has been resolved."

"Do you hear anything?" Corea asked, pausing the recording. The sides of his mouth were twitching. He was enjoying this, but John couldn't understand what he was getting at.

"No, sorry," John said, shaking his head.

Corea replayed the last sentence, slowing it down, but John didn't know what he was listening to.

"When you phoned and said you thought a Chinese man was somehow involved, I listened to the recording again. Do you notice how the man on the phone says 'there'?"

Corea replayed "There was a problem" even slower this time.

John shrugged. "There is a slight slur in the word 'there' but I don't understand the significance of it."

Corea shook his head. "No, it's not a slur. The speaker is having trouble pronouncing the 'th' sound in the word 'there'. That tells me the man on the phone is possibly a foreigner. He's probably been here a number of years, since his accent is almost indistinguishable from a regular Canadian accent, but the 'th' gives him away."

John shook his head. "I know where you're going, but it's not possible. I spoke to the Chinese guy who bumped into me. He had a very thick accent, so it couldn't be him."

"What if he put on the accent for you? It would be easy for him to fake."

"But aren't there a lot of languages that don't have the 'th' sound in their lexicon? What makes you think it's the same guy?"

Corea replayed "There was a problem" but this time he focused on the world "problem".

"Notice how 'problem' is spoken."

This time John did hear it. The speaker had difficulty with the word. "The 'R' and 'L' sounds aren't correct."

Corea nodded. "It's slight, but it's there. I would guess the speaker is of Asian descent but has been in Canada for at least five years and probably longer."

Madeline spoke up for the first time during the whole process. "You're basing this entire conclusion on a bloody accent?"

Corea looked uncomfortable for a moment. "Well, we'll have to send it off to the voice analysis experts to be absolutely certain, but I'm pretty sure I'm right about this."

"And you don't stop to think this could be racial profiling? My God, you cops are all the same."

Corea glanced at John as if to say, *where did you get this woman?*

D'Hereaux, however, was the one to answer. "Look, I don't know who the fuck you think you are, but this is how we do our job. We only came to you as a matter of courtesy, which I, personally, don't think you deserve. So if you don't like it, get the fuck out."

Madeline opened her mouth as if to reply, but when she looked over at John she closed it again.

John quickly took the opportunity to interject. "So you think that the CNOOC is not behind this?"

Corea said, "I wouldn't rule them out completely, but to me it looks like somebody is trying to set them up."

"What are you going to do now?"

Corea rubbed his chin. "We'll put the word out, but we'll do it quietly. If this guy is a Chinese national we don't want to scare him."

John nodded. "Hopefully he's still in the country."

Nowhere to Go

I T WAS FOUR-THIRTY. THE SKY was slowly getting dark, and the temperature was dropping fast. John entered the building and studied the list of addresses on the wall. Nerno only had three floors; the rest were populated by stock brokers, accountants, lawyers and even an architect firm.

"Can I help you, sir?"

John turned to face the security guard.

"Yes, I have an appointment with my accountant from Pacific Life."

The security guard smiled, swiped his card over the elevator's magnetic strip and pushed the button for the fifteenth floor.

"Have a good day, sir," he said, as John stepped into the elevator. John tried to change the floor number when he was in the elevator, but apparently it couldn't be done without a magnetic card.

The elevator opened and John stepped out into Pacific Life's office. Luckily, the receptionist wasn't at her desk, and so he slid off into a hallway to his right. He eventually found the stairwell and stepped in. He climbed the five flights of stairs until he reached the top. He tried the door, but it was locked. John sighed and went down a flight to see if he could open that door, but it was locked as well. He realized that to get out he would have to walk the thirty flights of steps down to the lobby. John examined the lock. It was a typical dead bolt lock. But then John saw a fire alarm next to the door. He went back up to the thirtieth floor, and taking his laptop bag, he smashed the glass with the hard bottom corner. He then pulled the alarm. Immediately a long, shrill noise filled the building.

John tried the door again, wondering if it was on some sort of central electronic control that would automatically unlock in case of a fire, but the knob still wouldn't budge.

John took several steps back from the door and waited. Eventually somebody opened it and stepped into the hallway. John reached out and grabbed the door before it closed. The businessman looked startled to see him there.

"Sorry, I forgot my phone," John said.

The businessman glared at him. "It's a fire, you can't go back."

"I'm sure it's just a false alarm," John said, manoeuvring himself around the businessman. "It'll only take two minutes."

John stepped into the Nerno office and quickly moved down the hallway. Groups of people passed him on the way to the stairs. John hoped that he didn't run into Andrea Drashkov or anybody who might recognize him. Luckily, he managed to get to Kahn's office without any incident.

The office still had police caution tape placed across it. John looked both ways, making sure that nobody was watching him, and carefully removed the tape from the door, which he found wasn't locked, and so he opened it and stepped through. He then carefully put the tape back up. Examining his work, he knew that it wasn't perfect, but it would fool the casual passerby.

John then closed the door and looked around the room. It was dark and eerie and smelled stale, choked with iron and decaying matter. It was a familiar smell—yet one he hadn't smelled in years. Immediately the bloody imagery reappeared in the corners of his consciousness. He thought of the explosion that he had witnessed in a Baghdad bazaar. John couldn't move. He felt paralyzed, as if the whole office would collapse in one seismic rupture.

Then the image of the bazaar crumpled in on itself and John was back on the top of the rollercoaster with Byron beside him. The cool wind was blowing strong, and the bone-white clouds rolled overhead like a conveyor belt. John looked at his son, so fearless, so stoic, bolt upright in his seat.

Suddenly John knew that this was what Sheila meant when she'd told him to listen to the wind. He was back on the rollercoaster. Byron was laughing, sitting next to him. John was gripping the bar, his knuckles white.

The image of Byron gave John the courage to concentrate. He looked around the expansive office. He took several deep breaths and forced himself to take several steps forward. Even in the darkness, John could see the bits of dried blood congealed on the desk and chair. But there was surprisingly little blood until John walked around the desk and saw the back of the chair.

Of course, most of the blood would have flowed out of the exit wound and down the back of the chair, John realized. He knelt down and looked at it. He wasn't looking for anything specific, and wasn't really hopeful that he would find anything the police hadn't.

John got up, careful not to disturb anything, and walked towards the window—the real reason that he wanted to examine the crime scene. John looked at it. There were two panels, each about a metre wide and three metres high. He grabbed the handle, unlatched it and opened it. It only opened about six inches. The cold air flooded in, immediately seeping over John's hands. He tried pushing the window open further. It opened another six inches or so. He stepped back from the cold and examined his work. The window gap was still too small for somebody to sneak through, but still . . . maybe another six inches. John took a deep breath and stuck his head out of the window.

He couldn't see any escape ladder, or any ledge to climb onto. John looked up at the rooftop, only about five metres away. It was possible that somebody could edge in from the rooftop if the window was left unlatched.

He eased his head back into the room and closed the window. His face felt like it was burning. He tried to wipe away the frost with his sleeve. He decided that it would have been highly unlikely for somebody to enter from the roof. Especially since Joyce Lancroft hadn't heard any noise, or any argument or scuffle.

John realized that his theory of murder was looking more and more unlikely, but he couldn't give it up.

Suddenly he heard the sound of footsteps in the hallway outside the door. Had they heard him? He froze and held his breath.

"You searched everywhere?" a deep voice said.

"Yeah, no sign of anything."

"The alarm was pulled in the hallway."

"Yeah, looks like a false alarm."

John supposed that it was the firefighters searching the building. It wouldn't be long before they let everybody back in. He would have to make his escape, but where would he go to then? He figured that he could find someone to stay with.

But then John wondered what would happen if he just stayed in the room until morning, maybe get a few hours of sleep. Nobody would be any the wiser.

He doubted that the police would come back, except to remove the tape and hand the room back to Nerno. They had gathered all the evidence that they needed.

Could he have fallen asleep with the sickening smell still permeating the room? He had slept in worse spots, but not for a long time. He could probably have come out later and slept underneath one of the desks.

John heard the groan of the elevator as it returned to service, and then made its familiar chiming sound as the doors opened and the Nerno staff went back to work.

The thought of sleeping underneath the desk suddenly triggered something in John's brain. He crouched underneath Kahn's large oak desk. It was clearly a big enough space to fit a person into. What if somebody hiding underneath the desk had shot Kahn? The bullet had gone through the bottom of Kahn's jaw, so that would be consistent with John's theory, and then when Joyce Lancroft opened the door she wouldn't have seen the killer because he or she would have been underneath the desk.

In the report, Joyce Lancroft had stated that she had gone to the bathroom to vomit. That would have given the killer ample opportunity to escape. But why hadn't Lancroft heard anything before that to indicate that somebody else was in the room? And for that matter, how had they got into the room in the first place?

John heard more voices and a rush of footsteps. He stood frozen, debating what he should do. He looked at the dried pool of blood on the floor. Could he crawl through that and hide underneath the desk as the killer could have done?

No, he decided. He didn't need to go anywhere. Nobody would think of looking for him in Kahn's room. John sat in the corner, exhausted, his limbs aching, but his heart thumping in his chest.

The sun was seeping through the closed blinds, scattering mysterious-looking shapes across the carpeted floor. He watched as the evening light slowly faded and he was left in darkness. John had been holed up in places that stank worse than Kahn's office before, but nevertheless, the stench was getting to him and he felt a strong urge to run out of the building. He wanted to phone Charles again, but he was afraid of making any noise, or alerting an astute secretary when the wrong light lit up on the phone line.

The voices from the office slowly faded until everything was quiet, and the only thing that John could hear was the hum of the heater.

He got up and opened the door a crack. Most of the lights were off. He didn't see anybody around. He peeled the police tape off, stepped out and then replaced it. He examined his work. The police would realize that it had been tampered with—that couldn't be helped.

John slowly, stealthily walked around the office, checking for anybody who might have been burning the midnight oil. Several of the offices were locked, but it appeared that he had the floor all to himself. He suddenly wondered if there was any alarm system that he should be wary of. He hadn't triggered anything yet, so he supposed that he was safe.

He sat in the office for a long time, debating what to do. It was warm, cozy and inviting. He could sleep there and wake up in the morning before anybody arrived. He wandered around, looking for something cozy to sleep on. He didn't find anything, but he did find a flask of whiskey in one of the desks. He supposed that it was used for some after-hours shindig, or perhaps to enliven some long, boring meeting. Whatever the purpose, John was grateful.

He went to the washroom, and when he came out he heard the distinct sound of footsteps. He froze, wondering who was there. The steps were soft and evenly paced. They didn't sound like the footsteps of a Nerno employee coming back. How did they know he was here? They must have heard him.

"Is anyone here?" a voice asked through the darkness. "Calgary Police. Identify yourself."

John still didn't move. He had to think fast. Was it really a police officer? He backed up against the wall, pressing his neck against the cement. The exit was just behind him, but if he ran, he would have had to leave his laptop, and then he would have been locked out and unable to get back in.

He evened his breath and tried to control his rapid heartbeat, which seemed to threaten to pop through his chest. Would he have a heart attack right here in the middle of the office?

John heard only one pair of footsteps. Then a thought struck him: where was the backup? There was no way that a police officer would be investigating an office floor alone. Maybe he was a security guard? But if so, why was he pretending to be a police officer? And why didn't he turn on the lights? Why was he still in darkness? The only answer John could come up with was that whoever was stalking him wasn't supposed to be there either.

The footsteps stopped. The hum of the computers seemed to grow louder until they were deafening in John's ears. John tried to concentrate. He listened for the footsteps again but didn't hear them. Should he make his move now? There was no need to rush things, he decided. In Afghanistan, John had spent several weeks with the Joint Task Force. They would lie in wait, motionlessly, for hours, sometimes even days, for the enemy to be in the perfect position before they struck.

The footsteps resumed. This time they were slightly quicker and heavier. They came closer. John visualized what he had to do—another soldier's trick.

Suddenly a hulking figure appeared around the corner, and John launched his entire weight against the man, hoping to take him by surprise. He was nowhere near as young as he used to be, and didn't think that he could last long in a fight. They both went tumbling to the ground. The man under John let out a loud grunt as air was expelled from his body, and beside him there was a muffled thud of something hard hitting the floor. John didn't have time to register who the man was. Instead he just started punching. John got several good hits in, effectively subduing his stalker. He stopped. His fist hurt where he had hit the man's jaw. John grabbed his stalker by the collar and stared at him. The first thing John registered was that he was old—older than him. Loose flesh hung from the man's cheeks and neck. The man opened his eyes and glared up at John, and only then did he recognize the Chinese man who had stolen his money in the restaurant.

"Who do you work for?" John asked.

The man didn't answer, but just stared up at John, blinking dumbly. John could see a gush of liquid coming from his face; he was bleeding from somewhere, but in the darkness John couldn't tell from where.

John reached for whatever had fallen, but he couldn't reach it. Suddenly he felt a swell of anger at being forced to pawn his watch, humiliated into asking for money, arguing with the hotel. This man had forced him into a corner.

John brought his elbow down on the man's nose. He heard a loud crunching sound, like glass, and the Chinese man screamed piercingly. Surely it would alert the police or security, but he didn't care. He leaned over and groped in the darkness until he found the thing that had fallen. He grasped his fingers around the cold, metallic thing and realized, unsurprised, what it was. A gun.

John put it against his captive's temple. The man was clutching his nose, trying to stem the flow of blood. John felt a wave of regret come over him, but it was too late to go back now. "Who do you work for?"

The man wouldn't answer. He seemed oblivious to the fact that he had a gun against his head.

"I won't ask again," John said. "You come to kill me? Is that it? How did you get in here?"

John got off of the man and searched through his pockets, finding a money clip with a hundred dollars in it and a key card for the elevator, but that was it. No ID, no cell phone.

John took a deep breath and wondered what he should do. Should he make a run for it, or wait for the cops to arrive? Should he call Detective Corea? If he phoned anybody, he would have to leave the Chinese man in the hallway, and he didn't think that that would be a good idea, no matter how incapacitated he seemed at the moment.

John had to wait for what seemed like an inordinate amount of time before the security guards arrived, and when they did, they seemed slightly dumbfounded and aghast to find one man clutching a semiautomatic, and another man lying motionlessly on the floor with blood beginning to pool around his head.

"Don't just stand there," John said. "Call an ambulance."

The two guards were both dark-skinned, slightly portly and grey-haired. They looked at each other before one took out his cell phone and started dialling. The other guard stared at John's gun. "What happened?"

"He attacked me," John said.

The Chinese man took his hands from his face and looked over at John. "You fucking kidding me? He jumped me." The man seemed to speak English well; his thick accent had all but disappeared.

"Listen," John said. "I need you to phone Detective Orlando Corea. He'll tell you what's going on."

"Can you hand over the gun, please?" the security guard asked, nervously.

John gave the weapon to the guard, who held it away from his body as if he had never held a gun in his life.

"We're just going to wait until the police arrive. They will decide what to do with you."

"Can I at least borrow your cell phone?" John asked. "I just want to make one phone call."

The security guard reluctantly turned his phone over to John, who dialled Corea's number. The phone rang five times before there was a sleepy answer.

"It's John."

"Do you have any idea what time it is?"

John didn't. He hadn't realized how late it was. "Sorry, but I've got our impersonator here."

Corea groaned on the other end. "What do you mean?"

"I mean I've subdued him. The hacker. The police are on their way. I don't think they'll believe me when I describe what happened."

"Okay, okay. I'll call them. Where are you?"

"The Nerno office."

"What are you doing there?"

John hesitated. He decided that there was no way to lie. He had backed himself into a corner. "I was checking out the crime scene."

"What the fuck? You contaminated it?"

"I have a theory. I think Kahn was murdered. There is ample space underneath his desk to hide. He was shot from underneath. It makes sense."

"John, I should let you rot in fucking prison."

"But what if I'm right? What if he was murdered? You can solve this."

"All right, I'm coming to get you."

Two police officers showed up about ten minutes later, and the paramedics shortly thereafter. The two officers split up. One interviewed John while the other interviewed the Chinese man. The two hefty security guards stayed back, but were intrigued by what was probably a highlight in an otherwise boring night.

John explained everything all over again but he could tell that the police officer wasn't buying it. He glanced over at the Chinese man who had managed to sit up, his back against the wall, while the paramedics were attending to him. He looked a sad and pathetic figure.

"What were you doing here anyway?" the police officer asked John.

"I was checking on a theory I had about the death of David Kahn, the former CEO."

"You were trespassing?"

"Look, he is the man who is responsible," John said, pointing his finger at the Chinese man. "Phone Detective Orlando Corea and ask him. He knows the details of the case."

The police officer leaned towards John and sniffed. "Have you been drinking?"

"No—well, a few sips, but that's all."

The two police officers came together and conferred quietly with each other. John could tell by their body movements that it wouldn't be a good outcome for him. His fears were confirmed when they advanced on him, and without warning swung him around and cuffed him.

"You are under arrest for trespassing and assault under the Criminal Code of Canada."

"No, you've got it wrong. He was going to kill me," John yelled.

Nobody answered him. John glanced over at the security guards, hopeful for an appeal, but they gave him disdainful looks in return.

One of the police officers recited John's rights, and then put on some rubber gloves to search his pockets, and found a voice recorder, a wallet and cell phone. They placed each item in a plastic bag and wrote down the contents in their notepad.

The paramedics took the Chinese man away to the elevator. John watched powerlessly as the elevator door closed behind him. John wasn't sure, but he thought that he saw a twitch of a smile appear on the Chinese man's lips, and then he was gone.

After the police officers had finished processing John they took him down in the elevator.

"Did you call Detective Corea?"

"You'll get your phone call," one of the officers said.

"I know you don't believe me, but he'll explain everything."

They didn't respond, and the elevator dinged cheerfully as they reached the ground floor. They walked through the lobby and out into the cold. The ambulance had disappeared, but the police car had parked right in front, its lights flashing.

The police officers shoved John into the back seat and climbed into the front. Futilely, John looked around for any sign of Corea, but he was nowhere to be seen.

John slumped over in the backseat of the cop car, wishing that he hadn't waited for the security guards. He should have just made a run for it, but instead he was going to be thrown in jail. Where had the Chinese man gone? To the hospital?

John was exhausted but unable to sleep. His eyelids were wide as he watched the buildings pass by.

"So, you're the journalist who has been writing about Nerno?" one of the police officers asked from the front seat. "I read your article about David Kahn. What a bastard."

John didn't know how to respond, and so he kept silent. Was this the start of the Good Cop, Bad Cop routine?

They arrived at the police station and John was put in a large, empty cell. John sat on the bench, wondering what time it was. Not that it mattered. He didn't know how long he had sat there, staring at the unchanging shadows against the wall. It must have been a slow night for the cops. There was nobody else in the holding cells. He listened for some sound, but there was nothing except for the slow drip of water hitting a pool somewhere in the distance.

Not that John minded being alone. It gave him time to think and reminisce about the almost mystical Afghan nights and the way the silver moonlight reflected off of the green-and-brown mountains. He hadn't appreciated the beauty then. Now beauty took on a special meaning that only the old seemed to understand.

At least it's warm here, he thought. He laid his head down on the bench and closed his eyes, but he couldn't fall asleep. His mind began to wander back to Hayden and Byron. They would be fast asleep, dreaming pleasant dreams. Maybe he should use his one call to phone them. He wanted so badly to talk to them. His back started to hurt, so he sat up again. He rubbed his eyes.

"You don't look so good," a familiar voice said.

John looked up to see Detective Corea standing at the door, looking down at John. He looked like he was trying to hide a smile, but he was unsuccessful at it.

"Took you long enough to get me," John said, grumpily.

"I went to the Nerno building first, but the security guards said you had been arrested."

"The hacker . . . did you get him?"

Corea shook his head. "He got to the hospital, but after the paramedics dropped him off he left. All the info he gave us was fake too."

"So you have no way of tracking him?"

"We have the gun. Hopefully that gives us a hit. We'll know by tomorrow probably."

"If only the two cops had listened to me."

"Well, you didn't give them a very convincing story. Our Chinese friend said he was working late when you attacked him."

John looked down at the cell floor. "I wonder where he got the key card to enter the building. Maybe he really does work there."

"It's possible, but even if we do find him, we don't have anything to charge him with."

"I'm sure you'll think of something," John said. "Now are you going to get me out of here?"

"I'm sorry, but there's still the matter of trespassing. I can't do anything about that. You'll have to wait until tomorrow."

John sighed. He didn't have anywhere to go anyway, so he supposed that it didn't matter. "All right then, I'll see you tomorrow."

"What? You're not going to try and convince me to let you out?"

"Just think about my theory for a moment. I'm going to phone you tomorrow."

"John, you keep forgetting one thing. It's not my case to think about." And with that, Corea turned and walked down the hallway.

John listened to his heavy footsteps as they thudded down the cement floor, and then the sound of a heavy door opening and closing. Then there was silence.

The Affair

"**N**OT YOU AGAIN," JOYCE LANCROFT said to John, who was once again standing on her wooden front steps in Dover Mews. Joyce's red hair was wild, falling over her face and neck. She looked a little better than the last time that John had seen her, but not much.

Lancroft attempted to close the door, but John stuck his foot in the door, keeping it open. "Please, just a couple of moments of your time. I know what happened to your boss. Just give me some time to explain."

"If you know what happened, why don't you tell the police?"

"I did, but they wouldn't listen to me. I need your help to try and convince them."

"If you can convince me, that is."

"Let me try."

"Do you always stick your foot in people's doors so they can't close them?" Joyce asked.

"It's an effective technique," John admitted.

Joyce Lancroft paused. She sighed, and John could see all the fight drain from her body. "All right, but this is the last time."

John found himself, once again, in Joyce's living room, sitting on the bar stool and having to explain how he had spent the night in jail and how in the morning a police officer had come and given him his wallet and deactivated cell phone back, telling him that the charges had been dropped.

"Do you have a boyfriend, Joyce?"

"Why do you want to know that?"

"Just curious I guess."

Lancroft shook her head. "No, nobody special."

"Somebody as young and as pretty as you? Come on, what are you doing living all the way out here? Shouldn't you be living downtown somewhere? Closer to where the action is?"

Joyce shrugged. "Are you proposing yourself as a solution to my old maid tendencies?"

John laughed. "No, of course not. I'm just curious, that's all."

"Tell me about your important theory. The one the police missed."

"I think your boss was killed and that his murderer hid underneath the desk."

Lancroft shrugged. "I already told you nobody went in or out of that room."

"Why are you protecting his murderer?"

Lancroft opened her mouth halfway, then ground her teeth together before answering. "I'm not protecting anybody. Your theory is crazy."

"You loved him, didn't you, Joyce?"

Lancroft hesitated, and in that nanosecond her face betrayed her, but she quickly tried to cover it up. "I don't know what you're talking about."

John remembered the pearl necklace that she was wearing the last time she came to the door. It had to be a gift from an older man. Only a lover gave pearls. "Did you have an affair with him?"

"Get out of here. I don't need to listen to this."

"Answer my question."

Lancroft got up and went into the kitchen. John got up from his stool and followed her. "He gave you the pearl necklace, didn't he? Why else were you wearing them with your bathrobe?"

"It's in the past," Joyce said. She grabbed her phone, but John reached out and held her wrist. His action seemed to surprise both of them. Joyce just looked up at him with a puzzled, dumbfounded look on her face.

"Don't," John said, softly, trying to ease the tension. "Whoever you're planning on phoning, don't."

"Why shouldn't I?" Joyce said. "You have been told to leave, but here you still are."

"I won't publish any of it. You have my word."

Joyce didn't say anything for a long time. "I need a drink. Would you like one?" she asked.

John released his grip on her. It was early afternoon. A bit early for a drink, but he could use one too. "What do you have?"

"I don't know . . . wine, I think."

"I guess that will do."

Joyce took two glasses from the cupboard and a bottle of wine from the top of the fridge. "I'm sorry, it's the ten-dollar type. Nothing fancy."

John smiled kindly. "You think I'm the fancy type?"

Lancroft studied John closely. "Judging by your clothes, definitely not."

John had on a well-worn pair of jeans and a dirty long-sleeve sweater. "Well, I spent a night in jail. What's your excuse?"

To John's surprise, Lancroft laughed. "Yeah, I suppose you're right. I've been holed up in my house for far too long."

Lancroft poured the wine and recapped the bottle. "Let's sit down again."

They sat back down in the living room. Joyce crossed her legs. She seemed a lot more relaxed. Perhaps the glass of wine helped. "When I wear the pearls it feels like he's close to me," she said.

"You were in love with him?"

Lancroft shrugged. "I don't know. At times I felt I was in love with him. Other times he was really cold and distant."

John remembered what it felt like to be young and in love. He felt a mixture of envy and pity for her. "Were you having an affair with him?"

Joyce looked down at the glass of wine and took a large gulp, almost choking on it. "This won't make it in the newspaper, will it?"

"We're just two friends talking. I give you my word."

Lancroft lowered her eyes and nodded. "I guess it was a stupid thing to do. He was just so . . . I don't know . . . handsome and doting—at least at first."

They spoke for another hour about David Kahn, and John told Lancroft about his family, Hayden and Byron. John didn't know why, but it felt good speaking about them. He hardly ever got a chance to talk about them. They finished the bottle of wine. John felt slightly flushed, but Joyce was having a hard time standing up.

"I think I need to lie down," she said. "It's good to have company. I'm beginning to hate being in this big house all alone."

Lancroft tried to stand up, but she was unsteady. John went over and grabbed her by the shoulders to prevent her from falling.

"You could do better than David Kahn, you know," John said. "You're young and pretty. You just need to get out more."

Lancroft collapsed back on the ground, stretching her slender legs out. "God, you sound like my mother."

"What are you doing?"

"I'm lying down."

"Don't you want to lie down somewhere comfortable?" John asked. "I could take you upstairs to your bed."

But Lancroft shook her head, laying her head down on the wooden floor, her chest heaving steadily like an ocean wave. "No, I don't think I would make it. Here's fine."

"Let me find you a pillow at least."

"Just stay with me," Joyce said, grabbing hold of John's arm. "I don't want to be alone anymore."

John couldn't think of anything to say to that, so he remained quiet. He tried crossing his legs and sitting beside her, but they were too stiff to bend in the way that he wanted, and so he just sort of flopped beside her.

"Remember when we first had lunch? I thought you were a recruiter." Lancroft gave a giddy laugh. "You're such an asshole. I couldn't believe it."

"You know, I could just leave."

"You really think David was murdered?"

John nodded. "You still haven't disproved my theory about his killer hiding under his desk."

"He could have."

John cocked his head. "You sound certain."

"Because I've hidden there many times."

Lancroft's eyes were closed. Her face was towards the ceiling. She showed no emotion and so John couldn't tell what she was thinking.

"I'm confused. Why did you hide under the desk?"

Lancroft opened one eye and peered mischievously at John. A half smile crossed her large lips. "Because I was naked."

John finally understood. "You were having sex and somebody interrupted you?"

Lancroft nodded. "One time he made me hide there during a presentation and give him a blowjob. It was awful. I told him I wouldn't do it anymore."

"As terrible as this sounds, Joyce, I think you are better off without him."

"But it hurts so much."

"I know it does."

Suddenly a thought occurred to John. "I have one more question to ask. It might be painful. Is that okay?"

Lancroft opened both of her eyes and stared at John. "Why do I think that if I say no you'll ask me anyway?"

John smiled. "I guess you know me well."

"Ask away, then."

"Do you think Kahn was sleeping with anybody else?"

Lancroft didn't answer for a long time. "I don't know. I guess anything is possible. What does that have to do with anything?"

John shrugged. "Maybe nothing, maybe everything." He paused to gauge Lancroft's reaction but she seemed numb, unable to respond to anything. "Was there somebody he spent more time with than anybody else? Some late nights?"

"He always worked late. A lot of people did."

"If I said Andrea Drashkov, what would you say? Did they spend a lot of time together?"

"Of course . . . you think she killed David?"

"It's possible . . . do you mind if I use your phone? Mine has been deactivated."

"No, of course not."

John went back into the kitchen and picked up Joyce's cell phone. He dialled Michael Chu's number.

"John? What's going on? I've been trying to get hold of you, but you're not answering any of your emails and your phone has been deactivated."

"Yeah, I'm having problems. I need a favour."

"Okay, but first you have to listen to what I have to say."

"You have something?"

"Remember you asked me to do a background check on Nerno?"

"Of course. You found something interesting?"

"Yes, one of my friends back in Toronto said somebody was buying up large quantities of Nerno stock through a numbered company in Switzerland."

"Really? Did you find out who registered the company?"

"I phoned a friend who works for Credit Suisse. I had to promise him my first born child but he came through."

"I'm going to guess Andrea Drashkov."

"How did you know?"

"Call me lucky. I think she set this whole thing up from the beginning."

"To wrestle control of the company?"

"Exactly. I think she also killed Kahn and made it look like a suicide. She snuck into his office while Lancroft was away from her desk. She shot him from under his desk, which is why Lancroft didn't see her when she opened the door."

John suddenly remembered Andrea telling him that she used to watch her father work on expensive cars in his workshop—cars like Lamborghinis. Her father had probably taught Andrea how the car's brakes worked. John was suddenly positive that she had caused the brakes to fail on George Hopkins' Lamborghini.

"But how did she escape without anybody seeing her? And how did she end up under Kahn's desk without him noticing?"

"Oh, he noticed all right. They were having an affair. Apparently it was common practice for Kahn to hide girls under his desk."

"Lancroft told you this?"

"Yes, my guess is that Drashkov snuck back to her office and then down the stairs so nobody would see her. Can you phone Detective Corea and ask him to send a Crime Scene Unit to Drashkov's office?"

"Okay. I'll phone you back on this line when I get hold of him."

John ended the call and went back to the living room, where Lancroft was passed out on the floor, snoring heavily. There was nothing for John to do but wait. He snooped around the house. He logged onto Lancroft's computer and checked his email. There were two emails from Michael, one from Charles Dana, and several from readers giving him story ideas or commenting on Nerno.

Lancroft's phone rang. It was Michael phoning him back.

"What did he say?" John asked.

"He said he would do it. He also said they have caught the hacker. He was boarding a plane to Ecuador."

"Really? What's his name?"

"You won't believe this. His name is Cheng Aiguo, and officially he works for the *Beijing Star*."

"He's a journalist?" John asked, astounded, thinking of Madeline, who worked for the same newspaper.

"Officially," Michael said. "But I've heard of China using journalists as spies on politicians and corporations before."

John thought of Madeline making her late-night call on Jerry Gottler. Was it possible that she had been planted as a spy all along?

"So China is still somehow involved," John said. "Is there something we are missing?"

"I don't know, but Corea said they were interrogating him."

"Okay, I've got to get over there."

John called a cab, and while he waited for it to arrive he gently scooped Joyce Lancroft up from the floor. Her head leaned back, her hair falling over his arms. She smelled wonderful, sweet, like coconut. Maybe it was the soap that she used. Even though she wasn't heavy—a hundred and ten pounds at the most—John had trouble moving her. He laboured to bring her up the stairs. His shoulder hurt, where he had been shot, but he ignored the pulsing pain and took her to her room, where he laid her gently down on her bed. He stared at her for a moment to make sure that she was okay before he closed the door. She didn't stir the whole time.

"You must be fucking crazy if you think you're going to get anywhere near that room," Detective D'Hereaux said. He had one hand up against John's chest.

"I just want to observe, that's all."

D'Hereaux shook his head. "No. If this thing goes to trial, we can't have you messing it up."

They were standing in the hallway on the third floor. The sunlight was streaming into the windows at the far end and splintering on the ground into square compartments.

John could tell that he wasn't going to win this battle. "Okay, I'm going to wait here until Corea comes out."

"Fine."

John was hungry, and wanted to go get something to eat, but he was afraid that if he moved he would miss Corea, and so he stayed put. There was a coffee machine just down the hallway, still in view of the interrogation room. John inserted a few coins and the machine spit out a cup of coffee. John took a sip from the Styrofoam cup. It was bitter and unpleasant but he drank it anyway. He had had worse.

Corea didn't come out for another hour. He walked past John without saying anything to him.

"What happened?" John demanded, walking after him.

"I need a smoke," Corea said. "Do you smoke?"

"No, I quit long ago."

"Well, why don't you join me anyway? Maybe you could take up the habit again."

There was a small overhang at the back of the building that protected them from the elements, but even so, it was still bitterly cold and neither of them were dressed for the temperature. Corea took out a pack from his jacket pocket, selected a thin cigarette and put it between his lips. He then took a lighter from the same pocket, and cupping it with his left hand he flicked it on, lighting the cigarette with it.

John watched this ritual without narrative. He knew that it was important for Corea not to be bothered as he gathered his thoughts.

"He confessed to everything," Corea said, finally. "He's so afraid of being sent back to China. Apparently he's wanted for treason. He didn't elaborate on why, but I suspect it's something to do with hacking. He says he'll testify."

"So he's responsible for hacking into my account. The whole thing?"

Corea took a puff from his cigarette. "He says his contact was a man named Patrick Oswald from the PR firm Walker and Thompson, and it wasn't actually the Chinese government. Do you know Oswald?"

"The name sounds familiar but I can't place it."

"I've never heard of him but I looked him up. Walker and Thompson is the PR for Nerno."

"Is that enough to tie it to Drashkov?"

Corea looked at John. "I don't know. We're bringing Oswald in for questioning. If he points the finger at Drashkov . . . meanwhile we'll go over her office and her houses with a fine tooth comb. Maybe we'll get lucky, but it will probably be too contaminated to get a conviction."

"There's something I don't get," John said. "What was he doing at the hotel? The first time I saw him."

"He said he was instructed to steal your phone and write down your last twenty calls and then replace it in your hotel room. He said the timing was important but he wasn't told why."

John shook his head. He remembered the incident vaguely. He thought that he had left his phone in the hotel room. He remembered going back to his hotel and finding it . . . was it just to keep tabs on him? Why was the timing important?

Then he remembered who he had phoned just before . . . Sheila McKinnon. That was why Cheng had stolen his phone. To get to McKinnon. The information hit John right in the gut and twisted in like a screw.

"What?" Corea asked.

"Drashkov leaked the information to Vince Parkerson. He did it to get to Sheila."

"What? You're not making any sense," Corea said.

"Andrea was Parkerson's source for the article in the *New York Times*, not Sheila. Hank Gates was going to break the story anyway. Andrea knew I would think Sheila had blabbed to Parkerson. She knew I would blow her cover. She just needed to watch me. That's how Nerno found out about her . . . it was me all along."

John felt like collapsing, and even had to put one hand on Corea to balance himself.

"Let's get you back inside," Corea said, crushing his cigarette into the snow. "You don't look so good."

Corea pushed the glass door open and helped John inside.

"I killed her," John said.

"Who?"

"Sheila. She was my source. Because of me she got blackballed."

Corea and John entered the hallway where the air was warm. "It wasn't your fault," he said, pressing the button for the elevator.

"I'll never forgive myself."

Corea gripped John on the shoulder. "It always surprises me when I find journalists actually have hearts."

The elevator door rolled open and Corea stepped in. He turned around to face John. His face was hard and unreadable. The door started to close, but Corea suddenly blocked it with his hand. The elevator made a disgruntled electronic whining sound and then opened again.

"Listen," Corea said. "When you start on a case, you start fresh and that is the best feeling in the world. Do you know why?"

John gave Corea a confused look and then shook his head.

"It's the best feeling because you haven't made any mistakes yet. Alternatively, do you know what the worst part of the case is?"

Again John shook his head.

"It's when you put the handcuffs on the guy, because you know you should have done it sooner. All I can think about is the damage done between the start and the finish, and how I could have prevented it. You understand what I'm saying?"

John didn't, but nodded anyway. He wanted to be alone with his thoughts.

Corea nodded, dropping his arm so that the elevator could finally close. "The feeling will slowly pass."

But John wasn't so sure. Afghanistan had never truly passed. The world had forgotten Amira, but John hadn't. It had become a part of his identity. The former war correspondent. The world would soon forget Sheila McKinnon too.

The Answer

A ndrea loved a crowd. The murmur of excitement. The electricity of anticipation. They were here to see her, to hear what she had to say.

Andrea had booked the Hyatt conference room again, judging that there would be a big turnout. She was right. About a dozen or so cameras were set up at the back of the room. She recognized journalists from all over the country.

She looked around for John Webster, but he was nowhere to be found. She tried not to feel sad. She knew it was unlikely that he would come, knowing his dislike for press conferences.

One of her aides introduced her as CEO of Nerno. Her? CEO of Nerno? She loved the sound of it.

Andrea stepped up to the podium and adjusted the microphone. She looked around slowly. The lights were glaring at her. She could feel the intense heat of the stage and she hoped that her makeup wouldn't melt, making her look like a mess for the cameras.

"Thanks all for coming," Andrea said, clicking through the slide that was on the big projector.

"I want to announce the grand opening of the Mackenzie Valley site in the Northwest Territories. We will start drilling in early February with a new type of drill Nerno has developed. This drill will go miles deeper than any existing drill on the market, allowing us to extract 300,000 barrels of oil a day for an estimated fifty years, making it the most significant source of oil in the history of humankind."

Once again, Andrea answered her first question from Josh McGuire from the *Calgary Herald*, and as predicted, it was a soft question.

"Don't you think this is an ambitious plan for a company currently coming back from the brink of bankruptcy?"

Andrea gripped the podium with both hands and nodded. "Yes, it is very ambitious, and one the previous leadership didn't approve of, but I believe we need to be ambitious to survive against the multinational companies that are our competitors."

More hands shot up, and a dull roar went through the crowd, but then somebody in the very back said something, and suddenly the whole room went quiet.

"What was that?" Andrea asked. "I didn't hear."

"I said, did you kill David Kahn, the previous CEO, to gain control of the company?"

Andrea shielded her eyes against the lights and stared into the crowd. She knew the voice, but she couldn't see the source of it in the crowd. "No, that is absolutely ridiculous. Next question."

"Then the police would be lying when they told me they found traces of David Kahn's blood on your desk?"

Andrea dropped her hands to the edge of the podium. She gulped, trying to remain calm. It was a bluff, wasn't it? The lights seemed to get hotter . . . she wanted to step down, but she knew how that would look.

"It's a lie," she said, weakly. "This is defamation."

"And when the police take a swab of your saliva, it won't match the saliva taken off of David Kahn's penis?"

Andrea frowned, looking at the crowd, hoping that somebody would save her. "Does anybody have a real question? Because if not, I'm leaving."

But the crowd was silent. She didn't want to think of what the cameras were picking up.

"Okay, thanks everybody for coming."

Andrea was about to step off of the stage, but somebody took her arm. She wrenched it away.

"Leave me be," she said.

"Andrea Drashkov?"

The way that the person said her name made her look, and she found that she was staring at a dark-skinned, small-eyed man. It took her a while to find his name in the back of her mind. Orlando Corea . . . Detective Orlando Corea.

"Yes?" she said, quietly.

"You are under arrest for the murder of David Kahn. Would you please come with me?"

Andrea hesitated. Why was this happening? This was supposed to be her moment of triumph. What had gone wrong?

Suddenly there was a loud bang, and screams, and the sound of footsteps scampering to the exit.

"That was for Sheila," somebody yelled.

Sheila? Who is Sheila? Andrea wondered.

Then there was another loud bang, and one after that. What was going on? Andrea looked around, but couldn't process anything.

She saw Detective Corea scanning the room, his gun up in the air. The room was practically empty now. She saw police officers trying to subdue somebody, knocking over chairs.

She felt very woozy. *It must be the heat from the lights,* she thought. She just needed some rest. She struggled to remain conscious. Something was wrong, she realized, and it wasn't just the heat. She put her hands on her stomach and felt a warm liquid. She took her fingers away and looked at them. There was sticky blood dripping slowly down them, hitting the freshly-vacuumed carpet. She stared at the blood as it escaped through her hands. How bright and smooth it seemed. Where was it coming from? Was it from her stomach?

She pressed both of her hands against her abdomen this time, and was surprised to find a sense of pain slowly swelling through her. She now could feel the blood flowing freely over her hands. She looked over at Detective Corea. He had a stern, concentrated look on his face. She stumbled towards him, but her dizziness overcame her and she fell to the floor.

"Somebody call an ambulance," she heard, but it was distant and muted, as though her ears were full of water.

Was she going to bleed to death? Was this the end, she wondered, just before she closed her eyes, succumbing to the darkness.

The Church

THE CHURCH WAS A SIMPLE wooden building on 7th Avenue. The paint was flaking, and the building was badly in need of a paint job. Except for a small wooden cross on the top of the building, it was barely discernible as a holy place.

John went in on a whim. He still had a few hours to kill before he had to be at the airport and return his rental car.

John parked and walked the two blocks to the church.

Was he getting used to the cold, or was it warming up? John couldn't tell. He pushed the door open, and it gave a loud moan that echoed through the cavernous building. John stepped inside and closed the door behind him.

He listened for a while for an indication of company, but when he didn't hear anybody he walked up the aisle and sat in the front pew.

There was a Christmas tree in the corner, populated with luminous round bulbs and decorated with silver tinsel, reminding John that in a month it would be Christmas.

Would he spend it with Byron and Hayden and Hayden's new husband Paul? No, he couldn't think of any conceivable scenario where that would work. Most likely he would go over to his mother's house and have some biscuits and a pot of Earl Grey tea, and listen to her as she talked about growing up in Scotland. The whole holiday was bearable only if he added a little bit of whiskey to the tea.

No, no more alcohol, John thought.

Earlier, John had phoned Doctor Kavita Nagi, his therapist.

"John, I haven't heard from you in a while."

"I fell off the wagon," John admitted.

There was a long silence before Nagi spoke. "Well, you want to come in and talk about it?"

"Sure. I'm in Calgary at the moment, but I should be home next week."

Nagi looked at her calendar. "How about next Thursday at noon?"

"Next Thursday would be great."

After he hung up, John drove out to Dover Mews again to visit Joyce Lancroft. There was a "For Sale" sign hanging in her window.

"You moving out?" John asked, when she answered the door.

"Yeah, I'm going back to the Maritimes. Visit with my family for a little while."

"I'm glad," John said.

Lancroft and John went into the living room.

"What are you doing here? I thought you were unemployed."

John shook his head. "No. The Icelandic Media Corporation went bankrupt. It was a shell corporation Andrea Drashkov used to buy the paper, but without her to funnel money into the corporation the whole thing collapsed pretty fast. John Pommeroy bought the *Daily Globe* back and is now taking it public."

"So you have a job again?"

"That's right. Most of the original staff were hired back."

"And you're in search of a story," Lancroft said, a hint of a smile around the edge of her lips.

"No, I have a question."

"What's that?"

"It always bothered me . . . who sent the recording of Kahn and Drashkov to Sheila's email account?"

Lancroft frowned. "I don't understand."

"I talked to one of the IT guys at Nerno. He told me it was company policy that once an employee was terminated, their email account was erased."

Lancroft shrugged. "I don't know anything about that."

344 | Joel Mark Harris

"That's kind of strange, since IT said you went to them and told them Kahn had specifically asked them not to touch Sheila's account."

Lancroft shook her head. "No, I never did that."

"They specifically remember it was you who told them."

Lancroft stood up slowly and went to the window. Her back was facing John, and the brightness of the sun hit her and cast a long shadow against the old carpeted floors. John watched her long, slender body sway against the sheen window, and he understood why David Kahn had desired her.

"You emailed the recording to Sheila's account using an account you thought was untraceable . . . did you want me to find it?"

"I thought the police would eventually find it. I didn't know you would be the first." Lancroft's voice was soft, hardly discernible.

"Did you record all of Kahn's phone conversations?"

Lancroft turned. Her eyes were red from tears. She nodded. "Yes. He told me to. David did. He was very paranoid."

"Why did you decide to email the recording?"

"I don't know. I guess it was something you said about doing the right thing."

John nodded. His suspicion had been confirmed. He stood up and gave Lancroft a hug, and on impulse, he kissed her on the forehead. She looked up at him but didn't say anything. John smiled.

"That's all. That's all I wanted to know. Thank you. Thank you for emailing it."

Lancroft still didn't reply, but instead stared back at him as if she didn't quite comprehend what he was saying.

John turned and let himself out. He got back into his car and drove off without looking back.

John thought of all the things that had happened to him recently, and he wanted to be reassured. But he never felt reassurance when he went into a church. Wasn't that what church was for? For reassurance, for forgiveness, for faith? Why did John just see an old, pointless building?

I killed Sheila, John thought.

He looked around. The church was still empty and quiet. John looked up at the white marble statue of Jesus crucified on the cross. A plaque to the right of the Jesus statue caught John's eye: *For all have sinned and fall short of the glory of God*, it read.

This was the church at which the McKinnon family had held the funeral service for Sheila. John tried to imagine the entire family congregating here to mourn her. What was said? How would she be looked on as a person? Would her end define her? Would she be remembered as the person who had stood up to the billionaires that controlled the oil industry?

And how would John be remembered for his role in this tragedy? Would he be vilified by the McKinnon family? John remembered knocking on the McKinnons' door, and the oppressive mood that had blanketed the entire house. He remembered being beaten by Kyle McKinnon.

What would happen now? How could they go on?

John had gone to visit Mathew McKinnon in jail. It took a lot of effort to get the authorities to agree to let John see him. Mathew McKinnon would probably plead guilty; about a dozen witnesses had seen him pull a gun and shoot Andrea Drashkov. His first shot had missed, but his second had found Drashkov's stomach.

"Too bad that stupid bitch survived," Matt had said to John.

Andrea Drashkov was still in intensive care, but the doctors said that she would pull through. What awaited her after? The police promised to put her on trial for David Kahn's murder and for fraud. Patrick Oswald, the PR man from Walker and Thompson, had apparently agreed to testify against Drashkov in exchange for a lesser sentence.

John couldn't help bitterly noticing that she wasn't being charged with financial fraud, the charge that the police had initially been investigating. He supposed that he couldn't have everything.

"Don't talk about that here," John said. "I'm not a lawyer. Whatever you say now might be used against you."

"I just wanted revenge," Matt said, slumping down in his chair, apparently not listening to John. He looked frail and gaunt, wearing the neon-orange jumpsuit prison garb. It looked foreign on him. He just wasn't cut out to be an inmate.

"You think the dead care about revenge?" John asked. "You think anything you say or do will stop you from feeling your own private guilt?"

Matt, who was hanging his head, suddenly snapped his neck up and looked up at John.

John nodded. "Yes, I know all about it. I have enough for several lifetimes."

"How do you deal with it?"

John sighed. "The only way I know how: keep on going."

Matt nodded, falling silent. His head bowed.

John had to ask the question that had been badgering his mind ever since the incident. He had been alternately intent on asking it and on not asking it. But Matt had opened the door and John intended to walk through, regardless of where it might have led. "Why her and not me? Why not blame me for her death?"

Matt didn't look up, and John didn't press for an answer. What answer was there?

"I wish you had shot me first," John replied, softly, getting up from his chair. "I wish you had killed me."

He knocked on the door so that the prison guard could let him out. As he waited, he looked back at Matt, but Matt wasn't looking at him. His head was lowered, seemingly lost deep in thought.

The door to the church opened, snapping John out of his thoughts. He stuck his whiskey back into his pocket and looked to see who had entered. It was an old woman and a younger woman. The old woman had a long wooden cane in one hand. The younger woman was holding the older woman's other arm.

John hadn't reactivated his phone. In fact, he hadn't spoken to either Charles Dana or Michael Chu since he had written the article about Drashkov's shooting. He had sent it in and turned off his computer, and hadn't looked back. He was sure that Charles would be trying to contact him, asking about follow ups, about new angles, new stories, et cetera, et cetera. But he wasn't interested in going back and facing the newsroom. Would he ever be? He didn't know. He was beginning to get used to the cold.

John took out a crumpled piece of paper. It was a printed version of the article that he had written about Amira, in what seemed like a lifetime ago. It had never been published, but he wrote it and kept it in hard copy. Why had he kept it for so long? Why didn't he just recycle it?

"I think I understand, you know," he told the lifeless black-and-white paper.

And in a way, he now understood Sheila as well. Their torments were now over, while his continued.

Mathew McKinnon had asked him how he dealt with the pain of loss and despair, and he had given him the only answer he knew: moment by moment, time after time, because really, what else was there to do?

But in the back of his mind, John wondered if there was a breaking point. A place the mind just couldn't return from. He had seen men and women lose everything that they had—husbands, wives, sons, daughters, homes, money, wealth, luxury—and still trek repeatedly on and on to the horizon of their lives. John thought of how Andrea Drashkov had dreamed of being American. In a way, America was the most tragic place of all. Such loss was so effectively kept at bay that when it did seep through the carefully laid defences, it was like a crack in a dam. The whole thing just came down.

John stood up, stretching his legs. He could hear the soft rumble of traffic outside as the world moved onward. The two women were on their knees, praying to a higher authority. But what for? And what did it matter if God granted their wishes or not?

John didn't have the power to save Sheila or Amira, or the other countless lives that had been destroyed. The past was gone now—to be remembered by only a few, but even then, the few would forget, or die, and everything would disintegrate and join the infinite cosmos.

John took his article about Amira and carefully put it back into his pocket, before walking out the door and into the wintry day.